CONVICTION

Also by Elise Title

Hot Property
Romeo
Chain Reaction
Killing Time
Inside Out

CONVICTION

ELISE TITLE

ST. MARTIN'S MINOTAUR
NEW YORK

www.minotaurbooks.com

Library of Congress Cataloging-in-Publication Data
Title, Elise.
    Conviction: a mystery / Elise Title.—1st ed.
        p. cm.
    ISBN 0-312-31820-0
    EAN 978-0312-31820-8
        1. Police—Massachusetts—Boston—Fiction. 2. Prostitutes—Crimes against—
Fiction. 3. Socialites—Crimes against—Fiction. 4. Boston (Mass.)—Fiction.
5. Policewomen—Fiction. I. Title.

PS3570.I77C66 2004
813'.54—dc22

                                                        2003069545

First Edition: June 2004

10 9 8 7 6 5 4 3 2 1

For David and Rebecca

acknowledgments

I continue to owe my gratitude to the many staff people of the Massachusetts Department of Corrections who opened their doors to me (and then released me!). Bill and Marilyn Dawber, my past boss and supervisor at MCI Norfolk's Counseling Center and my longtime friends, remain a source of inspiration and information. Thanks once again to my son David for being a first reader and pulling no punches. And equal thanks to my daughter Rebecca for her expert proofreading. Other colleagues and friends provided insight and guidance: Dr. Theodore Spielberg, Dr. Deanna Spielberg, attorney David Lazan, and Judi Lazan to name a few.

Deepest thanks to my editor Kelley Ragland for once again guiding me through the maze.

CONVICTION

prologue

"I SEE IT'S BEEN A WHILE." She smiles, her fingers skimming his bare chest.

He scowls. He doesn't like being read so easily. Is she belittling him? He definitely doesn't like that. Besides, what does she think? That he's made of money? Maybe some of her other "dates" have dough to burn, but her price is way out of his range. Not that he's let that stop him.

"Relax, darling. I'm very excited," she whispers against his ear, taking his hand, guiding it between her legs. "See? See what you do to me?"

He smiles back. His first smile for her. He's glad the lights are dim. He's a bit self-conscious about his teeth. Thirty-plus years worth of nicotine and coffee stains have them badly yellowed. His wife's been after him to have them whitened. She had it done last month. But he'd blown a gasket when he got the $1,100 bill from the dentist. That, on top of almost two grand for his son's crowns the month before courtesy of a brawl that ended with the kid's two front teeth scattered on the filthy floor of a bar in the South End. Kid! Sean was almost twenty-six. You'd never know it by the way he acted. Oh, sure, Sean swore he'd pay him back every dime as soon as he got another job. Yeah, right. He should live so long.

"Hey, honey, your mind is wandering." There's a hint of a reproach behind her smile.

"Isn't it your job to keep that from happening?" he shoots back. He's annoyed with her, but he's more annoyed with himself. What the fuck is he doing thinking about dentist bills at a time like this?

"Ooh, a man with a quick temper. I like that." She moves his hands to her full breasts. He wonders if that maneuver is primarily meant to keep his mitts otherwise occupied. Keep them from clenching into fists. Has she had guys who punched her out? Was she ever scared?

The possibility of her fear arouses him. Not that he plans to capitalize on it; he's never struck a woman in his life. It's just that he likes the sense of power it gives him. Men should be stronger than women. More in charge.

As her hand tightens around his hard-on, he quickly gets back with the program. He likes the way she grips him. He likes the way her pebble-hard nipples press into his palms. He likes that her tits are real. Would have lost interest if they were filled with silicone. Still, he isn't too far gone to note with a flash of disappointment that her tits aren't as firm and perky as those of a twenty-year-old.

How old is she? Twenty-five? Maybe even a few years older. But a looker, no question there. And even more to his taste, a woman with bearing. As promised. Even out of what he's sure is a designer outfit and the exquisite lace underwear, she radiates class. Doesn't matter that the silky blond hair could be a wig. He might have gotten a clue from the shade of her pubic hair, but she's shaved down there, smooth as a baby. He likes that. Likes it a lot. Likes everything about her right down to the expert manicure and pedicure, the nail polish a soft, creamy taupe. Not like his wife, who favors garish colors like fire engine red or hot pink. Of course, he never told Dana what a turnoff those shades were. For one thing, it would hurt her feelings. For another, there really was no point, since sex hasn't been much of an issue for them for a good five years now. Oh, sure, Dana lets him fuck her maybe once a month. But he can tell she doesn't enjoy it. Wonders if she ever has. Wonders, in fact, if *he* ever has. With her, that is. Not that he doesn't love Dana. He does. And he loves his two kids even though each in their own way has been a sorry disappointment.

"Do you want some more Champagne?"

"Huh? Oh . . . yeah, sure," he says, even though he knows he's already a little drunk. First the dry martinis—was it two? Three? He isn't sure because she never let his glass become empty. And then, after they got naked, she opened the Champagne. They've been working their way through the bottle for the past half-hour. Well, he was working his way through it. She hardly touched any of the booze. Not that he minds. He needs it more then he imagines she does. Needs it to relax. It isn't that he's never gotten a little on the side. Hell, he's had more than his share of hookers over the years.

But this is different. A whole different operation. Not so much as a whiff of sleaze. Very professional, everything top-notch. The gorgeous private brownstone on Joy Street in tony Beacon Hill, the first-class booze, the classical music, and most especially, the woman. Genevieve. Hell, even the name says class. Doesn't matter to him whether it's her real name. He doubts it is. He sure as fuck isn't Phil Mason. That's a little inside joke, in fact. Phil Mason is his price-gouging family dentist.

She reaches over to the bedside table for a flute half-full of the bubbly, lets it drip slowly down her creamy skin. "Go on," she murmurs. "Drink to your heart's content."

He starts to lean over her, but she grips his hair, yanking so hard his eyes smart.

"You forgot to say *may I*," she murmurs.

OCTOBER 16, 5:00 P.M.

The meeting with the commissioner of corrections, Warren Miller, left Deputy Commissioner Stephen R. Carlyle feeling out of sorts. Miller was from the old school, which Carlyle definitely saw as a plus. But there were some distinct negatives. Miller was always trying to play both ends against the middle. In one breath, he'd tell his staff he was determined to take a hard-line approach to the running of the prisons. In the next breath, he'd grant that over-crowding of inmates was a serious problem and innovative approaches needed to be explored.

Today, Carlyle witnessed Miller give the nod to Deputy Commissioner Russell Fisk when Fisk brought up the possible expansion of the prerelease centers. These centers provided a bridge between prison and the outside community. Inmates who were deemed a good risk and who had six months to a year left to serve based on either a parole date or the completion of their sentences would be placed at a center and assigned to a job in the community during the day. Beyond working in a supervised setting and attending authorized programs like AA or anger management, the inmate was remitted to the center, and for all intents and purposes, remained incarcerated. Any serious infraction of the rules resulted in a disciplinary hearing, and more often than not, a fast return to a walled prison.

There were eight centers total, scattered all over the state. The newest one was Horizon House, over in the South End of Boston. This one was Fisk's baby. Over three years back he had convinced the commissioner to okay Horizon House as an experimental coed center—an idea that Carlyle strongly opposed. And Carlyle presented even stronger opposition when the commissioner decided to appoint a woman as its superintendent—again, Fisk's influence. Carlyle's opposition to the coed center in general, and to Superintendent Natalie Price in particular, had been borne out in spades. There'd been two serious incidents at Horizon House in as many years, each garnering a slew of bad publicity. And Natalie Price had, in his estimation, been primarily responsible for each of those incidents. But for some reason that Carlyle would never understand, Miller not only hadn't given Price the ax but continued to throw his support behind Horizon House. And behind her.

Even now that the meeting was over Carlyle could feel himself getting worked up again. Feel the acid burning its way up his throat. He needed to get a grip. More than that, what he really needed to do was arrange another date with the divine Genevieve. For that evening if possible. To hell with the fact that he'd seen her only the day before. To hell with the cost. Since he'd begun seeing her in August, he'd managed at least one "date" every couple of weeks. It wasn't easy. She was expensive. Very expensive. He had to juggle finances, dip into funds that he shouldn't. But fuck it. He'd come to see these times with the sultry and inventive call girl as essential to his mental health. Not that he hadn't been talked into trying a couple of others when Genevieve wasn't available. They were fine. He certainly wouldn't—and didn't—throw either of them out of bed. But he didn't like meeting one of them in a hotel suite instead of the brownstone. Too risky. And neither of them was Genevieve. She was unique. She was worth the wait. Worth the big bucks. If she had an opening for that evening, he'd call his wife and say he had a late meeting. Dana probably wouldn't believe him, but he doubted she'd care all that much.

He was in his office, pulling his cell phone from his pocket—it wouldn't do to use his office phone and have a record of his private calls—when he saw a manila envelope on his desk. No stamp. Probably some interoffice crap. There were always newsletters and memos floating around. He probably wouldn't have bothered with it right away if his gaze hadn't fallen on the return address in the upper left-hand corner. Actually there was no address. There was only a name. Only a first name. Genevieve.

He froze. How the hell had she tracked him down? He'd been assured his cover would be absolutely secure. A man in his position had to be careful.

And why now?

He pulled a five-by-seven photo from the envelope.

His secretary knocked lightly on his door and then opened it wide enough to peer in. "Deputy Carlyle? Here's your tea. I put a good bit of sugar in it for energy. You looked kind of drained after the meeting." As she crossed the office to bring it over to him, he quickly slid a file over the photo.

"Here you are," she said brightly, setting the mug on the desk in front of him.

The collar on Carlyle's white shirt felt too tight. His whole body was clammy. His heart was pounding against his chest. A heart attack? The secretary thought he looked drained before. He must look like hell warmed over now.

No amount of sugar was going to give him a boost, but he swallowed down some of the overly sweet drink if only because the woman was watching him with such concern.

"Is the tea okay, Deputy?"

He gave her a glazed look. He was scared. Scared of dropping dead. Maybe even more scared of all that photo implied.

"Yes, Grace," he managed to croak. He finished off the tea in one long swallow to prove it. To get her out of there.

"There you go. You should feel better now. Is there anything else you need for that parole board meeting tomorrow?"

"No. No, thanks." And then, pulling himself together a bit, he said, "Oh, one thing. I . . . found a manila envelope. . . ."

"Yes, a delivery boy dropped it off while you were at your meeting with the commissioner."

"Did he . . . say anything?"

"No." The secretary hesitated. "Are you sure you're feeling all right, Deputy?"

He felt bile rise up in his throat. It took all his self-control not to break down right in front of the poor woman. "Just a . . . stressful day," he muttered. "Typical."

The secretary nodded. Grace Lowell, a tall, buxom woman with brown hair cut unstylishly short, too much makeup and the wrong shade for her olive complexion, was new. She'd only been with the deputy commissioner for a few weeks. She wouldn't know that, for him, this day was as far from typical as they got.

Ten minutes later Carlyle was again grimly staring at the photo. No chest pain now. He was too numb to feel anything.

God, he thought wearily, how grossly ugly the sex act could

look. This was nothing like those touched-up photos in porn rags he'd whacked off to more times than he cared to count. True, he'd never focused much on the men in those photos. But no question, they were buff.

In the photo, Stephen Carlyle saw that he looked like the overweight, out-of-shape fifty-seven-year-old man he was. He was kneeling on the bed. An unsightly roll of fat left several deep creases across his middle. The cellulite puckers in his ass and hips were repugnantly visible. The camera had even caught a cluster of pockmarks on his left shoulder, a reminder of a bad case of teen acne.

Genevieve's svelte naked body, on the other hand, looked great in the photo. She could grace the cover of any porn rag. Was it merely by chance, though, that her face was mostly hidden by a cloud of blond hair? He doubted it. Her identity, at least in this photo, remained secure.

What about him? He studied the photo intently. His face had been captured in profile. Was he absolutely recognizable? Maybe not. At least he doubted anyone could make an irrefutable ID from this shot.

But Stephen Carlyle knew there was no way this was the only photo. His stomach lurched even as his temper soared to the boiling point. He'd been set up. He'd been had. This was nothing more than fucking extortion. And like some horny country bumpkin, he'd walked right into the trap with his dick literally hanging out.

So, what did the blackmailing bitch want from him? Money? Since she obviously knew his real identity, she sure as hell had to know that civil servants, even at his level, got paid shit.

He slammed the photo facedown on his desk. And that was when he saw that there was something written on the back.

His body stiffened. His breath caught.

The note was brief. "I need a favor. Love as always, Genevieve."

His secretary's voice chirped from the intercom. "Well, I'm just going to finish up a few letters and then I'll be leaving, Deputy. Have a nice evening."

He heard her but he made no response. The chance of his having a nice evening tonight or any night soon definitely wasn't in the cards. His fury boiled over.

He'd kill her for this. He'd fucking kill her.

OCTOBER 17, 11:30 A.M.

"Hey, hey, where's the fire, baby? It's early. I thought we could maybe go another round or two."

"Sorry, Tommy. Can't today."

"Got another *appointment?*"

"No. But one of the other girls is due here very soon."

Tommy Thomson—the alias that the powerful criminal defense attorney Jerry Tepper uses—throws off the sheets, brazenly displaying his erection which is only partially concealed by a pair of red satin lady's panties. "You sure I can't entice you to let me stay just a little bit longer? I'll let you handcuff me again."

She grins. "You'll *let* me?" She heads for the bathroom, leaving the door open.

Reluctantly, he climbs out of bed, slips off the satin panties, reaches for his silk boxers. "What about next week? Same time? Same place?"

"Same time, but we need to meet over at the hotel suite," she calls out.

"Ah, shit, you know—"

She walks naked back into the bedroom, a placating smile on her face. "Just for next week, sweetie. An unfortunate scheduling snafu. It won't happen again."

She hands him his slacks, then helps him finish dressing. She needs him to get moving so that she can.

"You look nice, Tommy," she tells him as she pats down his comb-over, which doesn't begin to cover his bald pate. Men are so vain, she thinks. Not to mention so blind.

He takes hold of her arm, smiling. "We don't have to play make-believe, *Genevieve*. I can be Tommy for the others, but with you, Jess—"

She kisses him full on the mouth. "Make-believe is half the fun. See you next week, *Tommy*."

A shadow of annoyance moves across his face.

She chooses to ignore it.

11:55 A.M.

Jessica Asher was checking her diamond-studded Rolex as she dashed across the street to her shiny new silver Porsche. She caught a glimpse of a white SUV as it turned the corner and headed down the street in her direction, but she didn't give it so much as a thought since she was already well out of its lane, nearly at her car. She was just clicking her remote door opener when the vehicle veered suddenly and sharply to its left. Jessica looked back, startled. The SUV was bearing down on her. Her eyes widened in horror. The driver must be drunk. Or having a heart attack. There was no other possible explanation, surely.

But then she saw the face of the driver. And knew with horrified certainty there was, indeed, another explanation. Her mouth formed a name. But she never got to scream it out.

As the SUV plowed into her, she was literally lifted off her feet and would have been thrown a dozen yards or more if not for her own car blocking the expected trajectory. Her body slammed with incredible force into the driver's-side door of her Porsche, her lovely face shattering the glass window, her svelte body caving in the metal. The impact had to have been excruciatingly painful, but Jessica Asher was fortunate. She died quickly.

Even so, the SUV gave it one more for good measure.

one

THERE WAS A STUNNING BOUQUET OF a dozen long-stemmed yellow roses on her desk when Nat Price walked into her office. She wasn't happy about it, even though she wasn't absolutely sure who they were from. But she could make a good guess. Or two reasonably good guesses. The point was, Nat was hoping no one would be marking this day. She just wasn't big on birthdays, at least not her own. They depressed her. It wasn't so much getting older—in her line of work being older lent her weight, gave her more credibility—it was that where she was was never where she wanted to be when the next November 7 rolled around.

This year was no exception. She was still divorced, still involved with a man who couldn't commit, still making mistakes with another man she wasn't likely ever to commit to. She worked far too many hours. She was lonely more than not, still missing her close friend Maggie Austin even though she'd been dead now almost two years. She spent far too much time worrying—about her staff, her inmate residents, her sister, who naively believed her womanizing husband had learned his lesson. Nat even worried about her dog, Hannah. She seemed listless lately, off her food.

Oh, yeah, and now there was something brand-new to worry about. Her period was three weeks late. She'd gone into the pharmacy a half dozen times in the past few days determined to buy a pregnancy kit and put herself out of the misery of not knowing. But each time she entered the store, she walked out with everything but the kit. This wasn't her. Nat prided herself on being nothing if not resolute. She didn't go looking for problems, but she didn't duck them when they were coming at her.

This was different. This was a problem she'd like to make evaporate. But she couldn't. Denial worked for a lot of people she knew—her sister, Rachel, topped that list—but it was definitely not working for her. Try as she might not to think about the possibility that she was pregnant, she could hardly think of anything else. It had become a draining preoccupation.

Today was the day. Nat vowed that if she didn't get her period by the time she left Horizon House, she would definitely pick up a kit on her way home. Put herself out of her misery. Or deeper into it . . .

And to think, there was a time she'd ached for a baby. But that was a time when she'd had no doubt who the father would be.

There was a knock on her door. Sharon Johnson, Nat's employment counselor, popped her head in. "Happy—"

"Yeah, yeah," Nat muttered.

Sharon eyed Nat ruefully and stepped inside, shutting the door behind her. "How about coming over on Sunday for brunch? Ray's making her famous, or should I say infamous, blueberry pancakes." She patted her slightly rounded stomach. "That woman's been putting pounds on me like nobody's business."

"Give it a break. You're ravishingly beautiful and happy to boot," Nat said dryly, instantly flashing on the pounds she was likely to be gaining. And it would have nothing to do with blueberry pancakes, unfortunately.

The cocoa-skinned woman grinned. "If I didn't know you were straight as an arrow, girl, I'd think you were hitting on me."

"Believe me, if I wasn't straight and you weren't in a fantastic relationship with a fantastic woman, and you were not just a friend but my employee, I might just hit on you, girl," Nat teased. But behind her jaunty humor was open envy. Here was a woman who'd had a long list of knocks in her life including a stint in prison. It was largely because Sharon was an ex-con that Nat had wanted to hire her. Sharon's job would be to find placements for inmates at the prerelease center and supervise them once they were settled at work. Her hope was that Sharon would serve as a role model. Here was an ex-con who'd turned her life around—they could, too.

However, it was because she was an ex-con that Nat'd had to fight so long and hard to get her hired. The higher-up who gave her the toughest time was Deputy Commissioner Stephen R. Carlyle. But then Carlyle had given Nat a tough time at every turn.

"So, are we on for brunch? You can even ask that guy of yours."

Which one?

"How about a rain check?"

"You still not feeling great?" Sharon asked, giving her close scrutiny.

"What do you mean?" Nat was instantly defensive.

"You just haven't seemed your old self the past week or two."

Nat felt herself redden. "Just a lot of stuff going on," she said vaguely.

Sharon didn't push it. While there was no question the employment counselor and the superintendent had gotten friendly over the past couple of years, they were both very conscious of the lines drawn in the sand. Neither of them overstepped those lines.

"Hey, you should be smiling, Nat. You don't look a day over thirty-three."

Nat turned to her deputy superintendent, Jack Dwyer, who was standing in the doorway of her office. "Very funny." Jack knew perfectly well she'd just turned thirty-three.

He eyed the roses with an arched brow. "Leo?"

"Don't know. Just walked in." But she assumed if Jack didn't send the roses, it had to be Detective Leo Coscarelli—the man who wouldn't commit—to her, anyway.

Nat set her tote bag on the floor next to her desk. Still standing, her back to Jack, she checked her message slips.

"Don't forget. We got a disciplinary hearing at eleven," he said, ambling over to her. "Wanna go over the details?"

Nat gave him a blank look. Hard to forget a hearing she had no recollection of in the first place. Which of her inmates had broken one of the house rules? Better question still, where the hell was her mind lately? Nat was glad it was Friday. She needed the weekend to get herself back on track. If only she'd get her damn period already.

"Dennis Finn," Jack said to refresh her memory. "The inmate transferred here from Norton a month ago. Finishing up a three-five for larceny. He got into that little fracas with Hutch Tuesday night, remember?"

"Oh, right." Nat sighed wearily. "You'd think if Finn had to pick a fight, he'd have been smart enough not to choose an officer, especially Hutch." Not that Finn wouldn't have to go before the disciplinary board regardless of who he'd gotten into a scrape with since fighting was a definite house violation. But this was worse, since the man the inmate had hit—Horizon House's head correctional officer, Gordon Hutchins—would be one of the staff people determining his fate. There was a good chance the vote would be unanimous to ship Finn back behind the wall, but if there were extenuating circumstances—his girl sent him a Dear John, he just found out his kid had some serious disease, whatever—at least it gave them some wriggle room.

Throwing inmates out of the program was never easy for Nat. For any of them on staff. But they did it when they had to. Any sign of being soft on the rules not only put the program at risk but also jeopardized the safety of everyone involved—staff, residents, and the community at large.

"Is this Finn's first offense?" That would help some, too.

Jack squinted at her. "What's up with you, Nat? You're always the one with every little fact and figure about our residents at your fingertips. You feeling okay? I don't know. Lately, you've—"

"I'm fine," she snapped. And that was another thing. She'd not only been distracted lately, she'd become impatient and churlish. Nat was aware of it, but couldn't seem to control it. A bad sign for a control freak.

Jack's gaze drifted back to the flowers. "They must be from Leo."

Nat glared at him. "I told you. I don't know."

"Your man back in the doghouse?" Jack made no effort to hide the note of pleasure in his tone at this possibility.

She shot him a warning look. "We've already been through this, Jack. Many times," she added pointedly. "I'm not going to talk to you about my relationship with Leo."

"Okay," he said, edging a bit closer, "so talk to me about our relationship."

"There is no relationship," she said firmly. "No *personal* relationship," she amended, her irritability shifting to weariness and the day hadn't even gotten rolling. Another bad sign. Weariness was not usually a word in her vocabulary. Driven—yes. Unrelenting—yes. Unyielding—probably too much so . . .

Jack edged closer still, his shoulder now brushing against hers. "So that warm September night when you crawled into my bed and—"

She took a large step to the left to break contact. Jack stepped toward her again. Their little dance. They were both familiar with the routine.

"Drop it, Jack. We've been over that. It was a mistake. We agreed—"

"I agreed to let you pretend it was a mistake."

"Let it go, Jack. Please."

"It's hard, Nat." He grinned. "Pardon the double ententre. You do get me hot and bothered."

Nat sighed. "Well, I'll second the *bothered* part." But her tone softened.

"Yeah, it's a bitch." His tone, too, had softened. He remained on his mark, arms folded across his broad chest. He was wearing a white shirt, cuffs rolled up to reveal muscular forearms, and a striped tie that'd seen better days, which he wore loose around an undone top button. Somehow he managed to look tough and not sloppy. Hell, he looked sexy, that was the truth of it. He *was* sexy, that was even more the truth.

"How about lunch? I promise not to bring up anything personal."

Nat rolled her eyes.

"Hey, and we have more to celebrate than just your birthday. It's my anniversary. Three weeks on the wagon. Not one drop of booze has touched these lips in twenty-one days."

"That's great, Jack."

"I'm really cleaning up my act, Nat. Hey, none of us is getting any younger. I'll be turning forty-one in a couple of months. My mom was dead of a heart attack at forty-eight. My dad died of liver failure at fifty-three. I may only have a few years left. I want to spend them sober. And, hopefully, not alone."

Jack's struggle with booze was an old problem. It was a problem Nat was all too sadly familiar with, her father having lost his battle with the bottle at the end of a noose. She still hadn't resolved in her own mind if her dad took the easy way out or the hard way. Or, for that matter, if he fully knew what he was doing since the coroner's report on the alcohol content in his body at the time of his death was practically off the charts. Nat guessed the only thing she knew for certain was, her father took the *final* way out.

She looked over at her deputy, her expression softer. "I'm really glad that you're doing so well with the booze, Jack. You keep it up and you'll outlive your parents by at least thirty years."

He grimaced. "I don't think I can stand myself for that long."

She smiled.

"Unless, of course, you could stand me." His tone was only half-teasing. "So, what do you say, Nat? Lunch at La Maison? Surely you could stand me for that long. You can have Champagne and I'll toast you with a Perrier."

No Champagne or alcohol of any kind if I'm pregnant. . . .

"The hearing could run late," she said brusquely. "And I've got meetings all afternoon."

"Okay, dinner," Jack persisted, never one to let go easily of something he wanted. On this, they were very much alike. Too bad they didn't usually want the same things. "Then we don't have to rush through—"

"I can't, Jack. Leo and I—"

He held his hand up at her like a traffic cop, his lighthearted manner evaporating fast. "Sure. Right. I should have figured. You and Leo. Yeah. No problem, Nat—"

Before she could think of something to say to soothe her deputy's ego, her phone rang. "I've got to take this, Jack." Usually her inmate clerk, Paul LaMotte, picked up, but he'd been sick all week so she was manning her own phone.

"Nat?" A male voice that was all business.

"Yes."

Jack turned without so much as a wave or a nod and exited.

"Warren Miller here."

Nat experienced a tiny seizure of apprehension. Getting an unexpected call from the head of corrections wasn't an everyday occurrence. "Commissioner Miller. Yes. What can I do for you?"

"We have a situation, Nat. And I'd appreciate your help."

Apprehension quickly spiraled into anxiety. "What kind of a situation?"

"I'd prefer not to discuss it on the phone."

"Do you want me to come over to your office? I have a disciplinary hearing scheduled here at the center for eleven, but my deputy could take charge—"

"I need to see you now."

"Okay, I'll come right over."

"I'm not at my office." There was a brief pause. Nat heard him breathing into the mouthpiece. "I'm at the Fourteenth Precinct. It's just off Charles Street."

Her stomach lurched. She knew if she saw herself in a mirror right now her trepidation would be visible. "Is it one of my residents?" This was all she needed. Another of her inmates in trouble with the law.

Instead of answering her question, Miller said brusquely, "I'll see you in fifteen minutes, Nat."

Three minutes later, she was rushing out the door when her phone rang again. She pivoted back round, making a dash for it.

Maybe it was the commissioner again. False alarm? *Dream on, girl.*

"Did you like the roses, Natalie?"

"Yes. Yes, they're lovely, Leo." Nat realized she hadn't even glanced at the card. And she had no time now. "Look, I'm just on my way out. Are we still on for dinner?"

"I'm counting on it."

"Great—"

"Where are you off to in such a hurry?"

She hesitated. "Fourteenth Precinct. Do you know anyone over there?"

"What's up?"

"Don't know yet. But nothing good, I'm sure. So do you know someone there?"

"As a matter of fact, I do. Fran Robie. She's in homicide."

Nat shivered, her stomach taking a turn for the worse. "Let's hope I won't be needing her. But if I do, can I tell her I'm a friend of yours?"

"A friend? Yeah. Sure. You can tell her you're my *friend.*"

It was only after she hung up that Nat wondered whether Fran Robie was a friend of Leo's.

two

AS SOON AS NAT GAVE THE paunchy desk sergeant her name, he sprang up out of his chair and hurried round from behind his perch. It was clear she was expected.

"Right this way, Superintendent." His manner was brisk but polite. Nat followed him up a wide flight of stairs, dodging cops heading down. They went along a narrow hall passing several closed doors, then one that was open to a midsized squad room containing a dozen back-to-back desks. The sergeant stopped at a closed door just beyond the squad room. "Here we are, Superintendent. The commissioner is waiting for you."

The sergeant reached for the doorknob. Nat stared at the block letters on the glass window—Captain Francine Robie. And just beneath the name—Homicide Division. The seriousness of the situation hit home with a wallop.

"I think I'm . . . going to be . . . sick," she mumbled.

The sergeant quickly turned to Nat, but she wasn't really able to focus on him. "Bath . . . room?"

He pointed farther down the hall and she made a mad dash. She just barely got to a stall, partly missing the bowl as she sank to her knees and started to retch.

Five minutes later, splattered linen skirt washed off, mouth rinsed out, new lipstick applied, loose strands of hair tucked back into her French knot, Nat exited to three pairs of worried eyes in the hallway outside the bathroom. She recognized two of the pairs—the sergeant's and the commissioner's. She figured the third pair—given that it was a woman's eyes—belonged to Captain Francine Robie, Homicide Division.

"Must be a stomach bug," Nat mumbled, embarrassment overtaking apprehension over why she'd been summoned.

Commissioner Warren Miller approached her. He was in his early sixties, a tall, bony man with a prominent nose and pronounced jaw, neatly trimmed hair that was dark brown tinged with gray and combed straight back from his face. He was wearing a navy suit nicely tailored to his lean frame. He was not an attractive man, but he did have a definite presence about him. "I'm terribly sorry, Nat. If I'd known you were ill—"

"I wasn't. I'm not. It's . . . I'm fine now. Really." Nat could see by the three sets of concerned eyes still fixed on her that no one was convinced.

"Why don't you come into my office and sit down, Superintendent. Perhaps a glass of water?" The woman Nat had not officially identified gestured toward the office bearing the name Captain Francine Robie.

Nat nodded. Captain Robie guided her over to her door, which was now wide open, stepping aside for her to enter first. The commissioner followed close on Nat's heels. Maybe he was afraid she'd pass out and he wanted to be close enough to catch her.

Robie looked over at the sergeant before she joined them inside. "See about some ice water, Rick."

"Will do, Captain."

"Sit. Please, Superintendent." The captain offered Nat the choice of a maple rocking chair or one of a pair of armchairs upholstered in an earthy-colored paisley pattern. Dismissing the rocker instantly—even the idea of sitting on something that moved made her queasy—Nat opted for one of the upholstered chairs. The commissioner took the other.

Nat was a bit surprised to find a precinct office so well appointed. More than that—downright homey. Rag rug on the floor, cream-colored cotton curtains on the window, nicely framed photos—primarily seascapes and boats—on the wall, which, instead of the traditional institutional green, was painted a warm taupe. Even the desk wasn't the standard city-issue gunmetal monstrosity. Robie worked at a huge oak roll top desk that had the patina of age about it. She had the back of the desk placed against a side wall, with the curtained window to her right, the door to her left.

Under some circumstances Nat might have written the decor off to the fact that the office belonged to a woman. But in Nat's experience, the majority of women who opted for careers that were primarily male-dominated, like corrections and the police department, went out of their way to fit in. Or at least not draw attention to their differences.

Francine Robie appeared to have no such concerns. Not only as regarded her office but her appearance. Even were she to make an effort to tone it down, there'd be no hiding how attractive she was. But far from making any effort in that direction, she was quite out front on that account. Expertly streaked silky blond hair worn loose to her shoulders, dark brown eyes highlighted by perfectly applied liner, the lashes tinged with just the right amount of mascara to keep them from caking, and a glowing tan achieved either by a late autumn island vacation or a tanning salon.

The homicide captain's choice of attire was also anything but demure. Black leather boots with a good two-inch heel, snug fitting black velvet slacks, an apple green silk shirt that was eye-catching not only for its vibrant color but because the police captain had opted to leave the first two buttons undone.

Even if Nat hadn't puked all over her charcoal linen suit, she'd be feeling decidedly drab and dowdy.

"Better now?" the captain inquired solicitously. She was still standing.

"Yes. Thanks."

"I'm Fran Robie, Superintendent Price." She extended a hand after the formal introduction. Nat gave it a brief shake.

She had to admit it, she found Robie somewhat off-putting. Not only because of her looks, her dress, her interior decorating. It was also that she was younger than most police captains Nat had met. She guessed early thirties. Then again, Robie could be older than she looked. Nat wasn't great at guessing someone's age. Leo was a good example. When she first met him, Nat thought he looked far too young to be a homicide detective. But his youthful appearance was deceptive. Leo had definitely aged some over the past couple of years. Nat figured she was at least partly to blame. But she wasn't the only woman in Leo's life to put gray strands in his brown hair. His son's mother, Suzanne Holden, had done her fair share.

Nat felt Robie's eyes on her. She met her gaze. The homicide captain seemed to be studying her thoughtfully, likely trying to get a read on her.

Then again, maybe the captain was just nervous Nat might up and barf again.

Robie took the ergonomically designed tan leather chair in front of her desk, angling it so that she was facing both Nat and the commissioner. Commissioner Miller leaned slightly forward, elbows resting on his knees, hands pressed together.

Just as Miller started to speak, there was a knock on Robie's door. The desk sergeant entered with a glass of ice water. Nat accepted it and thanked him, watching him wait for the captain's nod before he made a quick exit.

Both Miller and Robie were silent. They seemed determined to wait until Nat drank some of the water, which she didn't really want. She took a few polite sips, anxious for them to cut to the chase. The anticipation of what was wrong was growing intolerable.

Miller cleared his throat. "Captain Robie is heading a murder investigation in which one of our people has been brought in for questioning, Nat. Needless to say, I am quite concerned."

Nat gave him a quizzical look. "One of our people?" Would the commissioner refer to an inmate as "one of our people"? And would a homicide captain be personally handling a routine murder investigation? The answer to both questions was—no. This was big-time. Either the victim was decidedly high-profile or the suspect was. *One of our people . . .*

Miller's fingers intertwined as he clasped his hands more tightly together. "Carlyle," he said, his voice dropping a notch.

Nat was sure she hadn't heard the commissioner right. Maybe that bout of nausea had nothing to do with morning sickness as she secretly feared. Maybe it was an inner ear infection.

"You do know Stephen Carlyle, Superintendent?" Robie interjected.

"The deputy commissioner of corrections? Of course, I—he's being questioned? He's a . . . a suspect in a homicide investigation?" Nat didn't even know who'd been killed yet, but that was beside the point at the moment. The possibility of the DC being a suspect seemed nothing short of ridiculous. Not that she was in any way fond of the deputy commissioner. Or thought much of his policies or personality, for that matter. But a murder suspect?

Well, one thing was for sure—no question it would make headlines if a deputy commissioner of corrections was arrested for murder. But who the hell did the cops suspect him of killing? Which was Nat's next question.

"Jessica Asher," Robie said, continuing to watch her.

"The hit-and-run victim?" Distracted though she might have been these past two weeks, that terrible event had not escaped Nat's notice. It had been splashed all over the media for days. Now it was even clearer why the homicide captain was involved. Not only was there a top-ranking corrections official as a suspect, they had a victim from a prominent Boston family. This was *seriously* big-time.

"Are you saying you think Stephen Carlyle was the driver of the vehicle that accidentally ran that poor woman down and then took off?" Nat emphasized the word "accidentally," shooting a glance at the commissioner, who was grim faced and pale. She was wondering if he was going to be sick now.

"A witness has recently come forward, Superintendent, who claims he saw the vehicle *deliberately* run Ms. Asher down."

"What?" If Nat was stunned before, now she was truly dumb-founded. "You're telling me you think the driver—" Nat couldn't bring herself to say "Carlyle"—"meant to kill this woman?" As if getting hit with vehicular homicide wouldn't be bad enough. Now the DA was likely to push for a charge of second- or even first-degree murder.

"Who is this witness?" the commissioner asked.

"A trucker based in the western part of the state who happened to be in Boston that day."

"Why didn't he report it immediately?" Nat demanded.

"He says he only just realized what he'd actually seen that day," Robie said. "At the time he only witnessed a white SUV backing away from a red sports car he'd obviously plowed into. The trucker didn't know a person had been hit. He's been on the road until this past Tuesday. When he heard about Asher's death on the news he says he agonized for a few days about whether to report what he saw and get involved, and fortunately for us, his conscience got the best of him. One of my men went out and got a full statement."

"Did he identify the driver?" Nat asked, hearing the shakiness in her voice. An eyewitness wouldn't seal the deputy commissioner's fate, but it would certainly make his situation more dire.

Robie didn't answer immediately. It's as if she was deliberately giving Nat time to ruminate. "No. He was too far away. He wasn't even sure of the make of the SUV. Thought maybe a Jeep Cherokee, but he wouldn't swear to it. He was certain of the color—white, and that it looked to be a recent model."

"What this trucker saw in no way indicates it was anything but an accident," Nat argued.

"There's more," Robie said. And Nat didn't like the way she said it. "After the SUV backed up, the trucker saw the driver hit the gas and ram into the sports car again. But, of course, it wasn't just the sports car he was ramming into."

Nat felt a shiver of revulsion.

"What do you know about Jessica Asher, Superintendent? The victim?" Robie asked her.

"Not much." Nat had read the obituary, but more vividly recalled the photo printed beside it. A photo of a beautiful, vibrant young woman. *Boston* magazine also was quick to get an article out that included color photos of the auburn-haired socialite at several charity events.

"Did you know that she was the daughter of the late Anthony Asher, attorney general of Massachusetts in the early '80s?"

Nat nodded. "Yes, I do remember reading that."

"And that she was only twenty-nine?"

"I knew she was young."

"Did you also know that her older sister, Debra Asher, is married to Eric Landon, CEO of DataCom and a city councilman? Although I suppose he's better known for his failed bid for governor in the last election," Robie said.

Nat nodded. Her ex-husband had been a big Landon supporter. He'd contributed enough to Landon's campaign to get an invitation to the Asher-Landon wedding around nine years ago. He went alone. Nat wasn't a Landon fan. Just one of the many issues she and Ethan hadn't seen eye to eye on. Another—bigger one—was his extracurricular interest in screwing other women.

Robie smiled. "I get the feeling you didn't vote for Landon."

Nat didn't smile back. She wanted to get back to the far graver matter at hand.

"I'm still baffled as to why Stephen Carlyle is being questioned. You've already said the witness couldn't identify the driver."

"If we had a positive ID we'd be doing more than merely questioning the deputy commissioner, Superintendent."

"Then what? The witness got the license plate number? You've traced the car to Carlyle? You have other evidence that—?"

Robie put up a hand to stop her. "This is early times in the investigation, Superintendent."

"Okay, then tell me this," Nat persisted. "If you believe the driver of that vehicle deliberately struck down Jessica Asher, and you believe that driver could conceivably be Stephen Carlyle, what's his motive? Why would he want to kill her? What's the connection between the victim and Carlyle?"

Since she wasn't actually expecting the captain to be particularly forthcoming, Nat was surprised when Robie answered without so much as a pause. "Ms. Asher's PDA was discovered under her car. Probably fell out of her purse at the time of the incident. She had a section of it password protected, but apparently she didn't realize that a password can be rather easily cracked. Very easily, in fact," Robie added.

"I'll keep that in mind," Nat said, given that she had certain information on her Palm Pilot password protected as well.

"It was an appointment calendar. Oh, there was also your typical appointment book in the unsecured section of her PDA. That one listed the usual. Hairdresser, dinner engagements, doctor's appointments, dress fittings."

"You saw Carlyle's name on this *other* appointment calendar—that's evidence that he was the driver of this SUV? So they had some kind of a meeting at some point. I still don't—"

"He saw her quite a few times. Starting in August of this year."

"How many times?"

"Eight. Approximately two weeks apart. The last date listed was Wednesday, October fifteenth. At seven P.M. Two days prior to the hit-and-run."

"And has Carlyle explained what these dates are about?" Nat asked.

Before Robie responded, the commissioner cut in. "It's possible Ms. Asher was involved in a series of meetings with the deputy regarding one of our prisoner programs."

It wasn't a bad hypothesis. Over her ten-plus years in corrections, Nat had met a number of women, many of them like Jessica Asher—young, quite attractive, well educated, and frequently well-off—who'd become involved with inmates. Sometimes it happened early on, at a defendant's trial, especially when it was a high-profile case. There could be a dozen or more women who would show up daily at the courtroom, dressed to the nines, vying for front-row seats, sending notes, flowers, doing whatever they could to get the defendant to notice them. Then there were women who got to know a particular inmate through a pen-pal program or, as the commissioner was suggesting, they got involved in an inmate volunteer program.

Nat had personally known a few women who'd gone so far as

to get jobs behind the walls—clerks, prison librarians, nurses, even ministers—in order to be close to an inmate. For certain women, men behind bars exuded a heightened sexual allure. It wasn't even that they necessarily believed the inmate was innocent. For some of these ladies, the very fact that the guy was guilty was a turn-on. Guilty and yet captive—making them safe. Or so these women thought. . . .

The problem with the commissioner's hypothesis was that Carlyle's primary role as deputy was administrative, his focus being on fiscal and budgetary matters. He also served as liaison between the Corrections Department and the Parole Board. If Asher was interested in doing some prison volunteer work she'd have been meeting not with Carlyle but with Russell Fisk, the commissioner's other deputy who coordinated and oversaw programs within the prison system.

Nobody was saying anything and the silence was getting to Nat. She turned to Robie. "Okay, so let's say the deputy commissioner of corrections did know the woman? So what? A lot of people knew Jessica Asher. Have you been dragging all of them down here for questioning? Are they all suspects?"

"That's what I'd like to know," the commissioner said indignantly. "You admitted to me earlier, Captain, there were a number of people whose names were on this locked calendar."

"A number of *men*," Robie said pointedly.

"How many?" Nat asked.

"Many," was Robie's answer. And then she unbent a little. "In the last week of her life, Jessica Asher had appointments booked with five men. Including Stephen Carlyle. And like Carlyle, these other men also appeared to be meeting quite regularly with the victim."

"Maybe she was counseling them," Miller muttered.

"I've heard it called lots of things," Robie said dryly, "but 'counseling's' a new one for the books."

The commissioner flushed even as he gave the captain a glaring look.

It was pretty obvious that Francine Robie believed Jessica Asher was engaged in sexual liaisons with these men. If she was right—and Nat was not yet in the know enough to argue for or against the hypothesis—the question was, why? Unless Asher was a raging nymphomaniac—and, in Nat's opinion, at least as far as Carlyle was concerned, a nondiscriminating one—it was a far more likely possibility that this well-educated, seemingly affluent young woman from a very prominent family was doing it for the money. Maybe she was into drugs or had a gambling addiction. If it was drugs, Robie would know about it from the autopsy. And it probably wouldn't be all that difficult to uncover a gambling addiction if there was one.

Then again, maybe Jessica was in it strictly for kicks. A rebel. A black sheep.

"Can I see that appointment calendar?" Nat asked.

"Sorry—" Before Robie finished turning down her request, there was a knock on the door. A heavyset middle-aged man in an ill-fitting gray jacket popped his head in without waiting for an invite. "We're just about ready, Captain. The lawyer's here."

"Okay, Wilson," Robie said, rising from her chair.

Miller got up as well. He looked over at Nat. "I've convinced the captain to let us observe the interview." He paused briefly. "I just want to have a word with you first. We'll only be a minute," he told Robie.

The commissioner waited for the office door to shut behind Robie. "I don't think I need to tell you what the ramifications could be in this situation, Nat." He began pacing the room. "All those men. A series of dates. There's very likely some kind of a sexual scandal brewing here."

"Do you think Robie would show you that calendar?"

"I already asked. And got a definitive no."

"I still don't get why Stephen Carlyle is being singled out."

The commissioner stopped pacing and turned directly to her. "Obviously," he said, "Robie knows more than she's telling us."

Yes, Nat was thinking. And she was curious to know what it was.

"The media's going to have a field day with this, Nat."

"It looks like the cops are managing to keep things under wraps so far. I didn't see any press hanging around the precinct. Hopefully, Carlyle will be able to provide an alibi and that it'll be the end of it. As far as the department is concerned." Nat was not sounding overly confident. Nor was she feeling that way.

"And if Carlyle can't provide an alibi?" Miller visibly shivered as he nervously raked his fingers through his hair.

Her eyes fixed on the commissioner's. "You mean, if he—"

"Don't misunderstand, Nat. I'm not saying for an instant that Stephen Carlyle is guilty of this heinous act." Now he was the one who wasn't sounding particularly confident.

"The point is," he started pacing again, "I need to be prepared for the worst-case scenario. If even a whiff of this gets out, it'll be exceedingly embarrassing for the department. We're going to have to run a hell of a lot of damage control. I'm going to need a person I can trust to be the eyes and ears of the department, as it were. Someone I can rely on to give me a heads-up so I'm not blindsided. I need you to get on top of this and stay on top of it, Nat," he said bluntly.

"Me?" Nat would have thought she'd be the last person on earth Miller would want sticking her nose in. For one thing he knew there was absolutely no love lost between her and Carlyle. For another, he himself had had her on the carpet not once but twice in the past three years, the first time after she'd almost gone and gotten herself killed during the apprehension of her friend Maggie Austin's killer, and again a year back, after she concocted and carried out a plan to catch the assailant who almost slashed one of her inmates to death—a plan that not only backfired but put her life at risk yet again.

The commissioner managed a faint smile, no doubt knowing precisely what was running through her mind. "You've had experience, Nat. You know people. You have connections within the police department. Professional and personal connections."

So much for assuming her private relationship with Detective Coscarelli hadn't been picked up on the department radar. But, still, it didn't make sense to Nat that Miller would actively encourage her involvement.

"There are a couple more reasons," the commissioner said after a pause.

"I thought there might be," Nat said.

"I don't know who else is on Asher's Palm Pilot. All I do know is that they're all *men.*"

Nat nodded. "So you can't be sure, if you asked a male friend or colleague for assistance, that his name wouldn't also be on that calendar."

"Sadly true."

"And what's the other reason?"

"Robie. I'm hoping, seeing as how you're two women of similar age, professional achievement—"

"You think I might be able to get her to confide me."

"Yes. If Fran Robie were to put her confidence in anyone, female or male, I think it would be you. People tend to trust you, Nat. Women and men. It's one of the reasons I thought you'd do well running a coed center, and despite a couple of, shall we say, unfortunate incidents, you've been doing an admirable job."

Nat felt Miller was spreading the butter on awfully thick. He must really be worried.

"Besides," he added, "I know that you'll be resolute in your determination to get to the truth of a situation."

And what if the truth was that Stephen R. Carlyle was guilty?

Nat doubted the commissioner was going to be showering her with compliments if that was the end result of her "resoluteness." Or did he think he could manipulate the truth if it came to that? Or more to the point—manipulate her?

A faint smile softened Miller's sharp features as he placed a hand on her shoulder. "Will you help, Nat?"

Despite all her concerns, there was only one answer to that question.

three

ROBIE WAS ALREADY IN THE OFFICE next door to the interrogation room when the commissioner and Nat entered. Nat was surprised the captain was there since she'd assumed Robie would conduct the inquiry. Maybe she just wanted to oversee at this point. Look, listen, watch. Sometimes you learned more that way. Nat was hoping that would be the case for her, as well.

Robie guided them to a pair of wooden chairs lined up next to each other in front of a glass window that was actually the other side of a one-way mirror. Through the glass Nat saw Deputy Commissioner of Corrections Stephen R. Carlyle and his attorney, Fred Sherman, seated across a worn wooden table from two detectives in a cell-sized room lit by fluorescent lighting that cast a yellow-green pall over all four men.

The older of the two detectives, Norman Wilson, the portly man who'd popped into Robie's office a few minutes back, was the one conducting the interrogation. The younger detective seated beside him fiddled absently with his mustache as he sat tilted back on his wooden chair, his gaze fixed on the deputy commissioner.

While Nat wouldn't say Stephen Carlyle looked composed, he didn't show any signs of being in a panic. He was sitting straight up in a wooden chair, but more in the way of being mindful of his posture than appearing rigidly uptight. He was dressed in a dark, tailored business suit and Nat was wondering if they brought him there from his home or his office. Probably caught up with him at home before he left for work. If two detectives had escorted him from the Department of Corrections, word would have leaked out in a matter of minutes and at least that much would have been all over the news by now.

"Let's start from the top again. You still claim you never met Jessica Asher." The older detective's tone was openly dubious.

"Not that I recall," Carlyle said in a well-modulated voice, seemingly ignoring the detective's tone of overt skepticism.

"So you have no idea why your name was listed in Ms. Asher's appointment calendar on her Palm Pilot? In a locked section?"

"Again, no. No idea."

"And the dates—let's see." The detective flipped open a note-pad. "August sixth, August twenty-second, September third, September eleventh—"

"I told you. Those dates mean nothing to me," Carlyle said, keeping his voice even, his expression bland. He never so much as glanced at his attorney. A strategy to demonstrate he didn't need guidance or coaching? "I don't know the woman. I don't know why in God's name you are questioning me about that tragic hit-and-run accident. This is all some horrible—"

"Let's talk about Friday, October seventeenth." The detective cut him off, his voice and tone matching that of the deputy commissioner's. Nat wondered if the cop was deliberately imitating Carlyle.

"Friday the seventeenth? What about it?"

"You were out sick that day, isn't that right, Steve?"

Nat saw Carlyle bristle for a moment, but she wasn't sure if it was because it was obvious the cops had already done some checking as to his whereabouts that day, or because the detective addressed him by his first name. Nat had known the deputy commissioner for close to eight years and she couldn't remember once calling him Stephen much less Steve. She wondered if even his wife called him Steve.

"I wasn't feeling well so I took a day of sick leave. That isn't a crime, Detective."

"What was wrong with you?"

"I woke up with a pounding headache."

"Hangover?"

A little flicker of irritation flashed on Carlyle's face. Sherman spotted it, gave the deputy's arm a little tap. "I don't drink. That is, I don't indulge to the point of suffering hangovers. It was a simple headache."

"And you felt it coming on the day before?"

"I . . . don't understand," Carlyle muttered warily. Sherman leaned closer to the deputy and whispered something.

"Your secretary, Grace Lowell, tells us she found a note from you on her desk when she arrived at work on Friday morning the seventeenth, that you wouldn't be in that day. Presumably, you left it for her after she left work on Thursday the sixteenth. You were planning on that headache?"

Another whispered word from Sherman.

"I don't know what you're talking about." Carlyle was visibly struggling to hold on to his composure. Nat was, too. This wasn't looking good.

"Are you saying your secretary lied?"

"I'm saying I never left any such note." Carlyle's tone was sharp. Nat had heard that sharpness in his voice on any number of occasions. Mostly when he was addressing her. The difference was, this time there was an overlay of fear dampening the sharpness. And if Carlyle was scared, she was scared. "She's new. She only started a few weeks ago. . . . She made a mistake. There wasn't any note."

"Pity you weren't at work that Friday," Wilson said sardonically. "Would have given you a solid alibi."

Carlyle blinked rapidly. Nervously. Sherman jotted something down on a legal pad.

"So, let's talk about what you did that day." Wilson tipped his chair back.

"I told you I woke up with this miserable headache, and besides, I had a dentist appointment for that afternoon, so I just decided to take the whole day off."

"So you went to your dentist on Friday afternoon?"

Sherman started to say something to his client, but Carlyle waved him off. He cleared his throat reflexively. "No. I checked my date book and saw I had the day wrong. The appointment was actually for Monday, not Friday."

"That's Dr. Philip Mason, right? Your dentist?"

Carlyle blanched.

Nat didn't understand the deputy's reaction.

"You must like the name," Wilson went on laconically. "Seeing as how you liked to call yourself Philip Mason from time to time."

What little color was left drained completely from the deputy commissioner's face.

"What did Jessica call you, Steve? Phil? Or Philip?"

Sherman started whispering furiously into Carlyle's ear. When he finished, the attorney addressed the detective. "My client has no comment."

Carlyle was sweating. So was Nat.

Wilson seemed unperturbed. "So, back to the seventeenth. You spent the whole morning home? Nursing this migraine?" he continued in a bland monotone.

The deputy nodded.

"And what about the afternoon? You never did go in to work that day. Just like that note—"

"I told you. I never wrote any note."

"That migraine—was it *killing* you the whole day?"

Sherman gave the detective a dirty look, but Carlyle said quickly, "No. No. Actually I felt better after a few hours and then I got a call from one of the nurses' aides at the nursing home where my mother stays. She thought my mom was looking kind of low and thought, if I had some time over the weekend, maybe I could pop down and visit her. I do try to go at least once every few weeks and it had been a while, and since I had already taken the day off, I decided to go that afternoon."

"This nursing home wouldn't happen to be over on Joy Street in Beacon Hill?"

Sherman slapped his hand on the table. "My client—"

Carlyle cut his attorney off. "It's in Plymouth," he said sharply. Then, as if realizing he'd come off too strongly, he repeated this information in a more subdued voice. "And the nurse's aide was right. My mother did brighten considerably when I showed up."

"What was the name of the nurse who called you?"

"Nurse's aide," Carlyle corrected. "And I don't recall her name."

Wilson let it go. "You were at the nursing home for most of the day then?"

"A large part of it, yes."

"What time did you get there?"

Another quick word from Sherman in Carlyle's ear.

"I don't remember exactly."

"Approximately."

"Maybe around lunchtime. Just after. Yes, I think it was early in the afternoon that I got down there. It's about an hour drive from my home—"

"And you stayed home until you went to visit your mother?"

"Yes."

"Anyone home with you?"

"No . . . no wait, my son Alan was home for part of the time."

"Which part?"

"He left at around eleven-thirty."

"No school? Work?"

Nat watched Carlyle's features tighten. "My son is a paraplegic. He was in a . . . a car accident a few months . . . actually it's been almost a year." A shadow of sorrow swept across the deputy's face. "Two days a week he goes for physical therapy."

Nat glanced over at the commissioner. She had never known about Carlyle's son. Actually she never knew he had a son at all. In fact, she realized, she knew almost nothing about Stephen Carlyle's private life. She vaguely recalled meeting his wife a couple of times at department functions, but Nat couldn't conjure up an image of her. Tall, short, thin, heavy, attractive, plain? No idea. But Nat was sure whatever the Mrs. looked like, she paled in comparison to Jessica Asher.

"Alan drive over to Meadowbrook himself?" the detective asked blandly.

"How do you know where he goes?"

"A van from the rehab center comes for him, isn't that right, Steve?" the detective continued.

Carlyle managed a nod. Sherman was wearing out the ink in his pen as he scribbled fast and furiously on his legal pad.

"What time usually?"

Carlyle cleared his throat. "I don't know. I'm not usually home on the days—"

"But that Friday, when you were home, you recall it coming at around eleven-thirty, isn't that what you said?"

"That's what the deputy commissioner said," Sherman broke in.

The detective rubbed his jaw. "Wasn't the van on the early side of eleven that morning?"

This time it was Carlyle who initiated a whispered word to his attorney. Sherman whispered something back.

"It's . . . possible. Yes, yes, maybe it was closer to eleven than eleven-thirty."

Now Nat could see the beads of sweat breaking across the deputy's brow. And she was sure she'd find perspiration stains under the armpits of her linen jacket when this was over. Even the attorney was looking rattled.

"Did you go outside with Alan? Help him get into the van?"

Carlyle rallied slightly, snapping, "Alan doesn't need help. He's very self-sufficient."

The detective merely shrugged. "So, let's see. We've got Alan heading off at ten-thirty-eight A.M.—"

Carlyle's shoulders slumped. His only response—

Nat heard the door to the observation room open behind her and she glanced around. A suave-looking man in a navy suit walked in, nodded to the three of them, remained standing behind them. It was District Attorney Joe Keenan. Quite the headline-making DA, he'd orchestrated several high-profile trials with a perfect track record of convictions. Some folks referred to him as a crusader, others likened him to Superman, a public official seeking truth, justice, and the American way!

Nat watched the way the DA smirked as Carlyle continued to be bombarded with questions. She was well aware that there was nothing in the way of good feelings between Keenan and the deputy commissioner. Keenan had spoken out many times about "our morally corrupt parole system." He believed the Parole Board was too soft and too easily pressured into letting criminals back on the streets long before they should be released. And since Carlyle was the Correction Department's liaison to the Parole Board, Keenan held him accountable as well . . .

"Then you headed down to see your mom at the Maple Hills Nursing Home—what time was it you said you got there?"

This time Carlyle showed no surprise that the cop knew the name of the nursing home. Nat, too, was well past being surprised.

"I'm sure you know precisely what time I got there." Carlyle's voice was now as drained as his complexion.

"According to the sign-in sheet at the nursing home, Steve, you got there at two-ten in the afternoon. Does that sound about right?"

Carlyle's hands were still on the table, but they were clenched tightly now. He didn't answer. The attorney gave his client a nod of approval.

It was making more sense by the minute to Nat why the police had dragged Carlyle down to the precinct house for questioning. They'd already done a lot of legwork and obviously believed they had a prime candidate here. That worst-case scenario the commissioner spoke about was starting to look like a more probable outcome than not. A quick glance at the commissioner's troubled expression confirmed he was having the same thought.

The older detective scratched his thinning hair. He seemed unbothered by the deputy's lack of response. "And it takes what?

You said about an hour to drive down there from your home in Milton?"

Carlyle remained mute.

"So between approximately ten-forty and let's say one P.M. you were home."

"Yes."

"Nursing a headache."

"Yes."

"You didn't take a drive—say around eleven o'clock—into Boston?" Wilson didn't wait for a response. "Let's see, it would take—what?—maybe a half hour, forty minutes tops—to get into town—"

"My client wasn't in Boston that day," Sherman said while Carlyle sat there clenching his jaw.

"Right. Right. You stayed home until you headed down to Plymouth. Wife wasn't at home with you any part of that time?"

"No," Carlyle said tightly.

"Oh yeah, right. She's a nurse over at Fairlane Hospital in Quincy. Seven-to-three shift." The detective's gaze was focused on his notes resting on the table. "And your other son? Sean, right?" He didn't even bother to look up at Carlyle for confirmation. "He works over at McGill's Auto Body. Got there at a little past nine A.M. that Friday. Not a stellar showing, since his boss wants him there at eight on the dot."

Nat saw Carlyle wince, but he remained silent.

"Anyone call or drop by during those three and a half hours you were home by your lonesome? Postman? Neighbor? One of those pesky religious nuts, maybe?"

"No."

"What kind of car do you drive, Steve?"

"I'm sure you already know the answer to that question, Detective." Carlyle's tone was flat. The man looked deflated, face drawn, shoulders sagging.

"Humor me."

Nat noticed the younger detective smile faintly.

"An Acura."

"Color?"

"I believe it's called Hunter Green."

"A 2001? Acura RT?"

Carlyle nodded wearily.

"Giving you problems?"

"What?"

"Car trouble?"

"No."

"So then why'd you rent a car for that day?"

"What? I didn't rent a car. I haven't rented a car in ages."

"Ever drive an SUV, Steve? A white SUV? Maybe a Jeep Cherokee?"

"No."

Wilson looked over at his sidekick. The other detective merely shook his head. Neither man spoke.

Nat was sure the silence was deliberate, a device to make the deputy squirm, but it actually had the opposite effect. Carlyle used the time to pull himself together. He looked over at his attorney. Sherman calmly regarded the lead detective. "Is that it?"

Neither cop responded. Sherman nodded. "Let's go, Deputy Commissioner." Both men rose to their feet.

A door opened and shut behind Nat. She glanced around. The DA was gone.

The lead detective looked over at his silent partner. "You got anything you want to ask the deputy commissioner, Deagan?"

"Not right this sec. Maybe later."

"Yeah, Deputy, maybe later."

The way he said it, there was no maybe about it.

four

FRANCINE ROBIE AND NAT WERE ALONE in the room, the commissioner
having exited right after Carlyle was let go next door. Nat was
sure Miller wanted to catch up with his deputy and have a serious
heart-to-heart with him. She was glad he hadn't asked her to join
in. Nat wasn't ready to converse with Carlyle. She'd learned a lot
watching that interrogation, but she was sure there was plenty
more the cops had up their sleeves. Nat wanted to know what they
had before she had her own little heart-to-heart with Carlyle.

"Can I see that calendar?" Nat asked Robie.

"Hey, I went out on a limb here just letting you observe Carlyle
being questioned."

Questioned? Nat would have called it interrogated.

"I'm guessing that the names of those men in that calendar
qualify as sensitive."

Robie made no comment.

"Men I might recognize. Have possibly heard about. Or, like
the deputy commissioner, even know."

No verbal confirmation from the captain. But sometimes silence could speak volumes.

It was becoming even clearer to Nat why the homicide captain was spearheading this investigation. No doubt she could be counted on to be discreet. It also went a long way to explain the district attorney's appearance so early in the investigation. Keenan must have seen that calendar. It was more than likely he knew or at least knew of the johns. This could be the case of a lifetime for the DA.

"Why single out Carlyle?" Nat persisted. "You've got these other men—four besides the deputy commissioner, you said, who were on her calendar that last week. How many others over the months?"

"The same five showed regularly. There were a few others that came and went," Robie said.

"And have any of them been questioned?"

"I'm very good at what I do, Superintendent. Just as I'm sure you are."

"Then I assume you're pursuing other possibilities as well. People—women as well as men—whose names weren't on that calendar. People with a motive—"

"Are you implying Carlyle has no motive?" Robie interrupted.

"I'm saying you have absolutely no concrete evidence—"

"Which is why he hasn't been charged. Yet."

"Was Jessica Asher a drug user?"

Robie smirked. "You think Carlyle was her pusher as well?"

Nat wasn't amused. "Did her autopsy—?"

"At least at the time of her death she was clean. But she'd just had sexual relations."

"With whom?"

Robie didn't answer.

"Was it on her calendar? Was the man she was with . . . booked?"

"You're still looking a bit pale, Superintendent."

No big surprise there. To either one of them. But Nat was suspicious as to why the homicide captain was commenting on her sorry appearance now. To stop her from pursuing her line of questioning? Who was the man Jessica Asher was screwing shortly before her death? Francine Robie knew. Or had a damn good idea.

Nat needed a way to ingratiate herself a bit, encourage Francine Robie to trust her. More to the point, confide in her. Woman to woman.

"By the way, Captain Robie, a mutual friend sends his regards."

"Leo? He passed them on already. Called me a few minutes before you showed up."

"Oh."

"By the way, happy birthday."

"You and Leo must have had quite the chat."

"We played a bit of catch-up," she said blandly.

So what were they catching up on?

Nat checked her watch. A little before eleven. Too early for lunch. She was about to suggest coffee when Fran Robie beat her to the invite.

Robie poured a heaping teaspoon of sugar into her latte and stirred leisurely. "Leo isn't happy about this."

"He isn't happy about what?"

"He says you have a tendency to get involved in criminal investigations. But I know that already. You've made headlines a few times, Superintendent."

"How about you, Captain? You worried about my interest in this case?"

She sampled her coffee, then set it down, giving no clue as to whether or not it was to her taste. "I'm not the worrying kind."

Nat wished she could say the same.

Robie took a bite of an almond croissant—a flagrant show of disregard for calorie counting. "Good," she said after she chewed and swallowed. "You sure you don't want one?"

"What I want, Captain Robie, is to know what you've got on Stephen Carlyle. Besides his not having an alibi for the time of the hit-and-run. Besides finding his name and those dates in Asher's PDA. As far as means and opportunity go, granted it's a gray area—"

"Gray? Must be one of us is colorblind."

Nat ignored the dig. "As is his supposed motive."

"Let's agree to disagree, what do you say?"

What she would have liked to say was that Robie's smug manner was beginning to grate on her. "What exactly is Carlyle's motive?"

What Nat got was another one of those impudent smiles. "Come on, Superintendent," Robie said. "I bet you've come up with a laundry list of possibilities already."

Nat pushed aside her barely touched cup of Earl Grey tea. "You're awfully quick to zero in on the deputy commissioner."

"Ah, the rush-to-judgment jab."

"If the shoe fits, Captain."

She grinned. "Hey, it's just us girls. How about I call you Nat and you call me Fran?"

Although Nat was suspicious of the reasons for the captain's sudden chumminess, she decided to try to turn it to her advantage. "Okay, Fran. So, how about—just between us gals—you level with me?"

Robie took another swallow of coffee, then demurely dabbed her peach-tinted lips with a paper napkin. "Does the name Griffith Sumner ring any bells?"

It took Nat a few moments to acclimate to this shift. "The Griffith Sumner doing time for murder?"

"That's the one."

Talk about high-profile cases. That one was all over the media for months. Even now, a good ten years later, Nat had a clear memory of the trial of the twenty-three-year-old golden boy. Griffith Sumner was a strikingly handsome young man from an affluent, upper-crust family, a graduate of Harvard, who was tried and, despite the efforts of one of Boston's premier criminal defense teams, convicted of the rape and murder of a seventeen-year-old prostitute. As Robie and Nat sat there in that Starbucks, Sumner was sitting in a cell at CCI Norton. And he was going to be sitting there for quite some time, having gotten a sentence of thirty years to life.

"What about him? What's his connection to Stephen Carlyle?"

"First ask me what Sumner's connection is to Jessica Asher."

"Fine. What's—?"

"Asher had Sumner's name and prison address on her palm. Just in the unlocked calendar, so it wasn't like she felt she needed to keep it private. Interesting to find him there, huh?"

"I'm not sure yet."

"She was a frequent visitor to the joint."

"I assume this is leading—"

"Seems Ms. Asher and Mr. Sumner go way back," Robie continued laconically. "Both attended Miss Hill's Academy in the Berkshires. One of those pricey private high schools for troubled teens."

"I'm not surprised Sumner was having problems even then, but why was Jessica Asher sent there?"

"I wondered the same thing. So I gave the headmistress a call. She wasn't terribly cooperative as to why either Asher or Sumner did time there. Gave me the big spiel about how all information regarding her students, present and past, was strictly confidential."

"Have you spoken to anyone in Asher's family? Her sister?"

"I've been trying. Seems Mrs. Landon is too distraught over her sister's death to answer questions just yet. As for the husband—hell, he wants to distance himself from this business as much as possible. Especially given his position as a councilman, not to mention that he's planning to throw his hat into the ring for the U.S. Senate."

"Just the kind of man this state needs to send to Congress," Nat said dryly, thinking that her ex would no doubt be overjoyed.

"Yeah," Robie said, "like it needs more taxes." There was a reason Massachusetts got dubbed Taxachusetts.

But Nat wasn't interested in getting sidetracked by politics at the moment. "Where does Sumner fit in concerning your investigation into Jessica Asher's death?"

"Don't you mean where does he fit into my investigation concerning the deputy commissioner, a.k.a. Phil Mason?"

"You're making this hard work, Fran."

She smiled, blithely finished off the last piece of croissant, then drank the rest of her latte. Nat ignored her tea. Her stomach was moderately quiescent at the moment and she didn't want to risk throwing it off kilter again.

"Actually, Nat, I'm about to head out to CCI Norton right now to have a little chat with Sumner."

"Mind if I tag along?" she asked.

Robie grinned. "I was hoping you'd ask."

Well, that was a switch. A cop *wanting* her along.

"I can even run you by your place first, if you'd like to change," she offered.

Nat might have forgotten about her less than spotless attire, but the fashionable captain obviously hadn't. Nor had she missed the opportunity to remind Nat of it.

"Good idea," Nat mumbled

As they were heading out of Starbucks, Robie said, "By the way, Sumner's new hotshot lawyer, Jerry Tepper, has apparently come up with enough new evidence in his boy's case to get the courts to grant him another appeal hearing. It's scheduled for January seventh. Tepper's pretty confident he can get Sumner's sentence reduced down to a first-degree manslaughter charge. If he succeeds, Sumner will be eligible for parole in March."

"Even if the appeal is granted, which I personally hope it isn't," Nat said, not eager to see Sumner back on the streets so soon after the heinous crime he committed, "I seriously doubt he's going to be granted parole first time up. Or even his second time." Unless, she was thinking, enough pressure could be brought to bear on the board.

Suddenly the fragmented strands of this budding investigation— victim, suspect, inmate—started to form a pattern. A very disquieting pattern. Because there was one man who could exert that pressure on the Parole Board. And that man was the liaison between the Corrections Department and the Parole Board. That man was Deputy Commissioner Stephen R. Carlyle.

five

DRIVING DOWN THE WINDING TWO-LANE country road, the rare November sun glistening off the fir trees, meadows on one side, rolling hills on the other side, you'd never for a minute imagine that just around a few more bends you'd be coming up on one of the state's medium-security prisons. Don't let the word *medium* fool you. CCI Norton was a concrete-walled prison and every inch of wall was ringed with electrified barbed wire. Towers on all four corners. Correctional officers in those towers—sharpshooters all—manned those posts round the clock. Inmates will tell you, for it all, Norton's a far cry from max—by which they mean CCI Oakville, a.k.a. the big house—and they wouldn't be lying. At least at Norton, they got to look at more than bars twenty-three hours a day. There were programs, although fewer and fewer as the economy got worse and worse and the propunishment lobbyists got stronger and stronger. Still, an inmate could get his GED in there, attend AA, go to therapy, and get to spend more than an hour outside of a locked cell. But an inmate had to earn a move to

Norton. And if he didn't go with the program he was back at Oakville before he could say "I'm innocent"—a line almost every inmate knows by heart. Some of them, as Nat knew only too well, could spout it with such conviction that you might actually believe them. Then there were the ones—not a lot, but some (as she also knew only too well)—who really were innocent.

Nat was pretty damn certain Griffith Sumner wasn't one of the latter. Not that he didn't have his supporters during the trial. Probably still did. Which wasn't to say they all believed he was innocent.

Nat guessed that Jessica Asher must have been one of Sumner's supporters. Did she believe he was innocent? Did she care whether or not he was? It wasn't as though Ms. Asher was all that pure and innocent herself.

Robie parked in a space designated Official Business, and they headed for a gray concrete slab building housing some of the prison's clerical offices, counseling center, private meeting rooms for inmates and counsel, and a large visiting room. That was another plus for the inmates in the medium-security prison. In max, they were separated from their visitors by bulletproof glass and had to use phones to communicate. At Norton, they not only met face-to-face with their visitors, they even got to touch them—as long as they kept it PG rated and they didn't give the officer on duty any grief.

The actual prison where the inmates were housed was behind the building where they'd be meeting with Griffith Sumner. Still, even getting into this first building, you had to go through a metal detector—no exemptions even for cops or correctional personnel. Robie had left her weapon locked in the glove compartment of her vehicle. Nat was unarmed. She did, however, set off the alarm thanks to the gold bracelet she'd forgotten to drop into the dish. She unclasped it and handed it over. It was a gift from Leo. For her last birthday. Nat grimaced—another reminder a whole year'd gone by and her life was, if anything, more complicated and messier than ever.

"You okay?" Robie was already through the security check and was watching Nat finally get the nod that she was clean.

"Fine," Nat muttered, feeling anything but—emotionally and physically. She made a mental note to place mark the bathroom, just in case.

A female CO met them outside the visiting room. "I'll show you to a private meeting room, Superintendent." And then, almost as an afterthought, she glanced over at Fran Robie. "Captain."

The officer made no effort to hide the disapproval in her eyes as she gave the flashy homicide captain the once-over, deliberately lingering at the open shirt that revealed a hint of a black lace bra, Bad enough, Nat was sure the CO was thinking, when the ordinary visitor dressed provocatively, but for a female member of the police force to be so inappropriate was inexcusable.

If Fran Robie picked up on the officer's overt disapproval, she gave no sign of it. Or maybe she simply couldn't care less.

"Shouldn't take more than a couple of minutes," the officer said, unlocking a metal door fitted with a small mesh window. She opened it and they walked into a windowless room outfitted with a wooden table and four chairs, two on each side. The only difference between this space and the interrogation room where Carlyle was questioned earlier at the precinct was that here there was no one-way mirror. There was nothing interrupting the drab institutional green painted walls save for the institutional gray metal door.

Even in the CCI Norton uniform of jeans and pale blue work shirt—both meticulously pressed—Griffith Sumner still looked much like the Ivy Leaguer he was ten years ago. His wheat-blond hair was shiny clean and stylishly cut—one of the inmate barbers had clearly given Sumner extra-special attention. Despite the parade of time, he was trim, buff, even sporting a tan. You'd almost think he'd spent the last ten years at a country club. Only Nat knew Norton was no country club. However, she also knew that some inmates—primarily those with outside heavy-hitter connections and access to money or goods that the money can buy—had an easier time of it. Getting your fellow convicts merchandise they wanted from the street—anything from candy to CDs to drugs—could literally save that inmate's ass.

Robie made the introductions. She was letting Sumner know she was the woman in charge here, and reminding Nat that she was just along for the ride.

Sumner looked openly nervous. Wary. It wasn't surprising, most inmates would feel the same if they were called before a police captain and a prison superintendent. Of course there were also the ones who hid those feelings behind a tough-guy or -gal stance. Especially when being confronted by a female in a role of authority. *I can take whatever you dish out, sweetheart, and I'm not gonna bat an eye.*

"I guess I don't have to introduce myself," Sumner said, attempting an engaging smile. Trying to convey the impression that they were meeting at some social gathering at the venerable country club. Nat caught his eyes stray for a moment to the homicide captain's cleavage—she was sure Robie noticed, too. But hey, who could blame him?

He quickly snapped his gaze back to their faces. The smile wobbled slightly, but hung on.

"I'm surprised you're so upbeat, Sumner." Robie's tone made it clear she wasn't charmed. "Mourning time over already?"

The inmate—who Nat wouldn't have described as upbeat—checked his watch.

"M-O-U-R-N," Robie spelled out each letter slowly. "You got a degree from Harvard so I figure you can spell."

Sumner's mouth twitched, but he swallowed down the gibe.

"You mean . . . Jessica Asher?" Sumner asked.

"Yeah, your girlfriend."

Sumner glanced in Nat's direction, giving her a befuddled look. Like she was going to translate what Robie'd said.

When she didn't, he returned his gaze to the captain. "She wasn't my girlfriend."

"How would you describe your relationship with Jessie? You did call her Jessie, right? Everyone close to her did."

Sumner was silent for a few moments, but then nodded.

"Jessie. Yeah. But we really weren't all that close. She was a friend, Captain. Just a friend. Still, I was broken up when I heard about the hit-and-run accident. Man, she was a beautiful girl. It's really tragic what happened to her."

"When's the last time you saw Jessie?" Robie asked.

The inmate shifted a bit in his chair. "Actually, just . . . just a few weeks ago." His voice cracked and tears welled in his eyes. He blinked them away. Turned his head from them. Nat couldn't tell if this was a true show of sorrow or if he was putting on a performance. *Look at me, ladies. I'm not a rapist, a murderer. I'm a sensitive, caring guy. If only you'd understand . . .*

Nat wondered if he'd tear up if they were two men.

Robie was looking bored. "She visited you a lot."

Sumner cleared his throat. "She was real good that way. Staying in touch, visiting a couple of times a month. Some of my old friends—" He shrugged. "Hey, I'm not blaming any of them for dropping me. If I were in their shoes, I'd probably do the same thing."

"So what'd you two chat about, you and Jessie?"

Sumner shrugged. "This and that. You know, news-from-Lake-Woebegone kind of stuff. Jessie was a real movie buff so lots of times she'd talk about films she'd seen. Me, I'm big on books, so I'd tell her what I was reading. I'm a major Clancy fan." He laughed. "But if I started talking techno-thriller stuff to Jessie she'd kind of blank out."

"And old times? You guys reminisce? Because you two were at Miss Hill's together."

"Ancient history," Sumner told Robie ruefully. "Neither of us cared to reminisce about high school."

"What landed Jessie at Miss Hill's?"

Sumner scowled. "Her dad railroaded her."

"Tell me more," Robie said.

"Jessie was seeing some guy Daddy didn't approve of. The boyfriend was from the proverbial wrong side of the tracks. And he was older."

"How old?" Robie asked.

"I don't know. Like in his twenties. Jessie hardly ever talked about him. I don't even know the guy's name. It was over before she got to Miss Hill's. Which was why she was so pissed at her father for shipping her off to reform school."

"What about you, Sumner? Why'd the folks ship you off to Miss Hill's?"

"What's all this about?" There was an edge in the inmate's voice that wasn't there before. He must have realized it himself, because he quickly lost it. "Look, Captain, I'm real sad about Jessie—real sad—but I don't see what her passing has got to do with me."

"Hey, Griff, you don't want to talk to us, fine," Robie said blandly. But her expression was saying something else altogether.

Sumner had no trouble seeing it and lifted his hands in an I-give gesture. "It's not a problem for me," he said, the bite as well as the charm going out of his voice. "I just don't get why. You want to know why I got shipped off to Miss Hill's, fine. I got mixed up with a wild group one summer out at the Vineyard. They thought breaking into some of the empty homes out there was a lark. It was stupid. Rich kids looking for a thrill. We took dumb stuff. And we were careless. Got caught red-handed maybe the third house we hit. Fortunately, we all had enough family clout to get off with a warning. My dad, however, felt I needed more than that. Hence, Miss Hill's. Not that I resented him for it. He was right. I really straightened my act out there. So much so that I got accepted to Harvard on early decision—"

Sumner perked up. He clearly liked telling this part of his bio.

But all Nat was thinking was, *Oh yeah, you straightened out your act all right. That's why you're sitting in the slammer on a second-degree murder conviction.*

Nat didn't know what Fran Robie was thinking, but she was obviously not particularly interested in what she was hearing because she cut Sumner off abruptly. "Tell me about Jessie's last visit, Sumner."

"Huh?"

"The one a few weeks back. A few days before she was killed."

"What do you want to know?"

"What did the two of you talk about then?"

The inmate pursed his lips. "Last time. I don't remember exactly. Same old."

"Nothing new?" Robie pressed.

Sumner thought for a minute. "No, not really."

"So if you weren't her boyfriend, who was?"

"What?"

"That a word you don't understand, Sumner?" Robie queried sarcastically.

The twitch came back. "She didn't talk about her love life."

"How about her sex life?" Robie challenged, locking eyes with Sumner.

Sumner looked shocked. "Of course not." The shock quickly gave way to open hostility. "You've got some nerve—"

"Was Jessie seeing someone, Mr. Sumner?" Nat asked quietly, wanting to temper the mounting warfare between these two.

He pulled his gaze off Robie. It was only slightly less hostile now that it was directed at Nat. "Why? What's it got to do with some drunk or crazy driver slamming into her?"

"We don't know that the driver was drunk. Or crazy," Nat said.

He stared at her for several long moments. Nat noticed Robie observing her as well. She didn't think the captain was pleased with her getting into the act. Robie was a woman who liked to perform solo, Nat got the feeling she had invited Nat along so that she could see her in action. And be impressed.

Only Nat wasn't all that impressed. She saw it as overkill. Both in Robie's flagrantly sexy appearance and her interrogation style. It shouldn't be the interrogator hogging center stage but the one giving the answers.

"Jessie may have been involved with some guy," Sumner said finally.

"Oh, she was *involved* with a lot of guys, Sumner," Robie cut in. "You know that."

"Don't fucking tell me what I know," the inmate said tightly.

"You forget your manners? There are two ladies present."

Nat was starting to get downright irritated with Robie. "Who was this man she was involved with?"

The inmate's dark gaze remained fixed on the homicide captain as he shrugged. "She didn't say who."

"How about *john*?" Robie said.

"Who? No. I don't know."

"She didn't tell you about all her johns?"

"You are whacked, lady."

"Oh, give me a fucking break, Sumner. You know your girlfriend was hooking. You know the deputy commissioner was one of her johns. Now wasn't that convenient, seeing as how the guy just happens to be mighty influential with the Parole Board."

"What's it to me? I'm not up for parole for years."

"Ah, come on, Robie. Let's not make this into an eight-hundred-page novel. You'd got the word from your big-time lawyer, Jerry Tepper, that you're going up for an appeal hearing. You telling me Jessie didn't know?"

"Yeah, sure I told her. But it's not like I made a big deal over it. I mean, sure, my new mouthpiece is hopeful, but it's far from a done deal, you know."

"But if you do get your sentence reduced, you'll be up for parole real soon."

"Yeah, well, I don't count my chickens before they hatch."

"Oh, I think you do. I think you and your girlfriend hatched yourselves a sure-fire plan—"

"For chris-fucking sake, how many times have I got to tell you? Jessie wasn't my girlfriend."

"Jessie must have had a reason for not telling you her boyfriend's name, Mr. Sumner."

He shrugged at Nat. "Maybe she figured it was none of my business."

Robie slammed her hand on the table, startling them both. "Stop bullshitting us, man. Who's the guy?"

"Honest. I don't know."

Robie looked at Sumner like he was some kind of a bug. "You wouldn't know honest if it hit you in the face."

Sumner gave Nat a pleading look. "Truth is, I didn't want to hear about Jessie's love life."

"Jealous?" Robie asked bitingly.

"Look, Jessie and I were never more than friends. Back in high school we were close, that's as far as it went. If I was jealous, it isn't because Jessie was with someone. It was that I'm not. Come on," he directed this at Nat, "you've got to know what it's like for someone being locked up, Superintendent. Not being able to live . . . a normal life."

"Annie Regan never got to live one either," Nat said soberly. "Thanks to you."

six

"**HAPPY BIRTHDAY. YOU LOOK WONDERFUL. SORRY** I'm late, Natalie." Leo planted a quick kiss on her lips, then slid into the chair across from her. Even in the trendy restaurant's dim candlelight Nat could see that he was looking harried.

"Work?" She knew Leo'd been putting in long hours on a recent homicide, a high school boy gunned down outside a pizza parlor. It was cases involving kids that always took the biggest toll on him.

He gave her a weary smile. "Jakey."

Jakey was Leo's almost-five-year-old son. A little boy who was both achingly adorable and exhaustingly precocious. Nat adored the child. But as with his father, her relationship with Jakey Coscarelli was complicated.

"He isn't sick. . . ."

"No," Leo quickly assured her. This was followed by a lengthy pause.

Leo's lengthy pauses all too often meant one thing. Or more

precisely, one person. Suzanne Holden. Jakey's mom. Jakey's ex–drug addict, ex-prostitute, ex-con mom.

No big surprise that Leo's relationship with Suzanne carried a lot of baggage with it. He'd met her six years ago when she was a resident at a drug treatment center where his mother volunteered. Anna Coscarelli took Suzanne under her wing, encouraged her to take some courses at a community college, and then encouraged her son to tutor her. Given that Suzanne had already done some time on drug and prostitution charges and given that Leo was a cop, in hindsight he was quick to admit it wasn't such a wise idea. Things got messy. Lines were crossed. Suzanne got pregnant. Leo offered to make it legal, but Suzanne was in no state, emotionally or physically, to take on marriage or motherhood. She wanted an abortion. The only way Leo could stop her was to agree to take full custody of the baby. As soon after the birth as she could, Suzanne dropped Jacob Coscarelli into his father's arms and fled. The next time Leo saw her, she was behind bars, convicted of the manslaughter of her pimp while under the influence of crack cocaine. She cleaned up while she did her time, and by now had been out for almost a year, reunited with her child and possibly wanting to reunite with her child's father.

Leo finally stopped looking down at the cover of his gold-embossed menu. "Jakey was really looking forward to spending the weekend at Suzanne's place, but she canceled out at the last minute. Jakey was upset." Again, Leo paused. "This is like the third time in as many months that she's blown him off."

"She's not back into drugs, is she?" Nat asked worriedly.

Not only was Suzanne enmeshed in Nat's personal life because of Leo but in her professional life as well. Suzanne had been an inmate at Horizon House prior to her parole, which made Nat's relationship with Suzanne doubly complicated. She was beginning to think there was no such thing, at least for her, as a relationship that was uncomplicated.

"I don't know," Leo said. "She swears she isn't. And either she's been damn lucky or she's telling the truth." He opened the menu and started to study it.

Suzanne still had almost a year to go to finish up parole.

Which meant random drug tests. So Leo was right. She was either clean or lucky. Nat was praying the former, since a positive test could land her right back behind bars, drug use being an automatic parole violation.

"What reason did she give for not taking him?" Nat knew it wasn't that Suzanne didn't care about her child. She'd seen mother and son together on a number of occasions, Suzanne spending more time than Nat would have liked at Leo's condo, which he shared with his mother. It was always awkward. For both Suzanne and Nat. Suzanne still related to Nat as the authority figure. It would almost be easier for Nat if the ex-con simply saw her as her rival for Leo's affections. Then they'd only have to deal with mutual jealousy.

He suddenly smiled, reaching across the table to take her hand. "Hey, birthday girl, this is supposed to be a celebration. I know you hate birthdays, but let's ignore that and have a good time. We haven't had enough of them lately. And they're important to me, Natalie. Being with you is important to me."

He held her gaze until she looked away.

But he wouldn't release her hand. "I guess I don't say that enough."

Nat could feel her chest constrict. *Oh God,* she thought, *if I am pregnant let this baby be his . . .*

Even as she had that thought, a voice in her head whispered, *Be careful what you wish for.*

"What gives with Suzanne, Leo?"

Nat had returned her gaze only for Leo to break contact. "Hey, they've got Dover sole on the menu. Your favorite." Leo was studying the menu as if he was about to be tested on it.

Nat waited.

Leo closed the menu. "She's seeing someone."

"Who? How long?" she blurted.

"A buyer she met at work about a month ago. He's got a place in Rhode Island and he asked her to come down for the weekend. She says she tried to change the date, but he travels a lot and this was the only weekend he'd be available until after Christmas."

"It sounds serious. I mean, if she's going away with him—"

Nat's mind was spinning with possibilities. Was it serious? Did this mean Suzanne was stepping out of the picture? And most important, how did Leo feel about this turn of events?

"Whatever," Leo muttered, reaching for the wine list.

His curt comeback didn't inspire confidence.

But he quickly offered up a smile, a sure sign that he wanted to appease her and that he wanted to end the conversation.

"Champagne?" he suggested, looking up from the wine list.

Nat almost said yes—wanting to drop the subject of Suzanne Holden as well since she didn't care to share her intimate birthday celebration with the other woman—before she remembered. Remembered, one, that she couldn't drink alcohol if she was pregnant. Remembered, two, that she'd somehow managed to forget to pick up that damn pregnancy kit what with all that had gone down that day.

"I think I'll stick to iced tea tonight," she said. "I might have a little stomach bug. Nothing serious," she quickly added. Leo worried about her. It was one of his qualities she found both endearing and frustrating, depending on the situation.

"Yeah," he said. "I know."

It didn't take her long to guess how. "Fran Robie?"

Leo nodded.

"Why is she reporting to you?"

Leo set down the wine list and eyed her straight on. "I wish you'd reconsider getting involved in this one, Natalie."

"Believe me, I didn't go looking for it. The commissioner him-self—"

"Yeah, I know that too. But there's getting involved and there's getting involved."

Nat didn't have to ask him to distinguish between the two be-cause she knew what he meant.

"Robie seems happy to have my help."

"Fran Robie's famous for using people to 'help' her."

Now she did need edification. "Meaning?"

"Meaning," Leo said, an edge in his tone, "the woman's very single-minded. Meaning she's not going to be watching your back. I'm not saying she'll deliberately put you at risk. But she's not going to stop you from putting yourself there. She's not even going to try to discourage you. Not if it means it'll get her closer to nailing the perp. This is a hot case. If Robie nails it, she's moving on up. Yet again. And that's what Robie wants. It isn't luck got her to captain at the age of thirty-six. And she has much higher aspirations."

"I thought the two of you were friends."

Leo smiled crookedly. "Did I ever say we were friends?"

The waiter approached, putting their conversation on hold. Nat ordered the Dover sole. So did Leo. And they both went with the iced tea.

"How strong a case does Robie think she has against Carlyle?"

"What makes you think she'd tell me?" Leo asked.

"Because if what you say about Robie is true, she'd use you, too."

"What use would I be to her?"

Her eyes locked with his. She was working on pure hunch here, but some of her hunches had paid off big in the past. "You tell me, Leo."

He paused again. So she was on the right track. After a few moments, he relented. Probably because he figured Robie would tell her if he didn't. "I know the sister."

"Jessica Asher's sister? Debra Landon? How do you—?"

"Chloe Landon was Jakey's girlfriend."

"What?"

He smiled. "The kids were in the same class in nursery school last year. They were like Siamese twins. When I took Jakey out of PlayDays, he was heartsick for weeks because he missed his best buddy. I finally called Debra Landon up and asked her if the kids could have a play date. She was all for it. Said Chloe was missing Jakey a lot too. Of course, she said she understood why I enrolled Jakey in another nursery school after . . ." Leo hesitated, his expression grim. It had been a year, but Nat knew the memory of Jakey being kidnapped outside of that exclusive nursery school was still raw for him. Thank God, they'd found Jakey quickly and he'd been unharmed. But while Jakey wasn't traumatized by the experience, all the people who loved the little boy—Nat included—were.

"Anyway, Debra invited Jakey over to play with Chloe. After that, the kids got together at either her place in Wellesley or mine in Boston once or twice a week for a few months. Then the passion kind of petered out," he added with a smile.

"And so you got to know Debra Landon a bit?"

His gaze narrowed. "You pumping me, Natalie?"

"Of course I am. I want to talk with her, Leo. Robie's been getting the runaround—"

"I know."

"Are you going to ask Debra to talk with Robie?"

"No," Leo said succinctly.

"Did you know her husband's planning to run for the Senate?"

Leo looked surprised. "I did, but how did you know?"

"Fran Robie told me." She gave him a curious look. "Is it a secret?"

"Not exactly, but there's been no public announcement. Debra made a point of asking me not to say anything." He shrugged. "Not everyone who's asked to keep something under wraps keeps their mouths shout."

"I'm not surprised that you do," she said with a smile. "So, how about it?"

"How about what?"

"I'd really like to talk to Debra Landon, Leo. It isn't like I'm a cop or anything. Griffith Sumner says Jessica was seeing someone, but he wouldn't say who. Debra might be more forthcoming."

Leo exhaled a loud sigh. "I plead with you to back off and what do you do?"

Before he could finish, she said, "I'm using you. No question about it, Leo. But I will watch your back. And I know you'll watch mine."

He smiled and Nat knew it was despite himself. Then he dipped his hand into the pocket of his navy jacket and pulled out a small velvet box. He slid it across the table and her heart started pounding, her eyes riveted on it. If this was what she thought it was, complicated wouldn't begin to describe her relationship with Leo Coscarelli.

"Happy birthday, Natalie."

She couldn't move. If she could have, she'd probably have made a race for the ladies' room and upchucked her iced tea.

And then suddenly Leo gasped with realization. "Oh, shit, Natalie. It isn't . . . I didn't think . . . The box . . . I . . . Hey, it's a pair of earrings, Natalie. The ones you almost bought that day we were at that antique shop looking for a gift for my mom, but then decided they cost too much money. . . . You loved them so much. . . . I wanted to give you something special."

He was watching her closely as if he were trying to discern whether this birthday gift was a relief or a disappointment. How to explain that it was both?

seven

NAT WAS JUST TURNING DOWN DESSERT, Leo trying to persuade her to share a crème brûlée—a particular favorite of hers, but not now—when her cell phone rang.

"It's Fran," the voice said on the other end of the line. There was a sense of urgency bordering on excitement in her voice.

"Robie?" Nat threw a puzzled glance at Leo. He didn't look puzzled. He looked annoyed.

"Sorry to interrupt the festivities, Nat, but I thought you'd want to know we're bringing Carlyle back in for questioning. My boys are picking him up as we speak."

"I don't understand. Why at this hour of the night? What's the urgency?"

"I'll tell you all about it when you get here." She paused for a moment. "Oh, and tell Leo he's welcome to come along."

Nat didn't bother to extend the invitation, knowing Leo would be coming whether or not he'd been invited.

. . .

"Where's Carlyle?"

"In a holding cell. Waiting for his lawyer to get here." Robie shifted her gaze from Nat to Leo, who walked in right behind her.

He glanced around Robie's uniquely appointed office. If he was impressed by the female touch he didn't show it. Same was true regarding Fran Robie's appearance. The sexy blonde had changed into a short, pencil-straight burgundy wool skirt and a champagne-colored fitted jacket. If there was a blouse—or anything else underneath—it wasn't showing. Only thing showing was that flash of cleavage she liked to display.

"Hey, nice to see you, Leo. Been a while. Too long. How are you?" She extended a hand. He took it and she held on for a few beats longer than necessary. In Nat's opinion.

"Great—until you called," Leo said dryly. He was the one to withdraw his hand. Good move. Again, in Nat's opinion.

"Yeah, sorry about that." But Fran Robie didn't look even slightly contrite.

She gestured to the armchairs the commissioner and Nat had occupied that morning, but Nat remained standing. So did Leo. "So tell me what you came up with between the time I left you this afternoon and nine o'clock tonight."

Robie reached behind her desk and retrieved a manila envelope. She handed it over to Nat. "Go on. You can handle them. They're copies. The originals are down at the lab."

Nat glanced over at Leo before she lifted the flap on the envelope and pulled out four photocopies of photographs. Two of them were solo shots of a naked man. In one of the photos he was standing at the foot of a bed. In the other he was lying on the bed, his face contorted in what could be either pain or ecstasy. The other two shots showed a couple on what looked to be the same bed. Here the man was on top of the woman, his face in profile, the woman's face mostly hidden thanks to both the angle from which it was shot and the blonde hair that had fallen across her face. In the final shot, also a pair having sex, the man was again lying on his back on the bed, the woman astride him. The woman's back was to the camera, but because of the way she was leaning over the man, his face was plainly visible.

In each photo, it was the same man. Stephen R. Carlyle.

Shit.

Nat passed the photos over to Leo and then sat down in the nearest armchair. She needed to. Leo looked through the photos quickly and silently.

"How do you know the woman in these photos is Jessica Asher?" she asked Robie.

Robie retrieved the photos from Leo, pulled out the one of the woman leaning over Carlyle. Then she lifted a small magnifying glass off the top of her desk. She handed both to Nat.

"Check her back. Left shoulder blade. It looks like a smudge until it's magnified," she said. "Then you can see it's a tattoo."

Nat focused the lens over the smudge. "A butterfly."

"Unless you'd rather I didn't, I'll spare you the Asher autopsy photos that indicate the same tattoo," Robie said.

She definitely wanted to be spared those grisly shots.

"Where did you find them?" Nat asked. "Or did someone give them to you?"

Robie's phone rang before she got an answer. If she'd found them at Asher's apartment, what else had the captain and her boys unearthed over there? Sexually explicit photos of the socialite with other men? Incriminating letters? A juicy tell-all diary? It could take a degree of pressure off Carlyle if some other suspects had also come to light. But Nat got the feeling, no matter what the homicide captain might or might not have dug up, she seemed to think that Stephen Carlyle was the most viable suspect.

Robie hung up the phone. "Carlyle's lawyer is here."

"Who's doing the questioning this time?" Nat asked.

Robie smiled. "I think I'll give it a whack." A chance to perform not just for Nat this time but for Leo too.

"Can I talk to him first?" Nat asked.

Robie's smile deepened. "And give him a heads-up? I don't think so, Nat. But you can join the party if you like."

It was going to be anything but a party, but she was in, all right. Despite Leo's sour expression. And her sour stomach.

eight

WILSON, THE LEAD DETECTIVE IN THE investigation—the one who interrogated Carlyle this morning—had not been called in to run the
show, or even sit quietly and observe it this time. Leo was observing, however. From behind the one-way mirror. Robie and Nat
were alone in the small, airless room, already sitting at their side
of the table when Carlyle and his attorney, Fred Sherman, entered.

"What's she doing here?" This was the first thing out of Carlyle's mouth. He glared at Nat with a look bordering on rage.

"If you'd rather I leave . . ." Nat started to say, but stopped
when Sherman leaned closer to his client and whispered something in his ear.

Whatever he said didn't make Carlyle look any less furious, but
he muttered, "Fine. Let's just get this over with."

The photos were on the table, spread out, facing Carlyle. Only
now that his inflammatory gaze shifted off Nat did he see them.
His reaction was both swift and dramatic.

He turned gray and started to sway. His lawyer, having also

gotten an eyeful of the photos, firmly gripped Carlyle's arm—no doubt to keep him from hitting the floor in a dead faint—and hastily guided him down onto one of the wooden chairs, immediately taking the one beside him.

Carlyle shut his eyes. Nat noted that the DC was no longer wearing the dark suit he'd worn that morning. He must have changed into the khaki chinos and pale blue polo shirt, when he got home. Nat didn't think she'd ever seen him out of a suit before. Never seen the paunch that extended over his waistband, a jacket having done an effective job of hiding the fact that he could stand to lose maybe thirty pounds. Something told her he might start shedding pounds now, given his current situation. And his situation was likely to get worse.

His attorney looked like he thought so. His worried eyes were fixed on his client, a hand on his shoulder. "Would you like some water, Stephen?"

Carlyle faintly shook his head.

Sherman set his briefcase on the table, right over half the photos—a deliberate move, Nat was sure—and said nothing more.

There was a palpable silence in the room. After a very long couple of minutes, Robie broke it when she pressed the record button on the tape recorder and said, "This is Friday, November seventh—" she paused, checked the clock on the wall—"nine forty-eight P.M. I am conducting this interview with Stephen R. Carlyle. He is accompanied by his attorney, Frederick Sherman. Also in attendance is Superintendent Natalie Price."

Carlyle's eyes remained closed during Robie's statement. Now he dropped his head into his hands. Again Sherman leaned over and whispered something in his client's ear. Carlyle was shaking his head even before the lawyer finished.

Robie appeared perfectly at ease. And in no hurry to begin the interrogation. Nat, on the other hand, was anything but relaxed. She not only wanted it to get started, she couldn't wait for it to be over.

Finally Carlyle lifted his head and opened his eyes, pinching the bridge of his nose as if struggling to regain some composure. An effort that wasn't successful. He looked so lost, so full of anguish, Nat almost felt sorry for him. Which wasn't easy, considering she was no longer thinking this was a man incapable of murder.

Carlyle's eyes flickered from Nat to Robie, then the sight of neither one of them being tolerable, he shut his eyes again.

"You familiar with these photos, Steve?" Robie asked.

Eyes still closed, he shook his head.

"Man," Robie mused, her voice taking on a husky tinge, "snaps like these could really tarnish a man's reputation if they got into the wrong hands."

"My client has already said—"

Robie cut Sherman off. "I know what he said. I want to know what else he has to say."

A quiver passed over Carlyle's face as he slowly reopened his eyes. "I was having an affair with her," he said in a flat voice.

Robie smirked. "An *affair*?"

Carlyle looked away.

"Since when?"

"Since August."

"Where?" She tapped the photos. "Where were these taken, Steve? Where'd the two of you hook up for your *affair*?"

Nat saw the deputy commissioner's lower lip quiver. "Ten fourteen Joy Street," he said in a bare whisper.

Robie eyed the deputy ruefully. "Not much joy for Jessica Asher when she was crossing Joy Street that Friday."

Still, Robie looked pleased. Until now, the police hadn't been able to zero in on how it was Asher had come to be on Joy Street the day she was run down. She didn't live there or anywhere close by. She had an apartment across town in the South End.

Robie got up.

"Are we done?" Sherman asked, starting to get up as well.

"We're far from done, my friend," Robie said wryly. "I just need to go powder my nose."

Nat was sure Robie had gone out to arrange to have a team of techs hightail it over to 1014 Joy Street to conduct a thorough search.

Carlyle's lawyer passed the time scowling and scribbling notes on a yellow legal pad. Carlyle passed the time by giving Nat a cold stare and the silent treatment.

Robie was back in less than two minutes. It felt to Nat like it was a lot longer.

As soon as the homicide captain sat back down, Carlyle's demeanor changed. He gave Robie an earnest look. "The last time I saw that poor woman was on Wednesday, October fifteenth. I didn't see her after that Friday. I didn't kill her. I have no idea who did. There's nothing else I can say."

Robie mulled this over for a few beats. "I doubt that, Mr. Carlyle."

Fred Sherman stowed his legal pad back inside his attaché case. "My client has made his statement. That's all you're getting, Captain Robie. Now, unless you intend to press charges against the deputy commissioner—" As he spoke, he lifted his briefcase off the table, preparing to leave.

Robie cut him off, zeroing in on Carlyle. "How much?"

Carlyle stared narrowly at her but made no response.

"Come on, Stevie. You're not gonna sit here and tell me she provided her services free of charge."

Carlyle continued glowering.

"I don't think Ms. Asher's family would appreciate your unfounded, not to mention vilely distasteful, innuendoes, Captain," Sherman said officiously.

"It's not an innuendo," Robie said blithely, her gaze still fixed on the deputy commissioner, who, despite his irate expression, was looking ill.

"Look, Captain. We were two consenting adults having sex. The only crime I've committed is a moral one—adultery. And I'm—"

"Did you also consent to being photographed, Stevie?"

Carlyle's hand pressed against his chest. He looked like he was in pain. Understandable. "I . . ."

Sherman put a hand on Carlyle's arm. "You don't have to say another word, Stephen."

Robie lifted up one of the photos, studying it thoughtfully. "Was she worth it?"

As if involuntarily, Carlyle's eyes fell on the rest of those lurid photos. Nat could almost feel him trying to look away, but they held him fixed.

"Yeah," Robie said with a provocative smile, "I bet she was."

Carlyle remained mute. Sherman, however, was getting ready to say something, but Robie cut him off before he got a word out.

"Superintendent Price and I paid a visit to Griffith Sumner this afternoon."

Nat was watching Carlyle closely for some sign of—what? Alarm? Fear? Wariness? Anger?

But the deputy looked only wrung out.

"We were discussing his chances for parole if the appeals court rules in his favor and reduces his conviction to manslaughter one. What do you think about his chances, Deputy?" Robie asked Carlyle in a deceptively nonthreatening tone.

Carlyle couldn't fully bury his emotions now. Nat saw a muscle in the DC's jaw start to pulsate and she was sure his teeth were clenched tight as metal clamps. There was another hurriedly whispered word from his counsel, no doubt cautioning him to keep silent. Nat didn't believe Carlyle had any intention of responding in any event.

"Is there anything else you want to ask my client, Captain?"

"Oh, I've got plenty more questions for Stevie, Sherman. But I don't want to hit the poor guy with 'em all at once," Robie said dryly. Even though Robie was the one saying this to Carlyle's lawyer, Nat was the one the deputy commissioner started to glare at with relentless intensity.

Sherman was already on his feet. "Then we're out of here." When the lawyer saw that Carlyle had made no move, he once again grabbed hold of his arm, this time helping him up from his chair. Carlyle continued glowering at Nat until the lawyer literally maneuvered him around to face the door.

Why was Nat left feeling that, somehow, she was the one who'd committed a crime?

. . .

"What do you think?"

Leo gave Nat a quick glance. "I think it's not looking good for *Stevie.*"

They were in her Subaru Outback, Leo having left his car at the restaurant lot so that they could ride over to the precinct house together.

"Don't turn here," Leo said.

"But your car—"

"We can pick it up tomorrow morning. Just go straight."

Translation? Leo wanted to spend the night at her place. The prospect of which sparked the nerves all over her body. In both positive and negative ways.

"What about Jakey? Won't he be upset if he doesn't see you when he gets up in the morning?"

Leo saw right through her. "Don't you want me to stay, Natalie?"

"Yes, of course I do. But you said earlier that Jakey was—"

"Jakey will be fine. My mom's going to take him to Pollyanna's Pancake House for breakfast. That put a big smile on his face. Plus, I'm going to try to cut out early tomorrow and take him to Chuck E. Cheese for supper. A total pig-out day for the kid."

Her stomach did a flip-flop at the thought of pancakes and pizza, both of which she usually loved.

"So, what's going on, Natalie?" he said after she'd been driving silently for several minutes in the direction of her condo in Brookline. "It isn't the earrings."

"No, they're beautiful. I love them. I love that you remembered." She was wearing the antique gold drops inset with tiny ruby chips. She reached out and touched his cheek. He placed his hand over hers.

"I always thought we could confide in each other," he said, not even trying to hide the hurt in his voice.

Nat was hurting, too. She wanted to confide in him. But not now. Not yet.

"It's this business with Carlyle," she said, only half lying. "No way is this going to stay hidden under the rug now. You can bet someone from the mayor's office is going to be on the phone to both Robie and the commissioner by the morning. Probably the mayor himself."

The recently inaugurated mayor was Daniel Milburne, a politico Nat had tangled with the previous year when she was trying to uncover who'd brutally slashed one of her inmates. Milburne made it to the top of her suspect list for a while. Winning her no favor with him. Which was just fine by Nat. The man might not have been guilty of murder, but no question he was ruthless and corrupt. And he ran one of the dirtiest campaigns in the city's gritty political history. Needless to say, Milburne hadn't gotten her vote.

Leo glanced over at her. "Where are you?"

Nat sighed wearily. "Carlyle and the whole department are going to get smeared across every tabloid in town. And Carlyle's family . . ." She paused, acutely aware that the scandal that was about to go public would affect a lot of innocent people, detritus polluting everyone who was close to both the deputy commissioner and Jessica Asher. That meant her as well as a lot of others. It wasn't fair, but that's the way it was. "God, Carlyle's wife . . . how is she going to feel when she finds out her husband's been screwing around—?"

"Maybe she knows already," Leo suggested.

"You think he told her?"

"There are lots of ways for someone to find out if their partner's been cheating on them."

Something in his tone sparked an anxious prickle at the back of her neck. Was Leo talking about Carlyle now? Or her? Did he know about her recent dalliance with Jack?

That worry was pushed aside when she pulled into her condo parking spot. Standing just outside the garage-level elevator was the last person on earth she wanted to encounter at the moment. Stephen R. Carlyle. He started toward her as she got out of the car.

"I have to talk to you, Superintendent. Alone." Carlyle addressed her with the same familiar bite in his voice she'd heard on plenty of occasions in the past.

She turned to Leo and extended her car keys to him. "Drop it off in the morning."

He ignored the keys in her outstretched hand. "I'm not leaving you alone with—" His wary eyes were fixed on Carlyle.

"I'll be fine," she cut him off, her voice resolute.

Leo knew when it was pointless to argue with her. He looked grim, but he took the keys.

Nat was looking pretty grim, herself.

nine

NAT'S BEAUTIFUL GOLDEN RETRIEVER, HANNAH, USUALLY a good judge of character, had made a place for herself at Carlyle's feet, her chin resting contentedly across the deputy's shiny cordovan loafers. So what positive vibes did her dog pick up from the DC that she didn't?

"Can I get you a drink?" she offered, mostly because she didn't know what to say and, so far, Carlyle was not saying anything.

"Scotch. Neat." His tone remained brusque, an unmitigated scowl on his face.

Nat got him the drink and poured herself some Coke, hoping it'd settle her stomach.

Carlyle took the scotch without a word and downed it in one long swallow. She didn't offer him a refill. An angry Stephen Carlyle was bad enough. She definitely didn't want to contend with him when he was both angry and drunk.

He looked down at Hannah. "Never did think it right for someone who's hardly ever home to have a dog. They need love and attention. You must come home to a lot of accidents."

Maybe it was the growing likelihood that she was pregnant that made the DC's remarks about her capacity for nurturing particularly disturbing, not to mention unjust. "I often zip home for lunch and take Hannah out. Plus I pay my neighbor down the hall to come in a couple of times a day—"

"You always have an answer, don't you, Price?"

"Unlike you, Deputy," she snapped. "Seems to me you're mighty short on answers to some very important questions."

She prepared herself for another attack, but he merely put the empty glass on her coffee table and scratched Hannah behind her ear. "Miller says you want to help me."

Interesting spin the commissioner'd put on it.

"I don't want your help, Superintendent. I don't want you involved in any way. Do I make myself clear?" Oddly enough, Carlyle sounded less belligerent than before. Maybe the booze was beginning to take the edge off his animosity. Having had no alcohol herself, Nat's animosity was very much intact. Still, she had made a commitment to the commissioner.

She took a sip of Coke. "What are you going to do?"

He rotated his neck as if to dislodge a kink. "Go home. Tell my wife."

So his wife *didn't* know about Jessica Asher. Or, remembering Leo's pointed observation, at least Carlyle didn't think she knew.

But then a new possibility struck her. Was Carlyle referring to his sexual encounter or the murder? Was he going to confess to his wife that he killed Jessica Asher? Was he feeling the need to come clean to someone? A wife was a good pick. Spouses couldn't be made to testify against their partners. Not to say Mrs. Carlyle couldn't opt to take the stand—

"After that . . ." Carlyle shrugged as if the rest was of small consequence. But at the same time he was eyeing his empty glass with open longing, indicating to Nat that he wasn't as indifferent as he appeared about what would happen next. More likely, he found it too humiliating to reveal his true feelings to someone for whom he held so little regard.

Nat watched him as he continued to fix his gaze on that glass. Shit, she decided, one more drink wouldn't get him soused.

Maybe it'd loosen him up some more and he'd drop his guard and decide to come clean with her. Make a full confession. Assuming he had something to confess that she didn't already know.

All this assuming she really wanted to know more.

She took the empty glass, headed to the kitchen to refill it, and brought it back.

If Carlyle was grateful for her hospitality, he certainly was keeping it to himself. He did, however, down the second shot without pause. When the glass was again empty, instead of setting it down, this time he held on to it with both hands.

"Miller said this morning he won't ask for my resignation. But that was before he knew. . . ." Another sentence Carlyle left unfinished. He craned his neck again. Looked idly around her living room.

"Did you know those photos existed?"

Nat could see his jaw muscles knot up instantly at her question. He smiled bitterly as he fixed her with an acid look. "You must be thoroughly enjoying this, Price."

"What? No, of course I'm not—"

"Hey, I don't blame you. If the tables were reversed, I'd be the first one laying into you."

Nat didn't doubt that for a minute. And no question, that rankled. Tempting her to give as good he'd given her. But the truth was, she wasn't finding an iota of pleasure in the man's misery. "That's not my intention—to 'lay into you'."

"Don't patronize me, Price," he said sharply. "You think you've got something over me now—"

Her irritation was fast turning into fury. "You're in deep shit, Carlyle."

"It's my shit, not yours. I don't like you, Price."

"I'm not crazy about you either," she blurted.

She actually caught a shadow of a smile pass over his lips.

"Robie thinks she's got her man, Steve. Does she?" Nat asked bluntly.

"Why should you believe anything I say?"

"Try me?" she challenged.

He offered another bitter smile, set the glass on the coffee table, then rose to his feet. Hannah, dislodged by his move, got up, too, lifting her head to give her new friend a baleful look.

Nat stayed seated. "Did Jessica Asher ever mention anyone that might want to do her harm? Anyone she was worried about? A boyfriend, maybe?"

His scowl morphed into a smirk. "We didn't do a lot of talking, Superintendent."

"How did you meet her?" she asked.

Carlyle glanced down at Hannah, who had begun nuzzling his pants' leg. His expression softened noticeably. "How old is she?"

"Eighteen months."

"We always had Labs when my kids were young."

His kids. Right. Two sons. One was a paraplegic, the other sounded like a ne'er-do-well. Whatever relationship Carlyle had with his boys, it was about to be tested to the limits, as with husband and wife. Guilty of murder or not, Stephen R. Carlyle had committed adultery with Jessica Asher. On numerous occasions.

"I think Dana will forgive me," he said, patting Hannah.

For committing adultery or murder?

"It's going to be hardest on my boy Alan. He's had this image of me as . . ." Carlyle's voice faltered at the mention of his paraplegic son. Hannah nudged him to continue patting her.

He bent and gave her one final rub, then straightened up. Hannah gave his leg a few more nudges, then, accepting that was all she was going to get from her new pal, she slunk over to Nat and deposited her head on her owner's lap.

So now you want me, you traitor, Nat thought as she caressed Hannah's silky ears.

"This time you'll be biting off far more than you can chew, Price," Carlyle said soberly despite the two drinks.

Nat was sure he was right. But it was interesting that he was presuming, despite his order, that she was not about to back off.

"I've told you that before," he reminded her even though she certainly didn't need any reminders. "I was right on those occasions. I'm even more right now." He leveled a finger at her as if it was the barrel of a gun. "Leave it be, Price."

She stood up, causing Hannah to bark in annoyance. "Tell me why."

Carlyle shook his head wearily. "You're a fool, Price. Either that, or you've got a serious death wish."

"I take that to mean you think someone will wish me dead if I pursue this investigation."

"Wish?" He gave a harsh laugh. "Yeah, like someone *wished* Jessica Asher dead."

ten

EVERYONE KNOWS THAT WHEN A PHONE rings at three in the morning it's invariably bad news. No one knew it better than Nat. The first ring and she was instantly awake. She lifted the receiver before the second shrill ring.

"Sorry to wake you, Nat."

She recognized the voice instantly. It was her head officer Gordon Hutchins. "What?" she asked immediately.

"It's Paul LaMotte. He had a stroke, Nat. He passed away before the EMT guys got here."

"Oh no," she said, her voice catching. Paul LaMotte had been her clerk since the second month she'd started Horizon House. An inmate trustee doing a life sentence with no possibility of parole, he was just about to turn fifty-seven. His last thirty years had been spent behind bars after a conviction for arson and two counts of murder in the first degree. His wife and his son. LaMotte turned himself in the day after his house burned down, admitting to having started the fire. But he swore his wife and boy were supposed to be staying over at his mother-in-law's home that night. He committed arson for the insurance premium. A meager ten thousand bucks, money he said he desperately needed to pay down medical bills resulting from his son's recent heart surgery.

Nat was always skeptical when an inmate claimed he was innocent, but she had come to believe Paul LaMotte. Not that he ever tried to have his case appealed. He told her once that he wanted to spend his life in prison because for all intents and purposes his life ended when the only two people in the world he'd ever loved died. And while he never swayed in his claim that he thought the house was empty, he nevertheless held himself responsible for their deaths. He spent most of his first couple of years of incarceration in the isolation unit at CCI Oakville—in those days known as Oakville Correctional Facility for Men—under a suicide watch.

Paul LaMotte was a quiet, reserved, dignified man who had learned one thing well: how to do time.

"Nat?"

Hutch's voice pulled her back to the present.

"I'm here."

"You okay?"

"Yeah," she said.

"I liked him, too, Nat. And you know I don't like a hell of a lot of 'em."

Hutch and Nat both knew he liked more inmates than he'd own up to liking. Her head CO maintained a tough-but-fair-guy image with the cons. Showed no favorites. Pulled no punches.

"There's no family left," she said quietly. "Paul's mother died last year. She was the last. . . ." She felt her throat constrict, tears filling her eyes. "We'll have a small service at the house on Sunday. I'll call Reverend Peterson later this morning and make the arrangements."

"I'll take care of that." Hutch hesitated. "And the interment?"

Nat swallowed hard. With no family and being a ward of the Commonwealth, LaMotte's remains would be placed in a plain pine coffin made at one of the correctional facilities and he would be buried at state expense in a prison cemetery.

"I want him buried next to his wife and son—"

"Nat, you know that's not—"

"I'll handle it, Hutch," she said firmly, already planning her call to Commissioner Miller at his home in Marblehead. He owed her.

"I'm afraid there's one more thing," Hutch said as she was about to hang up.

Nat could hear in his voice that he hated having to be the bearer of more bad tidings.

"Go ahead. Hit me with it," she said wearily. Why was it crises couldn't come one at a time with at least some breathing space between?

"It's about Finn."

"What now?" Nat already knew the outcome of Dennis Finn's disciplinary hearing, having gone back to the house for a couple of hours in the late afternoon. The vote had been unanimous to send Finn back to Norton. She read through the notes on the hearing and cast her vote in favor as well. Finn apparently seemed prepared for the decision and, according to the report, took the news with grim resignation.

"I guess it took a while to really hit him," Hutch said. "It finally did about an hour ago. Got himself good and worked up. His roommate, Leroy Gibbs, tried to calm him down and got Finn's fist in his mouth for the effort."

"Was Gibbs badly hurt?"

"Probably woulda lost a couple of teeth, but I suppose you could say he's lucky that he ain't got no teeth and that he takes his false ones out when he goes to bed. Still, he's gonna have a fat lip for a time."

"And Finn?"

"We got him in lockdown. He banged around there for a bit, but he's quiet now."

"We need to ship him back first thing in the morning, Hutch." It invariably created tension in the house when an inmate had to be returned to a locked facility. On the plus side, it impressed on the residents the harsh result of breaking house rules. On the minus side, it could stir up a lot of generalized anxiety and even resentment. The longer the inmate who was going back stuck around, the more problems could be sparked. And Nat had enough problems without adding this one to the mix.

"Not to worry, Nat. Go back to sleep."

"Yeah, right," she said wryly.

It was just past 8:00 A.M. Nat never did manage to get back to sleep. She'd showered and dressed and had already spoken on the phone to Jack Dwyer and Sharon Johnson about Paul LaMotte and Dennis Finn. And about the morning headlines. There was a leak. No big surprise there. And it was worse than she'd feared. Not only had the papers seized on the questioning of the deputy commissioner of corrections in the hit-and-run death of Jessica Asher, Nat had also been drawn into the act. Some reporter must have followed Carlyle when he left the precinct and was lying in wait in the shadows in her garage to see what was what. He or she not only saw but managed to snap a photo of Nat and Carlyle entering her elevator. Their backs were to the camera, so the photo itself couldn't identify them, but the reporter noted the pertinent info.

Still, the leak could have been even worse. Those lurid photos could have surfaced. So far, there'd been no mention in the papers of them or even about the sexual connection between Asher and Carlyle. But Nat knew it was only a matter of time.

Nat wished she could get Robie to confide in her. She believed there was a part of the homicide captain that wanted to, if only to show how much she knew. But Nat was sure Robie was being pressured from above to keep a tight lid on this investigation. For all Nat knew, someone who was on Asher's appointment calendar himself—a client with power and influence—was the guy issuing orders. Orchestrating the investigation. Using Robie as the front man.

And given Leo's assessment of Fran Robie, no question that she'd play along. But how far would Robie go to demonstrate her cooperation? Would she protect someone from being exposed even if he or she were guilty?

As Nat was grappling with this conundrum, her phone rang. It was the commissioner. He was understandably very upset, not just because of the story and photo of his superintendent and the deputy commissioner in the paper but because there were already a slew of reporters and cameramen lurking outside his home, hoping to squeeze a comment out of him the instant he showed his face.

"Which I have to do shortly," he said grimly, "because someone from the mayor's office called me five minutes ago to inform me that Milburne and the DA want to see me at nine this morning for a briefing."

"Do you know about the photos Fran Robie has—"

"Yeah, I know," Miller cut her off. "The DA's already seen them. So has Mayor Milburne."

Milburne. Talk about a man with power and influence. Talk about a man who could exert influence over a cop, especially one with big aspirations. Talk about a man who Nat could certainly imagine frequenting call girls. What if Milburne was one of the men in Asher's date book?

Talk about making a rush to judgment. Still, what Nat wouldn't have given to get a gander at Asher's PDA.

"Have you spoken with Carlyle?" she asked the commissioner.

"I called him at home right after I got the call from the mayor's office. Got the answering machine. He's probably been inundated with calls since the news hit, and isn't picking up."

Nat was wondering if Carlyle was still at home. If she were his wife, he wouldn't be. Nat would have handed him his walking papers and changed the locks on her doors. This thought instantly sparked unhappy memories of her own marital confrontation with her husband after finding out about his affair. And she had never even gotten the satisfaction of kicking him out. His bags were already packed. Still, Nat supposed she got the last laugh. Only she wasn't exactly laughing when Ethan tried to come crawling back to her after his pregnant girlfriend dumped him, first informing him that the baby she was carrying might not be his after all.

It hit Nat how closely her own predicament mirrored that of Ethan's ex-girlfriend as Nat, too, was unsure of her baby's paternity. *Who's laughing now?*

"I left a message for Carlyle," Miller was saying. "*Suggesting* he take a temporary leave of absence. Until this mess is sorted out. Otherwise it'll be sheer chaos at the department." He heaved a sigh. "This is getting too damn close to that worst-case scenario, Nat." He paused for a moment. "You talked to Carlyle last night. Did he say—?"

"That he ran the woman down? No. He didn't confess." Then again, he didn't deny it either. "He wants me to stay out of it."

"Yeah, well, he's not giving the orders here, Nat," the commissioner said pointedly. Immediately following this remark with a quick, "Not that I'm *ordering* you to pursue this, Nat. It's not an order. It's a request. You're under no obligation . . . there'll be absolutely no negative repercussions—"

"I know what you're trying to say, Commissioner. It's okay."

Nat decided not to mention Carlyle's none-too-subtle warning that it could be dangerous for her to follow Miller's request. She wasn't sure if it was because she was worried Miller would ask her to back off or because he wouldn't. In any case, it had gone beyond whether or not the commissioner, Carlyle, Leo, or Robie wanted her involved.

Nat didn't improve the commissioner's mood any when she asked him to let her make private burial arrangements for her inmate clerk. He didn't actually give her an answer, but she decided to interpret his nonresponse as a yes.

eleven

LEO SHOWED UP AT HER FRONT door at a little past 9:00 A.M. Nat was just about to leave. She wanted to get over to the house to oversee the Finn transfer. But first she was determined to make a stop at the pharmacy down the street. The anxiety of not knowing for certain had finally surpassed the terror of knowing. If she was pregnant, she needed to deal with it. How she was going to deal with it was another question. She was well aware she had a choice. She could end the pregnancy. End it before anyone knew. Her secret. Her right. Her burden to bear. Her loss . . .

But there'd been so many losses. And, with all the complications, Nat couldn't dismiss her maternal longing.

Quickly reminding herself that all these tumultuous thoughts could be for naught, she pushed them from her mind and eyed the newspaper folded under Leo's arm.

"Have you seen it?" he asked tersely, still annoyed with her for having sent him off the previous night. Not so annoyed, though, that he hadn't phoned her soon after he got back home to make sure she was okay. Carlyle had already left by then.

She nodded. "Do you want me to drive you to the restaurant lot for your car?" Okay, so she'd postpone her trip to the pharmacy for a bit longer.

"I took care of it already. Your car's parked out front. So's mine."

"Your mom?"

He hesitated. "Suzanne."

Nat felt an immediate ripple of irritation. "I thought she was in Rhode Island." *With her new boyfriend.*

"She came back early this morning. Said she felt bad about disappointing Jakey. They're both down in the car. I'm going to drop them off at her place and then I've got to go reinterview a couple of kids who were at the pizza joint when Manuel Rodriquez was gunned down."

"You still working on the gang-hit theory?"

"It's looking that way, but we both know looks can be deceiving," he said. "Speaking of which, you look like you didn't sleep much last night."

"I didn't. Paul LaMotte had a stroke." She could feel her eyes start to well up and looked away. "He died a little before three this morning. Hutch called me. . . . I didn't sleep after that."

Leo was drawing her against him. "I'm sorry, Natalie. I'm really sorry."

She gave in to his embrace, needing to feel their special connection, which seemed so tenuous lately, more her fault than his, she knew. Still, in the end, she was the one to break away. How ironic that just when she craved the closeness most, it was the most threatening. She knew all the psychological reasons—many of which stemmed from being raised by dysfunctional parents who were unable to nurture—but understanding why and being able to let it go required a leap of faith she still lacked.

"You better go, Leo. Suzanne and Jakey are waiting."

Leo looked at her askance. "This isn't just about LaMotte's

passing. Or about Carlyle. Or even Suzanne. Something else is going on here, Natalie. I wish you'd tell me what it is."

She might have to tell him, but not now. Not yet.

"Look, I've got to get going, Leo. The inmate who's getting shipped back to Norton this morning has been pretty testy and I want to make sure the transfer's made without incident."

He searched her face as if he were trying to break a code. But it was a failed effort.

"Okay. We'll ride down the elevator together. I'll run interference for you."

It took a second for her to get it. "Oh, shit. Reporters."

"Come on. You know your line. You've said it enough times in the past. 'No comment.' "

She hesitated. It would definitely help to have a cop escort to her car, but Nat didn't particularly want to do a meet and greet with Suzanne. But she also didn't want Leo thinking it was a big deal.

As they stepped out of the elevator into the lobby, Nat came up with a delay tactic for herself. "I've got to stop at my mailbox. Forgot to pick my mail up yesterday. Don't worry about the vultures. Like you said, 'No comment.' Say hi to Suzanne and Jakey for me."

Leo scowled faintly, but he nodded and headed off toward the exit.

Her mailbox was full. A bunch of throwaway flyers, a couple of professional journals, a few bills, a postcard from the library letting her know a book she'd ordered was in, and one letter. It was the letter that grabbed Nat's full attention. Rather, it was the return address. The upper left-hand corner was stamped CCI Grafton.

Quickly stuffing the rest of her mail into her tote bag, she opened the envelope. One piece of plain white stationery, folded in thirds. She unfolded it to see just a couple of lines of quite elegant script. There was no salutation.

I have information that may help in uncovering the identity of the driver of the hit-and-run vehicle that struck down Jessica Asher. Please come see me. <u>You're the only one I'll talk to.</u>

Sincerely,
Elizabeth Temple

Nat checked the envelope again, and found herself feeling more than a bit unsettled. How did the inmate get hold of her home address? Her phone was unlisted so it wasn't like Temple could just check the phone book. Someone must have told her where Nat lived. Who?

A whole slew of questions started zinging through her mind. Why did Elizabeth Temple decide to write to *her*? Why at home instead of at work? What did she have to say? And what did she want in exchange for the information?

Because information rarely came free.

Nat reread the brief note a couple of times, then focused on the signature. Elizabeth Temple.

Why did that name ring a bell?

Even before she completed the question in her mind, it came back to her.

And suddenly that note took on a whole new meaning.

In no time flat, Nat was back up in her apartment, checking through a long list of references to Elizabeth Temple that she'd pulled up on her computer.

A little over two years ago, Elizabeth Temple, a young, wealthy socialite, became a tabloid darling, making headlines from the time of her arrest and all the way through to her conviction on numerous counts of pandering as well as charges of drug and gun possession.

It didn't take a genius or an expert in sociology to understand why the Temple scandal made such a splash. It had everything the public craves: sex, violence, power, and the potential to incriminate the rich and famous. The media had a field day with the spunky debutante, comparing Elizabeth Temple to the infamous Heidi Fleiss, a.k.a. the Hollywood Madam, who'd also been brought down for running a luxury escort service to the movers and shakers. Temple even bore some physical resemblance to Fleiss. Dark-haired, petite, pretty, feisty.

Temple's girls were purported to be not just lookers but of social-register caliber. The girl who turned her in, Alison Bryant, was actually in the social register.

So, it hit Nat, was Jessica Asher.

Until this missive arrived, Nat had presumed Jessica Asher operated solo. But now she was wondering if Asher had, in fact, been one of Temple's girls. Maybe she went out on her own after Temple's arrest. Or maybe she joined a new service. It was possible that Asher could have been a small cog in a big wheel.

If so, who had been running the show since Temple had been taken out of the picture?

She went through at least a dozen sites. In none of them was there so much as a mention of Jessica Asher. But that meant little since neither Alison Bryant, the call-girl informer, nor Elizabeth Temple would reveal the identities of anyone else involved in the highly profitable, exclusive service, neither the other girls nor the johns.

As she started scanning some of the articles about the trial, one name popped out at her: Jerry Tepper. The same hotshot attorney who was now handling Griffith Sumner's appeal had represented Elizabeth Temple. Only he hadn't come through for Temple. The trial ran several weeks, but the jury handed in a guilty verdict after being out for less than two hours. She got ten to fifteen years. Meaning she'd have to do six years minimum at CCI Grafton. She'd be just in the early days of her third year now.

One editorial hypothesized that Elizabeth Temple could have managed a lighter sentence for herself had she agreed to cooperate with DA Owen Barry, who was gung-ho to get Temple to expose her clients. The writer postulated that Elizabeth Temple refused to cut a deal and maintained her silence because she was more concerned about what her life would be like when she did finally get out of prison than she was about her time behind the wall. Because when she was released, she wouldn't want to walk back into the community having made a lot of powerful enemies.

Nat checked through the sites to see who the district attorney had selected as prosecutor in the Temple trial.

Well, well, well. Assistant District Attorney Joseph D. Keenan. Winning that trial clearly put Keenan on the map and, when Owen Barry suffered a fatal heart attack a few months after the trial, Keenan had easily stepped in to fill his shoes. And now there was the potential for a new headline-making trial that could catapult the current district attorney to even greater heights. Not to mention getting the opportunity to drive the point home that the man who'd been charged with overseeing the Commonwealth's Parole Board was a criminal himself. Nat was sure Keenan was just chomping at the bit. And this time he had the names of several of the johns.

Not that plenty of rumors hadn't floated around at the time of the Temple trial as to who might have been some of the madam's high-powered clients. Nat found dozens of the Web sites that focused on the infamous Boston madam and suggested plenty of likely possibilities. Men who were senior executives of major companies, jet-setters, local TV celebrities, and a few politicians were bandied about. They were names Nat recognized, names most tabloid readers would recognize.

Nat knew better than to buy in to rumors, but she was struck by the mention of one name in particular that kept showing up on a number of the sites. The name of the man who was, at the very time of Elizabeth Temple's arrest, kicking off his campaign for governor of the Commonwealth of Massachusetts.

Eric Landon.

Eric Landon, who was also Jessica Asher's brother-in-law.

Eric Landon, who was very rich, ran a multinational company, was politically well connected in his position as a Boston councilman, and was now preparing to run for the U.S. Senate.

twelve

NAT FELT LIKE A THIEF IN the night—only it was shortly after nine in the morning—as she skulked down the aisle of feminine hygiene products in the pharmacy, looking over her shoulder and checking ahead of her to make sure she hadn't been followed as she headed for the shelf containing the pregnancy test kits.

As Leo had forewarned, no sooner had Nat stepped outside of her building than a swarm of reporters and cameramen started buzzing around her. Nat's "No comments" could hardly be heard over the din. Nor could she break free of the vultures. Fortunately, no more than a minute went by before a patrol car pulled up and two uniforms came to her rescue, dispersing the crowd and making sure she had an unimpeded route to her car. Then again, it probably wasn't fortune. It was more likely Detective Leo Coscarelli who'd arranged for her safe passage.

Nat spotted the shelf—make that shelves—displaying the pregnancy kits. Who would have believed there were so many of them? Was one more accurate than another? She scanned the boxes for clues. "New . . . Easy . . . Quick . . . Simple . . ."

"Shit," she muttered, snatching one at random. Then she hurried down the aisle already digging her wallet out of her tote bag. Her head was momentarily lowered as she extracted the wallet, which was how she ended up running into the man who was just coming around from the aisle on her right.

As they collided, the pregnancy kit dropped from her hand.

The man bent down to retrieve it and handed it back to her with a benign smile. "Good choice. My wife picked that one when she thought she was pregnant. Which, to our jubilation, she was. Wanna see the snapshot I carry around in my wallet of my boy, Kyle, Superintendent?"

Nat groaned audibly as she stared into the handsome and familiar face of Bill Walker, crime reporter on WBBS's local evening news.

"You're good," she said morosely. "I never caught a glimpse of you."

"Don't look so glum, Nat. We've helped each other out in the past. No reason not to do the same now."

It was true. Last year, Walker had helped her lay a trap for a killer. In exchange, she'd promised—and come through on that promise—to give him the early scoop.

"Wanna go get a cup of coffee, Nat?" He eyed the kit. "Or would you like to take care of business first?"

She gave him a plaintive look. "Could we talk later?"

"Sure. What time?"

She tried to think, but her mind wasn't working all that well at the moment.

"Probably best if we keep our get-together low profile. You know McGinty's over in the North End?"

"I can find it," she said in a raspy voice.

"I'll buy you lunch. Say one o'clock. Place clears out by then." Again his eyes dropped to the box in her hand. "We can celebrate." The way he said it made it sound half like a question.

"I don't think so," she mumbled. Positive or negative, she

wouldn't be feeling particularly jubilant. The way she saw it, this was one of those lose/lose situations.

"You just missed Finn," Jack said when Nat arrived at the House twenty minutes later.

"Damn."

Jack gave her an assessing look. Missing the transfer was yet another glaring red flag that she wasn't herself.

"How'd it go?" she asked.

"Quietly. He pretty much burned himself out in solitary."

She breathed a small sigh of relief.

"How are you doing?" Jack was studying her like she was a specimen under his microscope that he couldn't quite identify.

Nat was instantly defensive, that pregnancy kit, which was still unopened, burning a proverbial hole in her pocket. "I'm fine," she snapped.

"Shit, don't bite my head off, Nat. We all know you were real fond of LaMotte."

Guilt and shame fell over her like a shroud. Her distressing encounter with Bill Walker at the pharmacy had literally made her grief over her clerk's death slip from her mind.

Jack thought she was merely letting him in on her grief and went to put an arm around her. She started to sidestep him, but he caught hold of her sleeve. "Why is it so hard for you to let someone in, Nat? Or is it just me?"

"Not now, Jack."

"That's always your response, Nat."

She fought back a yawn of sheer exhaustion. "It's not just you, Jack. Okay?"

"More okay than if it was just me," he said with a hint of a smile.

He released her sleeve and she headed for her office.

"Hey," he called out, "it's Saturday. Finn's en route. Go home, Nat. Get some sleep. You need it."

"I just have to take care of a couple of things," she called back.

. . .

One of her few perks at Horizon House was a private bathroom attached to her office. She was just heading for it when Sharon Johnson poked her head into her office. Nat gave a start as she turned to face her employment counselor.

"You're jumpy," Sharon said, stepping inside.

"Lack of sleep," she muttered. "What are you doing here on a Saturday?"

"Catching up on paperwork. What about you?"

"Finn."

Sharon nodded. "Damn shame. He was actually doing real good at his placement."

"Jack said the transfer went smoothly."

"Speak of the devil—what's with Jack these past coupla weeks?" Sharon asked.

"What do you mean?"

Now her employment counselor was giving her one of those under-the-microscope looks. "I'm worried he's been drinking again, Nat."

Nat had trouble meeting Sharon's dark-eyed gaze. Sharon didn't know about her recent sexual encounter with Jack. At least she didn't know it from Nat. Had Jack said anything to her?

And what about Jack's big spiel to her about being on the wagon? Wanting to outlive his parents who both had serious problems with booze? What about wanting them to celebrate his three weeks of sobriety? Was she so self-absorbed, she didn't see that he was handing her a line?

"Are you sure?" Nat asked.

"Sure? No. Maybe he's just back into minty mouthwash all of a sudden."

"Shit."

"Hey, it's not your fault, Nat."

Wasn't it?

"Stress gets us all from time to time, Nat. Jack's pulled himself out of the gutter before." Sharon was trying to keep her tone light, but Nat had seen Jack on the skids. It was not a pretty picture. If Sharon was right and her deputy was starting to slide—

"I'll talk to him."

"Maybe you need someone to talk to you as well," Sharon said.

"You think I'm drinking?" Nat's tone mirrored her incredulity.

She smiled gently. "No, I think you're stressed. And, hey, you got plenty of reason."

Sharon didn't know the half of it.

thirteen

SHE SAT ON THE CLOSED LID of her toilet, trying to focus her eyes on the instruction sheet. It was not that the letters were too small. Even if they were, Nat had 20/20 vision. It was nerves, pure and simple. Only, if she'd been anything close to "pure" she wouldn't be here trying to read these damn instructions. And there was nothing "simple" about the way she was feeling.

She finally steeled her nerves.

The test was as easy and quick as the box advertised.

But then came the agonizing wait.

Amazing how the passage of a few short minutes could transport a person to a new universe. Nat stared at that blue strip that proclaimed the test positive, feeling every inch a foreigner in a land where she didn't speak or understand the language.

She nearly jumped out of her skin at the knock on her locked bathroom door.

"Nat?"

She stuffed the incriminating evidence into her tote bag, then opened the door to come face-to-face with a grim-looking Fran Robie.

"Sumner's dead," the homicide captain said without preamble.

"Griffith Sumner? Dead?" Nat felt like she'd stepped onto the killing fields. "How?"

"Stabbed with a homemade shank."

"Who did it?"

Robie shrugged. "No clue. Probably never will nab the guy. A scuffle broke out in the cafeteria between two rival gangs—"

"Sumner was part of a gang?"

"I don't know, I suppose it's possible. Or maybe he simply got caught in the crossfire," Robie said, but she sounded dubious about either possibility.

Nat's sentiment exactly. Coincidences might happen, but in her experience, more times than not there was something more purposeful behind an occurrence, especially when it came to murder.

As Robie and Nat made the second trip in as many days to CCI Norton, Nat found herself going over the interview they'd had with Griffith the previous day. Was there a hint in anything that was said that might give them a clue as to why someone felt it was crucial to kill the inmate, or arrange to have him killed? Did Griffith Sumner know or at least have a strong idea who ran Jessica Asher down? Of course, the first name that leaped to Nat's mind with motive and means was Deputy Commissioner Stephen R. Carlyle. There were a lot of inmates and even some staff people who might be persuaded by someone with Carlyle's influence to carry out a favor.

But Griffith Sumner also mentioned another man closely involved with Jessica Asher. Her mystery boyfriend. Was it true Sumner didn't know who this guy was? If he did know, he'd gone to the grave keeping it a secret.

Still, someone had to know who she was seeing. Nat needed to track this boyfriend down. Find out if he knew about his girlfriend's sideline. Could even be that was how he'd met her. That he'd started out as one of her clients. Which would mean he was probably someone important. Someone with a reputation to uphold. Someone who might go to great lengths to keep from being exposed.

There was also another angle to consider. It was possible the boyfriend was someone Jessica met outside of work. A guy who started out with no idea she was a socialite by day, a hooker by night. And then discovered the truth and in a fit of jealousy ran her down.

Or maybe he found out and realized that if his girlfriend's extracurricular activities came to light and he was linked romantically to her, it could harm him personally or professionally, or both.

Whatever scenario Nat considered, if this guy was the hit-and-run driver, he probably knew that his girlfriend visited her old friend Griffith Sumner. Knew or suspected that Jessica confided in this close pal.

Was the killer covering his tracks?

Vincent Morgan was the superintendent of CCI Norton. He was a large, robust man in his late fifties with a ruddy complexion and thinning gray hair, who'd been in the system for a lot of years. Like Deputy Commissioner Carlyle, Morgan wasn't keen on women having positions of power and responsibility in the prisons. He hadn't even liked having to hire female officers, which he was forced to do because of antidiscrimination rulings a number of years back. All this to say that Morgan didn't greet Nat or Robie with open arms when they walked into his medicinally clean office, an inmate having just finished swabbing down the linoleum floor with disinfectant.

"Like I told you on the phone, Captain Robie, we had a little flare-up between some boys who we've now targeted as gang members of the Latin Kings and the Twenty Loves," Morgan said brusquely as they took seats across from the large dark wood desk behind which the superintendent was sitting.

"I thought you folk keep rival gangs from mingling," Robie said.

Morgan's ruddy face reddened and his eyes narrowed. "We are doing everything within our power to clamp down on rampant gang activity in our prison system, Captain. Any inmate who we consider to be a member or leader of a gang is placed in a higher security level. But inevitably some inmates slip through the cracks. They manage to keep their gang memberships secret—no signature tattoos, beads, colors. That's what happened here this morning in the dining hall. It was only after my men broke up the disturbance that we were able to identify the gang affiliations. You'll be happy to hear that all of the men involved in the fracas are in lockdown and will be reclassified STG."

"STG?"

"Security threat groups," Nat explained to Robie before Morgan got the chance. She felt a need to establish her presence there.

Morgan cast her an acidic look. They'd butted heads at a number of meetings where the issue of STG classification had been heatedly debated. Nat had taken the position that labeling inmates as gang affiliated and placing them under extreme restrictions—twenty-three-hour-a-day solitary lockdown—could actually enhance gang cohesiveness. Better to have fair disciplinary policies that focused on inmate conduct, staff training, and constructive educational and training opportunities. Morgan didn't see it that way. He was far from alone in his opinion— Carlyle was strongly on the super's side—which was why STG classification still existed.

"And where was Griffith Sumner when this fracas went down?" Robie asked the superintendent.

Morgan hesitated. "I'm not quite sure. One of our officers found him under a table at the back of the room once order was restored. He was already . . . dead. There'll be an autopsy, but the prison doc figures death was practically instantaneous, the result of a stab wound to the heart."

"Griffith was found under the table where the men involved in the fight were seated?" Nat asked.

"In that general area," Morgan told her curtly.

"We'd like to have a word with the officers who were on duty at the dining hall this morning as well as any other staff—cooks, servers, whoever—who were there at the time," Robie said. "And with the men you've now got in lockdown."

Morgan stiffened. "You're talking about over a dozen personnel, Captain. And fifteen inmates."

"Twenty-seven people. No problem," Robie said blithely.

"No problem for you, maybe," Morgan retorted. "But I can't have—"

"We'll start with the staff people whose shifts are ending the earliest," Robie cut the superintendent off, or more to the point, ignored him. "We'll need a couple of rooms. Nat and I will split the group down the middle."

Morgan's complexion was getting redder by the second. "I certainly don't see where you or Superintendent Price have any authority—"

"A man has been murdered under your watch, Superintendent," Robie said, her sultry voice suddenly steely. "Naturally, you'll want to offer your full support and cooperation in this investigation."

Morgan's mouth twitched, but he merely nodded, looking neither at Robie or Nat.

Two fruitless hours later, Robie walked into the cubicle where Nat had finally finished her last interview—a young Latino man who'd insisted that he was not and never had been a member of the Latin Kings or any other gang. He claimed to have been unfairly rounded up simply because he was Spanish, and made it clear to Nat he was going to "sue the fucking bastard fuckers for all they're worth." Oh, and he had no idea who Griffith Sumner was, much less any information about who might have shanked him.

Robie had also come up with zip.

"A bunch of fucking monkeys, the lot of them," she groused. "Saw no evil, spoke no evil, heard no evil."

"Well, someone sure as hell did some evil," Nat muttered, feeling weary and exhausted. The only good part about this whole wasted morning was she'd had no time to agonize over that positive pregnancy test result.

But it was back on her mind now. Along with the realization she was never going to make it to that lunch meeting with Bill Walker. She called the reporter on his cell phone. When he didn't pick up, Nat left him a message apologizing profusely for having to cancel. And promising to reschedule ASAP.

fourteen

FRAN ROBIE DROVE NAT BACK TO Boston and dropped her off at Horizon House. Nat watched the captain round the corner, then headed straight for her car and started out for CCI Grafton. Admittedly, she felt a little guilty for not having told Robie about the note she'd received that morning from Elizabeth Temple, but then Robie hadn't exactly been forthcoming with her. And if Nat had shown her the note before meeting with Temple, she had no doubt the homicide captain would want to step in to run the show.

And this was one show Nat wanted to run.

Nat was taken back by Elizabeth Temple's appearance. Unlike Griffith Sumner, Temple was showing a considerable amount of the wear and tear of being incarcerated. Granted, the worn-out drab gray cardigan and baggy black slacks didn't do much for her petite frame. The attire was certainly a sharp contrast from the couture designs she'd once worn. Still, it wasn't just the clothes.

Her complexion was blotchy, her dark hair, once expertly cut and styled, was long and stringy, her lips were badly chapped.

"Have a seat," Nat offered congenially.

Temple seemed a bit unsteady on her feet as she crossed to a chair at the table. When she sat down, she looked straight at Nat. "Do you have a smoke?"

"No. Sorry." Nat didn't bother reminding her that there was no smoking allowed inside the institution.

The inmate studied her. And Nat, in turn, studied the inmate. Everything about Temple's appearance suggested, unlike Griffith Sumner, that she hadn't been receiving a lot of goodies from family and friends on the outside, items like fine-quality shampoo and conditioner, top-of-the-line skin cream, gourmet food packages. Had they all abandoned her? Or had she cut herself off from them?

"I guess you got my note," Elizabeth Temple said.

"This morning." Nat wanted to ask a slew of questions, but decided she might learn more by letting Temple set the pace.

The inmate looked around the room aimlessly, then zeroed back in on Nat. At this close range Nat could see that the whites of Elizabeth Temple's eyes had a yellow cast. This woman wasn't just unkempt, Nat realized. She was sick. Hepatitis? Something worse?

"How's it been in here up to now?"

"Not as bad as I expected, really."

"Oh?" She was looking plenty bad to Nat.

"I've suffered less than some," she said vaguely. "I was sure I'd be gang-raped before my first week was out. It happens in here, you know." She gave Nat a closer look. "Yeah, you know."

Yeah, she did know.

"You also probably know why it didn't happen to me."

"Tell me," Nat said.

"I still have a few friends in high places."

"Friends like the deputy commissioner of corrections, Stephen R. Carlyle?"

"I saw that photo of you and the deputy commissioner in the paper." she said.

"Do you know Stephen Carlyle?" Nat repeated.

"You mean did he ever use my escort service?"

"You can answer that, for starters."

"No," she said quickly. "He wasn't a client. And I don't know him."

"Why did you contact me?" Nat asked, coming straight to the point. "You could have written that note to someone with a lot more clout."

"Someone told me about you."

"Who?"

Her hazel eyes stayed fixed on Nat, but she didn't answer.

"A former client?"

"It's not important." Meaning, the inmate wasn't about to tell her.

"So what do you want, Ms. Temple?" Nat's patience was starting to wear thin. Plus she was beginning to feel a little queasy again. *Why the hell do they call it morning sickness, if it can go on all day long?*

"I'll tell you what I *don't* want, Superintendent. I don't want to spend the rest of my sentence in this hellhole."

"I thought it wasn't so bad."

"Once I spill the beans, my life's gonna be worth shit in here. Look what happened to Griff."

"Griff? So you knew Griffith Sumner?"

"He was at my coming-out party." She smiled slyly, showing a hint of the sassy woman she'd once been. "My debutante ball. Those were the days." She didn't say this with any sign of fond memories. "Not that we were ever close. Griff was too cocky for his own good. I knew back then he'd end up in trouble."

"What do you know about his murder?" So far all that'd gone public was that Sumner was stabbed in a gang fight in the prison mess hall.

"Griff and Jessie Asher were pals. Being her pal has gotten to be unhealthy for some people."

"Were you Jessica Asher's pal?"

"Not exactly."

"She worked for you?" Nat pressed.

"What difference does that make?"

Nat started to rise. "This is going nowhere, Ms. Temple. When you want to—"

"Yeah, she worked for me."

"Why?"

Temple appeared amused by Nat's question. "The money was good. Very good. The hours . . . well, they were pretty flexible. And some women are into the rebellious aspect of it—playing against the good-girl image their families expect them to project."

"Some women like Jessica Asher."

"Yes, like Jessie. Besides, she'd been cut out of the parents' will, so she needed the dough. And she only worked when she wanted and with whom she wanted. When I got taken down, she quit. For a while, anyway. Then I heard through the grapevine she'd gone to work again."

"Was she on her own or working for another service?"

"I want a transfer to Horizon House, Superintendent."

Finally—the deal. "You're not eligible for prerelease yet."

"I know that. But I can be transferred as a trustee."

"Trustees are usually lifers," Nat said, thinking of Paul La-Motte. And about the fact that her clerk spot was now vacant.

"But it's not a rule," the inmate challenged.

"No," Nat conceded.

"My time here has been exemplary, Superintendent. You can read my records, talk to Superintendent Moore, anyone on the staff. No fights, no contraband. And besides . . ." She stopped.

"Besides what, Ms. Temple?"

Her eyes skidded off Nat, darting around the room.

"Nothing."

"You're sick."

She smiled ruefully, still avoiding eye contact. "Sick and tired."

"What is it?"

"What does it matter?"

"Are you getting medical attention?"

"If you want to call it that. Sure, I'm getting top-notch care, Superintendent. By prison standards. Not that it matters much, in any case."

"AIDS?"

She nodded. "Okay, I've had some . . . issues. Not really bad though. I mean . . . I know I don't look all that spiffy at the moment, but I just started a new drug cocktail. I should be looking a lot better—and feeling a lot better—so if that's what's worrying you . . ."

"It's not your illness that's the issue. It's your physical safety, Elizabeth. If you do have information that puts you in jeopardy, what makes you think you'd be safe at Horizon House?"

All of the inmate's tough exterior gave way. "You have a rep for looking after your people, Superintendent. I can't think of a safer place to be than under your watch."

Great. Just what I need. As if I don't already have enough to worry about.

"You said in your note you had information—"

"I can give you the name of a person who witnessed the crime. And knows who was behind the wheel of the car that struck Jessie down."

"Go on."

Her focus stayed fixed on Nat, but she didn't continue.

"This witness told you this? Told you who the driver was?"

"No," Temple said. "The witness told a friend of mine that she was there, and saw the driver, but she wouldn't say who it was. My friend told me."

"*She?* The witness is a woman? And this friend of yours—who is that?"

"What difference does it make? My friend isn't involved. And doesn't want to be."

"How do I know you haven't made this up? How do I know there is a friend? A witness?"

"You don't. Yet."

"Did your friend tell you why this witness didn't report what she saw to the police?"

There was a substantial pause before she answered. "Fear, possibly. Two people are already dead."

"You say 'possibly.' Could there be another reason?"

Temple smiled faintly. "I was told you're very perceptive."

"You think she's blackmailing the killer."

"Possibly," Temple repeated.

"A risky business. Like you said, two people are already dead."

"I'm sure she's watching her back."

"What's her name?"

"So, we have a deal?"

Nat stood up. "I don't make deals. You want to negotiate, do it with your lawyers, Ms. Temple. Send a letter to the DA. Talk to your friend." She picked up her briefcase.

"Wait. Please."

"For what?"

"What if Stephen Carlyle wasn't the hit-and-run driver?"

"Are you telling me you know for a fact it wasn't him?"

She hesitated. "No. But isn't it important to find out the truth?"

"You do know, Ms. Temple, that withholding information in a criminal investigation—a murder investigation, no less—is a felony."

She looked beseechingly at Nat. "Wait. I'll give you her name. No strings attached. Okay? Just . . . just please think about it. About okaying my transfer. That's all I'm asking."

"Okay. I'll consider it."

She still hesitated. "One other thing."

"What?"

"What I tell you . . . you can't tell the cops."

"Why not?"

"Because . . . because you just don't know."

"Don't know what?"

"Who you can trust and who you can't." Her features took on a fierce edge. "I learned that lesson the hard way."

Nat assumed the inmate was referring to her claim that the police planted the drugs and weapons at her house when she was arrested. But Nat was wondering if there was more to it than that. Temple ran her very profitable call-girl service without police interference for several years before she got busted. The cops who could have brought her down must have looked the other way for quite some time. Were there payoffs? Were some of the cops clients of hers? Cops who were also clients of Jennifer Asher's?

Now, that would be quite the sensitive situation for homicide captain Francine Robie to have to handle.

"Look, I'm saying this for your sake as much as mine, Superintendent. If you're going to pursue this investigation, I strongly suggest you do it on your own."

"What's her name, Ms. Temple?"

"Alison. Alison Bryant." And before Nat could respond, Temple added, "Yes, that's right. The woman who ratted me out. The woman who's responsible for my being here. You're probably thinking I'm lying. Just like she lied. But this isn't payback, Superintendent. It's simply the truth. It's your decision whether or not to believe me."

It wasn't a decision Nat was ready to make on the spot.

fifteen

WHILE ELIZABETH TEMPLE GAVE UP ALISON Bryant's name, she held fast on withholding the name of the friend who had passed this information to her. Nat, however, wanted to have all the information she could get her hands on. So she decided to check the inmate's authorized visitor sheet to see what friends had been visiting her recently. The list contained a dozen names in addition to Temple's attorney, Gerald Tepper. That gave Nat pause. Not too many inmates would consider the attorney who failed to get them off to be a friend. On the other hand, Tepper had really been up against it in the Temple trial and it was doubtful any other lawyer would have fared better. Maybe Temple understood that and didn't hold it against him.

Nat scanned the dates on the sign-in sheet. Tepper's visits, though not frequent—once or twice every few months—had continued right up to a few days ago.

The parents' names followed right after the attorney—Dr. Henry and Miriam Temple. Miriam Temple visited her daughter once every two or three weeks during the first year or so of Elizabeth's incarceration. After that, the visits grew steadily briefer and more sporadic. There'd been no visits for several months. The renowned shrink had visited his daughter only once. Four days ago. Dr. Henry Temple came alone. The visit clocked in at twelve minutes.

Did Elizabeth Temple intentionally mislead her by saying it was a friend who gave her this information? Was it actually her father? Maybe the person who knew Alison was one of his patients. Of course, that would be an unconscionable breach of confidentiality, but then Nat had known some unconscionable psychiatrists.

Two more names on the inmate's approved visitors' list drew Nat's attention. Debra and Eric Landon.

What was the relationship between the Landons and Elizabeth Temple? Nat supposed the link must be through the two women, since both Elizabeth and Debra came from monied backgrounds in the Boston area. And Nat knew that Eric Landon grew up in Dorchester, which was definitely considered the wrong side of the tracks. His marriage to Debra Asher had certainly allowed him to move to the right side of the tracks.

According to the list, Debra had been paying Elizabeth Temple regular visits over the past two years, but her last visit was back in September. Eric Landon, however, paid Temple a couple of visits in October. One was on October 12. And the last one was on Sunday, October 21. Three days after Jessica Asher was run down.

It was shortly after 5:00 P.M. when Nat walked into McGinty's. Bill Walker was sitting alone at a booth in the rear of the narrow bar, nursing a beer. Nat slid in across from him.

"What'll it be?" the reporter asked.

"Club soda."

He cocked his head. "Does that mean congratulations are in order?"

"Yeah," she said, because any other response would be too complicated to go into. Assuming she'd want to go into it, which she didn't. "But it's just between the two of us, right?"

"Right." He called out her drink order to the bartender.

She folded her hands on the scarred wooden table. "Look, Bill, I don't have anything that you can go public with yet. But when I do—"

He nodded. "Yeah, yeah. I'll be the first reporter to know. But give me a bit of a head's-up here, Super. Let me know what I might have to look forward to."

She hesitated. Most reporters she wouldn't trust any further than she could throw them. But Walker—she might add a few yards past that toss. Still, a reporter was a reporter. Nat needed to be careful what she disclosed.

The bartender called out to Walker by his first name, pointing to the club soda on the marble counter. Walker slid out of the booth, got the drink, and brought it back to her.

Nat waited until he was back in his seat. "The police have no concrete evidence linking the deputy to the crime," she said firmly.

"Rumor has it he knew her."

Those lewd photos flashed in her head.

She gave the reporter a sharp look. "Rumor has it Elvis Presley is still alive."

He shrugged. "Hey, you never know. But leaving the King aside, did Carlyle know Asher?"

"The deputy commissioner is only one person being questioned, Bill."

"Oh, Nat, and here I thought we had an understanding."

"This isn't for publication?"

He held up his right hand in an I-swear gesture.

"Yeah," she said finally under Walker's watchful gaze. "They knew each other."

He smiled. "You're not going to tell me how."

"Not just yet."

He took a sip of his beer, then wiped a bead of foam off his lips with the back of his hand. "Anyone else under suspicion?"

"I'm hoping so."

His smile deepened. "Yeah, it wouldn't look so good for your department if one of your top-ranking dudes ended up in the slammer."

Nat didn't smile back. "No, it wouldn't. Especially," she added, "if he's innocent."

Walker arched a brow. "You think maybe he's being set up?"

It was certainly something she'd considered. Hopefully, she'd know better after she followed up on Elizabeth Temple's lead.

"Where does Griffith Sumner fit into all this? Correction— where *did* he fit in?" Walker asked as he ran his finger lightly around the rim of his beer glass.

"What makes you think he fits in at all?"

"For one thing, he's dead. For another, I covered the Sumner trial. Asher was in the peanut gallery just about every day. Sat next to his girlfriend—"

"Sumner had a girlfriend?"

"Jessica's sister."

"Debra Landon?"

"She wasn't Landon then," Walker said.

And, as if that wasn't enough of a bombshell, he added, "A bit incestuous, if you ask me. What with Jessica having had a fling with Debra's hubby." He smiled as he saw her eyes widen. "But hey, our esteemed city councilman wasn't Debra's hubby at the time."

"When were Eric and Jessica involved?"

"So now you're asking *me* questions," he teased.

"Come on, Bill."

He smiled. "Well, it's only rumor, Nat."

"Yeah, well, who knows? Maybe the King is still alive."

When Nat tried the unlisted phone number Elizabeth Temple gave her for Alison Bryant she got a recorded voice announcing that the number was no longer in service. When she tried to track down a new number she was informed it was also unlisted.

There were a couple of people who could get her the unlisted number. Francine Robie for one. Leo Coscarelli for another.

Nat opted for the one she knew she could trust. Even though she also knew she'd have to do some explaining to get it.

Meanwhile, there were two more people whose numbers Nat

tried. She did better with both, in the sense that the people were still at those numbers. However, she didn't have any luck getting to talk with either party. A recorded message from Jerry Tepper announced that he was out of town over the weekend. A rather snippy housekeeper informed her that Dr. Henry Temple was unavailable. If his daughter was any example, Nat would hazard the guess that the eminent shrink was often unavailable.

sixteen

SUNDAY, A GRAY, RAINY DAY, PASSED quietly and sadly. In the late morning, a small group from Horizon House gathered at a cemetery in Dorchester, where they laid inmate trustee Paul LaMotte to rest. While Nat had been prepared to cover the full cost of the burial site and the minister's fee, Jack, Hutch, Sharon, and several other people on her staff had insisted on contributing. A number of inmates also made small donations as well as helped organize a memorial service for Paul in the visiting room at Horizon House.

Nat gave a brief eulogy at the memorial service—brief because she found herself close to tears and so cut it short. Not that anyone in the makeshift chapel was likely to see her breaking down as a sign of weakness. Well, no one except herself. Nat was terrified that if she surrendered to the pain of this loss—any one loss—she might collapse under the agony of all the others.

As she was returning to her seat, Nat saw Leo standing just inside the entrance to the visiting room. He started towards her, but stopped abruptly when Jack, who was seated in the front row, got to her first.

"You did good, Nat," Jack said soothingly, taking hold of her arm and guiding her back to her chair, which was next to his. Nat didn't think Jack noticed that Leo had come in. But she was hyperaware of his presence.

A couple of inmates talked after her. Nat tried to concentrate on what they were saying, but she wasn't succeeding. Jack thought it was because of what was being said, so he grasped her hand to comfort her. Which only added to her discomfort. So did the scent of minty mouthwash she smelled on her deputy's breath.

When the service was over, Nat looked back.

Leo was gone.

Nat was back at CCI Grafton on Sunday afternoon for another meeting with Elizabeth Temple. The inmate gave her an anxious look.

"I was hoping when the guard told me you were here, that it was about my transfer. But you don't look like you've come here to bring me good news."

"We need to talk some more about Alison Bryant."

"You spoke to her?"

"No. The number you had for her was disconnected. Her new number's unlisted—"

"Look, I didn't know—"

"I got the new number. And Alison's current address. Only she never answers her phone. I went by her place several times and she doesn't respond to her outside buzzer."

"Maybe she's . . . out of town."

"Maybe you should ask your *friend* how I can get in touch with her."

"I'll do what I can."

"Then again, maybe I can ask your friend."

"I told you already. I can't tell you who—"

"How about if I tell you?"

"What . . . What do you mean?"

"Eric Landon is a friend, isn't he, Ms. Temple?"

"What? Yes . . . but it . . . it wasn't Eric."

"He was also a friend of Jessica Asher's."

Elizabeth Temple nervously smoothed back her oily hair. "He was her brother-in-law."

"The two aren't necessarily incompatible." Although, when it came to Nat's relationship with her womanizing brother-in-law, they certainly were.

"No. I suppose not," she conceded.

"He was more than a friend for a time, wasn't he?" Nat pressed.

She could see that the inmate was about to deny any knowledge, but then there was a sea change in her features. Like she'd come to a decision. "Yes. Eric was in love with Jessie. But it was a long time ago."

"When she was in high school, right?"

"Jessie was sixteen, Superintendent. Eric was twenty-seven. Eleven years her senior. Now, if Jessie were in her twenties, no one would have batted an eye."

"Eric Landon was the reason Jessie's dad shipped her off to the Berkshires to finish high school. The same high school for troubled kids that Griffith Sumner attended."

Temple nodded.

"Were they still seeing each other when Jessica was run—?"

"No. Not in that way. Debra and Eric are happily married, Superintendent."

"But Jessie did have a current boyfriend."

"If she did, it's news to me. I haven't seen or heard from her since I got arrested. And as far as I know there was no particular love interest when she worked for me."

"And neither Debra nor Eric Landon mentioned anything about Jessica having a boyfriend when they visited you."

"No. In fact, neither of them talked about her at all."

"Hard feelings?"

"No. It just never came up." But she looked away when she said this.

"Did they know Jessie worked for you? Did they know she was a call girl?"

"No. If they had known, I doubt they would have had anything to do with me."

"Especially Debra, being that she was Jessie's sister."

"True," the inmate conceded. "She would have been very upset. More so than Eric. But I'm sure he would have been pretty upset himself."

"Was it Eric Landon who told you Alison Bryant witnessed the hit-and-run?"

"Eric has nothing to do with this," Temple insisted.

"He came to see you two days after Jessica was run down. He came alone. Why?"

Elizabeth Temple looked uneasy. "He knew I was fond of Jessie. He came to see how I was feeling."

"How was he feeling?"

"Upset. How would you expect him to feel?"

"Why didn't Debra come with him?"

"She was too distraught. I did call her to offer my condolences."

"Was Eric Landon a client of yours, Ms. Temple?" Nat asked her bluntly.

Her features hardened. "I'll say it again, Superintendent. Eric has nothing to do with this. It wasn't Eric who told me about Alison. And it wasn't Debra, if that's your next guess."

"Actually, my next guess was Jerry Tepper."

She gave Nat a weary look. "You're wasting your time, Superintendent."

Nat sighed. "You're right, Ms. Temple. I am wasting my time. Worse, I don't appreciate being sent on a wild-goose chase."

"I told you the last time you probably wouldn't believe me. That you'd think it was just sour grapes, because Alison was the one who turned me in."

"You have to admit it's a logical conclusion to draw," Nat said.

"Don't you get it? She wanted to run the show. I had the best girls. The best johns. The only thing standing in her way was— me. More than that, she saw other, more lucrative benefits to the business. A way to make much higher profits. That was why we argued. The shit hit the fan when I found some photos of her in bed with one of our clients. She'd rigged a camera—"

"Who was the client?"

The inmate gave her the kind of look you'd give to an ingenuous child asking a supremely inappropriate question.

"We had a blowup over it," she went on. "That is, I blew up. Ali couldn't see what I was all worked up over. But she said she'd stop. Next thing I know I'm being raided."

"So, when you were running the show you never resorted to blackmail?"

"No. I would never do that. It would have been unscrupulous."

She gave Nat a rueful look. "I know what you're thinking. That pandering is illegal. Not to mention morally wrong. In some people's eyes, anyway. But I don't think it's immoral to fulfill someone's needs. Not when it's two consenting adults. I never hurt anyone, Superintendent."

"Didn't you?"

"No. My girls and my clients—"

"I'm not talking about your girls and your clients. How did you become HIV?"

The inmate compressed her lips. "I didn't get HIV from a john," she said finally. "It was before . . . before I got into the biz." She tried for a playful tone but fell way short and gave it up. "It was a boyfriend. A guy I met a couple of years out of college. He was in law school. A guy with the perfect pedigree. My parents were tickled pink. A match made in blue-blood heaven." She laughed harshly. "Little did they know what a scumbag he was."

"He knew he was infected?"

The laugh died. "You know what he told me when I found out I was positive? He said that . . . that it was better that way. He couldn't face it alone. This way we'd be in it together."

"That's awful. And criminal."

Tears spiked her eyes. "I was so . . ." She shivered despite the almost cloying heat in the interview room. "I hated Gene for what he did to me. And for a while, I admit I hated all men. But after a time I just . . . felt mostly numb. Ali was the first person I told . . . about being positive. We'd met at Vassar. She was already turning tricks there. I thought she was wild and a little crazy, but I was drawn to her like a magnet. I even tried it a couple of times. Hooking. It was before Gene. We didn't meet until I was twenty-three. Six years ago. Anyway, I found that sleeping with guys for money wasn't much fun. But . . . but after Gene, I felt so lost. And so scared."

"Did you tell your parents?"

"No."

"But surely they know now." Nat didn't want to say that just looking at her would be enough for them to know she was ill. Wouldn't they press her to tell them what was wrong with her?

"Only . . . just." She smiled ruefully and Nat wasn't sure how to interpret the expression.

"I haven't had any . . . flare-ups until this past month. And my mom hasn't been here in months. And my dad . . . Let's say he was pretty disappointed in me—well disgusted, to be frank. He never visited until . . ." She bit down on her chapped lower lip. "Gene died last week. Cause of death made it in the papers. My dad came to see me."

"That was a few days ago?"

She nodded.

"And you told him what had happened?"

She emitted another harsh laugh. "He told me. Seems Gene told his folks just before he died that he contracted AIDS from me. And given that I was already in prison for pandering, it was easy enough for them to believe him. Gene's dad confronted my parents, threatening to sue them. He couldn't very well sue me since I haven't a dime to my name at the moment."

"Did he sue them?"

"No. My father paid him off. And then he came here to make sure I knew how much suffering I'd caused them. In his language, suffering is always translated as costing him money."

Now Nat understood why she'd gotten that curt dismissal from the Temple housekeeper.

"Didn't you tell him the truth?"

Elizabeth Temple looked tired. "It's irrelevant, Superintendent. Forget about my folks. I have."

Nat didn't believe that for an instant, but she saw that discussing this painful relationship was taking its toll.

"Let's talk a bit more about Jessie."

The inmate looked relieved. "What else can I tell you?"

"She kept an appointment calendar of her dates. The police have it and they're not willing to share it."

Temple laughed harshly. "No, I don't suppose they would. I'm sure Jessie's clientele was top-rung. Men with a lot of influence."

"Given that she used to work for you, you have any idea who her clients might have been?"

"Other than your deputy commissioner?" She smiled faintly. "No."

"Would you tell me if—"

"No. I'm taking enough of a risk as it is, Superintendent," Temple said frankly.

"Do you think Bryant kept duplicate schedules for her girls?"

"I always did. I imagine she does, too. It's important for the head of the organization to know who's seeing who when. There could be some extremely embarrassing moments if the wrong people bumped into each other coming or going."

"You think all the clients were being hit up?"

"I doubt it. Ali is very greedy, but she's not stupid. I think she's selective. In terms of the girls she asks to cooperate as well as the clients she targets."

"Like Jessie."

"That would be my guess."

"Photos have surfaced of Jessie and Steve Carlyle in bed together."

Temple didn't look surprised.

"I'm figuring he wasn't the only client to be photographed."

"I'm sure he wasn't," Temple agreed.

"I think Jessie wanted Carlyle to make sure Griffith Sumner was okayed for parole when his hearing came up."

"Makes sense. Like I said, Jessie and Griff were good friends."

"So were Jessie's sister Debra and Griff."

Temple shrugged. "Ages ago."

"What I can't figure out is what Alison Bryant would get out of this blackmail venture. Why would she care if Griffith Sumner got paroled?"

Temple's gaze locked with Nat's. "I can't figure that out either."

"There are a few possibilities," Nat continued, having ruminated about this since her chat with Bill Walker the evening before. "One—there's something in it for Bryant that you don't know about. Two—you know and aren't telling me—"

"I'd tell you if I knew."

"Or, three—Bryant didn't know about it."

The inmate considered this thoughtfully. "Meaning Jessie was moonlighting."

"How angry would Ali be if she discovered one of her girls was hitting clients up for her own purposes?"

"I know how incensed I was when I found out that's what Ali was doing." Temple frowned. "But we all have different ways of showing our anger. I tend to explode, and then let go of it."

"And Alison Bryant?"

"She's the type who'll look you square in the face and smile like whatever it is that irritated her is no big deal, but as soon as you turn away she'll stab you in the back."

"Are you so sure your friend got it right, Ms. Temple?"

"You think Ali could have been the driver?"

"What do you think?"

"All I know is what I've been told, Superintendent. I guess you'll have to form your own opinion after you meet Ali."

"Even if your friend's right, and even if I do track her down, Bryant isn't going to voluntarily own up to being a blackmailer. Hand over the identity of the driver. Especially to a prison superintendent."

"No. You're right. You'd have to use—a different approach. But I'm not sure you're up for it."

seventeen

AT HALF PAST SIX ON MONDAY MORNING, Nat was once again awakened by the jarring ring of her phone. She peered blearily at it, hesitating as she tried to steel herself for what had to be another round of bad news.

"Nat? It's Warren Miller. Dana Carlyle, Stephen Carlyle's wife, just called me. From Boston General."

Her stomach dropped. It was bad news all right.

"Stephen's in the emergency room Suffering from chest pains."

"Heart attack?" Nat asked, her voice raspy from having been woken so abruptly. She reached over for the glass of water she'd taken to keeping on her bedside table, next to which was a stack of Saltine crackers. Bill Walker told her his wife swore by them during her first trimester. The crackers helped to settle her stomach and were often the only solid food his wife could keep down. So far, the crackers weren't working their miracle on Nat.

"Nothing conclusive yet," Miller said. "The docs are running tests. I'm going over there now."

"Will you call me as soon as you hear anything?"

"Of course. Oh," he added, sounding even more solemn if that was possible, "the DA is pushing hard for a warrant, but I've convinced the mayor to persuade Joe Keenan he'll have a stronger case against Carlyle if he gives the cops a little more time."

"And the DA agreed?"

"He agreed to forty-eight hours. I guess he'll extend it some if Carlyle's chest pains *are* a heart attack."

Great, Nat thought ruefully. And just think how lucky the deputy commissioner would be if he dropped dead!

They say bad news comes in threes. Surely Nat was over the limit by now. Nevertheless, not twenty minutes after the commissioner's call about Carlyle being in the hospital she got slammed with another piece of bad news. This time the call was from Joan Moore, Superintendent at CCI Grafton.

"Elizabeth Temple's in the infirmary."

Nat immediately thought it was AIDS-related. But it turned out she was wrong.

"She got into an argument with one of the COs and ended up trying to take a punch at him," Moore went on after a brief pause. "When the officer went to restrain her, Elizabeth tried to fight him off and in the process hit her head on the concrete floor and lost consciousness briefly. She's okay now," the super added quickly, "but given her medical condition, the doc wants to keep her in the infirmary for twenty-four-hour observation."

"And then what?"

"Forty-eight hours in solitary. And an incident report in her file." Moore hesitated. "This really is unfortunate, given that just yesterday morning Elizabeth requested a recommendation from me for a trustee position at your prerelease center. Before this incident, I would have given her one that was glowing. She's been a model inmate until now. I really don't understand what got into her."

"Neither do I."

Before Moore hung up, Nat asked to speak with the CO who was involved in the altercation.

"He's not on duty now. He works the eleven-P.M.-to-seven-A.M. shift."

Nat got his name and address. But she had an appointment she needed to keep first. She was sorely tempted to call and postpone it. But she knew that would be a very bad idea.

"I'll see you in my office in a few minutes."

Nat slid off the table, clutching the flimsy paper robe around her. The examining room was warm but she felt chilled to the bone. "Everything's all right, isn't it?"

The doctor smiled, but Nat couldn't decipher whether it was a smile of assurance or pity. "Get dressed and we'll talk." She opened the door and was about to step out into the hall.

"It's just . . . I always heard if you have bad morning sickness it's usually a sign that you're doing . . . okay. You know . . . that the pregnancy is going well. And I've had really awful morning sickness."

Dr. Louise Rayburn glanced back at Nat, smiling again. And again, Nat didn't know what it meant. Then she was out the door, shutting it quietly and firmly behind her.

Dr. Rayburn was the obstetrician who'd delivered all three of Nat's sister, Rachel's, robust, healthy children. When Nat called her office to make an appointment, the nurse told her there was over a two-month wait. But when Nat said she was Rachel Mercer's sister, she was put on hold for a minute. When the nurse came back on the line, she told Nat the doctor could squeeze her in Monday at 9:00 A.M.

Now she was wishing she'd put it off a bit longer. Maybe it was all in her head—but Nat felt certain she'd picked up some vibes from the obstetrician during the exam that all was not well. That terrifying possibility, coupled with her continued bouts of morning sickness, made Nat grab for a nearby metal pan. A nurse entered as she was standing there retching, still draped in her paper johnny, and guided her to the doctor's metal stool. When she was done vomiting, the nurse removed the pan and brought Nat a cool, damp washcloth. Then, despite telling her she was okay, the nurse helped her dress and personally escorted her down the hall into Dr. Rayburn's sun-filled consulting office. The obstetrician's ocher walls were covered with a myriad of framed photos of children of every shape, color, and size. One thing they all shared in common was that each cherub was the picture of strapping health. *Will a picture of my robust baby hang on the obstetrician's wall one day?*

Dr. Rayburn was seated behind a Queen Anne–style desk, a chart—Nat's chart—open in front of her. The doctor was a small woman with delicate features. Her white lab coat was now draped over the back of her chair, revealing a simple pale green jewel-necked sweater, highlighted by a small gold pendant in the shape of a butterfly—or was it an angel? Her short hair was threaded with gray, her face clearly showing both laugh lines at the corners of her lips and worry lines across her brow. The framed medical degree on the wall behind her indicated that she graduated Cornell Medical School in 1979. Which would place her somewhere in her late forties, early fifties. Giving her years of experience. Enough experience, hopefully, to have success with problematic pregnancies. Nat tried to tell herself she was letting her imagination get the better of her—

"Please, Nat, sit down."

But she felt rooted to the spot. "Is anything wrong? Please—"

The obstetrician got up, walked around her desk, and came over to Nat. Nat felt overlarge and gawky beside this petite woman. Worse, she felt as though the doctor was too small and too fragile to take care of her. Most disturbing of all was Nat's awareness that she wanted to be taken care of. She hated that feeling. Hated it—

Dr. Rayburn lightly placed her hand on Nat's arm. "Your blood pressure's a bit high, Nat. It's nothing to be alarmed about."

But of course she was alarmed.

"Have you been under a lot of stress lately?"

Nat swallowed hard. "I'm always under stress. It's the nature of my job."

The doctor smiled. "Yes, I'm sure it is. But you'll want to try to avoid taking on additional stresses now."

Nat pressed her lips together and nodded. "Yes . . . right. It's not always easy to do that." Talk about understatements.

"I understand. And don't worry."

Nat was quick to note that she didn't say she had nothing to worry about.

"I assume I'm right in thinking you intend to see this pregnancy to term."

Nat gave a start. "Have the baby? Yes. Have it, raise it, love it," she blurted. Her choice. From her heart. There really was no inner debate to be had.

"Hopefully," Dr. Rayburn said softly, "your reading will be fine by your next visit."

Nat gave her a weak look. "I'm not a very hopeful person by nature."

"What about the father? He could be a source of needed strength." But she stopped there, seeing Nat's expression, reading it fairly accurately. "He doesn't know yet?"

"I don't know yet."

Nat parked behind an old-model pickup truck in the Barker driveway, stepping around a Big Wheels as she headed up the concrete path to the house. A little towheaded boy who looked to be the same age as Jakey Coscarelli answered the door. He was still in his Ninja Turtle pajamas.

"My mommy's not here," he announced.

Nat wanted to say, *Hasn't your mommy taught you not to open the door if she isn't home?* but instead told the child she'd like to talk to his daddy.

"I think he's sleeping."

But then a husky male voice called out from somewhere inside the house, "Billy, who is it?"

"A lady."

"Mr. Barker," Nat called out. "I'm Superintendent Natalie Price. Could we talk for a minute?"

"Hold on," the officer groused.

Nat stepped inside, entering directly into a small, square living room cluttered with toys. She saw a bowl of cold cereal and milk on the coffee table, and the TV was on to a cartoon show, but Nat noticed that it was on mute.

Billy sauntered over to the coffee table, picked up the cereal bowl, and plunked himself down in front of the TV. Instantly, he was mesmerized by the show even though there was no sound.

There was a small table near where Nat was standing. On it were keys, a phone, a pile of mail, and a small notepad. There was something scrawled on the pad. A name. Hard to make out all the letters, but it looked like the last letter was an *m* or an *n*. Okay, it could be any one of a million people's names or not even a name at all, but then again the first letter looked like an *L*.

L-a-n-d-o-n?

Nat was about to snatch up the note when a shuffling of feet announced Frank Barker's entrance into the room. She quickly turned to face him. He was a pale, heavyset man with a faded and thinning version of his little boy's red hair. He was still wearing his khaki prison officer uniform, but the shirt was unbuttoned, the belt was missing, and he was barefoot.

He greeted her with narrowed eyes and thick arms folded across a barrel chest. Then he shot an irritated look over at his son. "Hey, Billy, how many times I tell you no damn TV when I'm in bed?"

"But you're not in bed, Daddy. And I don't have the sound on."

"Well, turn it off and go get some clothes on."

Billy sniffled loudly. "I'm sick, Daddy, Mommy said I can stay in my PJs—"

"Do what I told you."

Billy made a beeline for the kitchen.

Barker remained at the entry to the living room. He didn't offer Nat a seat, so she remained standing by the front door. And kept her eyes averted from the telephone table.

"I'd like to know what the argument was about between you and Elizabeth Temple, Officer Barker."

"I gave my incident report to Superintendent Moore," he said sullenly.

"I'd like to hear it from you."

"Why? What's it to you?" he challenged, tagging on "Superintendent" as a deliberate afterthought.

"Ms. Temple is being considered for a trustee position at my facility. Until this alleged altercation she had an exemplary record—"

"*Alleged?*" He unfolded his arms in order to jab a finger in her direction. "That's bullshit, pardon my French. She mouthed off at me and I told her real politely to cool it. And what does she do, she tries to knee me. Then in the process of trying to restrain her, she goes bonkers and ends up slamming her head—"

"I thought she tried to punch you."

"You know, I was gonna give her a break. I mean, what with the AIDS and all, you know. I was gonna, like, play it down, but hey, I don't need this grief. The state don't pay me half what it's worth doing this crummy job. You want to know what the argument was about, I'll tell you. Temple offered me a bribe to bring her in some coke. I ain't talkin' the soft drink, you know. I told her, no way, José. And she wouldn't let it drop. I got pissed. Said a few things, you know. Just to remind her who she was and where she was, you know. Guess she didn't like what I had to say and so the next thing you know, she's goin' for my balls. Okay, Super? So now you know what the *argument* was about."

His version, at any rate.

Naturally, Elizabeth Temple denied Barker's version when Nat visited her in the prison infirmary early that evening. Temple swore she not only never asked that CO or anyone for that matter to smuggle in drugs for her, but that she'd been clean, save for the heavy-duty AIDS meds, since she'd been incarcerated. That alone wouldn't have particularly convinced Nat that Temple was the one who wasn't lying. But, after Nat spoke with the doc in the infirmary, who confirmed that Temple had consistently tested negative for drugs each time there'd been random checks, the inmate's version did ring true. There was also the convenient timing of the incident. And that scribbled name on the pad in the officer's house. A name that kept popping up all over the place: Landon.

"If someone did want to keep you from being transferred to Horizon House," Nat asked the inmate, "do you have any idea who?"

A flash of fear shaded Temple's features, but she shook her head. "Who even knew? . . ."

"You asked the superintendent for a recommendation."

"Are you saying she set me up?"

"Was it a setup?"

"All I know is I didn't start that fight with the screw . . . officer," she hurriedly corrected herself.

"What about Eric Landon?"

"What about him?" she countered warily.

"What reason might he have to keep you here?"

"None. Absolutely no reason."

"If he was worried you'd rat him out—"

"I wouldn't . . . there's nothing to rat him out about. . . ." Temple's agitation was palpable. "My head is killing me. Please . . . no more."

"Sorry." Nat started to rise from the chair beside Temple's bed. The inmate caught hold of her arm.

"Does this mean I won't get the transfer?" she asked plaintively. And the flash of fear Nat saw in her features before was back.

Nat was afraid, too. Afraid of what might happen to Elizabeth Temple if she wasn't transferred to her care.

eighteen

"WHEN WILL MR. LANDON BE OUT of his meeting?"

"I don't know," his secretary told Nat over the phone.

"It's important I speak to him."

"If you'd like to leave your number—"

"I already did that yesterday. He never called back. Let's set up an appointment. Anytime today—"

"He's already overscheduled for the day. It isn't easy running a company and being a councilman."

"Tomorrow, then. Any day this week."

"I'm sorry, Ms. Price. Mr. Landon's booked solid all week."

"Did he tell you not to give me an appointment? Did he tell you not to—"

"If you'd like to leave your number—" she repeated as if Nat hadn't told her she'd done that already.

. . .

"No way, Nat," Jack Dwyer's tone was adamant.

Nat checked out Hutch and Sharon. Her other two key staff people looked equally opposed.

"Look, I need a clerk—"

Jack gave her a hard look. "The old one's barely cold in the grave."

Nat flinched, ashamed of how callous she must sound. But Sharon was quick to come to her defense. "Jeez, Jack, you can be a shit sometimes," she said hotly.

Jack looked mildly surprised by the job counselor's uncommonly blunt attack, but not particularly annoyed. "You first getting around to realizing that, Sharon?"

"No," she said coolly.

He grinned. So did Hutch. Even Sharon looked less pugilistic.

It took the edge off the tension they'd all been feeling. Well, Nat's tension was still way too high, partly because she couldn't look at Jack now without worrying that he'd gone off the wagon. She was hoping Sharon was wrong. Her deputy appeared perfectly sober at the moment. But how did he look at night?

Forget that thought, Nat. You want to avoid checking Jack Dwyer out after dark.

"What's the scoop, Nat?" Hutch asked, cutting to the chase.

"Okay," she admitted. "I haven't been completely straight with the three of you as to why I want Elizabeth Temple to clerk for me."

Sharon smiled crookedly. "We ain't first getting around to realizing that either."

"How you doing with that unlisted number I tracked down for you?" Leo asked Nat on the phone later that day.

"Not great. I've left a half-dozen messages on Bryant's answering machine. I was just about to try again when you called. But I'm not too hopeful."

"She screening the calls, you think?" he asked.

"Good possibility. I drove over to the address a few times and either no one's home or no one's answering. But I don't give up easily."

"No, you don't," Leo echoed.

"I'm not sure if you think that's a plus or a minus."

"I'm not always sure myself," Leo admitted. Nat had told him why she wanted Alison Bryant's number—it was a condition he placed on his getting it for her. She could have lied, but she didn't like lying to Leo. However, that didn't extend to giving him more information than was good for him to know. For instance, if he knew what Elizabeth Temple had suggested she do to get to Bryant, he'd be absolutely sure of her tenacity being a minus.

The inmate thought the only way Nat could make contact with the madam was to go undercover. Pass herself off as a society girl from some obscure place in the Midwest looking to be part of Bryant's exclusive service. Temple said she could give Nat some pointers. She didn't spell it out, but Nat was sure the ex-madam felt she needed a lot of help to pull off being a femme fatale. Temple would then put Nat in touch with one of her connections, someone who could provide Nat with an introduction to Bryant. Nat was still hoping a straightforward approach would bring results.

"My mom said you called last night," Leo said. "I got home too late to call you back."

Nat wanted to ask where he was, but she also knew not to ask questions if you weren't going to like the answers. And if the answer was that he was with Suzanne, Nat was not going to like it.

"You doing anything tonight, Natalie?"

"Other than try that number a dozen more times? No."

"Debra Landon's agreed to talk with you."

"With me and Robie?"

"No," Leo said. "She's not ready to be interrogated."

"Robie's not going to be happy about being left out."

"Now you're concerned about Francine Robie's happiness, Natalie?"

"What time?" she asked.

"Eight tonight. She wants us there after her little girl, Chloe's, asleep."

"Us?"

"Didn't I mention that? She wants me there as well."

"For emotional support?"

"I guess you could say that."

"Will Eric Landon be there, too?"

"I don't know. Debra was a bit vague when it came to the husband," Leo said.

"I wonder if that's the exception to the rule or the rule," Nat mused.

Minutes after Leo's call, Fran Robie rang up Nat.

"You hear the latest on Carlyle?" Robie asked.

Nat had received an update from the commissioner a short while ago. "They're still running tests. Nothing conclusive, yet."

"Yeah. Convenient."

No missing Robie's skepticism.

"And wise," Nat added pointedly. "On the physicians' part. Given the deputy's high profile, it wouldn't do to misdiagnose him. And end up with a headline-making malpractice suit."

"You can look at it that way. My bet is the family figures as long as Carlyle's in the hospital it'll keep the wolves from his door. But I can howl anywhere," she said dryly. "And will, if I get my hands on just one piece of hard evidence."

"You sound awfully confident that evidence, if you come up with it, is going to point to the deputy commissioner."

"Hey, Nat, maybe most of your bets don't pan out, but mine do."

"Always?"

Robie laughed. "Nobody's perfect, but some people are more perfect than others."

nineteen

AS THEY DROVE INTO WELLESLEY, AN exclusive suburb twenty miles west of Boston, Leo told Nat that the Landons were living in the home in which Debra and Jessica Asher were raised by their parents, Anthony and Margaret Asher. The large Tudor mansion, set on more than two acres of rolling hills, was bordered by a gated stone fence. There was a buzzer and speaker box at the gate, but before Leo reached out to press the buzzer, the electrified gate swung open.

Only then did Nat spot the discreet camera lens. Someone up at the house had been watching for them. As they wound up a wide cobbled drive, Leo's headlights momentarily shone on a greenhouse, a tennis court, and a covered swimming pool. Even on a dank, gray November evening, everything on the property appeared to shimmer. Especially the house itself, set majestically on the knoll of a hill, and adorned with lavish stonework, several ornate chimneys, half-timbering, and steep roofline. This estate had to be worth well over ten million bucks.

"A little gloomy for my taste, but I guess Debra and Eric see it as a nice place to hang their hats," Leo said as he pulled up to the front of the house.

"Mighty nice inheritance. What did Jessica get?"

"Zip," Leo said. "Debra did once mention that her sister was cut out of the will."

"How come?"

"She didn't say. But I got the feeling Jessica was always a handful and the folks didn't approve of the people she hung around with. I also got the feeling Debra didn't much care for them herself."

"I'd like to know who those people are," Nat said. "Debra didn't happen to mention any names in particular?"

"No, she didn't talk much about Jessica."

"How about her husband? Did Debra talk much about Eric?"

"No."

"You think they're happily married?"

"I think they've got their problems same as every other happily married couple," Leo said dryly.

Nat couldn't imagine the house didn't have servants, but Debra Landon greeted them at the door—well, she greeted Leo. As for Nat, *greet* was going some. She got a brief cool glance. Debra, three years older than Jessica, was a thin, elegant blonde, who looked very much the grieving relative in her black sweater and deep charcoal slacks. Only her freshly and expertly manicured nails, painted a discreet light peach color, gave a hint that Debra Landon was still attending to her appearance.

Before they even stepped across the threshold, she took Leo's arm, leaving Nat to fend for herself, as she led them through the dark wood-paneled hallway into an overlarge but surprisingly underfurnished living room. It had a musty smell that came with keeping the thermostat too low and the windows always closed. Nat doubted much living took place in this room that at one time had probably been a showplace.

Now it was more notable for what wasn't there than what

was. Like the large blank spot on the cherrywood paneling over the fireplace mantel. Nat could tell by the darker hue of that square that something did once hang there. A valuable painting? A pricey antique mirror? More dark squares on other walls indicated other paintings that must have hung in this room at one time. The wooden parquet floor was also bare, but here, too, only the perimeter was faded, indicating the floor had once been covered by some kind of carpet. Persian? Chinese? Expensive, Nat wasn't sure. Where had all the pricey accoutrements gone? And why?

Debra caught Nat doing her survey.

"I'm in the process of redecorating," she said. "Or I was . . . before . . . before my sister—" She looked away for a moment. When she turned back, she appeared composed. "I was working with a decorator, but we didn't see eye to eye. So I'm going to do it myself."

Nat didn't believe her. She smelled money problems in paradise. Maybe everything was being sold to fill Landon's campaign coffers. Or maybe Landon was being hit up for blackmail money by the still-elusive Alison Bryant. Of course, if Eric Landon was the hit-and-run driver and he was paying off Bryant, he'd know how to find her—

"Eric's all for it," Debra went on. "He wasn't particularly keen on the decorator's ideas either."

And speaking of the devil—"Where is Eric?"

"He had to go out of town," Debra said as she crossed the room toward a mahogany cart on which an assortment of high-end alcoholic beverages were on display. She poured herself a Dewars neat and then, more as an afterthought, asked them if they wanted a drink.

Leo and Nat both declined.

"How's Chloe doing, Debra?" Leo asked gently.

Debra turned slowly to face Leo, a harrowed look in her eyes. "She keeps asking for her aunt. I've tried to explain . . . Well, I've made up some garbage about Aunt Jessie being with the angels up in heaven, but how do I expect my child to buy that bullshit when I certainly don't?"

Nat wasn't sure if Debra was indicating that she didn't believe in angels or that her dead sister was unlikely to be one even if she did believe in them.

"When is your husband due back?" Nat asked.

Debra glanced Nat's way, but it was obvious she was only there on sufferance. Without Leo, she'd never have made it inside the house. "I'm not sure."

More trouble in paradise?

"This is such a difficult time. I still can't believe Jessie's gone. I'm not sure this . . . this meeting was a good idea," Debra murmured in a pained voice that served—deliberately?—to shift the focus away from her errant husband. Her eyes watered and she quickly took a belt of the whiskey.

Leo walked over to her. Taking gentle hold of her arm, he guided her over to the sofa and sat down beside her. Leaving Nat to the armchair. Odd girl out again. She should be used to that by now.

Debra closed her eyes. "I'm sorry. I promised myself I wouldn't. . . . It's just that I miss her, you know."

Leo placed his hand over the grieving sister's hand. She turned hers over so their hands were palm to palm, entwined her fingers through his, and gripped his hand tightly. Leo responded in kind. She was clutching the glass of booze in her other hand, but didn't bring it to her lips.

After a minute, she opened her eyes and loosened her hold on Leo's hand. Although she didn't let go.

"I'm truly sorry for your loss, Debra," Nat said softly. "I can only imagine how much you must be hurting."

Debra managed a weary half smile. "Leo says you wanted to ask me some questions about . . . Jessie. I don't know what there is I can tell you. I mean . . . the police seem to think they've . . . found the driver." Her voice cracked and her grip on Leo's hand tightened again.

"Did your sister ever talk to you about Stephen Carlyle?" Nat asked.

Debra shook her head. "The first I heard of him was when I saw the paper and read that he was being questioned by the police.

Jessie never mentioned him. I can't imagine what their relationship would have been."

Couldn't she?

"What about your sister's relationship with Griffith Sumner? Weren't they close?"

"Griff?" Debra bit down on her lower lip. "It's awful what happened to him. To be murdered like that."

"Did you know Jessica visited Griffith Sumner regularly up at Norton prison?"

Debra nodded. "I didn't approve. Jessie could be very naive when it came to men."

Nat kept her expression neutral. It wasn't easy.

"She never believed—never even contemplated the possibility—that Griff did rape that poor woman," she continued.

"I gather you thought he was guilty."

Debra eyed her grimly, but didn't answer.

"And yet you sat there at his trial every day."

Nat spotted a flash of irritation on Debra's face. "I was hardly there every day. Who told you? . . . Anyway, I just went there to support Jessie."

"You weren't dating Griff back then?"

"What? No. Absolutely not."

The woman really was a lousy liar. But, hey, Nat couldn't blame her for not wanting to be linked to a rapist. A *dead* rapist at that. Especially as she was now married to a man with very high political aspirations. And it wasn't going to help the councilman's Senate campaign any when word got out that his deceased sister-in-law was a high-priced hooker. His deceased sister-in-law who was once his lover, back when she was jail bait. And maybe long after that as well.

Men have killed for less—

So have their deceived wives—

"Did you know Sumner was about to have an appeals hearing? That his attorney, Jerry Tepper, was confident Sumner would get his sentence reduced? That he'd be up for parole in March?"

Debra gave Nat a blank look. "I didn't know. Why should I?"

"Jessie might have said something to you."

"About Griff? Not likely. She knew how I felt."

"But you and your sister did talk. About other things."

Debra looked a bit leery. "Yes, I suppose. Of course we . . . we talked."

"Your sister recently mentioned to Griffith Sumner that she was seeing someone she was quite serious about. Did she tell you about this guy?"

"Griff must have got it wrong. Jessie hasn't been seriously involved with a man since . . ." Debra stopped there, clearly having second thoughts about finishing her remark. She let go of Leo's hand and took several gulps of booze. The woman drank like a pro.

"Were you and Jessie close?" Nat asked after Debra cupped both of her hands around the glass.

"She was my sister. My only sibling. I'm devastated about losing her. And," she added stiffly, "I've had enough questions for one night."

Debra had managed not to answer her last question. She looked pleadingly over at Leo. "I'm sure you understand."

"I know this is hard for you, Debra. But we all want the same thing here. To find the person who ran down your sister," Leo said, soothingly.

"The police already know who ran her down."

"Just because someone's been questioned doesn't mean he's being accused," Nat said.

"And it doesn't mean he isn't guilty," Debra challenged. "Just because he works for the Department of Corrections doesn't mean he wasn't driving recklessly. Or that he wouldn't flee the scene of a crime."

"What do you suppose your sister was doing over there in Beacon Hill?" So far there'd been nothing in the tabloids about Jessica Asher's other life. But it would come out sooner or later. More likely sooner. Would Debra Landon truly be surprised? Would Eric?

Nat's question appeared to throw Debra off balance. "I . . . I have no idea. I suppose she was visiting a friend. What difference does it make?"

"Do you think it was an accident, Debra?"

"What else?" she said hoarsely, quickly finishing off what little was left in her glass, and then heading resolutely over to the bar for a refill.

Nat saw Leo about to rise as well to go over to her, but she gave him a quick shake of the head. Instead, Nat went, stopping just behind the agitated woman. "I didn't mean to upset you, Debra."

She reached for the Dewar's, but stopped midway, both hands going up to her face. She started to weep softly.

Nat placed a hand lightly on her shoulder. "I have a younger sister as well, Debra. I can't imagine how I'd feel if something happened to Rachel. It's not only that I love her, it's that . . . well, I'm the older sister, and there's that sense of responsibility older siblings feel towards their younger siblings."

She didn't say a word, but she didn't move away from Nat's touch.

"Sometimes Rachel does things that make me want to shake her. You know, shake some sense into her. She has this knack for getting herself into situations that only spell trouble. I try to make her see that, but she just thinks I'm being too judgmental. That I don't understand. That I'm jealous."

As Nat was talking, Debra's hands slid slowly down from her tearstained face.

"Jessica was like that," she said in a bare whisper. "She was so . . . headstrong."

"Debra, did Jessie have any enemies that you know of? Was there anyone she was afraid? . . ."

"Mommy?"

All three of them turned in the direction of the child standing in the arched doorway of the parlor in her pink pajamas, clutching a Sesame Street blanket against her small frame.

"Chloe, what's the matter, darling?" Debra rushed across the room and scooped her daughter into her arms.

Chloe spotted Leo. Her face brightened. "Is Jakey here?"

"No, it's late, Chloe. Jakey's tucked into bed, fast asleep."

"I miss him," the little girl said solemnly.

"Well, then," Leo said warmly, "your mommy and I will have to plan a play date real soon. Okay?"

"Who's that lady?" Chloe pointed a little finger at Nat.

"She's my friend," Leo said.

Friend, Great. Well, your friend may be pregnant with your child, Leo.

"Is she Jakey's friend, too?"

"Sure, she is," Leo said.

"Is she coming to our play date, too?"

"Enough questions, young lady. You should be in bed," Debra scolded her daughter tenderly.

"But I had a bad dream, Mommy. It scared me sooooo much."

"There, there, baby," Debra soothed, stroking Chloe's back.

As Nat watched the beautiful little dark-haired girl nuzzle her head into her mother's neck, and she felt a drawing sensation in her stomach. *One day, I'll be holding you, little one, comforting you, protecting you from bad dreams. . . .*

"That awful man was hurting Aunt Jessie again and making her cry—"

Debra quickly cut her daughter off. "It was only a dream, sweetheart. Only a bad dream."

twenty

"I TOLD YOU ON THE PHONE several times, Ms. Price, that Mr. Landon couldn't squeeze you in any time this week," the trim, middle-aged secretary said curtly.

"Maybe he'll have a cancelation."

"I'm sure he won't—"

"I'll wait," Nat said, turning from the receptionist's desk and heading for one of the smart-looking plum leather armchairs in the large skylit reception area of DataCom. She'd done some checking into the company, which was owned by a group headed by Eric Landon and Joel Hamilton. Hamilton was the chief operating officer and Eric Landon was the CEO. They had a very slick Web site in which they were described as one of the largest privately held information-technology consulting firms in the Northeast. *We pride ourselves in providing our corporate customers with end-to-end human resources management. . . .*

From the look of their high-end reception space as well as the fact that they had a slew of offices occupying almost the entire twenty-ninth floor of the prestigious Hancock Tower, the company must be doing very well. Again, Nat pondered the question of why the Landons were selling off family heirlooms. Again she thought about how blackmail could eat up a lot of dough.

"You're really wasting your time," the receptionist said as Nat picked up the current *Architectural Digest.* "Maybe next week—"

Before she could respond, the door across from her opened. She probably shouldn't have been surprised by who walked out of Landon's inner sanctum, but still she gave a start.

Fran Robie, however, didn't look the least bit surprised to see her. She didn't look particularly happy, either.

"Is that why you went to see him? Is Eric Landon one of the men on Jessica Asher's private appointment calendar?"

Robie continued to eye Nat grimly as they sat across from each other at a coffee shop off the lobby of the Hancock Building. As Nat had anticipated, she was on the captain's shit list for not having given her the heads-up on her visit with Debra Landon, information a much-disgruntled city councilman passed on to the policewoman. According to Robie, Landon accused Nat of browbeating his wife and causing her severe emotional distress. Nat supposed he was going to be even more disinclined to grant her an appearance now.

"This isn't a one-way street, Nat." Robie was eyeing her like the traitor Nat supposed she was.

"Give it a rest, Fran," she said wearily. "I've just spent the last ten minutes filling you in on every last detail of our meeting." Which wasn't quite true. Nat didn't mention Chloe Landon's bad dream. *"That awful man was hurting Aunt Jessie again and making her cry . . ."* Nat very much wanted to know the identity of *that* awful man. It was obvious, however, that Debra Landon very much didn't want her to know who he was. Which made Nat even more curious.

Fran Robie picked up her bagel, which was slathered in cream cheese, and took a large bite. How did the woman stay so damn trim eating that way?

Nat averted her eyes. Not only was she having trouble eating—or keeping down what little she did force herself to eat—she could barely tolerate other people eating in her presence. When she got on the scale that morning, she was alarmed to see she was down to 126 pounds. Too low for her five-foot-seven frame. And Nat was worried that the weight loss might harm the fetus. She resolved to start trying to eat a little more. But not right now.

"So what? You think Landon was screwing his sister-in-law before she was killed?" Fran Robie asked as she dabbed a smudge of cream cheese off her upper lip.

"What do you think?"

"I'll tell you this much—as a show of trust. Eric Landon's name wasn't on his sister-in-law's calendar. Not to mention that our councilman and U.S. Senate hopeful—"

"He isn't my hopeful. Is he yours?"

Robie grinned. "I try to avoid discussing politics whenever possible. It rarely makes for friendly conversation."

"Meaning he would have your vote." Why wasn't Nat surprised?

"Of course, just because he wasn't *booked* doesn't mean he wasn't getting it on with the sister-in-law," Robie said.

"Is that why you went to talk to him?"

"You always interview the people closest to the victim, Nat."

"I gather he didn't tell you he'd been intimately involved with his murdered sister-in-law." Nat wondered whether Robie knew about the relationship between Landon and Jessica long before she became his sister-in-law.

But Robie merely grinned. "What do you think?"

"Jessie did have a boyfriend whose name she was careful not to make public—"

"Before you run with the boyfriend being Landon," Robie broke in, "I should tell you the guy's provided a pretty tight alibi for October seventeenth. Seems the councilman was the guest speaker at a DAR luncheon down in Weymouth that day. I haven't checked it out yet, but he'd be real dumb to lie about it. And say what you will about the man, he isn't dumb."

"I'm sure he's smart enough to hire a hit man," Nat said caustically.

"Yeah, but we've got zip tying Landon to his sister-in-law's murder, Nat. Whereas we've got plenty more than zip tying Carlyle to Jessie."

"Did you come up with anything at the town house on Joy Street?"

"Nope. Place was clean as a whistle. Asher may have done business there, but either she cleaned up real good after herself or she had some service come in to tidy up."

"Or someone else did it."

Robie smiled. "Like minds think alike. It's doubtful Asher was the only one using that town house for salacious purposes."

"A service."

She nodded.

"How much do you know about it?" Nat asked bluntly.

"How much do you?" Robie was equally blunt.

A draw.

"You really don't trust me," Robie said after a brief silence, but she wasn't sounding particularly bothered.

"Nor you me." Nat was bothered, but she hoped it didn't show.

"I guess we both have our reasons."

"Can you tell me this? Who was the town house leased to?" Nat asked.

"The J. F. Rheiner Corporation."

"Who are they?"

"Good question," Robie said. "It's gonna take some time to track that down."

"Did you ask Eric Landon about it? Maybe it's a subsidiary of DataCom?" she persisted.

"You've really got it in for the guy. How come?"

"Can't you guess? I thought like minds thought alike."

Robie laughed. "Can't we get past this, Nat? I'd hate to think you were bent on conducting your own private investigation."

"Why is that, Fran? Because I might muddy the waters? Steer the investigation in a different direction? One that could be . . . let's just say, awkward for certain prominent men?"

"Surely I don't have to tell you of all people, Nat, that withholding evidence or even information that might aid in a criminal investigation is a criminal offense."

The same warning Nat had given Elizabeth Temple a short time ago. It gave her a disquieting feeling to be the recipient of the admonition this time around.

"I wouldn't imagine you're particularly worried about that, Fran. After all, you've already settled on a prime suspect. So has the DA. I know Keenan's just itching to file a warrant."

"Yeah, Joe has been breathing down my neck," Robie admitted.

Something about the way she said the district attorney's name—his first name . . .

"Are you and the DA chums?"

Robie laughed. "I doubt he'd call us chums."

"What would he call you?"

"His ex."

"Ex? Ex as in—"

"Wife."

Nat was about to exit the coffee shop when she passed a discarded tabloid paper on a table near the door. "Secret Love Tryst Uncovered."

But it wasn't the headline that stopped Nat cold in her tracks, it was the grainy lurid photo on the front page. She snatched up the tabloid and stormed back to Robie.

"You know about this?" Nat threw the rag on the table.

Robie gave it an idle glance. "Yeah. Not that I personally ever read that garbage—"

"Eric Landon knows, too?"

"He saw it."

"Was he surprised?"

"Stop beating on that drum, Nat."

"How'd the rag get their hands on that photo, Fran?"

"Believe me, I'd like the answer to that question more than you."

"Really? So how come you sound like you couldn't give a shit? Maybe because this helps your case—"

"Hold on. I give a shit, okay? And if it was someone in my employ—"

"*If?*"

"Hey, we don't know how many copies of those photos are floating around out there, now do we?" Robie challenged.

"Thought if I hung out here long enough you'd eventually show."

Bill Walker was leaning against the wall just inside the hospital entrance.

"Hi, Bill."

"How you feeling, Nat? Crackers helping?"

"Not much."

He nodded sympathetically.

"Still keeping secrets, huh?"

She knew the reporter was talking about more than her pregnancy.

"You saw the tabloid."

"Yep."

Nat took his arm and drew him over to a secluded spot in the hospital lobby. "Look, Bill, I still can't give you anything for publication, but just between you and me—for the time being—I'm working on a new angle."

His bushy brows lifted. "Oh?"

"I got word that there's evidence floating around that could point the finger at someone else."

"Who?" The obvious reporter question.

"I'm not there yet."

"What kind of evidence?"

"I'm not there yet either."

"You're *under*whelming me here, Nat."

"Precisely why I haven't been in touch."

"You heading up to see Carlyle, I presume. I don't suppose, if I hang around a little while longer, you'll have something for me that would be for publication."

"I hate to think of you wasting more time, Bill."

twenty-one

"HOW ARE YOU FEELING?" IF HIS appearance was any indication, Stephen Carlyle wasn't feeling too good.

"I've been better," he confirmed.

The deputy commissioner had been moved from ICU to a private room at Boston General. His wife, a small, plump woman with a smooth complexion, even features, very white teeth, and very red fingernails, was seated in a molded plastic orange chair beside the bed. Nat gave her a nod of sympathy and she, in turn, offered a half smile and a nod of recognition.

Over by the window, leaning against the wall was a sleek young man in beat-up jeans and a black leather biker jacket. To complete the ensemble, he was sporting a nose ring and several ear piercings from which dangled a cross, a string of silver studs, and several hoops. His dark brown unkempt and unwashed hair fell well past his shoulders. His fingers slowly caressed his scruffy beard as his icy blue eyes insolently checked Nat out. He reminded her of those predatory-looking punk rockers she'd caught, briefly, on MTV videos. Put this guy on a stage and girls would be throwing their panties at him before he got out his first note. But while Nat could easily identify his appeal, it didn't entice her. This young man was bad news. She'd seen enough like him to know. He knew it, too. Nat thought he reveled in it.

"My oldest boy, Sean, Superintendent," Dana Carlyle said awkwardly.

"Sean, go out in the hall and get a chair for the superintendent," Stephen Carlyle ordered brusquely.

Sean didn't move a muscle.

"Please, Sean." Dana gave her son a pleading look. Nat had a feeling it was a look she often gave him. But it had its desired effect. Sean pushed himself away from the wall and swaggered out of the room.

It was only when Nat heard a sharp cough behind her that she realized there was someone else present. Looking over her shoulder she saw a second young man seated in a wheelchair. Nat assumed this must be Alan, the son who'd been paralyzed in a car accident. What struck her first and foremost was the contrast between the two brothers as far as their appearance went. Alan had a scrubbed-clean, almost military look. His hair, a lighter brown then his brother's, was cut short. He was clean-shaven and there was not a piercing to be seen. He was wearing gray wool slacks and a pale blue crew-neck sweater. He might have stepped off the pages of a J.Crew catalogue. Except of course, he couldn't step anywhere.

So this was the gathering of the Carlyle clan. Mother, father, the two sons. None of them was looking too happy. Nat was wondering if they'd seen the tabloid yet. If not, they were going to be looking a lot grimmer after they did.

"Hi," Alan said politely. As their gaze met, Nat saw that he, too, had blue eyes. But they were a warmer blue than his brother's. And they lacked Sean's impertinence.

"My son Alan," Dana Carlyle said.

"Hi, Alan. I'm Nat Price."

"Yeah, I know," he said. "I met you once at a department picnic."

"Oh?"

"It was a long time ago. I was eighteen," he elaborated. "Before—" He waved his hand across his lap. "I played shortstop on your softball team."

"Did we win?"

He smiled sweetly. "No."

"Are you here merely to pay a condolence call, Superintendent?"

The deputy commissioner's voice had a familiar edge to it. Nat turned back to him, bristling at his tone. You'd think, under the circumstances, he'd have taken it down a notch.

"I was hoping we could talk a bit," she said. "If you're up to it."

Carlyle eyed his wife. She rose instantly. "I should be going anyway—"

"Ms. Price won't be long."

Dana Carlyle hesitated. "Well . . ."

"Wait," Carlyle said. "The boys, too."

Alan, who was already wheeling himself toward the door, almost collided with his brother who was sauntering in with another orange chair.

"We don't need it anymore," Carlyle said gruffly. "Wait outside with your mom and Alan."

Sean started to argue. "I've got to get to the garage—"

"Since when have you worried about whether or not you show up for work?"

Sean snickered, but dropped the chair to the ground, pivoted around, and walked out. Dana followed, and then Alan wheeled himself out of the room.

"Sit down," Carlyle barked.

"Well," Nat said wryly, "at least I know I'm not the only person you boss around."

She could see he was momentarily taken aback by her impudent remark, but then he laughed sharply. "Things must be going even worse for me than I thought."

Nat sat down. "They are."

The arrogance was gone. She was suddenly looking at a frightened man.

"I told my wife everything after I left your place the other night," Carlyle said grimly. "Not that it prepared her for . . ." His lips compressed into a tight line. "This morning, Sean brought in the tabloid to show me." He gazed wearily into space. "For once, he got the last laugh."

"I doubt he's laughing," Nat said quietly.

"You don't know Sean. Not exactly a model of moral turpitude himself. But my days of preaching virtue to my oldest son are pretty much over now since he knows I don't practice what I preach."

"Your wife seems to be sticking by you. And Alan—"

"So, what do you want from me, Ms. Price?"

"I want you to give me someone else to focus on," she said bluntly.

"I thought I told you to back off."

"You did."

"You're either dumber than I thought you were, Superintendent, or even more egotistical."

"Depends on how dumb and how egotistical you thought I was."

Carlyle stared at her and she could almost feel him calculating where to take this conversation from there. "If you're not careful, Ms. Price . . ."

"Don't worry, Deputy Carlyle, I'm more careful than you'd ever give me credit for."

"Bullshit," he said. But not in an abrasive way.

"Okay, score one for you," she begrudgingly admitted. Having been put in the position of opting for caution or action in the past, it had never even been a contest.

But it was different now. Nat had more than herself to look after.

"Anyway, before you interrupted," Carlyle continued, "I was going to say that if you're not careful I could get to like you."

Nat was not a woman easily at a loss for words, but every one of them deserted her now.

"Don't worry, Price, you aren't there yet."

"That's a relief."

They both actually smiled. And it struck Nat, to her complete astonishment, that she might possibly get to like Stephen Carlyle as well if this kept up. Well . . . maybe *like* was too strong a word. Especially as she was far from convinced the deputy commissioner wasn't a cold-blooded murderer. What was happening, though, was that she was finding herself wanting to be convinced. And not just because of the commissioner of corrections' mandate.

So she plunged right in.

"Do you know any of the other men Jessica Asher was involved with?"

"You mean, did I engage in threesomes?" Carlyle asked sarcastically. For once, Nat was relieved by the return of his acerbic manner. How true it was that what you knew about a person, even if you didn't like it, was more comfortable than what you didn't know.

"No," he answered after a pause.

"No, you didn't engage—?"

"No, I didn't know any of her other clients. It was a very discreet operation. If Gen . . . Jessica had a client before or after me, she spaced us far enough apart so that there were no accidental meetings."

"What about someone who wasn't a client? A boyfriend?"

"You asked me that already and I told you—" He stopped midway, and after a brief pause, said, "There might have been a boyfriend. One time when we were together, she did get a call on her cell phone. First time I ever heard it ring, which made me think she usually kept it shut off while she was . . . working." Nat had to give the man this much. He looked uncomfortable.

"She took the call?" Nat asked.

"Not exactly. She answered, but told whoever was on the line that she'd call back in a minute. Actually, I was on my way out."

"Did she address the caller by name?"

"Baby."

"What?"

"She said, 'I'll call you back in a sec, baby.' And there was . . .

I don't know . . . a kind of anxious note in her voice. Like she was afraid he might be annoyed that she wasn't able to speak to him right then."

"Him? How do you know it was a man?"

Carlyle shrugged. "The way she said 'baby.' I just assumed . . . What do I know, maybe she swung both ways."

"Did she ever mention any girlfriends?"

"We didn't chitchat. I knew zip about her personal life. And I stupidly thought she knew zip about mine. I didn't even think she knew my real name."

"How'd you find out she did?"

Carlyle's mouth twitched.

Nat waited him out. She didn't have to wait long.

"She messengered something over to me at my office."

"What was it?"

He looked away.

"The photos," she said, the proverbial light dawning. "She sent you the photos."

"Only one of them," he muttered.

"It doesn't help your situation that you lied to Robie when she showed you the photos and you said you didn't know about them."

"And how exactly would it have helped me to admit it?" He grimaced. At first Nat worried it was his heart. "I should have realized it wouldn't take long for the cops to dig them up."

If they did dig them up. Nat realized Fran Robie never had actually answered her when she'd asked the homicide captain how she'd got her hands on those lurid photos. Had she unearthed them at Jessica's apartment? Or had someone provided those photos for her?

"What did Jessica Asher want from you in exchange for keeping those photos from getting out?" Nat wanted to see if Carlyle was going to be straight with her or play her like he played Fran Robie.

"What do most blackmailers want, Price?"

"I doubt they all want what she wanted, Deputy."

"She wanted a favor," he said after a lengthy pause.

"To influence the Parole Board to approve a parole date for Griffith Sumner?"

"I don't know what she wanted. She died before she spelled it out. And don't forget, Price, I didn't know until that photo arrived that Genevieve . . . Jessica . . . knew my true identity."

"And if she had spelled it out?"

He hesitated. "I don't know what I would have done," he admitted.

"Where's the photo?"

He hesitated. "I burned it."

"Griffith Sumner was murdered last Friday."

He held a poker face, like he'd been practicing. "I know. It's all over the news. Knifed in a gang fight."

"Convenient."

He made no response.

"When did you receive that photo?" Nat asked.

"The day before . . ." His voice was a hoarse whisper. And he didn't finish the sentence.

"The day before Jessica Asher was killed?" *Shit.*

"Yeah, I know. It's looking worse and worse." And so was the deputy commissioner.

"What about that note you left your secretary? Saying you wouldn't be in the next day. This was after you got the photo, right?"

His eyes locked with hers. "I didn't leave any note. My secretary must be mistaken. Or the cop made it up to try to trap me. I left no note," he reiterated. "Talk to my new secretary. Her name's Grace Lowell. Maybe she can clear this matter up. She can't very well have found a note from me I never wrote," he insisted.

"But you were upset after you saw that photo."

"Upset? Yeah."

"And angry." Nat didn't pose it as a question.

He made no response.

"And you felt betrayed."

He looked back at her, his expression grim. "All of the above."

"Did you see Jessica Asher the next day?"

"No."

"Did you speak to her?"

"No."

"She didn't phone you?"

"No."

"And you didn't phone her?"

Nat could see her persistent questions were sorely trying his patience. But her patience was wearing thin as well.

"Didn't you want to get the details of what she wanted? Didn't you want to reason with her? Try to strike a bargain? Find out more about—?"

"I had no way . . . I didn't know how to reach her. I didn't know her real name, where she lived—"

"How did you know she didn't live in that town house where you had your assignations?"

He laughed harshly. "'*Assignations.*' You make it sound so romantic."

"And it wasn't?"

"No. Never romantic. It was sex. Down and dirty sex. The kind of sex men dream of having. The kind of sex they never have with their wives. At least the kind I never—" He stopped abruptly, as though he'd said more about this topic than he'd meant to. "Anyway, I knew Genevieve didn't live there because the closets and bureau drawers were empty." He smiled dryly. "Yes, I snooped. You got me. Guilty."

"But you knew she worked out of the town house," Nat persisted. "You knew where to find her—"

He cut her off. "I had no way of knowing who was using the place that day. I assumed a lot of the girls did business there."

"Assumed? Or knew?"

"I'm not in the mood for twenty questions, Price. I'm sure my cardiologist wouldn't approve."

"Did you meet any other women there?"

His answer was a glare.

"What about Alison Bryant? Did you ever meet her? Do you know her?"

"Leave it, Price. You're way over the line."

Nat doubted she was even in sight of the line, but she could see Carlyle was not going to volunteer info about his other sexual peccadilloes. "Why not just call the service that morning to arrange a time with Asher?"

He swiped a bead of sweat above his upper lip with the back of his hand. "I needed to get myself under wraps a bit before we met."

His answer sounded weak at best. At worst—

"I know," he said as if Nat had spoken her thoughts aloud, "but it's true. I really did wake up with a piercing headache. I'd gone to bed the night before with it as well. I did spend the morning at home and I did go to see my mother in the afternoon. I didn't speak to Gen . . . Jessica. I didn't drive over to Joy Street that day. I didn't have anything to do with her murder."

"How did you arrange your meetings with Jessica?"

"I had a phone number. That's all. A woman . . . the same woman . . . always answered. She booked the appointments."

After a bit of resistance he gave her the phone number—no surprise that he knew it by heart—and Nat jotted it down.

"How did you pay?"

"Cash. Strictly a cash business."

"You gave the cash directly to Jessica?"

He nodded.

"This woman you talked to on the phone. What was her name?"

"I have no idea."

"Was she the madam?"

He shrugged. "I'd guess a flunky. According to Genevieve, the madam kept a very low profile."

"Did she tell you the madam's name?"

"No. And I really didn't care who was running the service. Just that it was discreet. Only . . . only it wasn't after all."

"Did she say anything else about the madam?"

Carlyle started to look more interested in her question. "Is it important?"

"It could be."

He frowned. "There was this one time when Genevieve seemed very agitated. I asked her what was wrong. She made some obscure comment about it being bad enough coping with one boss, she certainly didn't need two of them tossing out orders."

So Alison Bryant wasn't running the service alone? This piece of news certainly gave Nat pause.

"After she said it, she seemed even more agitated. Told me to forget it. Asked me to give her a few minutes to pull herself together before . . ." He let the rest of the sentence drop.

"Did this woman who booked the appointments know your real name?"

"She never asked."

"Wouldn't she want to check you out before she booked you with one of the women?"

He shrugged. "I wasn't about to tell her my real name." He snickered. "If she'd asked I would have made up a name. Just as I did with Genevieve. Just as she did with me."

"Phil Mason?"

He laughed dryly. "My price-gouging dentist."

"Did you always use the same name? Phil Mason?"

"My little joke."

"Who were the other women?"

"What?"

"That you were with, besides Jessica? You just said you always used the same alias."

"Very good, Ms. Price. You led me right into that one."

"I'm not trying to trap you, Deputy. I'm trying to find a shred of light in a very dark tunnel. And you're not even willing to voluntarily flick on a flashlight."

"I only saw a couple of other women. And only when I couldn't book Genevieve. They were fine. First-class. But they weren't . . . Anyway, I don't know their real names either. I don't even remember what names they went by."

"So the name Alison Bryant doesn't strike a chord?"

"No. I told you—"

"Did you see all of the women at the Joy Street location?"

"All *three*? No. I met Skye at a hotel. Apparently the town house was already booked."

"Skye?"

"Jeez, that jumped out of my unconscious. Yeah, that was her name. Or the name she used when we were together."

"And you have no idea what name she went by when she wasn't working?"

"No idea."

"Nothing about her looked familiar?"

"I have no idea who she is, Price."

"What was the hotel?"

"The Boston Regency. A suite. I only went once. Too public for my taste."

"Who gave you the skinny on this call-girl service? Who gave you their phone number? I'm assuming you didn't come across it on a men's-room wall." Nat was also assuming that whoever was giving out the number was being very selective. It would explain why there was no need for real names or any overt background checks over the phone. That was all sorted out before the dates were arranged.

Carlyle darted his tongue across his chapped lips. "I met a woman at some black-tie benefit last spring. I guess I had a little too much to drink and I . . . hit on her and she gave me what I thought was her phone number. It ended up being a service."

"And did this service hook you up with her?"

"No. I described her and ended up with Genevieve . . . Jessica, instead. I wasn't sorry."

"Who was the woman you met at this benefit? It wasn't Skye?"

"No. I never got her name."

Nat gave him a dubious look.

Carlyle smiled wryly. "I didn't give a rat's ass what her name was, Price."

"Can you describe her?"

He gave her a wry smile. "She was a tall, stacked, beautiful redhead. A looker with class."

More likely a *hooker* with class.

"Was she there alone?"

He shrugged. "No idea. Like I said, I was a little bombed. I saw her mingling, but I don't know if she was with someone."

"How about you? Were you there alone?"

"You mean, was my wife with me? No. She hates those kinds of affairs. I went with the commissioner and his wife."

"What was the benefit?"

"The mayor's charity gala to benefit the American Heart Fund."

Ironic—a mayor without a heart hosting that charity.

"Must have been a lot of important people there," she remarked. "Did you see this classy redhead mingling with Mayor Milburne?"

"I can't recall. I do remember when we had dinner, she was at a table with Eric Landon and his wife."

Landon yet again. "Who else was at that table?"

"Jerry Tepper. Tepper was one of the speakers and then he sat down at that table." He paused, scowled. "Oh yeah, and the DA was at that table."

"Joe Keenan?"

He nodded grimly. No surprise the deputy wasn't feeling kindly toward the district attorney at the moment.

Nat did find it a curious combo, though. A defense lawyer and a prosecutor at the same table . . .

Carlyle's expression got grimmer, deep lines furrowing his brow.

"Shit," he muttered. "I knew she looked familiar the other day, but I couldn't place her."

"Who?"

"The woman sitting on the other side of Joe Keenan that night. It was that foul-mouthed cop, Robie."

"Fran Robie?" Keenan's ex? Or were the pair still married at that time?

"Yes. Come to think of it," Carlyle went on, "the redhead who gave me the phone number—she was on Robie's other side. Yeah, they were sitting right next to each other."

twenty-two

NAT WAS HEADING OVER TO THE bank of phones in the hospital lobby, eager to try the number for the escort service that she got from the deputy commissioner, when she spotted a much-agitated Sean Carlyle at the end phone. He was staring, or rather glaring, straight ahead so Nat quickly moved to a phone two walled-off sections from him. She lifted the receiver to her ear but held off dialing, intent now on eavesdropping.

"Look, don't start fucking with me or you know—"

He stopped, the caller apparently breaking in before he got to finish. But he came back even stronger.

"Yeah, well I can make your life fucking miserable, too, sweetheart."

Nat was guessing a woman.

"Leave her out of it. And you tell that little bitch Ali that if she—You there? Hey . . . hello . . . Fuck!"

She heard the phone slam and kept her face averted as Sean Carlyle stormed past. One word reverberated in her head. *"Ali."*

Okay, there was certainly more than one Ali in this world, but then again . . .

Nat heaved a sigh. As if things weren't complicated enough. Now she had to find out if Carlyle's punk son fit into this picture. And if so, how. She doubted Sean was going to fill her in. She could go back up to the deputy commissioner's room and ask him. Assuming he knew. Assuming he'd voluntarily involve his own child in this god-awful mess.

After taking a couple of moments to get refocused, Nat dialed the number Stephen Carlyle gave her. A recording came on after a couple of rings, informing her that the number had been disconnected.

No big surprise there.

But then she'd had enough surprises for one day.

"I'm only working here until the end of the week. Mostly fielding phone calls from reporters," Grace Lowell told Nat wearily. Her dull gray eyes, which were in no way aided by her heavy-handed application of mascara and black eyeliner, shifted to the telephone, which rang as if on cue.

"Department of Corrections . . . No, I am not giving any statements regarding Deputy Commissioner Carlyle. . . . Now, listen, you've called here before several times and each time I tell you the same thing. . . . *No comment.* Now, please do not call again." She slammed the receiver into the cradle and heaved a sigh, her ample breasts heaving beneath her blouse. The tall, heavyset secretary's overkill on her makeup was in keeping with her colorful although unflattering attire. Deep emerald green blouse two sizes too small, a pencil-thin dark purple skirt ending several inches above her knees—granted her legs were surprisingly thin and shapely by comparison to the rest of her bulk—and a scarf covered in bright red roses and giant emerald leaves on a mustard background, worn like an ascot. This poor woman was the ultimate candidate for one of those TV makeover shows.

"I'll be glad to finish up the week."

"Will you be transferred?"

"I'm leaving corrections. It's been a short but eventful experience. Only a month, but it feels like it's been a lot longer," Carlyle's secretary said dryly. "Actually, I'm starting a job in New
York City in two weeks. I lived in Manhattan for years. And then
I met this man who was moving here to Boston." She sighed. "I'm
afraid I got a bit carried away. Followed him out here. Letting
myself think he might want to pursue a relationship. He didn't.
No big surprise," she said bluntly. "Let's face it, I'm not exactly a
man magnet. I'm a plain, plump, thirty-two-year-old spinster
who . . ." She gave Nat an embarrassed look. "I'm sorry. You
didn't come over here to listen to my tale of woes. I suppose it's
about the poor deputy commissioner."

"Yes, I would like to ask you a few questions."

Grace Lowell nodded. "Of course. Commissioner Miller gave
me permission to tell you anything I know. Which, sadly, isn't
very much."

Nat pulled up a chair. "Sometimes, people know more than
they realize they do."

"I suppose." But she didn't sound confident. Or, for that matter, particularly interested.

"Let's start with the delivery boy who brought in that manila
envelope on Thursday, October sixteenth."

"Sorry, I don't remember. . . . We get packages all the
time. . . . Wait. You said the sixteenth. Wasn't that the day before
that poor woman was run over?" She pressed a hand to her chest.
"I can't believe he would ever do something so . . . so awful as to
run her down. He was a very nice boss. True, I was only with the
deputy commissioner for a few weeks, and I will admit he could
be a bit . . . well, abrupt, but believe me I've had many worse
bosses."

A not altogether glowing recommendation for Carlyle.

"Anyway, you were asking about a delivery. I remember now.
Because the deputy asked me about it later that day. Yes, that's
right. Now that I think about it, he seemed . . . a bit upset."

Nat bet he was upset.

"What exactly did he ask you, Ms. Lowell?"

"He asked who delivered it. Which I remember now, I thought

was sort of odd. I mean, what did it matter? It was just a delivery boy. Just like any delivery boy."

"Can you describe him?"

She looked perplexed by Nat's question. "I don't remember. I'm sorry. Is it important? Oh, it must be if you're asking. What was in the envelope?" She was suddenly looking more interested. Excited, even. Like this could turn out to be the highlight of her day. Or of her whole year. Grace Lowell definitely impressed Nat as a woman who'd had few highlights in her life.

"Didn't you have to sign for it?"

"Well . . . no. Now, that is odd, isn't it? Usually I do have to sign." She shrugged. "But not always. Not that time. Dear, I'm not being terribly helpful. I'm sorry, Superintendent."

The phone rang again. Grace Lowell rolled her eyes as she picked up. "Department of Corrections . . ." She used the harried tone of a woman too long put-upon. But then her tone changed ever so subtly. Nat could pick up the shift but she couldn't quite put her finger on what the change was. Tension? Irritation? "No, I'm sorry, but I can't talk to you. . . . Yes, that's right. . . . Yes. . . . No comment." She seemed to tack this last bit on as an after-thought before she hung up.

"Another reporter?" Nat asked.

"God, they just won't give up."

Nat's bullshit detector started going off in her head. She didn't think that was a reporter. Then who?

"You told the police you found a note on your desk from the deputy when you came into work on Friday morning, the seventeenth."

"A note. Yes. Right. From the deputy. On one of his pink message slips. Saying he wouldn't be coming in that day . . . the day that poor girl was killed." She began to shake her head slowly back and forth. "I didn't think anything of it at the time. To be honest, I was a bit relieved. I actually had a date that night, and, well, I figured since the deputy wasn't going to be in, I could leave a bit early and get ready—"

"Did you give the note to the police?"

"No. I couldn't. I tossed it out that morning. I mean . . . I had no idea it might be . . . well, evidence."

"Was the note in the deputy's handwriting?"

She looked perplexed. "Well, who else's handwriting would it be in?"

A question with no answer, thanks to the fact that the note no longer existed.

"Sorry I can't be of more help," Grace offered.

"Right. Well, thanks." Nat turned to leave when she decided to ask one more question. "I'm just curious. Did the deputy's son ever drop by to see his dad while you were here?"

"His son did come by a few times. We used to chat a bit if his dad was at a meeting or something." She scowled, her makeup caking across her brow. "But the last time he came by, well . . . not that I was eavesdropping, I assure you. It's just . . . well, they got a bit worked up . . . you know, yelling . . . well, not the deputy so much as his son."

"What was Sean yelling about?"

"Sean? Oh, it wasn't Sean. I only met that one in person once. First day I was here. Very surly. I'm talking about the other boy. Alan. Tragic to see such a young, nice-looking boy condemned to a wheelchair."

"What was Alan yelling at his dad about?"

The secretary shrugged. "I really don't know. I couldn't hear what . . . I mean I certainly didn't want to hear . . . it was just his tone . . . And he looked very upset when he wheeled himself out. Didn't even say good-bye to me."

"When was this? When was Alan here?"

"When? Oh, I remember that. It was the same day that delivery came for the deputy commissioner. I was just getting ready to leave—in fact I'd already said good night to Mr. Carlyle—when Alan showed up."

"Alone?"

"Oh yes. He's quite adept with his wheelchair."

"But someone must have driven him over."

She shrugged. "I don't know. I have a cousin who's a paraplegic and he drives his car without any problem. Just had it rigged so he could manage the gas and brakes with his hands."

Again, the phone rang. Grace Lowell picked up. "Department of Corrections . . . No, I am not giving any statements regarding . . ."

It was close to noon and since Nat had gotten a reprieve from her almost constant state of nausea, she figured she'd better try to eat something while she could. Across the street from the State Office Building was the Lone Wolf Grill, an upscale and concurrently pricey café catering to the government officials from the upper echelons. Nat had been taken there a few times, once by the commissioner and on several occasions by Deputy Commissioner Russell Fisk. As for Deputy Commissioner Carlyle, they'd never broken bread there on his dime or hers. They'd never shared a private meal together anywhere.

Nat heard her name being called as a hostess was leading her to a table for one. She recognized the voice.

Russell Fisk rose from his chair as she headed over to him. He was with an attractive middle-aged man.

"Join us, Nat. This is Keith Brockman. Keith, this is Nat Price, superintendent of Horizon House. I've been wanting the two of you to meet."

Nat shook hands with Brockman, who had also gotten up from his chair to greet her. Russell had told her in confidence that he'd been living with Keith for the past year. Given all the controversy that had swirled around the Department of Corrections the past few years, the deputy commissioner had opted to keep his sexual preference a private matter.

Nat declined the invitation and Russell didn't press it. He did, however, ask her if she'd been to see Steve Carlyle at the hospital.

"Yes. He seems to be holding up."

"It must be awful," Russell said sympathetically. "I may not always agree with Steve professionally or personally, but I do think he's been a hardworking and committed deputy. How are things going?"

"Not great," Nat admitted.

"Is there anything I can do to help?"

"You didn't happen to see a note from Carlyle on his secretary's desk on Friday morning, October seventeenth?"

"A note? On Grace Lowell's desk?"

"On a pink message slip. I know Lowell was strictly Steve Carlyle's secretary so you probably had no reason to be at her desk—"

"Actually, I did. My secretary, Janice, was out that week. The poor girl had a miscarriage—"

Nat literally felt a terrible pull in her womb. Sympathy pains?

"And so my mail was being left on Grace's desk," Russell was saying. "I remember I came in early on Friday. Before Grace got in. And . . . I mean, I certainly could have missed seeing it, but Grace keeps an admirably tidy desk—I'm sorry, Nat. I just didn't see any pink message slips. Is that a problem?"

"I'm not sure, Russell."

The waiter brought her a check, having already removed her barely touched omelette. Nat couldn't eat after all, too anxious now about the possibility of having a miscarriage, as if somehow it was a contagious condition that could strike simply because she'd been told it had happened to another woman.

She was putting some bills on the table when a man slid into the chair across from her. At first she assumed it was just some guy trying to grab an about-to-be-available table, but when she looked at him she realized he most definitely wasn't *just some guy*.

"I guess we both recognize each other from our photo spreads over the years. But it's time we met in person." He extended a hand across the table. "Joe Keenan. A pleasure to meet you, Superintendent Price."

As they shook hands, Nat noticed that the district attorney had a firm grip and that his nails were expertly manicured. In fact, Keenan was a regular fashion plate in his navy double-breasted suit, toothpaste white shirt, deep maroon jacquard tie. She'd only caught a brief glimpse of him when he showed up at the precinct observation room to watch Carlyle being questioned that first time.

Having the opportunity to see him up close and personal, Nat had to admit the DA had the trim, muscular build and the rugged good looks to carry off the slick men's couture. Like his ex-wife, Keenan was sporting an outdoorsy tan that blended very nicely with his dark brown eyes and expertly trimmed light brown hair. Nat bet Keenan and Robie had turned plenty of eyes whenever they stepped into a room. She guessed they still did, since their divorce apparently hadn't stopped them from spending time together.

"Do I pass inspection, Superintendent?"

Nat was sure the DA's query was meant to cause her some embarrassment, which would in turn give him an immediate edge.

She smiled faintly. "No loose threads or telltale lipstick marks showing on your collar."

Keenan showed a hint of disappointment at her comeback—possibly a dash of irritation as well. But he covered it with a provocative lifting of one eyebrow.

"Well, you certainly look even better in person than in your photos." He smiled sheepishly as he observed her less-than-flattered reaction. "Hmm, something tells me that was a bad line."

"All lines are bad lines, Keenan. I was just leaving, so if this was just a chance meeting—"

"I was hoping we could have a brief chat."

"It'll have to be very brief. I'm running late."

A waitress started to approach the table, but Keenan waved her off.

"Bow out, Superintendent."

Well at least he'd come right to the point.

"Murder inquiries are complicated enough without amateurs muddying the waters. And," he lifted his hand again, this time to forestall her, "you are not only an amateur, you've got a professional stake in the outcome of this investigation. That makes you biased as well. And biased people have very selective vision."

"And you're not biased?"

"The facts are the facts, Ms. Price."

"There are no facts in this case, Keenan. Only allegations."

He gave her a sober look. "You don't have all the facts. But I'll tell you this much, Superintendent. Carlyle's going to stand trial for the premeditated murder of Jessica Asher. That's murder in the first. I'm not claiming to be a soothsayer, but I can tell you with a fair degree of confidence that the jury will bring in a guilty verdict."

"Were you as sure of the verdict before the jury returned in the Elizabeth Temple trial, Keenan?" But Nat didn't wait for him to answer. "Yes, I suppose you were since you had such a strong informant testifying for the prosecution. Alison Bryant made your case for you. How's she doing, by the way? Or should I be asking—how's tricks?"

Keenan shrugged like he couldn't care less. "Last I heard, Ms. Bryant had retired from that oldest of professions."

"What's she doing now?"

"I haven't the faintest idea, Ms. Price."

But, given that little agitated twitch in his jaw, Nat was sure the district attorney had more than a faint idea. One of the *facts* he thought she didn't know about?

"Well, like I said, I'm running late. Take care, Keenan." She got up from the table. "Oh, and say hi to your ex for me. You and Fran are certainly proof that there really is such a thing as a friendly divorce."

Before leaving the café, Nat needed to make a quick stop in the ladies' room. On her way out of the café, she glanced back at the table where she'd left District Attorney Joe Keenan in a testy mood. He was looking more testy now. And he'd put her comment about his friendly divorce in question. Because occupying the seat Nat had vacated a few minutes before was his ex, Francine Robie. And neither one of them was looking particularly friendly.

How Nat would have loved to be a fly on the wall.

twenty-three

FIRST THING NAT SPOTTED WHEN SHE walked into Leo's office was a new cactus plant on his cluttered desk. His last one was a sorry sight, but this one was vibrantly healthy and starting to bloom. She doubted Leo had bought it. Not his thing. So who wanted to brighten the place up? Not his partner. Oates was even less into plants than Leo. Could be Anna Coscarelli. But a more likely candidate was Suzanne Holden. When Suzanne was a resident at Horizon House, she'd kept a colorful array of plants in her room. A woman with a green thumb. Particularly partial to cacti.

"You're in luck," Leo said, sounding less than enthused about it. "Kid's on probation."

"He's twenty-six. Hardly a kid." Nat scanned a copy of Sean Carlyle's rap sheet. He'd had several brushes with the law but managed to get off—Nat was sure in no small measure to his father's influence—until the last incident three months ago when he was arrested for driving under the influence of a controlled substance, cocaine. He was placed on two years' probation. Nat jotted down the name of his probation officer. Kerry O'Donnell. Another lucky break. She was a woman Nat had had good dealings with in the past. A tough broad who'd been with the system for twenty-odd years.

Leo handed her a copy of the incident report.

"Check out where he was stopped," he said.

"Cambridge Street," she read off the sheet. "Is there some special significance? . . ."

"Probably reading too much into it," Leo said in a way that she knew he wasn't, "but Joy Street happens to run right into Cambridge Street."

She told Leo about the snippet of Sean's phone conversation in the hospital lobby that she'd overheard.

"I don't like this," was Leo's response. "The kid—correction, man—is a sleazebag, Natalie. I want you to dump this in Robie's lap and walk away."

"I can't do that, Leo."

"Can't? Or won't?"

"Did you know Fran Robie was once married to our prominent DA, Joe Keenan?"

Leo scowled. "Yeah, so?"

"When did they split?"

Leo's scowl deepened. "What are you driving at, Natalie?"

She told him about the mayor's charity affair a few months back, focusing on the people sitting at the table with the woman who gave Stephen Carlyle the number of the escort service.

This info didn't brighten Leo's expression. "So what are you telling me? You think Robie's dirty? Along with Keenan, the Landons, Tepper . . . oh yeah, and this mystery redhead. Hey, and let's not forget our mayor. After all he brought this little group together. Well, honey, if you're right you got yourself one sizzling hot political sex scandal."

Leo wasn't big on endearments. The "honey" wasn't meant as one.

"Then we toss in the deputy commissioner into the mix. And, as if the murder scene isn't crowded enough, we squeeze in Carlyle's druggie son."

Nat knew Leo was mocking her, but the truth was, he was laying out a list of possible suspects.

"I saw Keenan at lunch today. He told me to back off."

Leo smiled wryly. "Poor bastard doesn't know how unkindly you take to being given orders."

Nat smiled back. "No, he doesn't."

"I had a visit this morning from Debra Landon."

"What did she want?"

"Three guesses, Natalie."

She only needed one. "She wants me to stop poking my nose into her husband's affairs—and I use that term broadly." Nat's gaze fell on that cactus again.

Leo followed her gaze. Was he also following her thoughts?

"Natalie," he said softly. And for a moment she believed they were going to have a heart-to-heart. They needed one badly.

He took hold of her hand. She was scared but ready.

"You can't blame Debra for wanting to protect her husband, Natalie. There's no evidence that Eric Landon is in any way involved in this ugly business, but still the man's already getting hit by the tabloids, what with that photo of his sister-in-law and Carlyle surfacing. He could find himself ousted from the city council. And his political opponents could turn this into a real smear campaign if he even ends up getting on the Senate ballot after this."

Scratch the heart-to-heart. Nat looked back down at Sean's incident report. And then she noticed something as Leo continued on.

"And it's not just Landon who could get smeared. You could be messing up a lot of influential people's careers—people could be ruined, Natalie. Innocent—"

"Leo, look at this. There was an unidentified passenger in the car when Sean was stopped. A woman."

"Natalie, are you listening to me? You're turning this investigation into a Kennedy-esque conspiracy."

"Leo," she countered, "are you listening to me? How'd she get to have her name kept out of the incident report?"

. . .

"Had to get out of that shithole for a breather," Kerry O'Donnell said in a husky voice that was the product of too many cigarettes over too many years. Nat followed her to a table at the end of a narrow deli in the North End a block from her office. The probation officer eased her bulky body clad in a navy blue tracksuit into a booth, slapped her tattered briefcase on the chipped red Formica top, and shouted out to the Latino man behind the counter, "Two hot corned beefs on rye, Miguel. And none of that lean crap."

"Unless you're planning to eat both sandwiches," Nat quickly piped in, "make it one."

Kerry peered at her over her rimless bifocals. "You dying?"

"What?"

"Nobody turns down a fatty, hot corn-beef sandwich unless they're dying. Or—heaven help us—on a diet."

"Stomach bug." One of the longest ailments on record.

She shrugged. "I'll take one back to the office. Unless you change your mind. So, we got us some interest in lover boy, huh?" The longtime probation officer was already pulling out Sean Carlyle's file.

"Is he?"

Kerry peered over at her again. "The ladies love him. And he loves the ladies. Personally, I like a guy who showers once a year whether he needs it or not."

They both grinned.

"How do you know so much about his love life?" Nat asked.

"I don't know that much. But it's more than I care to know. A few times, I showed up at his girlfriend's apartment for a spot visit. Before she tossed him out on his skinny butt a few weeks ago. Which, if you ask me, she should have done on day one. Anyway, a couple of times I showed up, there was a different girl with him. In various states of undress. A different one each time."

The probation officer referred to her folder on Sean Carlyle, which consisted of what Nat would describe as an impossible jumble of papers, index cards, and a variety of colors of Post-it notes. Somehow, the woman had her filing system down pat, and quickly pulled out just the slip of paper she needed.

"The girlfriend's name is Martha Cady. I'll say one thing. The slug picks 'em with not only looks but dough."

"Oh? Martha Cady has money?"

The two piping hot corned-beef sandwiches arrived, delivered by Miguel himself. The smell assaulted Nat like a sucker punch to her stomach.

Kerry was too busy digging into her sandwich to notice Nat edging her plate as far from her side of the table as possible. The probation officer hadn't quite finished chewing when she said, "Cady. As in Cady Electronics. The Phillip and Katherine Cady Foundation. Martha's rolling in it, Nat. Doesn't seem fair. She gets to be tall, gorgeous, stacked, and she gets to be rich. Oh well, fuck it. Bet she can't put her perfect white chops into one of these babies without being riddled with guilt. Of course, she could just barf it back up. You know, the model's diet."

Nat was wishing they'd stayed in O'Donnell's grim little cubicle of an office. . . .

"You okay? You're looking a little green around the gills there, Nat."

"What about the other two women Sean was with at Cady's apartment?"

Kerry was chewing another bite of her sandwich. Again, she didn't wait to swallow. "Their names? Can I ask why all the interest?"

Nat averted her eyes. "You can ask."

She grinned, a good-natured woman when she wasn't dealing with her wayward charges. Letting the question drop, she rifled through the folder in a purposeful fashion. Mustard from her fingertips stained the pages, but she didn't seem bothered. "Here we go. One gal gave her name as Mary Smith." Kerry quirked an eyebrow.

"And the other?"

"The other . . ." More rifling through papers. This time she came up with a bright yellow Post-it. "The other one—oh yeah, only got a first name from her. Real sassy-ass, that one. Jen."

"Jen? With a J or a G?"

"Geez Mareez, I didn't bother asking her to spell it." She filed the slip of paper back in the folder. Nat filed the name in her head. If it was Gen, it could have been short for Genevieve. First Ali, now Gen.

The family that plays together stays together. . . . Of course, it depended on who they were both playing with. If it was the same prostitutes, it could definitely strain a familial relationship. But where would Sean get the kind of money it would have cost for Genevieve's services? For a ladykiller like Sean there were a lot of possibilities. He could have hit up his rich girlfriend. One of his other lady friends. Or he could have had some kind of lucrative sideline. Like selling dope. Stealing. Taking illicit photographs?

Nat shivered with revulsion at the thought that Sean could have been the one who'd photographed Jessica Asher with his father.

"What about an Ali?" she asked Kerry. "Or Alison?"

"Nope," Kerry said after another search. "I think those two are the only names I got. One time I'm sure there was some gal in the bathroom showering. Sean said it was Martha. But who knows?"

"Do you think Martha knew Sean was cheating on her? Is that why she threw him out?"

Kerry smiled crookedly. "All I can say is the last time I went to do a spot check over at her place—which was also his last day living there, making it October tenth—I could hear them arguing while I was still in the hall. Actually, I didn't think it was Martha until she opened the door."

"Why is that?"

"He kept calling her Skye."

Nat instantly forgot about the offensive smell of corn beef.

"Skye?" She wanted to be sure she'd heard right.

"Yep. I remember because I asked Martha if Skye was her nickname and she gave me a look that woulda killed a weaker dame."

Nat's heart was racing and it must have shown in her face. Ali. Gen. Skye. No maybes here.

"So, is the Carlyle kid in trouble, Nat?"

twenty-four

MARTHA CADY'S INGRATIATING SMILE FADED THE instant she realized Nat hadn't popped into the Lanz Art Gallery on Newbury Street—Boston's equivalent to L.A.'s Rodeo Drive—to peruse the overpriced and unremarkable paintings. As soon as Nat mentioned the name Sean Carlyle, there wasn't so much as the memory of a smile on Cady's face.

"I have absolutely no desire to discuss the man," she said sharply, her clipped voice and patrician features well matched.

"I understand you were in the car with him a few months back when he was arrested for driving under the influence of—"

"How the hell—?" Her lips literally snapped shut. She was breathing hard. "Get the fuck out of here before I—"

"You must have a special friend or two on the force, Ms. Cady. Or should I say your parents must?" Nat leaned a bit closer to the steel-topped curved desk behind which the young brunette socialite was sitting. "I have a few friends on the force as well."

Martha blinked rapidly, trying not to look scared. And failing.

"You and Sean were coming from Joy Street that day." Nat watched her closely to see how close her assumptions—and Leo's—were to the truth. Pretty damn close.

"So?"

"Ten fourteen Joy Street."

"How do you—?" Anger colored with something else— fear?—suffused her features. "Get out of here."

"I'd like to talk to Alison Bryant. Maybe you could tell her. She seems to be avoiding me."

"I don't know anyone by that name," she practically spat out.

"How about Genevieve?"

"Never heard of her."

The tall, lithe brunette pivoted round and strode toward a back room without uttering a word.

"Skye," Nat called out.

She stopped as if caught in a freeze-frame. When she finally moved, it was only her head. She glanced over her shoulder at Nat. And Nat understood perfectly what Kerry O'Donnell had meant by Martha Cady, a.k.a. Skye's, killer look.

"I'd be happy to drive by and pick you up, Alan."

"No, that's okay, Superintendent," he told her over the phone. "I'd just as soon my mother didn't know we were . . . getting together."

"Oh? Why?"

"You know . . . this whole business has really upset her a lot. You're lucky you got through to the house. She's had the phone unplugged most of the time, but with Dad in the hospital, she reconnected it. I'm screening all the calls."

"What would be convenient for you?" Nat asked. "If you still drive—?"

"There's a bookstore right down the street from the house. They've got couches and chairs and they don't care if you read a whole book in there. Well, they don't care if I do. The gal who owns it used to be . . . Renée's a friend. An old friend."

Nat heard an undercurrent of sadness in his tone.

. . .

Alan was looking down at a book about the Civil War that lay open across his lap. He'd found a cozy nook in a corner of the bookstore, positioning himself between a worn green velvet love seat and an armchair that had a threadbare patchwork quilt tossed over it. On a small table beside Alan's wheelchair were two demitasse cups of espresso.

"I didn't add sugar," he said as she opted for the armchair.

"I'm coffee-ed out," Nat lied, glancing down at the sepia print of a war-torn battlefield covering both sides of the open book on Alan's lap. Bodies were strewn everywhere.

He closed the book. "Pretty gruesome."

She nodded.

He placed the heavy book on the table. "I guess in your work you come into contact with a lot of people who've done gruesome things."

"Yes. I do."

He looked directly at her. "Do you think my father ran down that woman?"

"I don't know."

He reached for one of the espressos. "I'm sure he didn't."

"Sure?"

He took a sip of the black coffee. "Oh, I can't prove it. He's hoping you can."

"Is he?"

"He won't admit he needs your help, but then Dad never admits he needs anyone's help." Alan smiled at her. "I'm a lot like him." The smile slipped. "Or . . . I was."

"Is Sean like your dad, too?"

"Sean? Sean's not like anyone in the family."

"None of us can fully escape the genes we get from our parents." She said this with regret.

"I'm sure you're right, Nat. Is it okay if I call you Nat?"

"Absolutely."

"The thing is, Nat, Sean was adopted."

"Oh. Well, that explains it."

Alan gave her a rueful look. "I wish you'd explain it to me. I've never been able to figure Sean out."

"What do you mean?"

"He's always been so hotheaded. And so . . . secretive. Hiding stuff. Sneaking off places. Never giving anyone a straight answer. It used to get my dad so frustrated."

"And your mom?"

"Oh, in Mom's eyes, Sean could do no wrong. It's like she felt she had to be doubly loyal to him because he wasn't her natural child. Like she had to bend over backwards to show him she loved him as much as she loved me."

"Sean must have a very strong bond with your mom."

"Yeah, I guess. But it's always been Dad whose respect Sean has craved."

"Really? But I get the impression Sean has always given your dad a rough time." Nat had seen a bit of it on display at the hospital.

"That's Sean's way. Mom calls it testing Dad's limits. The way Sean looks, dresses, acts—it's all a test." He smiled ingenuously. "But you didn't ask me to meet you to talk about Sean."

"Actually, I did."

The smile went. "Why?"

"Did you know Sean's girlfriend?"

"Which one? And why are you asking?" His hands shifted to the wheels of his chair. Like he was considering a fast exit if necessary.

"Skye."

He gave her a puzzled look. "Excuse me?"

"I thought Sean was involved with a girl named Skye."

"I don't know Sean's girlfriends. He didn't bring them home. He didn't talk about them. I told you, he's always been secretive."

"He was living with a girl until a few weeks ago. Martha Cady. Actually they split up a week before Jessica Asher was run down."

"So?"

"Did you know Martha?"

"No."

"Did your dad?"

"What?" Now his hands gripped the wheels.

Nat shifted topics. "Did you know your dad was involved with Jessica Asher, Alan?"

"Not until . . ."

"Until when?"

"I . . . I saw the picture on the front page of that disgusting rag."

"Not before then?"

"No. How would I?"

"You went to see your father at his office the day before Jessica Asher died."

"Huh? So what? Look, I met you here because I thought maybe there was something I could do to help you clear my father. Now I'm not so sure you even want to clear him."

"I do if he's innocent, Alan."

"Well, he *is* innocent."

"You got angry at your father that day you visited. Up at his office."

"No."

"His secretary heard you, Alan. You were screaming at your dad."

"No. No . . . I wasn't."

"What made you so angry?"

He started to push himself forward, but Nat grabbed on to one of the wheels.

A middle-aged man approached a bookcase nearby. He seemed to be looking for a specific book. A young woman, her hair pulled back in a girlish ponytail, wearing jeans and a black T-shirt, came along moments later. "Did you find what you were looking for?"

Before the man responded, she looked their way. "Hey, Alan. I didn't even see you come in."

"Renée." It was all he said by way of greeting.

"You need anything, Alan? Or your friend—?" She glanced at Nat, openly curious. Possibly concerned, since Alan looked agitated.

"I'm fine," Nat said politely.

"Oh, here it is," the customer said, pulling a book off the top shelf. "Can you ring this up? I'm in a hurry."

Renée reluctantly followed the man to the front of the store.

Alan stared down at her hand. "Please let go."

"What made you so angry at your father that day, Alan?"

He shut his eyes. He didn't say anything right away. "I accidentally bumped into the corner of his desk and a manila envelope fell onto the floor. A bit of a photo slipped out. Enough for me to see what . . . it was."

twenty-five

IT HAPPENED WHEN NAT WOKE UP the next morning. A sharp stab in her groin. She gasped, not sure if it was from the pain or from the panic that something was wrong. That she was having a miscarriage. Just as she'd feared . . .

But the pain disappeared as quickly as it struck. She told herself it was nothing. Indigestion. Or maybe she was being punished for all her lies about a stomach bug and she was really coming down with one.

But then it happened again while she was showering.

"You're fine." Dr. Rayburn's voice held a note of firm assurance. "I'd still like to see you get your blood pressure under control."

"But the pain?"

The obstetrician gave Nat an assessing look. "Any chance you can take a little R and R, Nat?"

. . .

Nat nearly jumped out of her skin when she walked out of the medical building to find Jack Dwyer leaning against her car.

"What the fuck are you doing here, Jack?"

"You don't curse unless you're real upset, Nat." He glanced over her shoulder at the building, then back at her. "What's wrong with you?"

"What's wrong with you?" she fired back. "Why did you follow me? What gives you the right—?"

"I care about you. I'm worried about you. That's what gives me the right."

"Maybe you should spend a little more time worrying about yourself," she snapped. This little encounter was not helping her blood pressure one bit. She stared hard at Jack. Had he followed her inside the building? Seen which office she'd walked into? Did he know—? Oh God.

Slow down, Nat. Okay, so worst-case scenario, he saw you enter an ob-gyn office. Women see gynecologists for all kinds of reasons. Checkups. Pap smears. Female problems. No reason to assume he knows you're pregnant. No reason to panic. Yet.

"What's that supposed to mean? I should spend more time worrying about myself?" Jack challenged.

"I have to get to the center." Nat started to pass him to get around her car and over to the driver's door, but Jack grabbed her arm.

"Are you sick, Nat? If you are, you can tell me. I'm here for you. No matter what it is. I'll take care of you. I'll be there for you, day and night. I'll do whatever you need—"

She shrugged off his grasp. "I need you to mind you own damn business. That's what I need, Jack." It came out sounding more like a desperate plea than an order.

"You are my business, Nat."

"No, I'm not. Get that through your thick skull, Jack. And if you can't, maybe you ought to think seriously about transferring to another center. Because I'm really reaching my limit, here."

"Jesus, you are some tough nut to crack."

"That's right, Jack. I am tough."

"Yeah, but not as tough as you want me to believe. Nobody's that tough, Nat. And don't forget I've seen you with your defenses down. I've seen you at your most vulnerable. Your most beautiful. You can't erase it, Nat. And I won't. It meant too much."

He was leaning close to her now. She picked up a pepperminty whiff. Breath mint? Mouthwash?

"Are you drinking, Jack?" Serious drinking, given that it wasn't even 9:00 A.M.

He laughed sharply. "That's your strategy? You feel threatened and attacked so you strike out. Oh, that's sad, Nat."

"No, what's sad is you lied to me. What's sad is you can't stay away from the bottle. What's sad is you say you're here for me and you can't even be here for yourself."

"Like I said, Nat. Nobody's that tough. We all slip up. We all make mistakes."

Yes, Nat thought. They sure did all make mistakes.

"Hey, don't bust my chops, Nat," Hutch snapped. "That's it. That's all she said."

Nat stared down at the message slip on her desk. Next to "caller" her head CO printed "Alison Bryant." Blank next to "phone number." And in the message section, two words. "*Butt out.*"

"Nothing else? Not another word?"

"Yeah, wait." He started to count off his fingers. "Four more. 'Tell your super to,' and then what you see there. 'Butt out.'"

"How did she sound?"

"You getting in over your head again, Nat?"

"Hutch, I'm asking the questions."

"You've been in a real pissy mood lately, you know that Nat?"

Yeah, she knew that.

"Now, if it was Deputy Commissioner Russell Fisk about to get fried for the Asher hit-and-run, I could understand why you'd be all worked up, but Carlyle? Or is something else going on? You got other troubles, Nat?"

"Please Hutch. Let's just focus on Alison Bryant's phone call."

"Yeah, sure. How'd she sound? Abrupt. Then she hung up on me. That was abrupt, too."

twenty-six

"CLUB SODA."

"Same for me, Phil," Tepper said. Then he smiled at her. "Trying to cut back on the booze." He patted his considerable gut. Jerry Tepper in no way resembled Nat's image of the dashing celebrity lawyer. He was short and pear-shaped with thinning gray hair, which he tried to mask with a comb-over. He did have on what was probably an expensive blue business suit, but at least the jacket could have done with being a size larger to accommodate his girth. Nat guessed he was in his late fifties, early sixties. He wasn't aging all that well.

"Thanks for meeting with me, Superintendent. Liz is very excited that her transfer to Horizon House came through. I imagine you had to pull a few strings to make it happen. Especially after that incident she had with the officer."

"Did she tell you about it?"

"Briefly. I'm sure it was a setup."

"So am I."

He gave her a closer appraisal, then leaned back in the tufted suede booth. "I'm glad we're on the same page."

Nat wasn't sure they were, but she kept that thought to herself. "How come you wanted this get-together, Mr. Tepper?"

"Firstly, to thank you on behalf of Liz. I know it can't have been easy to get that transfer through."

"You could have said thank you over the phone. Or mailed a card."

"I like to thank people in person."

"What else?"

He laughed. "Am I that transparent? That's a serious deficit for a criminal defense attorney."

"I'm sure you only let it show when it's to your advantage."

His expression turned serious. "I wanted to suggest that you have an officer assigned to Liz for a little while for extra protection. Someone you personally select."

"Too bad there wasn't an officer watching over Griffith Sumner."

Tepper squeezed the wedge of lime clinging to the rim of his glass into his club soda. "I know you'll make sure she's looked after, Superintendent."

Nat heard another voice in her head. Elizabeth Temple's voice. Saying almost the same words. "*You have a rep for looking after your people, Superintendent.*"

"Did Jessica Asher hire you to handle Griffith Sumner's appeal?" she asked the lawyer.

He deliberated before answering. "Yes. She hired me."

"Did she say why?"

"I'd like to think it's because I'm a very good lawyer."

"Why she wanted to help Sumner?"

"She said he was a friend."

"Just a friend?"

"If there was more to the relationship, I don't know what it was. Jess asked me to take the case, she paid my fee, and I was well on my way to getting Sumner's sentence reduced when—"

"How well did you know Jess?"

"Well enough. She was a mixed-up young woman. But very lovely. I liked her."

"Mixed up how?"

"She was a prostitute, Ms. Price. She used to work for Liz Temple and then she went to work for Alison Bryant."

He smiled at what Nat was sure must be her surprised look in response to his frankness. "Did you think I'd play dumb? Not my style, Superintendent."

"You know Alison Bryant?"

"Know her? That little snake in the grass cost me the Temple case."

"Of course. Right. I mean, have you been involved with her since then? Since she started running the escort service?"

"No."

"But you knew she took it over."

"Score a point for you, Superintendent."

"I heard that Bryant isn't solely in charge of the operation. That there's someone else involved in a key position. Possibly more key than Bryant."

"And who might that be?"

"I was hoping you'd tell me."

"Sorry, Superintendent. I have no idea."

"I'm having trouble getting in touch with Alison Bryant."

"No surprise there."

"No, I suppose you're right."

"I'd like to help you. I'd like nothing more than to see the bastard who ran Jessie down locked behind bars for a long, long time."

"But you have no idea who that bastard is?"

"No."

"Were you one of Jess's clients?"

He smiled indulgently. "I already told you I have no dealings with Alison—"

"You could have made private arrangements directly with Jessie."

"I could have, but I didn't."

"She told Griff Sumner she had a boyfriend. It wasn't you?"

He smiled ruefully. "Do I look like I'd be her boyfriend?"

Nat was momentarily at a loss for a response. Tepper supplied it for her. "There's no accounting for taste, so who knows? But in answer to your question, Superintendent, no. I wasn't her boyfriend. And in answer to the question you're about to ask, I don't know who it was."

"Did you know Jessie used to date Eric Landon?"

He scowled. "A long time ago, Ms. Price. Long before Eric married Deb Asher."

"Are you good friends of the Landons?"

"Friends," he amended.

"Do you recall being at a charity function a few months ago and sharing a table with them and the district attorney? Fran Robie was at your table, too. And you had a date. A very pretty redhead."

"I'm partial to brunettes."

"Was the redhead Alison Bryant?"

He eyed her thoughtfully. "An educated guess, Ms. Price? Or is it a trick question?"

"A simple yes or no will do, Mr. Tepper."

He chose this moment to take his first swallow of club soda. Something told Nat he was wishing it was something stronger. When he set the glass down, he lifted up a napkin and, with a surprisingly feminine motion, dabbed at his lips. "Yes. It was Ali. And I assure you she wasn't my date. If it wouldn't have caused an embarrassing scene, I'd have kicked the little bitch right out of the place."

"A minute ago you said you've had no dealings with Alison since the Temple trial."

"I said I've had no *involvement* with her. I didn't say a word to her at that dinner. Nor she to me."

"Who did she talk to at the table? The Landons? Fran Robie? How about the DA? I doubt he'd want to kick her out, seeing as how she was his star witness in the Temple trial."

"I don't recall her talking to anyone."

"When was the last time you saw Alison Bryant?"

Tepper looked as though she'd just pricked him with a hypodermic. He went for another swallow of his drink. "I haven't seen her since that function."

"She phoned me today."

Now the attorney winced, like the serum she'd pricked him with was burning through his veins. "What did she say? What did she want?"

Nat gave him a probing stare. "Do you have something you're holding over Alison Bryant, Counselor?"

"I don't know what you're talking about."

"Why else would she tell you?"

"Tell me what?" But he didn't wait for an answer. Blinking rapidly, quickly checking his watch even as he rose, he said, "I've got to get going. It was a pleasure to meet you, Superintendent." He extended a hand across the table.

Nat gripped it, held on. "You were the one who told Liz Temple that Alison witnessed—"

"Yes, yes, but I don't want it to get around," Jerry Tepper said anxiously. Then he started coughing fitfully and made a grab for his glass of water.

twenty-seven

IT WAS AFTER 8:00 p.m. WHEN Nat pulled into her designated space in the underground garage of her apartment building.

She got out of the car. Hit the lock button on her key ring.

Nat couldn't shake her nerves tonight. Maybe being pregnant was making her hypersensitive, messing with her hormones. And then there'd been that scare. Even though the obstetrician had assured her she was fine—

"Hey, Nat."

She nearly jumped out of her skin as a figure stepped out from behind the far side of the dark van parked beside her car.

The lighting was bright enough in the garage for Nat to immediately see who'd greeted her.

"Sean."

"Did I scare you, Nat? Sorry."

But Carlyle's punk son didn't sound the least bit sorry.

And Nat was starting to get a frightening feeling of déjà vu. She had been nearly gunned down in this garage a year ago.

Her car keys were still in her hand. She clicked the lock release gadget. Unfortunately, an interior light automatically flicked on as well, giving away her plan to make a fast getaway.

Sean sprang for her and had her pinned against the car before she even got her hand on the door handle. He was glaring at her, his pupils contracted into pinpricks.

"You're butting your nose in my business, Natty. And I don't like it. Grilling my dad, my brother, my fucking probation officer, my girlfriend—"

"I thought you and Martha split." Nat's voice was hoarse with fear but she was trying not to panic.

His fingers dug into the flesh of her shoulders.

"Please let go, Sean. You're hurting me. If you want to talk to me, we can go—"

"I don't want to talk to you, Nat. And I don't want you talking, even more. Not to me. Not to anyone about me."

"Okay."

"Why don't I fucking believe you?"

"Believe her, Sean."

As Jack Dwyer cuffed an arm around Sean Carlyle's neck and squeezed just hard enough to make his point, her deputy smiled at her. "Bet you're not pissed at me now for stalking you, Nat."

"Sean, if you cooperate, I might reconsider calling the cops."

Jack glared at Nat, definitely not pleased with her offer. But then he zeroed back in on Sean. "Cooperate, you little bastard, or I'll . . ."

"Take it easy, Jack." They were up in her apartment, Jack having literally dragged Carlyle's now-sniveling son up there. Nat had to shut her agitated dog in her bedroom. One sniff of Sean and Hannah had been ready to tear right into him.

Sean was on her sofa, his head in his hands, not the tough guy anymore. Nat sat down next to him. This didn't please her deputy too much either.

"You knew Jessica Asher. Maybe she called herself Gen. Or

Genevieve. Just like Martha Cady liked to be called Skye in certain situations. And then there's Ali. Alison Bryant. You're pretty pissed with Ali at the moment. And I think the feeling's mutual."

Jack wasn't following it all, but Nat could see he was paying close attention to what she was saying anyway.

She couldn't see Sean's face and he wasn't saying anything, but Nat was sure he was paying even closer attention.

"So I've been trying to figure out what your part is in this whole operation. I don't think you're a john. No money to speak of. And my guess is you don't have to pay to get laid."

He dropped his hands from his face, turned his head in her direction, and managed a cocky look even with his red eyes and badly running nose. "You bet your sweet ass."

Jack slapped him hard across the side of his head. "Watch your fucking mouth."

Sean let out a yelp of pain and shrank back into the sofa.

"Lay off, Jack," Nat snapped.

Sean tried to give her deputy a dirty look, but he couldn't manage it. He was too scared. And he had good reason. Nat had seen Jack Dwyer lose his temper. It was not a pretty sight.

"I hear you're into photography."

His eyes darted nervously to her. "Who told you that?"

Nat ignored the question. His reaction supported her assumption. "How did you meet Martha Cady, Sean? I wouldn't think the two of you traveled in the same circles."

"Yeah, well, you're wrong."

"Enlighten me."

"We met at a club."

"What were you? The busboy?" Jack piped in sardonically.

Nat saw Sean's hand reflexively squeeze into a fist. He was itching to take a punch at her deputy. Hey, she'd felt that itch a few times.

"What club?" she asked.

"The Bombay. Over on Charles Street. And I was no fucking busboy. I was a paying customer. Just like Martha and her girlfriend."

"Who was the girlfriend?" she rushed in quickly before Jack tried to teach him another lesson for cursing. She knew her volatile deputy would use any excuse to rough the Carlyle kid up.

Sean rubbed his nose vigorously. "Huh? Who knows? I was into Martha. And she was into me. In spades," he boasted.

"Was the other girl a redhead?" she persisted. "Tall? Very attractive? Well endowed?"

All signs of Sean's bravado vanished. "You're gonna get me good and fucked over, lady."

"By who?"

Sean clammed up. Scared again. Not of Jack now. Of her.

"You mean Alison Bryant will be good and pissed at you for talking to me about her."

"I'm not," he was quick to say. "I haven't said anything about anyone. Oh, man . . . why the fuck can't you just butt out? You're gonna get us both whacked, you keep this up."

She caught Jack's narrowed gaze on her now. Wondering what she was getting herself into this time. Worrying. *Here we go again. . . .*

Nat reached for the phone. "Maybe you're right, Sean. Maybe the safest place for you now is behind bars." She started to dial. "Then again, it wasn't all that safe for Griffith Sumner."

Sean's hand darted out. "Wait. Don't. Don't call the cops."

She paused middial, but didn't hang up.

"If I tell you what I know, will you make sure it doesn't get back to her? And . . . will you forget about what happened tonight?"

"Depends on what you know, Sean."

Jack cursed under his breath. Not so far under she couldn't hear him.

"I know plenty," Sean said, a glimpse of his tough-guy image returning.

"Go ahead."

He sniffed loudly, wiped his nose, then wiped his hand on the arm of his leather bomber jacket. "Yeah," he said. "Ali was the other girl that night with Martha. After Martha and I hooked up, she told me about . . . you know, working for Ali. Ali liked me.

She asked if I could use some dough." He laughed. "Like who couldn't?"

"She asked you to take photos."

"Not right off. Ali was looking for more girls. She kinda asked me if I'd like to do some recruiting. Martha took me to parties, clubs, you know . . . places where the beautiful people go. I have this knack . . . you know . . . for spotting 'em. Gals that want a little adventure, a little tax-free cash. Gals who wanna thumb their noses at Daddy and the trust fund he dangles over their heads. And those kind of girls dig me. So, it was easy, you know."

"Yes, I do know. In fact, so far, I'm not hearing anything I don't already know, Sean. I want to know about Jessica Asher— Genevieve."

"I don't know who ran her down, I swear."

"You knew your dad had dates with her. And with Martha. Although he probably only knew your girlfriend by her working name. Skye."

His bloodshot eyes narrowed. "I didn't know about the old man and them. I swear. Not until it all came out in the papers."

"You didn't take that photo? All the photos?"

He looked shocked. Nat wouldn't have thought anything would shock this guy. "No fucking way. I woulda never, man, never done it. Ali musta got some other stooge."

"Martha never told you? Jessica never told you?"

"No. I don't think either of 'em even knew. The old man didn't use his real name."

"Ali knew who he was. So did Jessica."

"Yeah, well, they didn't inform me."

"What about your brother?"

This really seemed to throw Sean. "Alan? You telling me Alan knew about the old man? No fuckin' way, lady. How the fuck would he? You better check your sources. Somebody's feeding you bullshit."

Hannah started barking. Nat thought it was the harsh pitch of Sean's voice that set her off again. Or maybe she was picking up on her deputy's escalating anger.

"Jack, could you go bring Hannah a treat? Maybe she'll calm down."

"She'll calm down when the cops cart this foulmouthed little prick off in a squad car," he snapped.

"Jack . . . please."

Hannah began slamming her large body against the closed bedroom door and her barking was reaching a fever pitch.

Before he stalked off to tend to her frantic dog, Jack glared at Sean. "If it wouldn't make the dog sick, I'd feed you to her."

"So what happened when you did find out about your dad?" she asked Sean, once Jack got a dog treat from the kitchen and brought it into the bedroom. "After you saw the tabloid?"

"What happened? I was furious. I confronted Ali, really laying into her. And you know what that little bitch did? She laughed. Told me it was her little joke. That when she met my dad at some charity shindig and he propositioned her, she couldn't resist setting him up with the service. Wanted to know didn't I think it was kinky that my dad and I were fucking the same ladies? That I should feel like I really had one over him 'cause I got 'em for free. That I got the last laugh. Only I wasn't laughing. I was pissed."

"Ali told someone she was there when it happened. When Jessica Asher was run down. That she saw who was driving."

"Well, she didn't tell me. We aren't exactly chummy right now."

"You have any idea—"

"No."

"Jessica had a boyfriend. Was it you?"

"Maybe she thought so. Lots of ladies think so. I was into Genevieve . . . Jessica, I won't deny that. She was hot. Like, no inhibitions. But Martha was my special lady."

"Is that why Martha threw you out? Because she knew about you and these other ladies? Like Genevieve?"

"If Gen wouldn't have opened her trap about it, I'd still be with Martha. I really love that woman."

Jack, who had returned and was standing outside her bedroom door, laughed dryly.

"You must have been good and pissed at Jessica."

Sean eyed her warily. "Look, I didn't run her down, okay? I was at the garage when she got plowed into. You can check with my boss if you don't believe me."

"But you admit you were angry at her," Nat said.

"Yeah, so?"

"Did you confront her?"

"No."

"I don't believe you."

He relented. "Okay, okay. We had words. That was it."

"You didn't get a little rough?"

He squinted at her as if he were trying to figure out if she already knew the answer to her question. Nat didn't know, but she had a good guess.

"I didn't go looking for her or anything. It was like a chance meeting, you know. I ran into her at a park a couple of days after Martha gave me the boot. I got a little pissed, you know. Kinda got in her face. And she shoved me away. I got more pissed, okay? I lost my temper. I smacked her. Just once. Not even all that hard. For fuck sake, how was I supposed to know she was there watching her niece? I didn't know it till I heard this kid on a swing start shrieking to beat the band."

"Chloe." The child's nightmare. The mean man who'd hit her aunt. It was Sean Carlyle.

He shrugged. "I don't know the kid's name." He paused to sniff again. "And then that fuckin' hard-on starts to come after me like I'm some kind of fucking woman beater."

"Who?"

But Sean realized he'd said more than he meant to. "No one. Some guy. How the fuck should I know—?"

"Eric Landon."

"I didn't see who it was. I was . . . like . . . running. You gonna throw me outta the frying pan and into the fire here, lady. Just drop that whole thing."

"I want to find Ali. Can you help me, Sean?"

"No. I mean, I would if I could, but she's like gone."

"Gone? Gone where?"

"Got me."

Jack started for him. Sean cowered, preparing to be slammed again. "I swear, I don't know where she is."

"Isn't she the one who told you to come after me?"

"No. No. It was like I said. I don't appreciate your questioning people about me—"

Jack was within a foot of Sean, hands clenched.

Holding his hands up to his face in a protective gesture, Sean said, "Okay. Yeah. Yeah, Ali called me on her cell. Sounded like she was in a car. Voice was like real staticky. She's the one told me you'd been talkin' to my probation officer. Then my brother said you two had a powwow."

How did Bryant know she'd talked to Sean's probation officer? Had the madam—or one of her girls—been tracking her? Did Kerry O'Donnell mention it to someone, not knowing she was passing along information that could put Nat in jeopardy? Who might she have talked to? A cop?

"What exactly did Ali tell you to do, Sean?"

"Do?"

"She told you to come after me and what?"

"Just . . . threaten you is all. I wasn't gonna hurt you. I swear."

"Like you weren't going to hurt Jessica Asher, you little shit?" Jack hissed.

"But you were pissed at Ali," Nat said. "For hooking your dad up with the service behind your back. For letting him take the rap for Genevieve's murder. Why would you still be following orders for her?"

Sean looked ill. "I . . . had to."

"She's blackmailing you."

Sean glanced nervously up at Jack who was still standing way too close for the young man's comfort. "No."

"Did you run the hooker down, Sean?" Jack asked in that low, slow voice that could set the hairs on your arms on end.

"No. No, I swear. I told you. I got an alibi."

"So why are you doing Alison Bryant's bidding?" Nat persisted.

Sweat was running down Sean's face. "She . . . she said she could clear my old man, okay? Look, me and him, we got our problems. He can be a real bastard, you know. I mean, sometimes he can really drive me up a wall—"

"Blah, blah, blah," Jack cut him off. "She tell you your old man didn't run Asher down?"

Sean nodded.

"But she didn't tell you—?"

Sean finished her question. "Who was driving? No."

"How is she going to clear your father?"

Sean gave her a baleful look. "I don't know how. I don't want to know. I don't think you do either." He shot Jack a quick look. "That's not a threat. It's a piece of advice. Fucking good advice."

"You're getting soft, Nat. There was a time not so long ago you wouldn't have let that punk walk. Is it that he's the deputy commissioner's kid? Is that why?"

"He didn't do anything to me, Jack."

"He scared the shit out of you, Nat. And that scares the shit out of me. Because if anything happened to you, Nat—"

"Nothing has happened, Jack. Look, it's late. I'm beat. Go home. Let me get some sleep. You look like you could do with some, yourself."

But Jack wasn't done. "Are you going to listen to that shit's warning? Will you drop it?"

"Steve Carlyle didn't run that girl down, Jack. He's being set up."

"How do you know that? How do you know Bryant wasn't bullshitting the kid? Or that the punk wasn't bullshitting you?"

"I don't want to have this discussion now, Jack."

"Yeah, right. You don't much like having any discussions lately. With me, anyway."

"This has got to stop. It's not going to happen for us, Jack. I'm sorry—"

"For what? Fucking me?"

"Yeah. Okay. For fucking you," she snapped.

They glared at each other, Jack backing down first. He rubbed his face with his hands. Erasing the lines of anger. Leaving him looking hurt and frustrated.

"You know what you need, Nat—"

"What I need? You don't have a clue, Jack. Not a clue." Damn it, she could feel the tears start to fill her eyes. "If you did, you'd leave right now. You'd back off. You'd leave me alone. Because that's what I need. Okay? Okay?"

twenty-eight

FRAN ROBIE SHOWED UP AT NAT'S office shortly before ten Friday morning. She wasn't looking like a happy camper.

"Why didn't you tell me Elizabeth Temple's being transferred here from Norton, Nat?"

"Why would I tell you, Fran? I mean, what's it got to do with you?"

"She's due today. Has she arrived yet?" Robie asked, ignoring her question.

Nat in turn, ignored hers. "What's your interest in the inmate?"

Robie sighed. "What I can't figure out, Nat, is why you're so hell-bent on going it alone. You want the glory, is that it?"

"Glory? Hardly."

Robie made herself comfortable on Nat's sofa, giving her short taupe wool skirt a little tug as she settled onto the cushion. She folded one shapely leg over the other and clasped her hands around her knees. "Okay, here's my interest. And yours. Elizabeth Temple ran a call-girl service employing beautiful, classy young women from the upper echelons. Women much like Jessica Asher. If I want to toss out a wild guess, I'd say Asher herself worked for Temple."

Robie eyed her with smug amusement. "Only it's not a particularly *wild* guess, is it, Nat?"

Sometimes the best response was no response.

"You went to visit Temple at Norton several times last week. The last time was this past Sunday when she was in the infirmary after she'd gotten into a fracas with a screw."

"Officer," Nat corrected her coolly.

"Sorry. Screw is pretty derogatory."

Robie didn't sound particularly apologetic. Nat was finding herself both trusting and liking the woman less and less. And yet they had so much in common. Two smart, strong, determined women in their thirties, working in a male-dominated profession, both of them having had to fight for every smidgen of respect as they'd clawed their way up the ladder.

At least Nat certainly did plenty of clawing. Maybe Robie's climb was easier.

"I'm curious about something, Fran. Are you and your ex trying for a reconciliation?"

"Why this sudden interest in my love life?"

"I saw you and Joe at the coffee shop across from the State Building."

"That was business," she said curtly, Robie's look telling Nat she didn't intend to give her any further information.

"You and Joe both also attended one of the mayor's benefit galas last spring."

"Hey, Nat, not every divorced couple ends up as enemies."

"No, that's true. But," Nat added, "most don't continue dating after the papers are signed. The divorce was final last January, right?"

"Dating?" She laughed, but it had a hollow ring to it. "I didn't even know Joe was going to be there. It was someone's little joke to put us at the same table. We simply made the best of it."

"Whose little joke?" Nat asked.

Robie eyed her narrowly. "You want to tell me what this third-degree is about?"

"I'm just curios, that's all. Carlyle thought you looked familiar when you were giving him the third-degree. Then he remembered why. He was at that same function. You and Joe Keenan were at a table with Jerry Tepper and the Landons."

"So?"

"Oh yeah, and Alison Bryant."

"Is there a point here?"

There was a point, all right. More than one. But Nat was suddenly not so sure she wanted to make any of them.

When Nat didn't respond, Robie seemed content to let the subject drop.

"What say we share divorce stories another time. I just dropped by to try to mend some fences, Nat. I'm not sure how they got damaged, but I'd really like us to work together on this case. I'm not out for the glory either, believe me. I could use your help. I'd like your trust." Robie paused, waiting to see what her comeback would be. When Nat didn't provide her with one, she got to her feet.

"Anyway, I'll give you a buzz later, Nat. Hey, maybe we can get a bite to eat, share a little downtime, have a few laughs. All work and no play make for bags under the eyes." She pointed a finger Nat's way.

As if Nat needed reminding that she was starting to look like hell. And here she'd thought pregnant women were supposed to look radiant.

Elizabeth Temple arrived at Horizon House less than twenty minutes after Robie left. Nat was glad they hadn't run into each other, but she was sure they would before long.

Elizabeth Temple looked better than she did when Nat saw her at the infirmary a few days back. Her hair was clean and less stringy. She even had a bit of lipstick on. According to the medical report that accompanied her arrival, the new drug cocktail she had been put on was starting to work, and her AIDS-related symptoms had abated. Also, she'd fully recovered from the slight concussion she suffered in that tussle with the CO.

Nat's new trustee's attire also added to her improved appearance. The inmate looked considerably more attractive in those expertly tailored tan slacks and teal blue sweater than she did in the drab, ill-fitting clothes she wore when she was in CCI Grafton. Nat wondered who provided the pricey new outfit for her. Someone with deep pockets. It didn't take a fashion maven to see that the outfit was of designer quality. Maybe it was a gift from her lawyer, Jerry Tepper. Nat had tried to reach him after their charged meeting the day before, but supposedly he was out of town again. Something told Nat he was going to be out of town a lot where she was concerned.

"Please sit down, Ms. Temple." Nat gestured to a chair across from her desk.

"Could you call me Liz? Ms. Temple seems so formal. And I will be working for you."

"Okay, Liz."

Liz crossed the office and sat down. Nat took the chair beside her.

"I can't tell you how much I appreciate you okaying the transfer, Superintendent. I won't let you down, I promise."

"Did Jerry Tepper tell you we got together?"

She nodded. "He called me early this morning. Told me he asked you to give me some extra protection. I guess that explains the officer who brought me here and is waiting for me out in your reception room. I gather he's going to be my guardian angel while I'm at Horizon House."

Nat certainly hoped so. "You and your attorney must be very close."

Temple looked uneasy. "He's been there for me throughout my long ordeal, if that's what you mean."

"It was Tepper who told you about Alison Bryant." Nat didn't pose it as a question.

The color faded from her face. "He . . . told you?"

"Why did he tell you, Liz?"

"He felt he owed me. You know . . . for losing the case. And . . . because he felt I got a raw deal. The drugs were planted in my home. So were those guns. Jerry believed me. He believed I was set up. He believed it was Ali Bryant who did it."

"And he'd been a client of yours." Nat made this a statement, as well. Because she was pretty sure Tepper had been lying to her.

Thinking she was stating fact, Temple saw no point now in denying it so she nodded.

"Was Genevieve his favorite?"

"His only," she said. "It was kind of a game with them. Usually the clients don't know the girl's true identity."

"But the girls know who the johns really are—even if they use an alias."

"Not always. Not when I was running the show, anyway," Temple said. "But a lot of my clients were in the public eye, so, sure, my girls knew. They could be trusted to keep their mouths shut."

"All but Alison Bryant."

Temple scowled. "Right. But at least as far as Jerry was concerned, he only saw Genevieve."

"But he knew Genevieve was really Jessie Asher."

"Right. They knew each other from way back. Jerry was a close friend of her dad's. I think maybe he was in love with Jess. Not that he ever expected anything more than what they had. He's old enough to have been her grandfather."

"We can still want something pretty badly even if we don't expect it to happen," Nat said quietly.

"I suppose that's true. I certainly wanted that jury to find me not guilty even though I didn't expect them to."

"Why would Alison Bryant tell Jerry Tepper that she saw the driver who hit Jessie? I'd think he'd have been the last person on earth she would have confided in."

"He didn't tell you?" Now she was looking reticent.

"He got a call on his cell and had to leave before he could finish filling me in." Nat was getting better at lying. And worse at minding.

"Jerry was with Jess. That day. The day . . . she was killed. He was her last client. When he left the town house, he saw Ali pull up."

"In a white SUV?"

"I doubt it. She's more a Porsche or BMW type of gal."

"Was she alone in the car?"

"I don't know. Jerry didn't say. And I never thought to ask." She seemed annoyed at herself, but then she went on. "When Jerry drove off he noticed that Ali was still sitting in her car. He knew another girl had an appointment at the town house because he'd wanted an extended session with Jess. . . . Maybe she'd still be alive if she'd been able to stay with him."

"Was Ali there to do a spot check? Or did she see clients herself? I thought the madam simply ran the show."

Temple laughed harshly. "Not Ali. She liked to mix it up with the johns. Of course, she was very discriminating."

"I still don't follow why Ali would have told Tepper she witnessed the hit-and-run. And that she saw who was driving."

Temple hesitated. "She didn't volunteer the information. Jerry drove off, but when he was a few blocks away he realized he didn't have his wallet, that it must have fallen out of his jacket at the town house. So he turned back. He saw . . . Jess. On the street. It was after . . . after she'd been run down. He said it was . . . horrible. And then he saw Ali. She was hurrying into the town house. He jumped out of his car and caught up with her. He told me she was white as a ghost. In shock. I guess that's why she blurted it out . . . about having seen Jessie get struck down. She didn't actually say she saw who was driving. But from the look on her face, Jerry was positive she had. And equally positive she knew the driver. When he pushed her on it, she almost told him. But then she pulled herself together. Wouldn't say who it was. Warned him to forget he ever saw her or he'd be sorry. She did let him back into the town house, he got his wallet, and was gone before the cops got to the scene. I imagine Ali was gone by then as well."

"She phoned me the other day."

"Ali spoke to you? What did she say?"

"I wasn't here to take the call." She told Temple the message.

Beads of sweat appeared above the inmate's upper lip. "Jerry heard from her as well."

"When?"

"Last night. Late. She knew the two of you met. And she warned him not to meet with you again."

"Right now it's Ali I want to meet with. And," Nat added after a weighty pause, "I guess there's only one way I'm going to manage that."

Temple gave her a close look. "Are you sure?"

"No. Experience has taught me that being too certain about anything can be very dangerous."

"What you're planning to do could be dangerous as well. You do know that," Temple said pointedly. "Maybe you should think about it over the weekend. If you still want to go ahead with it on Monday, I'll help you as best I can."

twenty-nine

ON MONDAY MORNING, WHEN NAT WALKED into her outer office, she saw Elizabeth Temple on the phone. Her new trustee looked up. "Yes. She's just walked in, Terry." Temple put her hand over the mouthpiece. "The mayor's secretary."

Nat was never happy when she got a call from the mayor's office. If it had been LaMotte who'd answered the phone, he would have known this. He'd have told Milburne's secretary he'd give the superintendent the message and that she'd call back. Nat felt a flash of irritation that Temple hadn't thought to follow protocol. But how could she since she couldn't have a clue about protocol?

"Is something wrong?" Temple asked, looking worried.

"Next time, just—"

Liz was straining forward, lips compressed, eyes wide with anxiety.

"Never mind. I better take that call."

Nat took a few steadying breaths as she headed into her office, reminding herself of the obstetrician's concern about her stress level. Hard enough to control her escalating blood pressure when she was confronted with serious matters; she certainly couldn't afford to sweat the small stuff.

"This is Superintendent Price." She looked down at several pink message slips on her desk. Calls from Commissioner Miller and Leo, both asking for call backs. Leo had also called her at home and on her cell several times that weekend. As had Jack. But Nat let her answering machine take all her calls. And she'd returned none of them.

"Just one moment, Superintendent. I'll put the mayor on."

Nat still couldn't believe Daniel Milburne had won the mayoral election. It really grated—

"Hello Nat."

She gritted her teeth. It also totally ticked her off that Milburne addressed her with that unctuous tone of familiarity. And Nat was sure he knew it ticked her off. Which was precisely why he did it.

"What do you want, *Dan?*"

"I understand you're involved in the Asher investigation."

"Is that right?"

"I don't think that's such a good idea, Nat."

"Oh? And why is that, Dan?"

Milburne cleared his throat. "I thought I'd give you a heads-up. The DA's issuing a warrant for Steve Carlyle's arrest as we speak."

"What? But I—"

"Some new evidence has surfaced." Milburne gave a low laugh. "Sorry. A play on words."

Nat wasn't following. But she doubted she'd be amused even if she was.

Milburne turned serious fast. "Believe me when I tell you, Carlyle's chances of not going down for Asher's murder are slim at best, Nat. Word to the wise? You would do best to start distancing yourself, pronto."

"What evidence?" she demanded, ignoring his *word.*

Milburne, in turn, ignored her question. "You'll be getting a call from your commissioner shortly. He'll be telling you to back off as well. You take care now, Nat." His tone had a definite edge to it. He clicked off without waiting for a response.

"Hey, can I get in a word edgewise there, Nat?" Fran Robie broke in as Nat paused for a breath, her fingers clenched around the telephone receiver. "I wasn't keeping anything from you. It just came down the pike this morning. Joe was over here at the time . . . and, no, it wasn't a date. Ironically, he dropped by to talk about the Asher case and see where we were at with the investigation."

Nat still got the feeling that for a divorced couple, Robie and her ex were unusually chummy.

"So what is this supposed nail in Carlyle's coffin?" Nat asked her.

"A white Ford Explorer."

Nat's breath caught in her throat. Robie had to be referring to the SUV that ran Asher down. "Carlyle rented—?"

"No, he didn't have to rent it. Just borrow it."

"From who?"

"His son. The one who's a paraplegic. Poor kid can't drive it anymore. He's kept it garaged at a friend's house since the accident. I guess it was too upsetting for him to see it parked at home, but, according to the friend, Alan couldn't bring himself to sell it."

"So it wasn't the car he was driving when he crashed?"

"Guess not."

"And this friend says Alan's father took the car out of his garage on October seventeenth?"

"No. No, the friend says the car was stolen on October sixteenth. Only he didn't tell Alan Carlyle. He was afraid the kid would be too upset. So he phoned up Alan's dad at work. And Steve Carlyle told him not to worry. *And not to report it stolen.* That these things happened. Oh yeah, and that maybe it was all for the best."

Nat heard a dry laugh over the line. And then Robie said, "I don't think that's the way it's gonna turn out, though. Do you, Nat?"

. . .

"I need to track Bryant down, Liz."

"It's too bad you had that testy exchange at that gallery with Skye—Martha Cady. She's probably your best lead to Ali, but I can give you an introduction to a man who owes me a few favors and who knows a lot of the girls who are with Ali now. If any of them know where she's hiding out, though, they're not about to pass that information on to a prison superintendent."

"Exactly."

Just then her deputy walked into the reception room.

"Shit's hitting the fan, Jack. Carlyle's being arrested for the Asher murder." They went into her office, Nat quickly filling him in about the new evidence. "The commissioner called and I've got to call him back. He must be at his wit's end over this."

"I knew that little prick was handing you a line. I hope to hell you're gonna go after him now. Have his skinny ass thrown in the clink along with his no-account daddy."

Nat was going to go after someone, but it wasn't Sean Carlyle. Nat reached for the phone.

He knew her too well. "You still don't think he did it."

She let her hand rest on the receiver. Jack was looking at her from across her desk.

"It was Carlyle's kid's car, Nat. How many people knew it even existed, much less where it was being garaged?"

It was a damn good question.

Temple's voice came over the intercom. "It's Detective Coscarelli on the phone, Superintendent. Should I say you're in?" The way her new trustee said it, Nat knew she'd gotten her earlier unspoken message.

"I'll take it," she said.

As soon as Nat said hello to Leo, Jack headed out of her office. Always a surefire way to get her deputy to exit.

"They're closed on Mondays. It'll have to be tomorrow night. Or you might need more time—"

Nat cut Temple off. "Tomorrow night is fine." She already had plans for tonight anyway.

"But you'll need time to . . . get everything together."

"You said everything I need is in your storage unit in Framingham. And that Jerry Tepper has the key. Give him a call." Nat had no doubt the attorney would be "in" for Temple. "Tell him I'll—"

"I already called him. He's having the key messengered over. You'll have it within the hour."

"Do you think I'll pull it off?"

Her trustee gave her an assessing look, then smiled. "I'd have hired you on the spot."

Nat reexamined her appearance in her office bathroom mirror. This was only the dress rehearsal, but she was actually feeling surprisingly confident. With the exceptionally fine blonde wig, the nonprescription blue contact lenses she'd purchased, and the expertly applied makeup, even Nat could hardly recognize herself. Not only did she look different from the neck up but from the neck down as well. Her 32B bra had been replaced by a 34D thanks not only to amazing padding but to special added inserts that greatly enhanced her previously limited cleavage. And although none of Elizabeth Temple's own clothes would have fit Nat, Temple had quite a collection of stunning designer garments she'd kept for her girls packed away in her storage unit. Nat selected several in her size, not knowing how many outfits she'd need.

Liz looked at Nat's reflection with a mixture of admiration and amazement in her eyes. "You know something? I bet even Martha Cady wouldn't recognize you the way you look now."

Nat met her gaze in the mirror. "I was just thinking the same thing."

Nat was leaving work when she nearly collided with Bill Walker at the door.

He grinned. "We gotta stop running into each other like this,

Nat." He glanced at the black garment bag that was slung over one arm. "Going somewhere?"

"Dinner date."

"So, how are things going?"

A multifaceted question if ever there was one.

"Still no news to report, Bill."

"Come on, Nat. You could have given me the heads-up that Carlyle was going to be arrested."

"I could have used a heads-up, myself," she muttered.

"And you could have told me about the car."

"How do you know about the car?" As far as Nat knew, the discovery of the alleged vehicle hadn't been made public yet.

"Not from you," he said, wagging a finger at her. "I thought we had an understanding."

"It sounds as if you don't need me to feed you the latest." She shifted the garment bag from one arm to the other. "Hey, I really do have a date, Bill—"

"Coscarelli?"

She gave him a narrow look. "Yeah. Leo. And no—I haven't told him yet." She started past him on the front porch. He trailed behind her.

"The district attorney thinks he's got himself an open-and-shut case against the DC."

She stopped in her tracks and turned back to Walker. "Keenan gave you a statement?"

"You want to give me one as well, Nat?"

"Yeah, I'll give you one, Bill. This case is far from open-and-shut. Far from it. You can quote me."

thirty

"SINCE WHEN DON'T YOU WANT A second helping of my lasagna?"
Anna Coscarelli gave Nat a scrutinizing look that made her feel
utterly transparent. Nat knew she shouldn't have agreed to this
Monday night family dinner. But Leo really pressed her and, as he
often did, played the trump card—Jakey. Jakey missed her. Jakey
kept asking when she was going to come over. Jakey wanted to
know when Leo and she were going to take him to the zoo again.
Jakey painted her a special picture in kindergarten. Nat gave in.

Now she was sorry. Every time she looked over at Jakey, she
thought, *Will the baby I'm carrying bear any resemblance to this
adorable child?* Every time she looked at Leo, she thought, *Are
you the father?* And following quick on the heels of that thought,
And if you are, what happens next?

And what happened next if Leo wasn't the father?

"Leave her be, Mom," Leo said in that gentle but firm tone of
his. "She's got a lot on her plate."

Jakey giggled. "No, she doesn't, Daddy. Her plate is all clean."

Leo grinned, ruffling the boy's hair. "How about your plate, kiddo? I see some broccoli there just crying to be eaten."

"Vegetables don't cry." But Jakey was grinning back at his dad to let him know he was making a joke. At nearly five, Jakey Coscarelli wanted to show he was a big boy now. He quickly shoveled the remaining broccoli into his mouth and even before he swallowed, asked about dessert.

"In a little while," his grandmother said.

"Can I go watch cartoons?"

"There are no cartoons on at night," Leo said.

"Oh yes. *The Simpsons* is a cartoon."

Leo wagged a finger at him. "You know that's not a cartoon for children, Jakey."

The little boy shrugged as though he were giving it his best try. "Okay. I'll go draw Natalie a new picture for her 'frigerater. A T-rex just like I drew for Mommy."

"Great," Nat said, trying to fabricate a bright smile, but she was sure it fell short.

Anna Coscarelli cleared away Nat's plate. "No wonder you have no appetite," she said. "Leo told me your deputy commissioner was arrested this afternoon for that hit-and-run. And, of course, it's all over the news. The police seem pretty sure they've got their man."

Leo was eyeing her. "Natalie isn't so sure."

Anna frowned. "You're not taking on another cause?"

"Well, at least you didn't call it a *lost* cause," Nat said, trying for a light tone.

Mother and son both regarded her with open consternation. Neither of them was happy at the thought that she might continue to pursue this case.

"They found the car, Natalie," Leo reminded her. As if she needed reminding. Lab work was still in process but she doubted Keenan would have issued any statements to the press if he wasn't already pretty confident that Alan Carlyle's 1999 white Ford Explorer was the vehicle that ran down Jessica Asher.

The car was found thanks to an anonymous tip—at least Robie told Nat it was anonymous. The SUV was dredged up from the

Colby Pond in Plymouth in the wee hours of the morning. The pond was less than two miles from the Maple Hills Nursing Home where Stephen Carlyle's mother resided.

Robie and Keenan were floating a couple of theories. One was that Carlyle drove the SUV down to Plymouth after he plowed into Jessica, dumped it, hiked over to visit his mother, then took a bus back up to his home in Milton—the cops were checking into that. Their other theory was that an accomplice drove Carlyle back. Meaning a second car either followed the deputy commissioner to the state park or met him there as planned, helped him dump the SUV in the pond, drove Carlyle to the nursing home, waited while he visited with his mother to establish an alibi, then drove him back to Milton.

"How about a little dessert, honey?" Anna asked her as she finished clearing the dinner plates. "I've got cannoli. Your favorite."

"No, thanks." Nat checked her watch. "I really need to get home. I've got a pile of paperwork waiting for me."

Anna Coscarelli sat back down at the table. "Okay, so who do you think killed that poor girl if it wasn't your deputy commissioner?"

"I wish I knew."

Leo scowled. "And I wish you weren't so damned curious."

thirty-one

NAT WAS AT CARLYLE'S ARRAIGNMENT ON Tuesday morning. So were the commissioner and Fran Robie. Carlyle's wife and two sons, however, were conspicuously absent. After hearing lengthy, emotionally charged pro and con arguments from both Carlyle's attorney, Henry Fisher, and District Attorney Joe Keenan as to the deputy commissioner's potential danger to the community, Judge Gwen Mossier set Stephen Carlyle's bail at an exorbitant $800,000.

Looking grim-faced and frail despite his bulk, Carlyle stared straight down at the floor as he was led out of the court in handcuffs and remanded to a cell in the county jail. Either bail would somehow be met or he'd be held behind bars until his trial.

There was nothing grim-faced about Joe Keenan. Or Fran Robie. Nat was sure they were seeing nothing but bright futures ahead of them. Robie might be aspiring to step into her ex-husband's shoes down the road. And there were already rumors starting to surface that Keenan had his eye on the state attorney general spot.

To avoid being swarmed by the press lying in wait for a scoop outside the courthouse, Miller and Nat were escorted by a bailiff out a back exit. Once they were outside, the commissioner extended a hand. "Thank you, Nat. You did all that you could. Now it's in the hands of justice."

Yet another way of Miller informing Nat that her help was no longer expected or required. Or—desired.

"In fact, I think you deserve a bit of time off, Nat. Take the rest of the week. Maybe go up to the mountains or take a drive down to the Cape. It's quiet but lovely there even in November."

Nat had no intention of taking a trip. But she was definitely up for having some time to herself.

A svelte brunette smiled up at her as she stepped into the art gallery. Nat had to admit that she felt a flash of relief that it wasn't Martha Cady behind the northern teak reception desk this time. Her confidence in her disguise was much weaker than it had been during her dress rehearsal.

"Hi. Can I help you or would you prefer to look around on your own? We have some very fine Clifford West oils."

"I was looking for Martha Cady. A friend of mine told me to look her up when I moved to the city."

"Sorry. Martha isn't in."

"Oh, she doesn't work on Tuesdays?"

The woman hesitated. "Well, she's supposed to, but she didn't show up. I had to come in yesterday, too. I usually just work weekends."

"Martha wasn't here yesterday, either?"

Nat was starting to get that queasy feeling in the pit of her stomach. Nothing to do with morning sickness now.

"What about last Friday? Was she here—?"

A bell tinkled over the door. A well turned-out middle-aged couple entered the gallery. The pretty brunette scurried around from behind her desk and beamed at them, both hands extended. "Mr. and Mrs. Nicholson. I'm so pleased to see you again. I knew you'd be by when you heard we'd gotten in some Wests."

She barely glanced at Nat as she hurried over to them. Mr. Nicholson was glancing in her direction, however. With a glint in his eye. Until his wife gave him a not-so-subtle nudge.

As she left the gallery Nat was feeling more confident in her new look.

And more worried about Martha Cady.

Leo called her cell as she was driving over to Martha's apartment.

"You okay?" He sounded a little worried. And a lot irritated.

"Fine. Sorry I had to leave your place so early last night, but—"

"I know. Piles of work. And this past weekend—"

"I needed some time to myself, Leo."

"What's going on, Natalie? If you're pissed at me for some reason—if this is about Suzanne—"

"I'm not. It's not." She almost went through a red light and needed to slam on her brakes. The driver in the car behind her hit the horn.

"Where are you?"

"On the road."

"I gathered that much, Natalie."

"I'm taking a few days off, Leo. Courtesy of the commissioner. Maybe I'll drive down to the Cape."

"I know you don't tell me everything, Natalie. But I didn't think you'd start lying to me."

"Leo, I can't drive and talk."

"Where are you driving to?"

Nat was afraid to tell him. What if he decided to meet her at Martha's place? She wondered if even Leo would recognize her if he did show up there.

"I can't say, Leo."

"You're worrying me, Natalie."

She smiled. "So what else is new?"

"Hi."

Martha Cady opened the door as wide as the chain lock would

reach and scrutinized her from the tip of her blond wig to her Manolo Blahnik black boots. Nat's altered appearance must have passed muster because Cady didn't finish her survey by slamming the door in her face.

It was nearly two in the afternoon, but Martha was wearing a robe. From the way her hand was clutching the lapels at her neck Nat was thinking she had nothing on underneath.

"What do you want?"

"My name's Samantha Mills—"

"My doorman already told me that," she said sharply. "And that Sean's a mutual friend. Sean doesn't live here anymore." She made no effort to mask the bitterness in her voice. And yet her ex-boyfriend's name had gotten Nat past the doorman.

"I didn't mean to bother you at home. I did go by the Lanz Gallery—"

"Yeah, well, I'm sick."

"Sorry to hear that. Hope it's nothing serious."

"Look, get to the point. I want to get into bed."

Nat bet she did.

"Well, like I told Sean, I just got back from a year studying sculpture in Florence. I was hoping for another few months, but my boyfriend got tired of bankrolling my artistic endeavors. And I got tired of him. And Florence. So I decided it was time to come home.

Martha was growing more impatient as she droned on.

"Anyway, a couple of days after I got back to the city, I ran into Sean over at this club, the Bombay. We got to talking and he said that his girlfriend, Martha—I guess you were still together then—anyway, he told me you could help me get into a line of work where I could earn very good money and have fun doing it." Nat was watching her face closely. She could see Martha was getting her drift.

Nat sighed. "The thing is—I'm kind of desperate. I've been staying at a friend's house since I got back, but he's kind of a shit, you know."

Someone coughed inside the apartment. Martha glanced back

for an instant. "Look, if you give me a number where I can reach you—"

"Any chance you could put me in touch with your boss now? Sean said she's the one who'd have to . . . interview me. I'd really, really like to get started—"

"I'll see what I can do. What's the number?"

Frustrated by her failure to get an immediate connection to Alison Bryant, Nat dutifully recited her unlisted home line. "Will you remember it?"

Martha nodded and started to close the door. The gesture required her to stop clutching her robe closed. And that's when Nat saw the dark bruises on her neck. They looked raw. Fresh.

"I don't suppose I could trouble you for a cold drink."

"There's a coffee shop right across the street."

Another cough sounded from inside as the door shut in Nat's face.

Nat took a seat at a window table with an unobstructed view of the entrance to Martha Cady's building. She ordered a large pot of tea, preparing to sit there for as long as it took.

Twenty minutes later, halfway through her second cup of tea, a figure darted out of the front door. But thanks to a baseball cap pulled low and the unbelted trench coat that didn't even give Nat a hint as to his build, she couldn't make out the fleeing man's identity. She couldn't even be certain he was the man who had been coughing in Martha's apartment, although the furtive way he made his exit certainly hinted at it.

Before Nat could throw down some money on the table and get out of the coffee shop, her mystery man had already darted down the street and around the corner.

By the time she turned the corner, he was nowhere in sight.

thirty-two

NIPPON WAS AN UPSCALE SUSHI BAR off the lobby of the Boston Regency Hotel. It was the kind of spot frequented by local and visiting movers and shakers on expense accounts. It was a little past eight o'clock and even on a Tuesday night, the place was quite full, a number of diners seated along the long, low bar expertly guiding assorted sashimi and sushi tidbits with their chopsticks into their mouths.

Although there were still a few tables available in the sparely decorated, narrow room, Nat deliberately opted for a spot at the far end of the bar. She was led there by a stunning young Asian hostess dressed in traditional geisha garb. Minutes later, a diminutive Asian waitress wearing black trousers and a crisp white shirt presented her with a steaming hot washcloth on a tray. The waitress waited while Nat cleansed her hands and deposited the used cloth back on her glazed tray.

She returned a minute later with a menu. "Can I bring you something to drink?" she asked. "Perhaps some saki?"

"Tea." Nat was watching the two Asian men making up the sushi behind the bar. While they were both intent on their creations, one of them—the older of the two—glanced in her direction. Their eyes met for only the briefest instant, but everything that needed to be said was said. Liz Temple had made the connection as promised.

The waitress brought a pot of steaming tea and poured some out in a lovely earthenware cup. "Do you know what you'd like?"

Most definitely. "A California roll."

She gave a formal bow and Nat watched her place the order slip in front of the older Japanese man behind the counter who was putting the finishing touches on an exquisitely decorated sushi platter. He glanced at the slip, then at the waitress, but he didn't look Nat's way again

Someone was, however, looking at Nat. The man sitting at the next stool. When she looked back at him, he smiled as though he knew her.

Or as though he wanted to.

"Hey," he said. Nat spotted a shiny gold Rolex watch on his wrist. It went with the perfectly tailored suit, the diamond-studded tie clip, the expert haircut that managed to play down the receding forehead. There was nothing particularly attractive about him. Save for his money.

Nat gave a curt nod. And caught the older sushi chef scowling.

"Sorry for staring. Guess I'm just a sucker for beautiful blondes." A man who didn't take a hint. Even when the sushi chef approached him and slapped down a check beside his unfinished maki roll.

"Isn't that right, Kazuo?" He kept smiling, his gaze fixed on Nat. Was this just his standard pickup or did this guy presume she was for hire? Liz Temple had told Nat that the sushi bar was a kind of watering hole for some of Ali's girls and that they frequently met their dates here. Liz also told her that Bryant had recruited Kazuo Shindo to see that arrangements went smoothly. After all, he'd done a good job for her former boss when he'd been a chef at a sushi bar near Temple's home in Weston. What

Bryant didn't know was that Kazuo kept in touch with the ex-madam. Unlike Bryant, he valued loyalty. Not that it extended to turning down the generous money the current madam paid him. Far more than his salary as a sushi chef.

"Give the lady a reference, Kazuo," the man beside her urged with a wink.

"The lady has another appointment tonight, Mr. Adams," the chef said pointedly.

Open disappointment showed on the man's face. But he accepted defeat with good humor. "Ah well, there's always another day. Can I have your name, beautiful blond lady?"

"Samantha."

"Very beautiful name." He popped the last maki roll in his mouth, then scribbled his name on his check. Apparently Mr. Adams kept a running tab.

Nat breathed a little easier when he left. And she was anxious to get what she came here for before someone else decided to hit on her. Being a blonde wasn't all the fun it was cracked up to be.

Kazuo placed both her California roll and a check on the bar. She glanced around before she turned the check over. At first she thought it was her tab. Fourteen dollars and thirty-five cents. Pretty damn pricey for what she'd ordered. And didn't even plan to eat. Not to mention that it wasn't what she came here for.

Or was it?

When she looked at the number more closely she saw there was no decimal point between the 4 and the 3. It wasn't 14.35. It was 1435.

Still puzzling, though, since she didn't know the significance of that four-digit number. She gave Kazuo a questioning look.

He surreptitiously pointed upward with his thumb then turned away from her, walking back down to the other end of the bar.

Nat stood there for a few more moments until she pieced the number and gesture together.

Nat was just getting off her stool when who should she see entering the sushi bar but Mayor Daniel Milburne. She hastily sat back down. No way she wanted to have to walk by him and take the chance that he might see through her disguise.

The sushi chef looked a little uneasy himself. He motioned to the hostess. She immediately hurried over to the chef. Nat couldn't hear what Kazuo said to her, but the hostess gave him a nod of understanding.

Milburne was standing alone at the entrance. There had been gossip of marital problems. Knowing—and liking—his wife, Beth Milburne, Nat wasn't surprised that the relationship was in trouble.

Then again, maybe he was meeting Beth here. Or meeting someone else. Like a high-class hooker?

Could the dishonorable mayor have been one of the names that showed up on Jessica Asher's private appointment calendar? Was he one of her johns? It wouldn't surprise Nat. She wondered if she'd be surprised by any of the names on Asher's calendar. She wondered if any of the names surprised Fran Robie. Robie was as likely to tell Nat that as she was to show her Asher's PDR. But if Alison Bryant kept a duplicate copy of all her girls' appointments—

Nat surreptitiously watched the hostess head toward the doorway.

"Good evening, Mayor Milburne. So nice to see you again. I have your usual table."

"Some friends are joining me tonight, Takasha. I'll need a table for four."

"No problem, Mayor."

She started to lead him to a circular table in a front corner of the restaurant, one that was positioned in such a way as to allow Nat to make an exit without notice. Unfortunately, Milburne didn't like the location.

"Something in the back, Takasha."

Nat drank some more tea as the mayor passed within a few feet of her.

Out of the corner of her eye, Nat spotted some new arrivals at the entry. She recognized all three. It was quite the group—Councilman Eric Landon, his wife, Debra, and District Attorney Joe Keenan.

She heard Milburne call out to them and they headed in his direction—and hers.

Nat lifted the menu in front of her face as if deliberating what to have for dessert.

Behind her, someone coughed.

Unfortunately, Nat didn't know which of them had coughed. It might even have been the mayor. Not that it would prove anything if she could ID the cougher. It wasn't as if the guy in Cady's apartment was the only one in the city with a cold or allergy. Still, the possibility that one of the people at the mayor's table was the man in the baseball cap and trench coat did give Nat pause.

As well as goose bumps.

Nat popped into the ladies' room down the hall from the sushi bar to touch up her face—lipstick, gloss, a bit more rouge, her complexion having gone a shade whiter at the sushi bar. It was still jarring to see herself as a blonde, but the wig was of such extraordinary quality that even she was hard put to see that it wasn't her real hair. She also gave her runway-couture outfit a check—the soft turquoise silk tank top with its deep V and Versace label, the slim black crepe Dior skirt falling midcalf but slit at each side to midthigh, the sumptuous Dolce & Gabbana spiked-heel backless pumps that not only added several inches to her height but somehow made her legs appear more shapely. And thanks to those high-rising slits in her skirt, far more noticeable.

Much to her dismay, someone was taking notice as she stepped out of the ladies' room into the hallway.

"You look familiar. Do I?" His gaze traveled slowly from her legs up to her face.

"No. Sorry." She started to move around him, but the hall was narrow and he was blocking her path.

"Eric Landon. And you're—?"

"Late," she said curtly.

"Eric?" a voice called out. "Did you make your call?"

"Yes, darling."

"Your sushi's on the table."

"Coming, darling." Landon donned his unctuous vote-getting smile as he turned from Nat to his wife. From the grim expression on Debra Landon's face, Nat had a feeling he was going to have to do more than smile to get her vote.

thirty-three

SHE KNOCKED ON THE DOOR OF suite 1435.

There was no response.

She knocked a little harder.

The door gave way, opening a few inches.

Nat was instantly on alert, her breath catching in her throat and her blood pressure soaring. She took in a few steadying breaths. At least she told herself they were steadying her.

Remaining in the hallway, she pushed on the door until it opened wide enough for her to peer inside. The room was dark, but there was enough light coming from the hallway for her to see a well-appointed sitting room.

"Hello?" she called out.

And got no reply.

She reached in and felt for the light switch, clicking it on. Light flooded the room from an ornate overhead crystal chandelier. Deep blue velvet curtains were drawn across a window wall. Two brocade settees divided by a glass and gold-leafed coffee table faced each other. Nat always knew the Boston Regency was an upscale hotel, but surely this was one of the establishment's top-of-the-line accommodations.

Her gaze fell on an upturned Champagne bottle protruding from a silver ice bucket on the coffee table. Beside the bucket were two crystal flutes. They were empty as well.

To the left of the sitting room was a closed door, which Nat presumed led to the bedroom of the suite. Stephen Carlyle had told Nat he'd been with Martha Cady—or Skye, as he knew her—at this hotel. Possibly in this very suite.

Nat stood perfectly still, listening for any sounds coming from behind that bedroom door. All she heard was the pounding of her own pulse.

"Hello?" she called out again, louder this time.

If there was someone in the bedroom, the occupant(s) were either deaf or dead. The instant that thought crossed her mind, a chill washed over her. As for her blood pressure . . . Nat didn't even want to think about what the reading would be if her obstetrician took it right that second.

She was still standing there at the door debating what to do when she heard a faint squeal of hinges and saw the bedroom door slowly open a crack.

"Alison?" Nat's voice was raspy.

The door opened wider. She felt her mouth go dry with anticipation. And fear.

Until she saw the figure in the doorway.

The child—she couldn't be more than seven or eight—was wearing a flannel nightgown covered in hearts. Her hair looked like fine spun gold, so blond that it appeared almost white in this light. Her face—the only way to describe it was angelic. Nat didn't think she'd ever seen a child more beautiful than this little girl.

"Is Alison here?"

"She's sleeping."

Sleeping? It wasn't even 9:00 P.M.

Nat stepped inside the suite. "I'm sure she won't mind if I wake her."

"Oh yes, she will," the child said emphatically.

"Well, how about if you wake her?"

"No way. She'd blow a gasket."

"You could just take a peek. Maybe she's heard us talking and woke up on her own." She'd deliberately raised her voice for that purpose.

The child glanced back into the dark bedroom. "Nope. She's still asleep."

"You can see in the dark?"

"If she was up, you'd hear her."

Nat glanced at the upturned Champagne bottle. Good chance the madam was smashed and out cold. And what about her drinking buddy?

"Is Ali all by herself?"

"No. She's with me," the child said, like Nat was either blind or retarded or both.

"Are you Ali's little girl?"

She giggled. "No way. She's Mom's friend. But Ali's okay. I hang out with her when Mom's not around."

"Where is your mom?"

"Drug rehab. For a change."

It was the kind of rueful remark Nat would have expected from a much older child. Could Nat have misjudged the girl's age? Or was she simply wise beyond her years?

"What's your name?"

The child eyed her with a wary curiosity. "What's yours?"

She almost said "Nat." "Sam."

"That's a guy's name."

"It's short for Samantha. Like Ali's short for Alison. Do you go by your full name or do you have a nickname too?"

"Daisy. Just Daisy."

"I like that name."

"I don't."

"How old are you, Daisy?"

She smiled. "Old enough." She started to giggle. "Whenever I say that, everybody has the same look on their faces that you do on yours. Ali and I always crack up."

A sour taste rose in Nat's throat. It had nothing to do with morning sickness. It was this little girl. And *Ali*. There was something terribly wrong here. Something acutely disturbing with this baby-sitter–child relationship. And Nat was an expert when it comes to warped adult-child relationships.

"Who was visiting Ali tonight?"

Daisy shrugged. "I don't know. I was asleep." She pointed to one of the brocade love seats. "I fell asleep over there."

"But you were in the bedroom."

Another shrug. "I guess one of them must have carried me into bed."

"Probably the man."

"Probably."

"Are you sure you never saw Ali's friend at all, Daisy?"

Although Nat tried to sound nonchalant, the child scowled. "I told you, I was sleeping."

Abruptly, Daisy stepped from the doorway back into the bedroom. Still frowning at Nat, she said, "You better go. Ali needs her beauty sleep."

She slipped back into the bedroom and slammed the door shut loud enough to wake the dead.

Nat's throat went dry. "Daisy?"

"Go away," the child shouted.

Nat hurried across the sitting room to the closed bedroom door. "Please let me in, Daisy. I think maybe Ali's . . . sick." She tried the knob, but the door wouldn't give. The child had thrown the lock.

"No, she's not. She's fast asleep. Go away. Go away right now or you'll be sorry. I'll call Tony and he'll come up here and . . . and throw you out."

"Tony?"

"He's a cop, so you better go or you'll be in trouble."

A cop?

"Tony could arrest you, you know." She was trying to frighten Nat, but Nat could hear in the child's voice that she was the one who was frightened. Frightened of Tony?

"A person can't be arrested if they haven't done anything wrong, Daisy." Okay, so she was stretching the truth here.

"Oh yes, they can." Daisy said this with absolute assurance. "Tony can put you in jail. And you wouldn't like that very much, now, would you?"

"No. No, I wouldn't. But all I want to do is come inside and make sure Ali's okay—"

"Who the fuck are you?"

Nat spun around. A large man in a black suit, the jacket stretched across overdeveloped pecs and a barrel chest, was standing at the open door of the suite glaring at her.

"Who are you?" she countered, trying not to sound intimidated. Or downright scared. No question about it, this guy was both intimidating and scary.

"I'm asking the questions."

Nat forced a smile. "Let me guess. Tony?"

"How the fuck do you know my name?"

How the hell did he happen to show up here? Daisy couldn't have called him as she'd threatened because she'd been talking to her the whole time.

Did this "cop" chance by? Or did someone send him up here?

Then Nat remembered Debra Landon asking her husband if he'd made his call. And his response indicating that he had.

"Don't put her in jail, Tony," came a frightened plea from behind the locked bedroom floor. "She didn't even wake Ali. She's still fast asleep."

Tony was momentarily distracted. "What are you doing up at this hour of the night, Daisy?" The bruiser's voice softened noticeably.

"I had to go to the bathroom, Tony."

"Well, get back into bed right now."

"Okay, Tony. G'night."

Daisy attended to, Tony focused his full attention on Nat. "I'm still waiting for an answer to my question, lady. Who the fuck are you and what are you doing up here?"

Everything about this guy—the way he talked, his appearance, even how he carried himself—didn't say cop to Nat. It said con. She'd seen lots of his type in the prisons. And most of them weren't doing time for nonviolent offenses.

"I wanted to talk to Ali."

"Only her friends call her Ali. You're not a friend."

"How do you know that?"

"Because I know all of Ali's friends."

"Actually, I was hoping to become a friend."

This gave him pause. "Is that right?"

"I am a friend of Skye's. She's the one who suggested I come by. I guess I didn't expect Ali to be asleep this early in the evening."

"Yeah, well, she keeps odd hours."

"Right."

Leering now, he started toward her. "Ali usually has me kind of screen ladies who want to be her friend. If you want to stick around—"

It was the last thing in the world Nat wanted.

In fact, the only thing she did want was to get out of the suite. But she didn't feel at all comfortable leaving Daisy alone. Or worse, leaving her here with this goon and the supposedly sound-asleep madam in the bedroom.

Tony moved swiftly. Before Nat could even think to get out of his path, he had his clammy paws on her shoulders.

"You're not bad," he said leeringly. "Maybe a little old—"

"Gee, thanks a bunch," she said coolly, desperately hoping he couldn't feel the tremor coursing through her body.

This was a bad idea—

"It's okay. Some guys like women with a little age on them." He let one hand trail seductively down her arm. Good thing she was wearing long sleeves or he'd be feeling her fast-rising goose bumps.

She stood her ground—not easy with her knees fast-turning to jelly. "You want to play, you got to pay, Tony. One thing my mama taught me, never give anything away for free. I don't even do *screenings* for free."

"You do if you want to hook up with the best in the business." He curled the hand that was on her shoulder around the back of her neck. He had an iron grip.

"You talking about Ali or her boss?"

This threw him off his game. At least momentarily. "Know what? Skye's got a big mouth. And a pea brain."

"Hey, Skye never said a word," Nat was quick to counter, not wanting to get the call girl in Dutch with this goon.

"Who then?" he demanded. Both hands were at her neck. Seconds ago she was terrified of being raped. Now she was terrified of dying.

"I have a lot of friends in high places, Tony. Friends who wouldn't be too happy with anyone who treated me badly."

"Is that right? What friends?"

"If I told you their names, they wouldn't be my friends anymore." Nat knew she was giving a pale performance compared to Elizabeth Temple, but it seemed to be having its desired effect. Tony was looking a bit hesitant.

"How much?"

"What?"

"Your mama was right. You shouldn't give it away free. I got plenty of loose cash on me—"

"There's a child in the next room." And possibly a dead woman. Or at least a very drunk one.

"Daisy? She won't come out. She don't do anything she's told not to do."

And what about what she's told to do? Does she obey those orders as well?

Bile literally rose up in Nat's throat.

"Tell you what, beautiful. I'll see how good you are and pay accordingly." The goon leered.

"I'm going . . ."

His fat, wet lips were within inches of hers when she spewed all over his fat, ugly face.

Shock and revulsion thankfully hit him before the fury. And Nat used that brief window of opportunity to bolt from the suite.

"Hold it," she shouted out as she saw a couple of men stepping into the elevator at the end of the hall.

She was making a mad dash out of the hotel just as homicide captain Francine Robie was arriving. Nat caught her breath, but Robie looked right through her—through "Samantha"—as they passed just outside the main entrance.

"Danny," Robie muttered in distracted greeting to the doorman as he held the door open for her.

"Captain." Danny was solicitous even though he barely got so much as a glance. And the doorman, with his dark, curly hair, bedroom blue eyes, and all-round hunky good looks, was a guy who would get glances. He was probably an aspiring actor or model waiting for his big break.

As Robie stepped inside the hotel, the doorman turned his focus on Nat, donning an approving smile as he gave her the once-over. Whether or not blondes had more fun, they certainly did seem to attract more notice from the opposite sex.

"Can I get you a cab, miss?"

"No, thanks." Nat glanced back inside, watching Robie head straight for the sushi bar. She looked at the doorman and pointed in Robie's direction. "Captain? As in the armed forces?"

He grinned. "As in Boston PD."

"And here I thought this was a high-class joint," she teased.

His grin broadened. "Oh, it is. Never a whiff of trouble."

Must be the folks here have olfactory problems.

"Captain Robie just likes sushi. And we've got the best."

"Oh, so she pops in on her own for a quick maki roll when she's in the neighborhood?" Nat asked lightly.

"Nah, there's usually a whole gang of 'em hangs out here. A really classy bunch."

"I bet my friend is one of that classy bunch. Ali Bryant? This place is like her home away from home."

"Miss Bryant? She's a friend of yours?" The doorman's interest was piqued.

Nat winked at him. "Is she a friend of yours?"

"In my dreams."

Nat would have liked to ask the chatty Danny a few more questions, but a very disgruntled Tony was storming across the lobby and heading for the exit. The goon was on a tear.

thirty-four

"WHAT DO YOU MEAN, THEY WEREN'T there?"

"The suite was empty," Leo told her over the phone. As soon as she'd left the hotel and got into her car, Nat had called him on her cell and told him about Alison Bryant and Daisy. And about Tony, although she didn't mention how it was she'd gotten away from the creep. For once, she was truly grateful for her morning sickness.

"What about those goblets?" If they were still there, they'd have a chance of finding out the identity of the man who'd been with Ali before she—

"No goblets. Not so much as a tissue in the trash can."

"Shit."

"There's more," Leo said after a pause.

"What?" Nightmare visions started to crowd her imagination, a cold fist of dread grabbing her around the middle—a particularly sensitive region to say the least.

"According to the desk clerk, that suite's been empty for several days. No guests are due there until tomorrow."

"Then the clerk's on the take. Alison Bryant was there this evening, Leo. She was in the bedroom either passed out drunk, drugged, or dead. And that little girl was in there with her, thinking she was asleep. And earlier tonight, there was a man there, too." Nat's voice was rife with agitation. Her temples were pounding. Which meant her blood pressure was in the red again.

Guilt mixed with her anxiety. *How am I going to take care of a baby if I can't even protect my fetus?*

But Nat couldn't shake the image of Daisy looking so young and vulnerable. She couldn't stop hearing the sound of panic in the child's voice when Tony showed up.

"And what about this Tony character?" she asked.

"No one by the name of Tony or Anthony is employed at the hotel."

"I didn't say he was, I told you that Daisy said he's a cop."

"Doesn't mean he wasn't a dick for the hotel. Anyway, I asked around, giving the description you gave me, and got zip. Nobody knows this Tony character. Nobody saw him—"

"I not only saw him in that suite, Leo, I saw him storming across that damn lobby."

"I checked with the desk clerk, the concierge. They didn't see anyone fitting Tony's description. I also drilled the doorman outside the hotel, Natalie. He doesn't remember talking to you, much less seeing this goon."

"He knows Alison Bryant, Leo—"

"Says he never heard of her."

"Maybe it was a different doorman."

"He said his name was Danny. And he's been on since six P.M."

"He's lying. He told me to my face—" Only it wasn't exactly her face . . . "What about Daisy? He doesn't know her either? He didn't see a beautiful blond-haired little girl leave the hotel?" Even Nat could hear the escalating note of dread in her voice.

"No. No one saw the child," Leo was saying. "Which doesn't mean—"

"I'm going back to the hotel—"

"Oh no. Leave it, Natalie."

Leo was laying down orders. Nat had learned over time not to come back at him straight on.

"Tell me Danny didn't see Fran Robie—"

"He saw her. I saw her, too."

"At the sushi bar? With Milburne and his little power group?"

"The mayor was gone. So was Joe Keenan."

"So it was just Robie and Eric Landon?"

"And Debra. She was still there, too."

"No doubt celebrating the arrest of the deputy commissioner."

"Hey," Leo said a little defensively, "you can't blame Debra for being glad the man who ran her sister down is behind bars."

"The man who *allegedly* ran her down," Nat corrected sharply.

"Sorry. You're right, Natalie."

Nat heard his apology but her mind was on something else. "I wonder where the mayor went. Maybe he didn't leave the hotel. Maybe he went up to the suite." Maybe, she was thinking, he was there earlier as well. Drinking Champagne with Alison Bryant. Possibly slipping something into her glass. Something that would knock her out.

Or worse.

"Milburne left the hotel," Leo interrupted. "Danny says he saw him get into his limo."

"And Keenan?"

"Got into a cab."

"What about the sushi chef. Kazuo? The guy who gave me the number of the suite? He knew Bryant was up there."

"Claims he never saw you, much less spoke to you."

Right. He spoke to Samantha.

"He's not going to tell a cop anything, Leo. But I have the proof. I've got that order slip where he wrote down Bryant's suite number."

"Hold on to it for me. I'll have another go at him tomorrow."

"I don't like this, Leo. People are dying, going missing. Bad enough when it's grown-ups, but now a little girl—"

"We don't know that this kid's gone missing, Natalie. We just know she's not in suite fourteen thirty-five at the Boston Regency."

Nat told herself that Leo was right. She told herself not to jump the gun. It was way too soon to panic.

"Maybe Ali woke up and took the kid home," Leo said.

"That's true. Or Tony drove them both there."

"I'm going with you to Bryant's place, Natalie." No surprise that Leo'd figured out her next move. No surprise that he didn't want her going off on her own. "Where are you?"

"I'm on my way home," she said as she pulled out of a parking spot a few blocks from the hotel. With Leo coming along, she was going to have to do a Superman/Clark Kent switcheroo back at her place before they met up. "I'll wait for you outside Bryant's apartment building."

"Wait for me at your place. I'll pick you up."

Nat felt a surge of irritation at being issued yet another order. But then, remembering how freaked she got at the hotel, she didn't argue. Having Leo along might help keep her blood pressure in check. Besides, being a cop gave him more clout than she had. And they might need it. Because she was determined to get into Alison Bryant's apartment one way or another.

As soon as she was settled in the passenger seat of his unmarked black coupé, Leo leaned over and kissed Nat on the lips. The kiss, brief but intense, took her by surprise.

"Where did that come from?" she asked a bit breathlessly.

He put his hand on his heart and Nat was instantly reminded of why she was nuts about this guy.

Unfortunately, these feelings were clouded by guilt and anxiety. She was going to have to tell him. Soon.

thirty-five

"I SUPPOSE IT'S POINTLESS TO TELL you to wait here in the car," Leo said as he switched off the engine, having pulled his car into a yellow zone in front of an expertly rehabbed Back Bay brownstone on Beacon Street.

She already had her door open.

When they got to the portico outside the building, Nat saw that her business card was no longer stuck in the slot next to Alison Bryant's name. Which didn't tell her much. Anyone could have removed it. Or the card could have been blown away by a gust of wind. The wind was brutal at the moment and she pulled up the collar of her wool jacket.

Leo pressed the buzzer beside Alison Bryant's name. They stood there waiting. Getting no response. Nat might have looked more apprehensive than Leo, but she knew his anxiety level was also on the rise. The possibility of a child in jeopardy hit him hard, just as it did her.

He tested the outside door to the four-story brownstone. It was locked.

He gave Nat a quick glance.

"We need—" She didn't have to finish the sentence. Leo was already pressing another buzzer. There were only four, so Nat assumed each tenant occupied a whole floor. Nice to be loaded.

It was only a few minutes past ten, but a groggy and irritated male voice answered.

"Yeah?"

"Boston police. Buzz me in," Leo said with just the right note of authority. The disgruntled tenant didn't even question his credentials. The buzzer went right off. Nat pushed the door open.

"She's on the top floor," Nat said, already heading for the stairs. There was an elevator. But she didn't want to wait for it.

Leo grabbed her arm and pulled her to a halt at the base of the stairs. He was not concealing his anxiety now. "Natalie, please—"

"I'll let you take the lead, Leo," she assured him.

Leo moved in front of her and she followed him up the stairs. A bare-chested young man in jeans was standing at an open door on the second floor. No doubt, this was the disgruntled and now nervous tenant who'd buzzed them in. When he saw them start up the next flight, Nat caught a glimpse of relief wash over his face before he quickly ducked back into his apartment and shut the door. The guy was probably guilty of something.

But then weren't they all?

Without having to be ordered to hang back, Nat remained at the top of the fourth-floor landing while Leo headed alone down the hall to the solitary apartment door. He rang the bell. Then without waiting to see if someone would respond, he also banged loudly on the door.

"Police, Ms. Bryant. Open up."

She saw Leo's hand move around to his back and slip under his leather jacket. Nat knew he sometimes kept his gun in the waistband of his pants rather than get holstered up. She felt a wave of relief as she saw him step to the side of the door so he wouldn't be in the range of fire should there be any.

But there was no gunfire. There was nothing.

Leo tried the door. No give.

He knocked again. Loud enough so that the elderly female tenant from the third floor came out of her apartment and was looking with worried consternation up at Nat from the bottom of the stairs. "What is going on up there?" she demanded. "I'm going to call the police if you don't—"

"We *are* the police," Nat told her. "Now go back into your apartment and lock your door."

The tenant gave her a dubious look, but she did as ordered.

Nat looked back down the hall to see Leo pressing an ear to the door. She started to approach, but got only a few feet closer when Leo raised his hand in a stop gesture.

Leo had his gun out now. As he pressed his back against the wall to the left of Bryant's door, he frantically motioned her to duck out of sight. Nat quickly turned on her heel and hurried several steps down the stairwell so she couldn't be seen.

For several long moments she heard nothing but her own ragged breathing. Then a loud splintering noise—a door being kicked in. She risked a peek around the corner and down the hall just in time to see Leo disappear into Bryant's apartment.

She stayed put for several moments, worried for Leo and wrestling with her need to know what was happening in there versus her fear of stepping into what could be a dangerous situation.

Before she had the chance to actually decide whether or not to make a move, she heard the thumping of footsteps approaching from down the hall. Next thing she knew, Leo was rushing past her in a blur as he practically careened down the stairs. A man in pursuit. But who was he pursuing? No one else had whizzed by her.

Nat heard him shout back at her, "Stay there."

Seconds later, she picked up the faint whir of sirens. A common enough sound in the city. But they seemed to be growing louder. Had Leo called in reinforcements? Or an ambulance?

What had he seen in Alison Bryant's apartment before he took off?

A shiver spiked down her spine as Nat pictured Alison lying

dead or dying on the floor in a pool of blood. And what if it was the little girl, Daisy, lying—?

Nat clutched her stomach.

The sirens were getting louder.

And all she could think was, *I don't want to bring a child into this world. It's too dangerous. Too many terrible things can happen. I can't do this. I can't—*

Two uniformed cops came barreling up the stairs, stopping dead in their tracks when they saw her.

"You the lady called nine-one-one?" the older one with the beer gut asked. He was breathing heavily from the climb.

Nat shook her head.

"You live here?" the same cop barked, a wariness creeping into his tone.

"No."

"Look, lady, I think maybe you should come with us," he said, edging closer cautiously.

"I'm here with a police detective."

Both cops kind of looked around. "Where is he?" the younger one asked.

"I'm not sure. I think he saw someone in that apartment—" she pointed up the stairs—"and took off after him. Or her." Not that Nat knew this for a fact, but she was figuring the assailant must have exited out a window and down a fire escape and Leo was hoping to get outside in time to meet up with the escapee. It was the only explanation that made sense.

At least it made sense to her. As for the two cops, they both looked skeptical.

"Romero, you stay here with the lady," the older cop ordered. "I'll go check things out up there."

Romero didn't look too happy with his assignment. "You sure you don't want backup, Pierce?"

The older cop eyed Nat as if she were either a loony or a criminal. Either way, he clearly saw her as someone who his partner should be watching closely. Romero got the picture. "Yeah, okay. But be careful, Pierce."

The older cop was still eyeing Nat warily as he answered, "Yeah, you too, Romero."

If Nat wasn't so worried about what—or who—Pierce was going to find in Alison Bryant's apartment and if she weren't such a wreck in general, she could have almost laughed.

Leo arrived back on the fourth floor landing to find Officer Romero attempting to calm down the distraught elderly lady from the third-floor apartment and Officer Pierce grilling her.

"What's going on here?" Leo demanded.

Nat rolled her eyes. "These officers think we were caught in the middle of a B and E and that you hightailed it out of here, leaving me to take the rap." Her tone was slightly lighthearted now that she knew that Officer Pierce hadn't found any dead or dying bodies inside Alison Bryant's apartment. Then again, he hadn't found any living bodies in there either, so Alison and Daisy were still missing. Or at least they were still unaccounted for.

Leo went to reach for his ID, but Romero used surprising quickness to unholster his gun and point it at Leo's chest.

Leo lifted his hands in the air as he introduced himself.

"I told you she said they were cops," the elderly tenant hissed.

"That's because he *is* a cop," Nat said.

Romero was concentrating hard on his target while Pierce approached Leo cautiously. "That's right, son. Keep those arms raised high, now, and don't give me any trouble."

"Wouldn't dream of it, Officer," Leo said politely.

The older uniform expertly patted Leo down, looking almost gleeful when he hit pay dirt. "What do we got here?" He was pulling a police-issue .38 out of the back of Leo's waistband.

Romero scowled as he eyed the weapon and recognized it for what it was. "Hey, that's—"

"If you reach into the inside pocket of my jacket, you'll find my wallet and police ID," Leo said calmly.

Pierce hesitated.

"Do it already," Nat snapped. Time was passing and she was growing increasingly agitated about the still-missing little girl. She was planning to go back over to the Boston Regency and make some more inquiries. Maybe the sushi chef knew where to find them.

Pierce gave Nat a grim and deliberately lengthy look before he retrieved Leo's wallet. He opened it slowly and studied Leo's ID for an overlong minute, carefully comparing the photo with the man in front of him who still had his arms in the air.

Finally, Pierce motioned to Romero to back off and handed Leo back his wallet.

"Ok, Detective," Pierce muttered. "Better safe than—"

"Yeah, no problem, Officer."

"You catch the guy did the B and E in there?" Pierce asked, pointing down the hall in the direction of Alison Bryant's apartment.

Leo gave Nat a quick glance. "No. No, he got away."

"Druggie looking for stuff to pawn, you think?" Pierce pressed.

Leo shrugged. "Probably."

The elderly tenant gasped, one blue-veined hand covering the other on which her ring finger was sporting a glittering diamond ring.

Romero, who was standing close to the woman and no longer holding his gun, gave her shoulder a comforting pat.

"Did you see anyone enter or leave the—?" Leo started to ask the tenant.

"This building is supposed to have excellent security," she snapped. "There's never been a break-in before. I can't imagine how an intruder even got inside."

"You didn't buzz anyone in?"

The tenant gave Nat a sharp look. "Certainly not. And I'd like to know who it was buzzed you in," she said sharply.

"You want we should question the other tenants?" Officer Pierce asked Leo, all eager beaver now.

"There are only two others. Christopher Nickerson on two, and the Brimmers on one," the tenant from three announced.

"See if either Mr. Nickerson or the Brimmers saw anyone around the place," Leo told Pierce. "Other than myself and Ms. Price," he added with a hint of a smile.

"Gotcha," Pierce said. His partner nodded.

"If you come up with anything, we'll be in the apartment up there." Leo gestured down the hall.

The two uniforms looked pleased to have an assignment and hurried off down the stairs.

The elderly tenant remained where she was.

"I don't suppose you know whether anyone other than Ms. Bryant had a key to the building and to her apartment," Leo asked her

"I have no idea. I mind my own business and I expect others to mind theirs."

"When is the last time you saw Ms. Bryant?" Nat asked.

"Why?"

"I've been by several times this past week and she hasn't responded to her buzzer."

"What's she done? Is it about that child?"

Nat felt her throat constrict. "Daisy?"

"What about the child?" Leo asked evenly.

"What about her? I'll tell you what about her. I for one would not have given my vote of approval when that woman came before our co-op board to purchase her apartment had I known she intended to have a child living with her. She said she was single and that she would be the sole occupant—"

"How long has Daisy been here?" Nat asked.

"She's been here since the beginning of the summer. Apparently her parents are off on some grand world tour."

A stay in a drug treatment center was about as far a cry from a grand world tour as Nat could conjure. At least that was where Daisy's mom had supposedly been all this time. And what about Daisy's dad? Where was he, Nat wondered?

Who was he? she wondered even more.

"I, for one, will be glad when they get home," the tenant said with increased irritation. "Do you know, that woman even lets that child roller-skate inside the apartment. Plaster has literally fallen off my ceiling. And I've had to ask her a hundred times if I've asked once not to blast that god-awful music—"

"When did you see them last?" Leo asked sharply.

"Haven't seen either of them all week. They must be away on vacation. And here, I foolishly thought—thank heaven, a little peace and quiet. And what happens? She gets herself robbed. Now the police are swarming all around—"

"Vacation? Isn't Daisy in school? It isn't school break." Nat said.

"As if that woman would care." The tenant snickered. "She drags that poor little thing around at all hours of the day and night. I bet that child has missed more days of school than she's attended. One time I even said something to the woman and she almost bit my head off. I can't for the life of me imagine parents so irresponsible as to leave their child with such a capricious person. I even considered reporting that loathsome woman to the child welfare people."

"Why didn't you?" Nat asked accusingly. Maybe if she had, Daisy would be safely ensconced with a foster family right now. Instead of being. . . . Instead of being God knew where.

thirty-six

ALISON BRYANT'S HUGE FLOOR-THROUGH APARTMENT with its interior-designer blend of fine period pieces and Italian modern, had had a thorough going-over.

"I wonder if they found what they were looking for," Leo mused.

"Found *what* is the question," Nat muttered.

"It's possible the break-in has nothing to do with the hit-and-run," he pointed out. "If Bryant was into blackmail like Temple claims, the search could have been for something else altogether."

Nat's mind flashed on those lewd photos of Jessica Asher and Carlyle. How many other clients were secretly caught on film with their pants down?

Leo walked over to a French door that led out to a terrace. The door was flung open. "The intruder got out this way."

"He jumped four stories?"

Leo flicked on a light that illuminated the terrace that looked out over the Charles River and the gleaming lights of Cambridge across the river. He stepped outside.

"Leave the door open," he cautioned as Nat followed him out. "It locks automatically."

He walked straight to the far right side of the terrace where there was a railing visible.

"Fire code," Leo said, pointing to the metal stairs that ran down the building to the narrow road below which was more an alleyway-cum-parking area.

"Must have had his car there. Could have even had a partner waiting behind the wheel with the engine running. Easy enough to drive straight forward and zip out onto Beacon Street via an alleyway. There's one a few buildings down. By the time I got to the street, it was way too late."

Nat went back inside, the chill night air cutting right into her flesh.

"Did he get in this way as well?"

Leo was examining the locking mechanism. "I don't think so. No sign of forced entry. Here or at the front door. And I doubt the door was ajar, given the weather."

"You think he had a key?" she asked as Leo joined her in the living room.

"We don't know it's a he," Leo pointed out. "And it's possible he or she was let in."

"Bryant? Letting in her blackmail victim? Thinking he or she was here to make a payment? But if Ali was here—here with Daisy—"

"Hey, Natalie. This isn't like you."

"What isn't like me?" she retorted. "I'm only trying to consider every possibility—"

Leo stopped her by putting his hands on her shoulders. "It's not what you're saying, Natalie. It's how you're saying it."

"And how's that?" But Leo didn't need to answer that question. Nat could hear the escalating agitation in her voice. She was losing it. She was running a mile ahead of herself. And it wasn't helping her think more clearly. Or helping her blood pressure.

"Look, Natalie. I'm concerned about the little girl, too. We'll find her."

She nodded, wanting to believe him.

He gave her a light kiss, a promise, then guided her out of the living room and down the hallway to survey the rest of the apartment.

They passed the bathroom. The door was open. The lights were on. Whatever was in the medicine cabinet was scattered, and some glass bottles shattered, on the tile floor. It smelled like a perfume factory. The CSI team would check it all out and catalogue everything.

They continued on to the bedrooms. There were two. Both spacious. Both with views of the river. The first one was a guest room. No way to tell if someone had been in the bed earlier because it'd been torn apart. The contents of the drawers in the bureau and desk were strewn on the burgundy carpet. Papers, books, clothing, children's clothing, in haphazard piles. A few stuffed animals as well. Nat's throat tightened.

Leo took her hand. Steered her out of there quickly. Led her down to Alison Bryant's bedroom, which was at the end of the hall. Here, too, chaos. Mostly clothes. Definitely of the couture variety. Silks, fine woolens, linens. A lot of black.

There was no question, given all the chaos, that much of the search had to have occurred before she and Leo got to the building. And since Leo heard the intruder inside, he or she must still have been looking when they arrived. Either the intruder found what it was in the moment before fleeing or never found it. If the latter was true, then whatever it was, was still there. Or never was there. In any event, they'd need to wait for the crime-scene team to give the apartment a thorough going-over.

Leo was already back out in the hall and Nat was about to exit the master bedroom when something out of character and color, given Alison Bryant's clothing taste, caught her eye and held her fixed.

"What is it?" Leo asked.

She pointed at a piece of fabric protruding from a heap of

mostly white and black lacy underwear on the floor beside an antique Japanese bureau.

Leo moved to the object, bent down to pick it up. Nat noticed he was careful to touch only a bare edge of it. He held it out. "A scarf. What—?"

"I've seen it before."

"Okay," Leo said patiently. "So?"

"Steve Carlyle's secretary was wearing that scarf or one just like it when I went to see her at his office." You didn't forget a garish item like that. Bright red roses with oversize emerald green leaves on a mustard background.

"Carlyle's secretary?"

"Grace Lowell. She was new. Told me she'd only been there a few weeks. A tall, overweight, top-heavy woman who wore enough makeup—" As Nat pictured the woman in her mind's eye she wondered what Grace Lowell would look like without all those heavy-duty cosmetics. And while it would be difficult for a fat, busty woman to pass herself off as svelte, easy enough to go in the opposite direction. Some padding and voilà! A complete transformation. Unrecognizable . . . and then Nat recalled the secretary's long, slender, shapely legs.

"I think Grace Lowell was Alison Bryant, Leo."

"But Carlyle had met Bryant at that charity event, even if he didn't know her name. Wouldn't he—?"

"Recognize her? No. Men don't look at women who look like Grace Lowell. They don't even notice them. It would have been easy for Bryant to pull off the masquerade."

"Why?" But even as Leo asked, Nat could see he knew the most likely answer as well as she did.

Her gaze stayed fixed on that scarf, her mind shifting into overdrive. "Grace Lowell told the police that Steve Carlyle left her a note saying he wouldn't be in the day Jessica Asher was run down. That note implies the hit-and-run was premeditated. Carlyle insisted he never wrote any such note. And Grace Lowell claims she tossed it."

"And you think she lied about the note."

"I think *Grace Lowell* lied about a lot of things. Starting with her true identity." With this realization came another one that'd been troubling Nat for days. "The car."

"What car?"

"The SUV. That's what was stumping me. Who else but the Carlyle family even knew that Alan Carlyle's car existed, much less where it was being kept? Grace Lowell *a.k.a.* Alison Bryant could have known as well. She mentioned something to me about a cousin who was a paraplegic who drove a car. And she told me she sometimes chatted with Alan. He could have told her. Or it could have been Sean."

"I guess we better have a little chat with *Ms. Lowell.*"

She gave Leo a wan look. "I'm sure she's gone. Just like Alison Bryant." Nat didn't say "gone" as in "*dead*" but she couldn't shake that worry.

"What I'm wondering," Leo said slowly, "is how she got the job with Carlyle. If it was a setup, who arranged it?"

"I don't suppose you could use your pull to get through to Carlyle at the jail. Ask him directly."

Leo checked his watch. It was after 10:00 P.M. "At this hour? Why not wait until morning?"

"I know who I can reach now, though," she said, pulling out her cell phone. "Alan Carlyle. He can at least tell us for certain if he told Grace about his car."

She dialed the Carlyle's home phone. It rang four times, then the answering machine clicked on. Nothing else to do but leave a message asking Alan to call her as soon as he came in.

Nat yawned, exhaustion setting in.

"I need to wait here for a CSI unit, Natalie. Why don't you take my car and go home. I'll have one of the guys drop me off."

He didn't say where he'd asked to be dropped off. His place or hers?

If it was hers, Nat hoped it'd be a while. Because, tired as she was, she wasn't ready to settle in for the night.

thirty-seven

IT WAS TEN-THIRTY AND THERE were only a few diners left in the sushi bar—two couples in their early thirties were now occupying the table where Milburne and his little power group sat earlier. A few solitary diners, spaced a stool or two apart, were seated at the long, low bar. Two men in business suits, attaché cases at their feet, were facing each other at a small table near the front of the narrow room, working their way through a huge platter of sashimi.

Behind the bar, a young Asian man was wiping down his work station. A different hostess from the one who'd seated her and the Milburnes' party earlier approached.

"I'm sorry, but the restaurant is closing. We're not seating any more diners—"

"I'm looking for Kazuo."

"He is gone."

"Gone?"

"He was not feeling well. I'm sorry."

So am I. And it must show.

The hostess gave her a closer study. Her expression changed. "He was expecting you?"

Sure. Why not? "Yes."

She nodded sagely. "I believe your friend is already up in the suite," she said in a low voice, a faint smile playing on her lips.

The current occupant of suite 1435 gave her a flustered look as he opened the door. "Oh, I was expecting . . . someone else."

So was I, Nat was thinking.

She forced a smile. "Ali?"

He took a cautious step back into the suite and started to close the door. Wrong pick.

"Ali sent me," she said to quickly cover her mistake. And hope that she wasn't making another.

He kept the door ajar. But he was still leery. "What happened to Skye?"

"She's under the weather. Are you going to ask me in?"

Jerry Tepper, wearing a white terry robe courtesy of the hotel, moved aside, smoothing down his comb-over.

"Hope you haven't been waiting long." Nat said as she once again stepped into the suite. She saw another Champagne bottle and two empty flutes on the coffee table. Only this bottle was upright in the silver ice bucket and hadn't yet been opened.

"Long enough," Tepper said, coming up behind her, his fingers trailing down her back.

Nat shivered with repugnance at his touch, but the eminent attorney took her response for arousal.

"Are one of those glasses for me?" She made a beeline for the coffee table. Not an easy feat in those spiked-heel backless pumps.

Jerry Tepper came over and popped the cork on the Champagne bottle. He filled both crystal flutes. After handing her one, he took his and sat down on one of the love seats. His robe fell away so that his bare hairy legs showed.

Nat was about to take a large swallow of Champagne to quell her escalating revulsion when she remembered—no alcohol during pregnancy. She brought the glass to her lips, pretending to take a sip. The attorney chugalugged his. Nat guessed he'd decided the hell with his gut.

"So," he said, when he finished drinking, "what do I call you?"

"Samantha."

"Very pretty name. Very pretty girl. Even if you are a blonde."

"Oh? Don't you like blondes?"

"I used to. One in particular." He looked momentarily saddened.

"Genevieve?"

The sadness clicked into wariness. "Ali told you?"

She shrugged in an effort to keep her response vague.

"Ali has a big mouth," he said acidly.

"Actually, when you opened the door before and looked flustered, I thought maybe Ali was still in the suite. She was here a few hours ago. With the kid."

"Daisy?"

"Adorable, isn't she?"

"You talked to Ali?"

Tepper was starting to sound more attorney than john.

"No. She was sleeping. I figured Ali and Daisy were going to spend the night here."

"Well, they weren't here when I arrived."

"Weird. They didn't go home. I called over there to confirm my appointment with you and the answer machine picked up."

Tepper rose from the settee and took her untouched glass of Champagne out of her hand. "I don't give a fuck where Ali is. She could be in hell for all I care."

"Gee," she said dryly, "you must really love my boss."

He gave a harsh laugh. "In any event, I have nothing against you, beautiful. Come on. The clock's ticking. And whatever I may think about your madam, she does provide top-quality merchandise." He placed his pudgy hand over her ass.

Well, if she'd ever wondered what it was like to feel like little more than a piece of meat . . .

"It's really awful about Gen," she said, edging away to break contact. "I knew her a bit. One time, when I showed up at the town house a little early, she was still getting her stuff together and . . ." She put her hand to her mouth as if she'd said too much.

"And what?"

"Gen was crying."

Tepper scowled. "Crying about what?"

Nat deliberately hesitated. "I shouldn't tell tales out of school."

"You can tell me, Samantha. I'm very good at keeping confidences."

"So am I."

Tepper smiled up at her. He was even shorter than she'd estimated when they were seated across from each other at that bar the other evening. Standing in his bare feet, he couldn't be more than five foot four. In her spiked heels, Nat towered over him. He didn't seem intimidated. Then again, a criminal lawyer as successful as Jerry Tepper had to be expert at concealing his true feelings. They did surface, briefly, however, when she mentioned Genevieve.

"So?" he coaxed. "Why was Jess . . . Genevieve crying?"

Nat pretended not to notice the slip. "Boyfriend trouble, what else?" she said wryly.

"What kind of trouble?"

"She didn't spell it out. Just that he was giving her a hard time."

Tepper's eyes narrowed. "Yeah, I bet he was."

She was fast learning that pretty much everything the attorney had told her during their tête-à-tête at that bar was a lie.

"You know him?" She tried to make the question sound offhanded, but the attorney eyed her suspiciously.

"It wasn't just that Gen was upset," she went on quickly. "She seemed . . . scared. Maybe . . . maybe she had some kind of premonition. Maybe she knew something was going to happen to her. Maybe that boyfriend of hers—"

"The fucker," Tepper snapped. "The whole rotten bunch of them should be strung up."

"Who would you start with?"

Tepper gave her a hard look. Another bad question.

"You know what I liked the most about Genevieve, Samantha?"

"What?"

"She didn't go in for chitchat." He slapped her hard on her ass. "Now, let's put my money where your mouth is, beautiful."

"Hey, pal. Gen may not have gone in for chitchat, but I don't go in for spankings," she snapped, giving her blond locks an irate toss. "I think Ali sent over the wrong girl."

Nat started to sidestep him, but he shoved her and she stumbled backwards onto the settee.

He opened his robe. He was naked except for a pair of ladies' red silk panties.

"I need to visit the little girl's room." She wasn't lying.

"Hey, Samantha, you're taking a long time in there."

Before Nat could think of a response, she picked up the faint sound of knocking.

"I'll go see who it is," Tepper said.

Oh, God, what if it was Skye?

There seemed no end to the problems she'd created for herself.

She threw the bolt and inched open the bathroom door. Tepper had left the bedroom door ajar. Nat could just make him out as he went to see who was out there in the hall. He'd put his robe back on.

"Yeah, yeah, hold your horses," he muttered, his grumbling followed by a brief spate of coughing.

The sound sent chills streaking through her veins. Was Jerry Tepper the man in Skye's apartment? The man who'd inflicted those bruises on Skye's throat? Rough sex play? Or something more sinister?

Nat opened the bathroom door wider, her eyes darting nervously around the bedroom of the suite, hoping there was a second door so that she could make a run for it.

But there was no exit from the bedroom. She was trapped.

She didn't know how long she had her eyes off Tepper, but it was long enough to miss seeing him actually open the door. Her gaze was drawn back to him when she heard him gasp as if in shock. He was standing at the open door—

There was a pop.

And then Jerry Tepper was falling back.

A silent scream shaped his lips.

One hand clutched his ample gut.

One hand reached out, grabbing only air.

As his 200-pound body hit the floor the impact literally reverberated under Nat's feet. His body was jerking with spasms.

Nat staggered backwards, nearly losing her balance and almost falling as well. She grabbed on to the bathroom doorknob to steady herself.

Her first impulse was to dash into the bathroom and lock herself in.

But that would be like waving a red flag if the shooter came into the suite to check on whether anyone else was in there.

She was scurrying under the king-sized bed when she heard a second pop—a sound Nat now was certain came from a silencer-fitted gun. The shooter finishing the job?

She was too frightened about her own life, and the life of her unborn child, to give even a thought right now to Jerry Tepper's life. Or lack thereof . . .

She had no idea how long she lay there huddled under that bed. Time felt irrelevant. It was a lifetime.

Finally, the steady silence giving her some measure of confidence that the shooter was gone, Nat crept toward the foot of the bed and peered out. Her vantage point from this position didn't give her a view of the front door. Or of Jerry Tepper.

She inched out slowly, listening intently for suspicious sounds, surveying more and more space as she emerged. And then she was fully out from under the bed.

She could see Tepper now. Maybe five feet back from the front door, which she could also view clearly. The door was now closed. Either the shooter was inside the sitting room, motionless, silently lying in wait, or he was long gone.

Tepper was on his back, the robe splayed open. There was no line of demarcation separating the red blood spread over his belly and his red silk panties.

She hovered in the bedroom for some more incalculable time.

She took off her shoes. No way she'd be able to make a run for it in spiked heels.

She got to her feet. Tiptoeing, she started across the room towards the bedroom door.

She got within range of it when, once again, someone started knocking on the door to the suite.

Nat froze.

More knocking. No, pounding.

And then—

"Nat? Nat, open the damn door."

"Drink this. Come on, Nat." Jack tried to coax her into sipping on some Scotch he'd taken from the suite's mini bar.

She pushed his hand away. "I don't want it."

They were sitting side by side on the bed. Jack had been quick to guide her out of the sitting room of the suite as soon as she'd let him inside. He went back out there briefly and then returned; firmly closing the bedroom door. Closing off the sight of the dead attorney.

Jack wanted to dial 911 but Nat convinced him to call Leo directly. Leo was just finishing up at the Bryant apartment. They were waiting for him to get there.

"How did you know where to find me?" She'd tugged off the blond wig and tossed it on the floor.

"I followed you," Jack said unapologetically.

Nat wasn't about to give him another lecture on stalking. Not now, at any rate. But it was a serious problem. And there would be a showdown.

"I went over to your place to see how you were and saw your car parked out front on the street," he went on. "At first I thought it was just that you were spooked about parking in the garage, but then I saw that you were in a No Parking zone. So I figured you were going out again. Next thing I know, this dynamite blonde steps out of your building and gets in behind the wheel of *your* car. So I got curious and took off after the blonde.

Followed *her* here to the hotel. Saw *her* go into the sushi bar, come out, take the elevator. I've got to hand it to you, Nat. You were almost unrecognizable."

"Almost? What gave me away?"

Jack lifted an eyebrow. "You asking so you can correct it for next time? Because there isn't going to be any next time, Nat."

She didn't want to receive a lecture any more than she wanted to give one. "How did you know I was in this suite?"

Jack gave her a provocative smile. "I worked my magic charm on a pretty Asian hostess down at the sushi bar." His smile vanished. "I wish to hell I'd worked it a little quicker. Before that shooter showed up."

"I don't," she said soberly. "You might have been hit as well."

His smile returned. "Nice to know you still care, Nat."

"Damn you, Jack." But she managed a smile in return. A moment of truce.

"You didn't even get a peek at the shooter?" he asked when the moment passed.

"No. I just heard. . . ." She swallowed hard.

"That cop, Robie, talk you into this? Going undercover?"

"No. It was my own brilliant idea," she said dryly.

Her sardonic response sparked instant fury in Jack. "You know you could have gotten yourself killed as well tonight, Nat. You could be lying out there in your own pool of blood right next to that poor bastard, Tepper."

She shivered involuntarily.

Jack took pity on her and let up.

thirty-eight

A HISTORIC MOMENT: JACK DYWER AND Leo Coscarelli were united. In their frustration, fury, distress. And Nat was the fortunate one who'd brought the two men together. She was the catalyst for their alliance. As well as the focus of their like-minded feelings.

But the union hit the skids before too long.

"Are you nuts?" Leo shook the blond wig at her. They were still in the bedroom of the suite, awaiting the arrival of yet another CSI team. They were having a busy night, those boys and girls. So would the slew of cops who'd be going door-to-door asking guests and employees at the hotel if they'd seen anyone suspicious. Nat wasn't holding out great hope.

"Sure, she's nuts," Jack said. "If you knew her as well I do, you wouldn't have to ask that question."

"It was rhetorical," Leo snapped at her deputy. "I know she's nuts."

"Thanks. Both of you." Nat rose from the bed, upset, angry, weary beyond description. "You've got my statement, Leo. You know where to find me if you have any more questions. Now I'm going home."

"I'll drive you," they said in unison.

Nat drove herself home.

Considering the fitful night she'd had, nightmares filled with endless scenes of death and dying, Nat was amazed that she didn't wake up at the crack of dawn on Wednesday morning exhausted. Her relief, however, was short-lived, thanks to the arrival of a very miffed cop.

It was a little past eight. Nat had just finished dressing for work.

Francine Robie didn't wait to be invited in. Hannah started toward her as the homicide captain entered, wanting to check out the new arrival. Robie ignored her. Clearly not a dog person. Hannah backed away, feeling slighted, regarding Robie suspiciously. Nat's Lab didn't trust folk who disregarded her.

"We need to talk, Nat."

"Speak for yourself, Fran."

"You were at a murder scene last night."

"I gave my statement to the police."

Nat could see Robie was trying to hold on to her temper. And that she wasn't doing too well. Hannah saw it, too, and snarled low in her throat. Nat's dog also didn't like folks who were angry. Especially when they directed their anger at her beloved owner.

"This is my investigation, Nat. Not yours. Not Leo Coscarelli's. I don't appreciate finding out hours after the fact that a material witness of mine's been gunned down—"

"A *material witness?*"

Robie glared at her.

Hannah emitted a low, rumbling warning growl.

As Robie unzipped her stylish mushroom-colored leather jacket to reveal an ivory silk blouse tucked into sleek chocolate brown leather pants, she stared down Nat's dog. Hannah was the first to look away, her growl transmuting into a whimper.

Cowed by a cop . . . Hannah, I'm ashamed of you.

Hannah sunk off down the hall. Probably in search of a comforting chew toy. Nat wished she could find comfort so easily.

Robie slipped off her jacket, flinging it over one shoulder. Letting Nat know she was planning to stay awhile.

"You got some coffee left over?" she asked.

Actually this was the first morning in weeks Nat had considered trying coffee again. Even made a pot. But in the end, not wanting to tempt the fates, she'd decided to stick to tea.

"How do you take it?" Nat asked, resigned to the visit.

"Black."

"Go have a seat in the living room. I'll bring it in." Sitting together at her kitchen table felt too chummy.

Robie followed her down the hall to the kitchen anyway. Maybe to let Nat know she wasn't taking orders. From her, at any rate.

Nat poured her a mug of coffee. Robie took it and leaned against the counter. Well, she was certainly not about to sit down if the police captain remained on her feet.

"You want to tell me what went down at that hotel suite last night, Nat?"

"It's all in black and white. I'm sure you've read my statement."

She took a sip of coffee. "You didn't say much about what you were doing there in the first place."

"I'll answer your question if you answer one for me."

"Shoot."

"What were you doing at Nippon last night?"

If she was surprised Nat knew she was at the restaurant, Robie didn't let it show. "Eating sushi." She drank some more coffee, eyeing Nat over the rim. When she lowered the mug, she said, "Now it's your turn to answer my question."

"I was having a chat with Jerry Tepper. What makes you call him a material witness?"

Robie smiled, but she put no effort into making it look genuine. "I think you can guess. In fact, I think you know the answer to that one."

"His name was on Jessica Asher's appointment calendar for that day. Her last appointment before she was run down." Nat could show her she knew even more than that, but she was not about to give Robie any information that the captain wasn't already likely to have. Especially after that flip answer to Nat's question about what she was doing at Nippon.

"What I don't know is why Tepper met you at that hotel suite. In a robe and ladies' panties, no less. And why he confided in you. He wasn't doing you any favors, Nat."

Just like knowing whatever he knew hadn't done him any.

"You sure you never caught even a glimpse of the shooter?" Robie pressed.

"Not a glimpse. Anything turn up at the scene?"

Robie shook her head. "Nobody saw anything. Nobody heard anything. Nobody knows anything."

"The Boston Regency seems to have that kind of reputation," Nat said dryly.

Robie let the comment slide. "We're figuring the shooter exited via the fire stairs two doors past the suite. Probably went straight down to the basement and left the building through a service entrance."

This had been Leo's theory as well.

"So who do you think our shooter might have been, Nat?"

"I can tell you who it wasn't. Stephen Carlyle."

"Is that right?" Robie smirked, milking this moment for all it was worth.

Nat felt a sinking sensation as she added two and two. "He's out?"

"Made bail yesterday afternoon."

Shit.

"He's back inside now." Robie was enjoying herself. At Nat's expense.

"He's being charged with Tepper's murder now?"

"He's being held for questioning on this one. And it's not looking good given his wobbly alibi. The poor bastard claims he was home with his crippled son all night."

"And Alan confirms that?" Nat was remembering the call she'd placed to the Carlyle home at a little past ten the previous night. The answering machine clicking on after four rings. Not that it proved no one was there. Unfortunately, it didn't prove the opposite either. . . .

Robie gave her a pitying look. "Sure, Nat. Sure the dutiful son is backing daddy's alibi."

"So what you're telling me is you have no—"

Robie cut her off. "What I'm telling you is Joe's pretty confident we can go for a two-fer."

"Oh, I bet your ex would just love that. Two for the price of one. And not just any two run-of-the-mill victims. He's got himself a socialite call girl and a renowned criminal attorney. And a defendant who's a corrections official. What a lucky break. Keenan pulls this one out of the hat and it'll get him from DA to attorney general in a hop and a skip."

Robie smiled, setting her cup on the counter. "Nothing wrong with having aspirations, Nat."

"You finished with that coffee?" Nat asked abruptly, dumping the contents in the sink before Robie responded. Nat turned on the hot water, giving the cup a thorough rinsing. As if it were probably contaminated.

Robie reached across and shut off the faucet. "I understand you're looking for Alison Bryant."

Nat turned sharply to her. "Who told you that?"

Robie drummed her fingers lightly on the granite countertop. "She did."

Nat could feel herself do a double take.

"We've got her, Nat. Tucked away in a safe house."

"Since when?" Nat asked, her head reeling from this bombshell. Well, she was thinking, at least Bryant was alive. . . .

"We'd have had Tepper there, too, if he wasn't so cocky. And I use the word in its broadest sense. Bryant, on the other hand, was smart. Smart enough to—"

"Make a deal? Oh, Alison Bryant's real good at making deals, Fran. Did your ex offer her immunity? She did come clean about taking over Elizabeth Temple's escort service, right? And I use the term escort service in its broadest sense."

Robie was unperturbed. "There are worse crimes, Nat."

"Yeah, like blackmail."

"Like murder," Robie shot back. "I'm going to do you a favor. Give you another heads-up. Alison Bryant is our key witness, Nat. She is going to take the stand and ID Stephen Carlyle as the driver of the hit-and-run vehicle that killed Jessica Asher. Only question now is—is the former deputy commissioner of corrections going down for one count of murder in the first degree or two counts?"

Nat was starting to get seriously nauseous. "Bryant's lying, Fran. Ask her about Grace Lowell. Ask her about Daisy."

"Who?"

"The little girl. Do you have her at the safe house, too? Did Bryant bring the little girl?"

"I don't know what you're talking about, Nat."

"Last night. At around eight. At the Boston Regency. When you were going into the sushi bar. Daisy was in that suite. With Alison Bryant."

"You saw Bryant? Last night?"

Nat pressed her palms to her pounding temples. "No. She was . . . sleeping."

"Alison Bryant may have been sleeping, but it wasn't at the Boston Regency, Nat. You've got my word for that. Bryant's been at the safe house since yesterday morning."

Nat stared at Robie, her mind in high gear again. If Robie was telling the truth, then Daisy had to have been lying. But why would the child lie? Someone must have put her up to it. But who?

Nat was so caught up in trying to take it all in that she didn't even hear her phone ringing until Robie offered to get it for her.

Nat pulled herself together and snatched the receiver off the hook. "Hello," she said abruptly.

"Is this Natalie Price?"

"Who's—?"

"It's Ali. Alison Bryant."

Nat's surprise and confusion must have shown on her face because Robie was regarding her with curiosity bordering on suspicion.

"Right. Sorry. Hold on, Sharon." Nat looked straight at Robie. "It's my employment counselor from Horizon House." She held the receiver out towards her. "You want to confirm that?"

Robie shrugged. "I'll be in touch, Nat. Take care."

Nat nodded. "Okay, Sharon. I was just saying good-bye to Captain Robie. I should be in soon, but why don't you give me a brief rundown on what Finn did that his boss was so upset about. . . ."

All she got was a hastily given address and a hang-up.

On her way out of Nat's apartment, Robie's cell phone rang. She picked up, listened briefly, then let out a string of curse words that rivaled any sailor.

The door slammed hard behind her.

thirty-nine

NAT PARKED HER CAR IN FRONT of an Asian grocery store that was wedged between two six-story apartment buildings. It was shortly before 10:30 A.M. and there were several customers inside the shop. All women. All Asian. As were the middle-aged couple behind the counter.

She turned off the engine but remained behind the wheel, sorting through a jumble of possibilities. If it had been Alison Bryant on the phone, and she was upstairs in the apartment of the sushi chef from Nippon's, then she must have managed to bolt from the supposedly safe house. Which would explain that string of curse words Robie spewed at whoever was on the other end of her cell phone line on her way out of Nat's apartment.

Then again, Nat had no way of knowing if it was Alison Bryant on the phone since they'd never even spoken. It could have been anyone.

It could be a setup.

Her cell phone rang.

"Nat, where are you?"

"Problem at the house?" Nat asked immediately. Jack knew she had the rest of the week off, courtesy of the commissioner.

"Are you sick again? Are you at the doctor's?"

"No. And no."

"Temple's pretty broken up here, Nat. I guess Jerry Tepper was more than just her mouthpiece."

"I guess so." But exactly what was their relationship? Was the attorney lying to Temple like he'd lied to her? Or were they co-conspirators? Nat was starting to feel as if she could be a lot of people's patsy.

A car horn tooted behind her and she waved at Leo as he pulled in to the curb.

"Jack, I've got to go. I'll stop by the house and talk with Temple later. Just keep a close eye on her."

She hung up as Leo headed over. She'd called him for backup.

The outside door to the building in which Ali had asked Nat to meet her wasn't locked and there were no buzzers to press. The lobby was dark and narrow, dingy but spotless. There was no elevator.

As they climbed the stairs, strong scents of Asian spices almost but didn't quite cover the smell of mold and mildew. Still, the building was remarkably clean. No whiffs of urine. No scraps of trash on the stairs.

"She's expecting me to be alone, Leo. So this time you need to hang back."

"You haven't a clue *who's* expecting you, Nat. And I doubt you need reminding that last night Jerry Tepper opened a door and got himself one hell of a surprise."

"Did you get any info on Carlyle's status?" Nat asked him.

"Joe Keenan's been working on him for a few hours already. The DA's hot to trot."

"He may not be so hot if Alison Bryant had a change of heart."

There was a bare lightbulb that couldn't be more than twenty-five watts lighting the third-floor hallway. If you could call it lighting. Nat needed to shine her key ring flashlight on the doorjamb to make sure they were standing in front of apartment 3C.

She knocked as they both stood to the side of the door—out of gunshot range—then knocked again.

"Who there?"

And before Nat could answer—"Go away. We no want."

It was a woman's voice. She had a heavy Asian accent. Nat couldn't tell if she was merely annoyed or fearful.

"It's Natalie Price. I'm here to see Ali."

"No Ari. You go."

"Is Kazuo home?"

"No. Go."

"Are you his wife?"

"I no talk English."

"Please open the door. I know Kazuo from Nippon. He's a friend of mine. Ali called me twenty minutes ago and told me to come see her here. Please tell her—"

"She not here. Kazuo not here. Now you go."

"What about the little girl? Daisy?"

"No little girl."

"Was Ali here? Please, it's very important."

"They go."

"*They?* Ali and Kazuo?"

"Not know."

Nat's chest constricted. Why would Ali leave when she'd told her—? "Did somebody come for them? Did they leave with anyone else?"

Silence.

Leo nudged her aside and rapped hard on the door. "Police, ma'am. Open the door now."

The door inched open revealing a diminutive Asian woman with dark hair tinged with gray and a fearful expression. "Please. Want no trouble. My husband get call. They go. That all I know."

"Who called? Did your husband say who called?" Nat asked.

"No."

"When did the call come?" Leo asked.

"Ten minutes. Maybe little more. Okay?"

"Whose car?"

"I no understand. Oh . . . oh, husband car. Yes."

"What does he drive?"

"Big car. Silver. Too much money. You go now, okay?"

Leo's pager went off as they were heading back onto the street. He checked the number. "It's Oates." He called his partner when they got into his car.

"Yeah, what's up?" Leo listened, a scowl taking hold.

"Positive ID?" More listening. Deeper scowl.

"Yeah, we're on our way." A brief pause as he glanced her way. "Yeah, Natalie."

"Who is it?" Nat asked anxiously when he clicked off and revved the engine.

"Martha Cady."

"Dead?"

He nodded.

"Who found her?"

"A tenant in her apartment building."

"What made the tenant go into Martha's apartment?"

"She didn't." He hesitated. "She found her in the laundry room down in the basement."

"The laundry room?"

"The tenant went down to do her wash. One of the large dryers had an out-of-order sign on it. Tenant said she saw what she thought were some clothes inside."

"Oh, God. Someone stuffed her in the dryer?"

"How long does the coroner think she's been dead?" Nat was waiting up in the lobby of Martha Cady's apartment building. The doorman was kind enough to get her a Coke, which she'd been sipping on slowly.

"Twelve to fifteen hours anyway. Possibly longer."

She clutched the Coke bottle as a tremor coursed through her body. She'd seen Martha Cady yesterday at two in the afternoon. Was she the last one to see her alive?

No, not the last one. The last one to see her alive was her murderer.

Was it the man in the apartment with her while Nat was at her door? The man in the trench coat and baseball cap who'd fled the building not ten minutes later?

Last night, when she'd heard Jerry Tepper cough, Nat thought he might have been that man. But if he was Martha Cady's killer, why would he have been expecting Skye to show up at the hotel suite last night? Unless he didn't know Martha and Skye were one and the same . . .

"What are you thinking so hard about, Natalie?"

"How was she killed?"

"Gunshot to the chest."

"Like Jerry Tepper."

"Could be the same shooter. Bullet's same caliber."

"Oh, shit," Nat muttered. "They can pin this one on Stephen Carlyle, too. He fit the time slot for Cady as well as Jerry Tepper." She could picture DA Joe Keenan dancing on poor Martha Cady's grave. As if trying Carlyle for the murders of two celebrated victims wasn't enough of a coup.

Leo rested a hand on her shoulder. "I wish you really would take that trip down to the Cape for a few days, Natalie."

The door to the building flew open as Fran Robie barreled past the doorman. She glared at Nat, then at Leo.

"Why the fuck am I always the last one invited to the party?"

forty

"WHERE IS BRYANT?"

"I don't know," Nat told Robie. "I wish to hell I did."

"I've just about had it with you, Nat." Robie was so angry spittle was gathering at the corners of her mouth. "You must have had yourself quite the chuckle this morning if my guess is right and it was Alison Bryant on the phone."

"I wasn't chuckling, believe me," Nat said.

The admission didn't improve Robie's mood an iota. "There I am, standing in your kitchen, going on about having Bryant in a safe house, and you're talking to her on the telephone. You knew before I got that call from Joe that she'd made a run for it. Know what that's called, Nat? Obstruction of justice. Maybe sweating out a couple of days in a jail cell will give you a taste of—"

"Calm down, Fran," Leo said, moving in between them like a referee.

Robie turned on him. "Don't fucking tell me what to do, Coscarelli. I'm going to have your ass, too."

A uniform tapped on the open laundry room door. One of Robie's men. The homicide captain had arrived on the crime scene with a battalion. They were swarming like ants all over the building. "Excuse me, Captain. The parents are upstairs."

"Well, don't fucking bring them down here," she snapped. Then she ran a restless hand through her hair. "I'll be up in a minute," she told the cop, her voice only a degree less sharp. He nodded and seemed happy to make a quick departure.

Nat wanted very much to make one as well. She thought Robie had deliberately dragged her down to the laundry room to get back at her. Thankfully, the body of Martha Cady, a.k.a. Skye, had been removed, but the odor of death remained pungent in this airless room.

"I should have told you this morning that the woman on the phone identified herself as Alison Bryant," Nat told Robie as calmly as she could, considering her physical and emotional upset. "But, hey, you'd just told me she was in a safe house. And you left my apartment without telling me what that call you got was about. So I asked Leo to meet me over at the address she gave me in case . . . in case it wasn't Bryant."

"Talking about *omissions,* you also never told me the sushi chef at Nippon's was a pal of Bryant's."

"I thought you might have known that already."

Robie ignored her comeback, remaining on her tear. "And you didn't call me after you found out she'd been at his place because—?" She waited for Nat to fill in the blank.

Nat eyed her levelly. "Because I don't trust you, Fran. You hang with some very questionable people. People like Eric Landon, Daniel Milburne—"

"Oh, give it a rest, Nat. So you don't like their politics, big fucking shit."

"Were either or both their names on Asher's client calendar, Fran?"

"It's none of your damn business, Nat. And you'd be wise to take that to heart."

"Is that a threat, Fran?"

"Yeah, it's a threat. You better believe it's a threat."

. . .

"I still can't believe Jerry's dead," Elizabeth Temple said in a raspy voice. She looked like hell, her skin blotchy, her eyes red from crying, her hair uncombed.

"You take your meds this morning?" Nat asked as she sat beside the inmate on the couch in her office.

"Yeah."

"There's more bad news, Liz."

Fresh tears spilled from her eyes even before Nat got it out.

"What?" she asked, sounding like a woman desperate not to hear the answer.

"Martha Cady was found dead this morning. She was shot. The coroner says it was the same caliber weapon that was used on Jerry."

Temple buried her face in her hands. "When will it stop? When will it stop?" A mourner's chant.

Nat drew her hands away. "Maybe it'll stop when you stop holding back, Liz."

The inmate's face was a study in anguish. "Jerry Tepper didn't tell me who the driver was, I swear. He told me Ali wouldn't tell him."

"Ali did tell the cops, however."

"What?"

"She identified Stephen Carlyle as the murderer. She said she was prepared to swear to it under oath. The DA placed her in a safe house."

"So it was Carlyle. Then I don't understand—"

"Bryant was lying. She knew who the killer was long before Jessie was struck down. She was part of the setup to frame Carlyle."

"I don't follow," Temple said, looking as lost as she sounded.

Nat told her about Grace Lowell. She told her about the scarf in Bryant's apartment. As she started to construct her theory, Nat could see that the fog of confusion on her trustee's face was beginning to lift.

Not that Temple saw the whole picture. But then neither did Nat. Yet.

"Why pick the deputy commissioner?" Temple asked her.

"I don't know. Maybe it was just Carlyle's bad luck. Someone in the wrong place at the wrong time. An easy mark. Or maybe Alison Bryant had some kind of score to settle with him. Bryant's the only one who can answer that question."

"Did you tell the cops all this? Are they going to confront Ali?"

"She bolted." Nat told her about the phone call she got from Bryant that morning. And about the phone call that sent the pair running from Kazuo's apartment soon after.

"I don't know why Bryant fled the safe house. And I don't know why she and Kazuo beat it out of his apartment. Were they running away from someone or to someone, Liz? Do you know?"

The tears were silently running down Temple's face, but she had her hands folded in her lap. She didn't answer.

"Four people are dead, Liz. Jessie Asher, Griffith Sumner, Jerry Tepper, and Martha Cady. And two people are missing—Alison Bryant and Kazuo Shindo." Nat gasped audibly.

"What is it?" Temple asked her anxiously.

"Not two. Three. Daisy. Daisy's still missing, too." Nat grabbed Temple's arm as she spotted a flicker of recognition in the inmate's eyes. "You know the child?"

"She's the daughter of one of my girls. Charlotte Hamilton. But what does Char's daughter have to do with this?"

Charlotte Hamilton. The name struck a bell, but Nat couldn't place why it was familiar. Liz Temple helped her out.

"Char's dad is Lowell Hamilton. He's Eric Landon's business partner."

Eric Landon kept cropping up like a virulent weed in this investigation.

"Char and Jess were good friends." Temple hesitated. "Char was the one who got Jess interested in coming to work for me way back when."

"Where is Charlotte Hamilton now?"

"She's dead."

Nat felt the color drain from her face. "Dead?"

"Oh, it's got nothing to do with these murders. She died over a month ago. OD'ed. At a rehab center, no less. Somehow managed to get her hands on some bad dope."

"Daisy told me her mom was in rehab. Nothing about her having died."

"You saw Daisy? Where?"

Nat filled Temple in on her encounter with the child in the hotel suite at the Boston Regency last night.

"Maybe she hasn't been told the truth yet," Temple said.

"And what about Daisy's father? Does he know she'd dead?"

"I have no idea."

"Who is Daisy's father, Liz?"

"I don't know."

"Was Char working for you when she got pregnant?"

"Yes. And I was very upset when she told me. I was real strict about my girls having safe sex. Condoms were absolutely required. I'm sitting here with AIDS because I was stupid."

"You didn't ask her who the father was?"

"I did. If it was a client, I'd have made sure he wasn't welcome back. But she insisted it wasn't. I did try to press her, Superintendent. I felt the father should at least provide some support. But she told me to mind my own business."

"Was she on drugs then?"

"Yes. In fact, she told me about her pregnancy while she was sitting in a jail cell. She'd been picked up with a significant amount of coke on her."

"Did she serve time?"

"No. The charges were dropped. She was lucky. Extremely lucky."

"Could Eric Landon be Daisy's father, Liz?"

"No. No, I'm sure he isn't. Char was his partner's daughter."

"And Jessie was his wife's sister."

Temple couldn't meet her gaze head-on. "Eric and Debra are good friends of mine. They've been married eight years. They have a child. Eric's planning to run for the U.S. Senate. Debra is backing him with not only emotional support but with most of her inheritance. I'm not going to be the one responsible for destroying their lives."

"I think Eric's done that already, Liz. I think he's an addictive womanizer. I don't think he cares if the woman is his partner's daughter, his wife's sister, or a hooker. He may have a social conscience, but he sure as hell doesn't have a moral one."

"I'm certainly the last one to throw stones," Temple said in a hoarse whisper.

"Was Jessie still in love with Eric?"

Temple swallowed hard. "First loves never fully die, Superintendent. Even if the guy ends up treating you like shit. Even if he ends up destroying you."

Nat knew Elizabeth Temple was talking as much about herself now as she was Jessica Asher.

"Liz, you said before that Char and Jessie were close friends. Char might have confided in Jessie. Told her who the father was."

"Jessie and Char had a falling-out a couple of months before Char got knocked up. They didn't have anything to do with each other for years. Char wouldn't have told her." Temple stopped abruptly, her hands going up to her mouth.

"What is it?"

"Something Eric said. The . . . the last time he came to visit me at Grafton. He mentioned that Jess had gone to see Char at the rehab center a few days before Char died."

"How come?"

Temple hesitated. "I don't know. Maybe Char asked her to visit."

Nat's mind started racing. What if Char told Jessie about Daisy? What if Jessie confronted Eric? All this time, Char had kept their secret. And keeping that secret had kept her alive. Had Charlotte Hamilton set off a horrible domino effect?

Could this whole case revolve around that little girl? Was Daisy the key?

forty-one

"THANKS FOR COMING RIGHT OVER. DID you see my dad today?" Alan
asked Nat anxiously as soon as she followed his wheelchair into
the Carlyles' living room.

"No. I tried, but I was told he was in being questioned by the
DA and that he'd be there the duration of the visiting hour. I'll see
him tomorrow, though." Nat looked around the large, spotless
room, the traditional furnishings in keeping with the colonial
style of the home. It was tasteful if bland. Lots of rust, beige,
cream. There were built-ins on either side of the fireplace, knick-
knacks, books, photos meticulously placed on the shelves—a
place for everything, everything in its place.

"I'm really worried about Dad's health, Ms. Price."

"Fran Robie said you told her that you and your father were
home all last night."

"Yes, we were. Dad's lawyer picked him up at the county jail
after his bail was made and drove him straight here."

"Who put up the bond?" Nat asked

"We mortgaged the house." He gave her an earnest look. "We were home, I swear it. Let them give Dad a lie detector test. Give me one, as well."

"What about your mom? Your brother? Were they home, too?"

Alan rolled his wheelchair so that it angled slightly away from her. He stared off across the room. "No."

"Should I try to read between the lines, Alan?" she asked softly.

"My mom moved out on Sunday. She's staying with my aunt in Connecticut. It's all been too much for her."

"Does she believe your dad's guilty?"

Alan shot her a reproving look. "He *is* guilty. Of infidelity."

"What about Sean?"

"Good question. Haven't seen him in days. Probably found himself a new squeeze. Another rich, pretty one, you can be sure of that." There was an edge of bitterness in Alan's voice.

"His ex-girlfriend was murdered yesterday. Her body was found this morning."

"Yeah, Martha Cady. I heard on the news. Probably gonna pin that one on my dad, too. But I know he couldn't have shot Martha or that lawyer. I was with him the whole day. And night. But the DA isn't taking my word or Dad's. Either is that police captain, Robie. It's like they're bound and determined to pin it all on my father. Doesn't matter that he couldn't have been in two places at the same time."

"I called here last night, Alan. At around ten. No one picked up. I left a message."

"Yeah, I know. I heard it. Dad was sleeping. And I . . . just didn't feel like talking. I wish to God I had." Tears welled in his eyes. "I wish I'd answered, got my dad up, and put him on the phone. Then they'd have believed me. They'd see they had the wrong man. And if they saw he had an alibi for yesterday, maybe they'd realize that they've got it wrong about who ran down Jessica Asher, too."

"It's the SUV that is a big stumbling block, Alan. There's no question it was the vehicle that ran down Jessica Asher. Who else knew about your car?"

Alan frowned. "Me. Sean. My mom. My pal, Rob."

"Rob? He's the one who kept your car garaged?"

"Yeah, but I was going to get it back. Get it rigged so I could drive again."

"Did your dad tell you the car was stolen?"

"No. He didn't know about it."

"I think he did, Alan. Rob told the police your father told him he didn't want you to know because it would upset you. And that maybe it was all for the best."

"It's not true. Rob told me he spoke to Dad's secretary about the SUV having gone missing. Maybe Grace told him all that crap about keeping it from me. I'd stupidly mentioned to her this one time how I was going to start driving again and she told me she thought that was a bad idea. The cops must have misunderstood."

Not the cops. Homicide Captain Francine Robie. And Nat didn't think she'd misunderstood.

"Something's wrong here, Ms. Price," Alan was saying. "Rob could straighten it out, only he's off in the wilds of Montana for another week, leading a bunch of troubled teens on a mountain trek. There's no way to get in touch with him. But we can talk to Grace Lowell. She'll tell the cops—"

"Is there any way Grace could have known where your car was kept, Alan?"

"What do you mean? That it was at Rob's place?"

"Yeah."

"Why?"

"It could be very important."

He thought for a minute. "Yeah, I guess it would be easy enough. Dad sent Rob Harris some dough each month for garaging the car. I know for a fact his old secretary, Lillian, took care of it. Writing out the checks, mailing them. Grace probably did the same."

Nat smiled. It was all starting to fall into place.

Eric Landon stepped out of the elevator into the lobby of the Hancock Building at 7:15 P.M. and sauntered over to her.

"Well, fancy meeting you again," he said seductively. "Must be serendipity."

Nat smiled. "Must be."

She caught him quickly glancing at his gold Rolex.

"Got an appointment?" she asked.

He winked. "I do now. Just give me a sec."

"I'm in no hurry."

He took out his cell phone, hit a number, his eyes never leaving her. Only they weren't focused on Samantha's face. They were glued to her cleavage. *Oh, the wonders of a push-up bra.*

"Hi, sweetheart . . . Yes, I know . . . but I have to work a little longer. . . . No, don't put Mommy on. . . . What friend is that? . . . A sleep-over? Well, don't stay up too late. . . . Okay, you have fun, now. . . . Love you, too."

"How old is she?" Nat asked when he clicked off.

The smile that he'd donned while speaking to his daughter died on his face. *Okay, got it. Doesn't like talking about the family. Or his little girl, anyway . . .*

"I never did get your name last night. So, who do I have the pleasure of dining with tonight?" he asked, ever the suave vote-getter.

"Samantha."

He coughed. "Sorry. Allergy."

He must have picked up a change in her expression because he quickly added, "I promise it isn't contagious, Samantha."

Nat forced a smile.

He seemed satisfied. "And you already know who I am."

"I know more than that. Ali's told me all about you."

There was a flicker of wariness in his eyes.

"Don't worry. She only said good things."

His wariness grew more intense. Nat was only making things worse.

"I'm hungry, Eric. How about you?" She let the tip of her tongue slide across her upper lip and gave it her best shot at projecting an image of pure wanton desire.

In a tug of war between suspicion and lust, at least for Eric Landon, the latter won out. His smile returned big-time.

"So, what will it be: Italian, Greek, room service?"

Nat smiled coyly. "Let's start with some pasta. I'll take you to my favorite restaurant in the North End. We'll talk about dessert after."

"What's the matter, honey? You've been twirling those few strands of linguine around your fork for almost a minute."

"It's just . . . well, I've had a shock today. You did hear about Martha Cady being murdered? Well, you probably know her as Skye."

Landon set down the fork and knife that he'd been using to dig into his chicken parmigiana. Nothing wrong with his appetite. Until now.

"Can you believe that some animal shot her and stuffed her in a dryer in the laundry room of her building? Isn't that the most hideous thing?"

His expression darkened. "Awful. This whole city is so goddamn riddled with crime."

"First Genevieve and now Skye. I'm starting to get a little nervous myself. But Ali says—"

Landon shoved his plate away. "Ali talks too much."

Nat reached across the table and placed a sympathetic hand over his. "Please, don't be angry. I know you're grieving over your sister-in-law's murder."

He yanked his hand away. "Hey, let's not turn this into a wake, Samantha. The bastard who killed Jessie's in jail. And I heard it straight from the horse's mouth, that Carlyle's going to get the book thrown at him for it. And maybe for Martha Cady's murder as well."

"The horse's mouth, huh? Is that the mayor?" She leaned closer, showing off her cleavage to her best advantage.

"Milburne?" Landon chuckled sardonically. "Milburne's not a horse, honey. He's a horse's ass."

"Oh, not a big supporter of the mayor, then," she teased. "And yet, weren't you and your wife dining with him at Nippon last night?"

"One thing's got nothing to do with another. Politics and personal likes don't always go hand in hand."

"So, who is this horse? Maybe I want to put some money on him to win."

"You want to put money on someone to win, put it on me, baby." Another big vote-getting smile. "You're sitting across from your next junior senator from the great Commonwealth of Massachusetts." His appetite regained, he brought his plate closer again, picked up his fork and knife, and resumed carving into his chicken.

"Well, when you do, I just hope you'll be really tough on crime. And drugs," she added. "I know you try to do your best as a councilman, but once you have a broader canvas than the city of Boston, you'll have a lot more power and influence."

He nodded and chewed. Clearly loving the snow job.

She sighed. "I guess you know I'm thinking especially about Char Hamilton. I think it's so tragic. Here she was trying to clean up her act and she ends up OD'ing at a drug rehab center, no less. They ought to close that place down. Too bad the center isn't in Boston. You could get it shut down. Maybe when you get to be a senator you'll do something about it. And what's to become of Char's little girl, Daisy? Don't you love that name? If I have a girl . . . I mean if I ever have a child . . ."

Landon stopped nodding and chewing as she was talking. And it looked like he was having trouble swallowing.

"You okay?" she asked solicitously.

He managed to get down whatever was in his mouth, hastily following it with a big swig of Chianti.

He didn't suggest room service for dessert. He didn't suggest dessert at all.

And the only dessert Nat was interested in was to see that Eric Landon got his just deserts.

Hannah wasn't the only one to greet Nat as she entered her apartment at half past nine that evening. But her dog was the only one who was happy to see her.

Leo was anything but happy as he gave Nat—or rather her alter ego, Samantha—a dark, intense scrutiny.

"You are nuts, Natalie."

She brushed past him, pulling off her blond wig. For a lot of reasons, she was regretting having given Leo a key to her condo. But when Nat gave him that key over a year ago, Suzanne Holden was still in prison, she hadn't screwed her deputy, and she wasn't pregnant. . . .

Leo didn't stop her, but he did follow her into her bedroom.

"Go home, Leo. I'm beat, I want to take a nice hot bath and go to sleep."

He sat down on her bed. "You're going to tell me what you've been up to sooner or later. Let's make it sooner, Natalie."

"Isn't Suzanne home waiting for you, Leo?"

"So it is Suzanne." He leaned back against her padded headboard. "I'm not sleeping with her, Natalie. It's not a sexual thing with us."

"Is that supposed to console me?"

And what if Leo was sleeping with Suzanne. Like Liz Temple had said to her that afternoon—"*I'm the last one to throw stones.*"

"I'm not going to lie to you and tell you there's nothing there." Leo looked prepared to settle in for true confessions.

She stopped him. "I don't want to hear the truth right now, Leo." Her agitation and weariness must have shown on her face because he got up from the bed, gently turning her in the direction of her bathroom.

"Go take your bath," he said softly.

Nat hesitated. "I know who did it, Leo. I know who killed Jessica Asher. And all the others. I know where it began. I know why—"

He kissed her gently on the lips. "Tell me all about it while you're soaking. I'll wash your back, if you like."

She felt tears threatening. "I like," she whispered. *I like too damn much.*

It wasn't ruminating over what Nat had told Leo that made her spring out of bed, it was what she hadn't told him. Not because it was something she was keeping from him, but because it hadn't registered at the time. But it not only registered now, bells were going off in her head.

It was the conversation Landon had had with his daughter on the phone when they were in the lobby of his office building. *"What friend is that? . . . A sleep-over?"*

What friend was that, indeed? His partner's granddaughter? Charlotte Hamilton's daughter? Very likely Eric Landon's daughter as well? Did Debra Landon know about Daisy's paternity? How much would Debra tolerate to see her husband win a seat in Congress? Did she have dreams of seeing him go even farther? All the way to the White House? Did Debra Landon have aspirations of one day becoming a First Lady?

Another remark echoed in Nat's mind. This one from Fran Robie. *"Nothing wrong with having aspirations."*

Well, Fran, that depends on what you're willing to do to achieve them.

Eric Landon might have an ironclad alibi for the time of Jessica Asher's murder, but what about Jessica's sister? Was she doing her husband's bidding? Or was it Debra's own idea? If, as Nat strongly suspected, Eric and Jessica had resumed their affair, Debra would have had more than one motive for wanting her sister out of the picture.

Nat checked her bedside clock. Nearly midnight. Her gaze shifted from the clock to the open foil wrapper beside it. Then she glanced over at Leo.

She could have told him then—when he was ripping the foil, extracting the condom—she could have said, *Hey, guess what? We won't need condoms for the next eight months. Because, surprise! I'm pregnant. Isn't that great, Leo? There's just one little catch. . . .*

For the first time with Leo, Nat had faked her orgasm.

Why not something else to feel guilty about?

forty-two

"THERE SHE IS, LEO."

"Are you sure?"

"Yes. Yes, it's Daisy," Nat insisted, her voice flooded with relief. "Follow them."

It was a little past nine on Thursday morning. Nat and Leo had been parked on the street beyond the gate leading to the Landon estate since seven. He was covered in sugar-doughnut crumbs and had long finished his king-sized cup of coffee. She still had her tea bag floating in her untouched small tea.

The silver Lexus sedan turned left as it passed the gate. Leo and Nat could both see that it was Debra Landon behind the wheel. Daisy was in the passenger seat beside her. They didn't spot anyone in the rear seat.

Leo waited until Debra's car was a half block away and then pulled out.

Debra pulled out of her street and turned onto Route 9 East, then onto 128 South, and cut over to the Southeast Expressway into Boston.

Twenty-five rush-hour minutes later, when Debra slipped a card into the slot allowing her entry to the parking garage under the Hancock Tower, Leo pulled his car over to the curb in a red zone and stuck a police ID plaque on the dashboard.

They hung back in an alcove in the lobby as Debra and Daisy headed for the bank of elevators. Daisy was chatting away like mad, but Debra seemed to be only half listening. Her expression was taut and when one of the elevators opened, she hurried the child inside.

"She's taking Daisy to Eric. Let's go up there," Nat said as another elevator was boarding.

Leo hung back. The elevator doors slid closed. "What exactly is the plan, Natalie? Daisy hasn't been kidnapped. She doesn't appear to be in jeopardy."

"We don't know that for sure. I want to see Daisy. If you don't want to come up with me, fine."

He followed her into the next available elevator. They squeezed in with a dozen or more men and women starting off their workday. A messenger boy stepped in right after them. Nat didn't realize she was staring at the boy until he winked at her before stepping out on the twenty-third floor.

She leaned closer to Leo. "There might not have even been a messenger."

"What?"

"Grace . . . Ali . . . she could have brought that photo in. For all we know, Jessie didn't even know those photos existed. It could have been part of the setup the Landons worked out with Alison Bryant. We have to find Bryant, Leo."

The elevator doors slid open onto the vast reception area of DataCom.

Debra, who was standing at the elevator about to board, gave the pair a startled look as they stepped out.

"What are you doing here?" Her eyes darted from Leo to Nat, then back to Leo again.

"We came to see—" But before Nat finished, a door opened and Daisy called out to Debra.

"Papa wants me to give you this," she said, running over to Debra and handing her a business-sized envelope. "And he said I can sleep over again tonight, so tell Chloe, okay?"

Debra nodded, but she looked distracted. She'd also missed getting on the elevator. It went down without her.

Daisy gave Nat and Leo the most casual of glances. She'd never seen Leo before and she'd only seen Nat when she was Samantha. She turned away to go back to Papa. They were of no interest to her.

"Daisy," Nat called.

The child stopped and turned. "How did you know my name?"

Debra appeared eager to know the answer to that question herself.

"Your papa told me about you," Nat lied.

"You know my papa?"

Debra's brow furrowed.

"Where's Ali, Daisy?" Nat asked.

The child shrugged. "Who knows?"

"I think you told a fib the other night, Daisy. Ali wasn't really sleeping in the bedroom, was she?"

"What's this about, Leo?" Landon's wife demanded.

"We need to talk to your husband, Debra," he said evenly.

"To Daisy's papa."

"You need to talk to who? Eric or my papa? 'Cause if it's my grandpa, he's pretty busy right now."

The Landons presented a united front.

"These accusations are not only ludicrous and cruelly insensitive, Ms. Price, they're downright slanderous," Eric Landon said, only barely containing his fury as his wife gripped his hand. "I hope you have a good lawyer."

"I might have hired Jerry Tepper," Nat hit back, "only he's dead."

"Leo, I will never forgive you for this," Debra said, her frown becoming a hard look. "That you could even contemplate the possibility—" She didn't finish. She merely turned away from both of them, still clutching her husband's hand.

"If one word of these preposterous, utterly unfounded accusations get printed or aired, I swear, Price, you and your boyfriend here will live to regret it," Eric Landon hissed.

"Considering all the people who you didn't let live to regret it, Eric, I guess Detective Coscarelli and I should count ourselves lucky."

Landon was breathing hard, hanging on to his temper by a thread. If a police detective hadn't been standing there in that office, Nat had no doubt Landon would have been taking a swing at her. Or worse. And his wife would probably be cheering him on. Shit, she'd probably be helping him.

"Do you know a corrections officer by the name of Frank Barker?" Nat asked him.

"No," he snapped. "Never heard of him."

"Then how come your name was scribbled on a notepad beside his phone at home?"

"I don't know what the fuck you're talking about."

"How much did you have to pay Barker to frame Liz Temple for that fight he instigated? I hope it wasn't too much, seeing as how your plan didn't work out the way you wanted."

Landon eyed his wife. "This is completely crazy. This woman is a lunatic."

"Frank Barker's going to be brought in for questioning, Mr. Landon," Leo said quietly.

Landon shrugged. "Nothing to me. Question him all the fuck you want."

Debra nodded in agreement. She was 100 percent behind her husband. Who'd expect otherwise, since if he went down so did she.

"Are you also going to deny you know Alison Bryant? That you're not only a silent partner in her prostitution business, you've been having sexual relations with a number of her call girls?"

"I certainly am going to deny it," he said between clenched teeth.

"You never spent time with Skye? Or Genevieve? How about Samantha? Do you deny knowing that call girl as well?"

"I most definitely do," he said tightly.

Nat smiled her sexy alter-ego smile. "Greek, Italian, or room service?' " She had him at "Greek."

Guilty as charged.

Even his wife saw it. She let go of his hand. Took a few steps back. Nat could see Debra Landon using every ounce of strength she could muster to maintain control.

Landon glared at Nat. "You little bitch. That's entrapment. You won't get away with it. I swear, I'll—"

He stopped as he saw his wife head towards the door. "Deb. Deb, wait."

She ignored his plea and she strode purposefully out of his office.

An apoplectic Landon picked up the phone and called security, but Nat and Leo left before the bouncers arrived to boot them out.

forty-three

CORRECTIONS OFFICER FRANK BARKER REFUSED TO sit down, remaining standing as Leo explained why he'd been called in for questioning. The whole while Barker listened, his arms were folded across his chest, feet apart, eyes narrowed. The same stance he'd taken with Nat that day at his home.

"I don't mean any disrespect to the super here, but she was seeing things if she saw the name Landon scribbled on that notepad. I don't know any Landons. I sure as hell don't know Eric Landon."

"You know he's a city councilman. And that he ran for governor in the last election," Nat said.

Barker shook his head. "For all I know Bugs Bunny was on the ballot, too. I don't pay attention to politics. I don't vote. What difference does it make which crook gets into office?"

"So if we subpoena all of Landon's phone records—home, office, cell—for that period of time, we're not going to find your home number listed?" Leo asked.

"Not unless my wife's been carrying on with this guy behind my back," Barker said sardonically. "And considering my wife's seven months pregnant, I kinda doubt she's fooling around on me."

The man looked like he'd aged a good ten years in the past couple of weeks. He didn't even glance up as Leo and Nat entered the small, square interview room. Shoulders slumped, head bowed, wrists cuffed, and wearing a Day-Glo orange jumpsuit, it was almost impossible to recognize the deputy commissioner.

"Have you been checked over by a physician, Steve?" Nat asked softly as they sat down across from him at a rectangular wood table.

"I'm fine," he muttered lifelessly. The arrogance that had been his trademark was not only gone, it seemed to have been drained out of him.

"I saw Alan yesterday."

Carlyle's head dropped lower. "I want him to go stay with his aunt."

"And with your wife?"

"I suppose he told you she left me." He seemed unconcerned. This was a man who believed he had lost the battle. There seemed to be no fight left in him.

Nat wanted to shake him. She wanted the old infuriating, insulting, frustratingly irritating deputy back.

"Look at me, Steve," she said sharply. "There's a lot I've got to tell you and then there are some important questions I need to ask you."

"What's the point?" he mumbled morosely.

"The point? The point is you're innocent. I know it. Leo knows it. And we're going to prove it."

His head jerked up. He stared at her as if he couldn't have heard right. Then he looked over at Leo who'd been sitting silently at her side.

"We're going to try to prove it," Leo qualified.

But it appeared to be enough for Carlyle. He returned his gaze to Nat. She saw signs of life.

Fifteen minutes of explanation later, there were not only signs of life but of rage.

"Alan is absolutely right. I never spoke to Rob. It had to have been Grace he spoke to. Grace." The deputy commissioner's face was red with rage. "What I'd give to get my hands on that deceiving little bitch—"

But there was no time to let him vent. "How did you come to hire Grace Lowell, Steve?" I ask.

Carlyle got himself in check. He, too, realized he had more important matters to attend to right now. "I didn't actually hire her. She told me she'd been called in by Personnel to replace Lillian."

"What happened to Lillian?"

"She walked into my office one day and said she'd come into some money and decided . . ." Carlyle stopped, his eyes narrowing. "She was paid off to leave the job. My God, they'd been planning this for over a month. Why?"

"I was hoping you'd have the answer," Nat said.

"Did you confirm Grace Lowell's appointment with Personnel?" Leo asked.

Carlyle scowled. "No. I didn't see the need. She had a letter from them. She gave it to me to read. It had the proper heading. It looked perfectly legitimate. I never thought . . . I never thought."

"What did you do with the letter?"

He shook his head in self-disgust. "I asked Grace to file it."

"Steve, think back to the day before Jessica Asher was killed." Nat said. "Did you make some comment to Grace that you weren't feeling well? Was there any way she could know you weren't likely to be in the next day? That you wouldn't have the alibi that you were at work when Jessica was struck down?"

"I wasn't sick. I mean I wasn't physically sick. I was distraught about that photo. Now that I think about it, Grace did comment that I wasn't looking well. She brought me in a cup of tea before she left for the day. Stood there while I drank it down. Which I only did to be polite, because it was so damn sweet. She'd put a ton of sugar in it. For energy, she said."

"Sugar," Nat repeated, eyeing Leo.

"Did that headache and upset stomach start that evening?" Leo asked.

Carlyle got the full meaning of the question. "You think she drugged me. That the sugar wasn't for energy. It was to cover the bitter taste of whatever shit she put in the tea." He laughed harshly. "She was so garish and unattractive, I considered trying to get her transferred to another department. But I was feeling so guilty about what I was doing outside the office that I didn't want to compound my guilt by getting rid of a perfectly good secretary just because she wasn't pleasing to the eye. Funny, isn't it?"

But none of them was laughing.

Carlyle looked wanly at them. "Why me? Why'd she pick me to frame? What did I ever do to her?"

"Alison Bryant may not have been the instigator, Steve," Nat said. "She may have simply been following orders. We believe Eric Landon is behind all of this." She caught Leo's scowl. Okay, so he was not as convinced of Landon's culpability as she was. Yet.

"Landon? I don't know the man from Adam. Shit, he even got my vote when he ran for governor. It doesn't make any sense. What would he have against me?"

"Who might have something against you, Steve?" Leo asked.

"No one. There's no one—"

"What about your son?"

"Alan? Alan wouldn't . . . he couldn't . . ."

"I mean Sean," Leo said quietly.

But his words gave Nat a start. Had she been on the wrong track? Had she overlooked someone who was an even more viable suspect than Eric Landon? Had Leo been focusing on Sean Carlyle all the while she'd been fixating on the councilman?

Carlyle sighed. "I'm ashamed to say I considered Sean at one point. I know the boy's been involved with drugs and God only knows what else. And even though Alan swore he didn't tell his brother about seeing the photo of me and Genevieve in my office that day, I . . . I couldn't be sure he hadn't. Sean and his mother are very close. It's understandable he'd be enraged at my infidelity. And if he were on drugs at the time . . ." He rubbed his face hard.

"The boy knew where Alan's SUV was kept. He knew I was home sick that day. I'm surprised no one but myself—until now—even questioned the possibility . . ."

Carlyle paused, staring down at the handcuffs circling his wrists. "I told myself, if it was Sean, I'd take the rap for him. I love him. I love my whole family. I've betrayed them all. At least I could do one decent act." He blinked away tears. "But it wasn't Sean. I contacted Hal Thomas, Sean's boss at the garage. I knew Sean had left for work that Friday at around eight-thirty, and the police did check that he got there at nine, but . . . he could have left later on. I had to know. Just for myself. Hal Thomas vouched for Sean. He swore to me they spent the whole day together putting in a new engine in a Mercedes. The boy never left the garage." His voice wavered. "I should have thought to ask Hal not to say anything to Sean. It was the final blow for the boy to learn I suspected him. The ultimate betrayal of trust. He told me he never wanted to see me again. And . . . that I could rot in hell for all he cared."

No amount of blinking could stop the flow of tears. They fell down Stephen Carlyle's face in a flood of guilt, regret, and despair.

Nat recognized the plainclothed cop as he approached her and Leo outside the Boston City Jail. It was Norman Wilson, the lead detective in the Asher investigation, the one who'd first grilled Carlyle.

"Natalie Price?"

She nodded.

"I got a warrant here for your arrest, Ms. Price."

"What the fuck for?" Leo snapped.

"Obstruction of justice, withholding evidence, collusion, using undue influence . . ."

forty-four

FRAN ROBIE MIGHT WELL HAVE LOOKED smug, but she didn't. "I was really hoping it wouldn't come to this, Nat."

"It does make your life more complicated."

"My life? Yeah, I guess it complicates my life, too."

"So, what happens now?"

"I want to show you something." She extracted a sheet of paper out of a file and slid it across the table in the interrogation room where Nat now sat on the wrong side of the table.

Nat looked at a typed and signed report. The signature belonged to Debra Landon. She scanned Debra's statement. What amounted to a solid alibi for Friday, October 17. In brief, Debra was a parent leader on her daughter, Chloe's, class trip to Plymouth Plantation that day. The group left at 8:00 A.M. and returned at 4:00 P.M.

"She came in of her own accord," Robie said. "She wanted to press charges against you for harassment."

"Did you tell her to get in line?"

Robie smiled faintly. "More or less."

"Was this Eric Landon's idea, Fran? Well, I guess I should be grateful he merely wants me thrown in jail. But I guess the body count is getting way too high. A person can take just so many chances. Besides, this time Stephen Carlyle definitely does have an airtight alibi. Of course, Landon could always frame someone else."

"Landon's got an alibi. So does his wife."

"He could have gotten his goon, Tony, to do it."

"Tony?"

"Alison Bryant's bodyguard, pimp, bouncer. Take your pick."

"You don't let go, do you?" Fran said with mostly frustration, but Nat detected a glimmer of admiration.

"You're holding on pretty tight yourself, Fran. But there are two people out there who could cut your line."

"What are you talking about, Nat?"

"I'm talking about Alison Bryant for one."

Robie's mouth tightened. "Do you know where she is?"

"I know she's scared. I know she lied about Carlyle. I know she knows the truth. The whole truth. And once the truth comes out, Fran, a lot of people's reputations are going to be smeared. And that's just for starters."

Robie didn't bite. "You said *two* people."

"That's right. There's also Rob Harris."

"Who?"

"The young man you claimed told you he'd informed Steven Carlyle that his son's SUV was stolen a few days before the hit-and-run. Rob Harris never spoke to the deputy. He only spoke to Carlyle's secretary, Grace Lowell. Well, he thought he was talking to Grace Lowell. Actually, he was talking to Alison Bryant, who was pretending to be a secretary by the name of Grace Lowell."

Fran Robie grimaced like she'd just been sucker punched. "Oh, shit. Shit, shit, shit."

She walked out without another word.

A uniform entered and took her back to a holding cell.

Forty minutes later, Nat left the precinct house on bail. Leo and her attorney, Laurie Belson, were waiting for her outside.

"You okay?" Laurie asked her.

She nodded.

Leo took proprietary hold of her arm. "Come on, I'll drive you home."

"I'm not going home. I'm going back to the center. I need to talk to Liz Temple."

His hold tightened. "What do you want, more charges thrown at you, Natalie? And by the way, Fran showed me Debra's statement. So there goes that theory up in smoke. Now, come on. Get in the car."

"Let go of me, Leo." It was a tone Nat didn't use a lot. It was one she didn't think she'd ever used with Leo Coscarelli.

He dropped her arm like he'd been badly burned. In a way, he had.

"It must be ESP," Elizabeth Temple said when she saw Nat walk into the office. "I was just going to phone you."

"Why?"

"I remembered something."

"About Alison Bryant?"

"Yes, not something current. Something that happened about a month before my arrest. But it could have some bearing on what's happening now."

"What is it?"

"Ali showed up at my house one day and the side of her face was all swollen, one of her eyes black and blue. I thought it was a john who'd laid into her and I was going to lay into him for it, but Ali swore it wasn't a client. She told me it was a guy she'd started dating a few weeks back. That she'd met him on Cape Cod. I told her she ought to find herself a new boyfriend. But she just said something like, 'He has a few loose screws, but who doesn't?' I said he didn't sound like husband material, that's for sure. I said it as sort of a joke, you know. Because Ali was always saying how she never wanted to tie the knot. Anyway, she said not to worry. He was already married. She also said he was a big honcho."

"Eric Landon?"

"She wouldn't say who it was."

"Did the Landons spend time on the Cape?"

"They . . . they have a place in Falmouth. But Eric wasn't there a lot that summer. He stayed in Wellesley with Debra. She was pregnant with Chloe. In her eighth month. So she wanted to stay in town to be close to the hospital."

She paused, then smiled hesitantly. "What month are you in, Superintendent?"

Nat's mouth dropped open. "How did you know?"

"I guess I shouldn't have used your private bathroom without permission the other day, but you weren't here. . . ."

"What tipped you off?"

"The info sheet from the pregnancy kit. It was on the floor behind the toilet. I. . . . Well, it doesn't take a great detective to figure out."

"Have you said anything to anyone here? To anyone anywhere?"

Liz also didn't have to be a great detective to detect the frantic edge in Nat's voice.

"No, I promise. I haven't said a word. And I won't."

"Okay, let's just drop it," Nat said abruptly. "Tell me why you were going to phone me. It wasn't just to say Bryant had a married big-shot boyfriend with a violent streak five years ago. And that you don't think it was Eric Landon."

"No."

"Then what?"

Temple hesitated. "I know how you can find out who it was for sure."

"If this is another wild-goose chase like my hunt for Alison Bryant—"

"This will be a cinch by comparison."

"A cinch" was an overstatement.

Getting in to see Dr. Henry Temple at his office on Charles Street in Beacon Hill took some hefty persuasion. It was only after

Nat convinced the psychoanalyst it was a life-and-death situation that he finally relented. He could squeeze her in between appointments. That meant ten minutes, he told her.

So she talked fast. "Liz says you keep records of everything, professional and personal. You have a cottage in Truro on the Cape. Liz and a friend of hers stayed there quite often during the summer before her arrest." She saw Dr. Temple wince, but he quickly adjusted his face back to analyst-neutral. "I need a copy of the phone bills for that period of time."

"Why?"

"Because someone a friend of hers was calling quite frequently from the cottage could be a murderer. If he is, I need to stop him before he kills again. There's a child at risk. As well as your daughter."

Daughter. That triggered another wince.

"Liz is on a new drug cocktail. She's doing well, Dr. Temple. There's something you should know about how Liz contracted—"

"I'll get you the phone bills, Superintendent. You'll have them tomorrow morning. Leave your address with my secretary. My next patient is here."

When Nat got home she took Hannah for a walk and then phoned Leo. She wasn't sure if she planned to apologize for being so sharp with him or not. She knew he wanted her out of the fray. He wanted her safe. He cared about her. She thought he loved her. But whoever said love was neat and tidy?

It was nearly 7:00 P.M. when she called him.

Jakey answered. The child loved getting the phone. It made him feel very grown-up. Nat smiled as he said in his little-boy voice, "Coscarelli residence. Who's calling, please?"

"Hi, Jakey, it's Natalie."

"Hi, Natalie. Are you coming over?"

"Not tonight. You need to be in bed soon."

"Oh, I can stay up. Nana lets me. Daddy says she's a pullover."

Nat laughed. "I think he means a pushover."

"Oh yeah. So, will you come over? I have a new puzzle. One hundred pieces. Mommy and I only put twenty-two . . . no, twenty-three pieces together. So there's lots more."

"Is your . . . mommy there now?"

"No. She and Daddy went out for a grown-up dinner. I told them I was grown-up so why couldn't I go? Mommy said, okay. If I wanted to eat raw fish. Yuck. Isn't that yucky, Natalie?"

Nat tried to laugh, but it came out strained. "Yeah. Yeah, it really is yucky, Jakey."

Shortly before eight Friday morning, Nat was buzzed from downstairs. When she hit the intercom a female voice told her she had the package Nat had requested. Nat buzzed her in, telling the messenger she'd be right down to pick it up and to leave it on the lobby table for her.

When Nat stepped out of the elevator a few minutes later, she was surprised to see that the messenger had waited for her.

"Superintendent Price?"

Nat nodded, studying the small, delicate woman who was so much the older and healthier version of Liz Temple that there was no question in Nat's mind that this was Liz's mom.

She extended a hand. "Nat."

Mrs. Temple's response was a bit delayed but when they did shake hands, her grip was firm. "Miriam." She handed her the envelope. It was thick.

"The girls made a lot of calls."

"Would you like to come up for some coffee? Or tea?"

"Yes," she said. "I'd like that very much. Either would be fine."

They didn't chitchat on the way up to Nat's apartment, but the silence didn't feel strained. As they entered her foyer, Hannah was right there to check out the new arrival. Miriam held out her hand, palm down for Hannah to sniff. Hannah liked Miriam Temple's smell. She liked the head rub Miriam gave her even more. Nat's dog had a new friend.

It wasn't until Miriam sat down at her kitchen table that Nat realized she had a little pile of Saltine crackers next to her mug of tea.

Nat didn't know if it was just that every woman who had ever been pregnant saw those crackers as a surefire giveaway—lots of men and nonexpectant mothers must eat Saltines—or maybe it was the flush that burned her cheeks when Miriam looked from the crackers to her. Whatever the reason, Nat was sure Elizabeth Temple's mother knew her secret.

"Going on two months," Nat said, turning on the burner under the kettle.

"I lived on Saltines until my sixth month. When Lizzie was born I expected her to come out covered in salt."

Nat laughed. But she stopped abruptly when she saw the sadness cloud Miriam Temple's eyes.

"Lizzie was such a beautiful baby. So sweet. When she'd smile up at her father and me from her crib, it was like being bathed by the rays of the sun," she said in a whisper.

Nat reached a hand out and squeezed Miriam's. The older woman dabbed at her eyes, then observed Nat with motherly regard.

"Are you taking vitamins?"

"Yes." The whistle in the kettle sounded. She made Miriam tea and brought it to the table. "I do have bagels and English muffins."

"This is fine."

Nat sat down, eager to get to those phone bills, yet wanting to let it go for a bit. "Other than my obstetrician, the only other people who know I'm pregnant are a reporter, you, and your daughter."

"I see."

And Nat sensed that she did.

"I know Lizzie's . . . sick," Miriam said, her voice strained. "And that her father blames her."

"He's wrong," Nat started to say in Liz's defense, but Miriam cut her off.

"We need to talk, my daughter and I. And we will. Very soon. But let's leave that for now. I can see you have a great deal on your mind."

Nat found herself telling this woman she'd never met before all about her predicament. She must have gone on for over an hour because when she finally went to swallow her tea it was cold. Nat felt oddly uplifted even though she still didn't have the slightest notion what to do about it all.

"You could find out before the child is born," Miriam Temple said. "There are tests that can be done in utero. You'd just need both Jack and Leo to submit to blood tests."

"Which means I'd first have to tell them."

The older woman smiled. "Yes."

"Yes," Nat echoed. And then she repeated it. "Yes."

She glanced at the thick envelope on the table.

"Can I help?" Miriam asked. Nat could see it wasn't an idle offer.

"I'm especially interested in calls that were frequently placed to other numbers on the Cape from mid-July to the end of August. I'm especially interested in the week of August fourteenth to the twenty-first. Your daughter let her friend Alison Bryant use the cottage that week and—"

"Alison Bryant is no friend of Lizzie's," Miriam said with a ferocity one would never guess she had, to look at her.

"No. You're right. But Liz thought she was a friend at the time. And Ali was seeing a man who was also staying on the Cape. He was married so they might not have been able to see each other all that often. I believe they spent a fair amount of time on the phone."

The phone bill didn't list the numbers in the local calling area, but there were calls to areas of the cape outside the designated area.

The task didn't take very long, especially as Nat could eliminate numbers that didn't show up at all during the particular week she was focusing on.

In the end, there was only one that met the criteria.

Nat dialed the number. She wasn't surprised to learn it was no longer in service. She'd been here before. Only this time she was not inclined to turn to Leo for help.

forty-five

JAKEY HAD A PUZZLE WITH ONE hundred pieces. Suzanne had helped him fit together over a quarter of them.

Miriam had helped Nat with her puzzle as well. But the picture was still far from complete. Nat hoped Liz Temple might be of some help. She phoned her from her condo.

"Sorry, Superintendent, the number doesn't register." The inmate hesitated. "You say my mother gave the phone records to you?"

"Both of your parents have been very helpful, Liz. Your mom's coming to see you. Whatever you want to tell her, I think she'll be very receptive."

There was a long pause before Nat heard a scratchy "Thank you." And then, after a brief pause, "Sorry I couldn't help with the phone number."

Alison Bryant's mystery caller wasn't the only problem Nat was trying to solve. She also wanted to know why Stephen Carlyle had been selected for being framed. Was it only that he could be linked sexually to Jessica Asher, and that it was relatively easy to set him up?

What drove the killer to pin the murders on Carlyle? Hatred? Betrayal? Revenge? All of the above?

Nat shut her eyes, hoping to see light in the darkness. Certain it was there . . .

Nat very much wanted to visit with Steve Carlyle again, but as she'd now been charged with a crime, she'd be refused admittance to the jail as a visitor. So she headed down to the Department of Corrections.

Commissioner Miller looked harried and not particularly pleased to see her.

"If only you'd left well enough alone, Nat—"

"Don't you mean 'bad enough alone'?"

"Let's not argue."

"I agree. Listen, I want to talk with Carol Nelson. ASAP."

"The head of the Parole Board?"

"Yes."

"Can you tell me why?"

"A hunch."

"That's not much of an answer, Nat."

"It's the best I can offer."

He didn't look pleased with that response either, but he phoned Carol Nelson personally and handed her the receiver.

Nat told the head of the Parole Board that she wanted a list of the inmates who had been paroled over the past year.

"That's a mighty long list," Carol Nelson said.

"Which is why I need it ASAP. It's going to take me time to sort through it." And time was at a premium. "I'll come pick it up. Say in an hour?"

"What are you looking for?" Nelson asked.

"A killer."

. . .

Nat stared at the three names she'd circled on the long list—Peter Grayson, Alvin Cooper, William Boomer. Three men paroled from different prisons across the state. Men who had no personal connections with each other. Men granted paroles at different times over the year, Grayson in February, Cooper in mid-May, Romero in September. They were currently living in different parts of the state and it was unlikely they'd had any contact with each other since release.

But for all the differences, Nat had circled their names as a group because these paroled inmates also shared several things in common. All three had committed violent crimes; all three had had headline-making trials; all three had received long sentences and yet had received relatively early parole dates. Also, the release of each of these inmates had stirred hornets' nests of outrage— from the victims' families and friends, the prosecutor's office, the community at large. Scathing editorials had hit the newsstands on each occasion. Nat was able to read them on-line by doing a search of the *Boston Tribune*'s archives. There were also news articles that mentioned that the members of the Parole Board, including Carol Nelson, had received death threats. So had Deputy Commissioner Stephen Carlyle, not only because of his role as liaison to the Parole Board but because he'd given statements to the press in full support of the Parole Board's decisions in each of these instances.

Nat wondered if Carlyle had done more than support the decisions. Had he taken an active hand in guiding them?

Was this the key reason why Stephen Carlyle had been singled out to be the patsy? Payback?

Stephen Carlyle didn't know it, but Nat was growing more and more convinced that the deputy commissioner most definitely had an enemy. A very powerful and dangerous enemy.

But the only person who could confirm Nat's suspicions— other than the killer—was the woman who knew the killer's identity. Alison Bryant.

. . .

Leo called her while she was packing. Nat told him she was going away for a few days.

"Where?"

"The Cape."

Nat could picture him rolling his eyes, certain she was lying again.

"No, I mean it this time, Leo. I really am going." The doorbell rang. Hannah barked and made a run for the door. "That must be my neighbor, Inez. She's going to watch Hannah for me while I'm gone."

"Where will you be? I can't get away today, but I'll try to clear the boards for tomorrow and meet you down there."

Nat was heading for the door. "I'm not sure yet where I'll be staying, Leo. I'll call you when I know."

She opened the door expecting to see Inez. So was Hannah. But her dog was happier to see who was there instead. Nat was not.

"I have to go, Leo."

"Natalie, call me."

"I will."

As soon as she clicked off, Jack asked, "Go where?"

"To the Cape."

"In November. It'll be dead there."

She hoped not. "Quiet, anyway. And I need that."

"Robie called the office. Did she call here?"

"No," Nat said, immediately on edge.

"She had some good news for you."

"That's a switch."

"All charges against you have been dropped. You're a free woman, Nat."

She was relieved, no question about that, but she was thinking, no one's ever really free.

"I'll drive down with you," Jack said.

"No."

"I'll come back in the morning."

"Jack—"

"Don't argue with me. We can sleep in separate rooms if that's what's worrying you."

"That's only a small part of what's worrying me."

"Then what else is it, Nat? Is it my drinking?" He breathed in her face. "I've been sober since that day outside your obstetrician's building."

Her breath jammed in her throat.

"I feel like a total idiot now for not having realized what was up sooner. It wasn't until I caught a snippet of your conversation with Liz Temple yesterday—"

"You mean you were eavesdropping, you bastard."

"I don't really think you want to cast stones, Nat."

Cast stones? She felt like she couldn't even lift a pebble at the moment, she felt so weak.

"Is it mine, Nat?"

The question, asked with such heartwrenching feeling, made it impossible for Nat to hold on to her anger. And the anger had helped her keep all her other emotions at bay. Now they rose to the surface and there was no lid in sight to stop them from bubbling over.

Her eyes met Jack's. "It could be."

He nodded. "Your suitcase in your bedroom?"

"Yeah."

During the summer it could take upwards of four hours because of high season traffic to get to the picture-perfect seaside village of Truro, which was almost at the tip of the Cape. On a chill, rainy day in November, the time was cut by half.

Still, two hours alone in a car with Jack was a long time. He didn't once bring up her pregnancy. Nat was sure he had a hundred questions he'd love to ask her, but he didn't ask a single one. Maybe he knew she didn't know the answers yet. Maybe he wouldn't want to hear them if she did have answers.

Jack did the driving and Nat filled the hours telling him everything she'd found out about the murders. He listened intently without interruption. When she was done, he, too, saw the whole picture. It was clear to both of them who had committed the string of murders.

"And if Bryant and this sushi guy aren't holed up there, what then?" Jack asked as he turned onto Hedgehog Lane.

Nat was thinking more about if Alison Bryant was hiding out at the Temple cottage, what then? Would she come in? Give a new statement? Tell the truth? Place the real driver of that SUV behind the wheel? It would mean implicating herself big-time. And cutting a deal with the state wouldn't be the cinch it was back when she turned in Elizabeth Temple.

The few summer homes they passed on Hedgehog Lane had been boarded up for the winter. The small weathered gray shingle two-story Cape-style cottage belonging to the Temples sat at the end of the lane. Nat's heart sank when she saw wooden shutters affixed to every one of the windows facing the driveway.

"Look," Jack said as they pulled up to the right of the cottage. He was pointing to a side window on the second floor. The shutters for that window were open.

"Stay in the car," Jack said.

Nat didn't need persuading. She gripped his arm. "Be careful."

He flashed her one of his rare but endearing smiles. "Hey, don't worry. I got a lot to live for."

Both the smile and his words left her with a big lump in her throat.

It was still wedged there when he came back out a few minutes later. "Place is empty now. They were here, though. No question. Maybe they went for a drive. A person could go stir-crazy in all that gloom."

Nat started to get out of the car, prepared to wait in hopes that Bryant and the sushi chef returned.

"Hold it," Jack said, getting back in behind the wheel. "Let's pull the car deeper into the woods. Might as well take advantage of the surprise factor."

forty-six

THERE WERE FOUR MESSAGES ON NAT'S cell phone. They never rang through because there was no reception out there in that back road of Truro. One message was from Fran Robie telling her what she already knew, that the charges against her had been dropped. The other three messages were from Leo. Wanting to know where she was. Wanting her to call him back. And in the last message that came through less than twenty minutes back, telling Nat that he loved her. Love was not a word Leo Coscarelli bandied around. He took it seriously. It meant something significant.

Jack was watching her closely as she replayed and listened to that last message as they stood in the living room of the Temples' now-deserted summer cottage.

"Leo," he said.

"Yeah."

"He doesn't know?"

"He will. Soon."

They both heard the creaking sound at the same time. A loose floorboard on the porch. It had creaked when they'd walked over it forty-five minutes ago. Jack hurriedly gestured for Nat to duck out of view. Easy enough for her to do as she was standing near the door that opened to a tiny half bath.

But Jack—

Jack was out there in the middle of the room. There was no place for him to duck. No time.

Déjà vu in the most horrifying way imaginable played itself out as Nat hovered in that bathroom.

The grunt of surprise. The pop. The groan. The body falling backwards. Stumbling. Hitting the ground so hard the tiles reverberated under her feet. And the blood. So much blood.

Only the scream was new. Nat's scream, as she rushed blindly to Jack Dwyer's side.

District Attorney Joe Keenan merely looked annoyed that he'd wasted a bullet on the wrong target. He stepped closer to Nat, giving only the briefest glance to the unmoving man at his feet.

Keenan looked straight down at Nat as she cradled Jack to her breast.

This time he aimed his silencer-fitted gun at his intended target.

"Don't do it, Joe."

Nat's gaze sped past Keenan to the armed woman standing at the open door of the cottage. The DA smiled, but he didn't take his eyes off Nat. "I thought that was you following me down here, Fran."

"It's over, Joe. Put the gun down."

"Please," Nat pleaded. "Jack's still alive. Let me get him to a hospital. Please, Joe."

"You should have stayed out of it, Price. It was all nice and tidy until you started sticking your nose in," the DA snarled.

Nat was sick with anguish. "Nice and tidy? Was Charlotte Hamilton's murder nice and tidy, Keenan? You murdered the mother of your child."

His eyes actually lit up. "Daisy's one doll of a kid, isn't she?" He gave his ex-wife a quick glance over his shoulder. "Eventually cost me my marriage to Frannie. Not that she knew the whole story then. Just a lot of suspicions."

"I know it now, Joe," Fran said somberly. "Alison Bryant turned herself in this morning. She told me the whole sad, sorry, sick tale. About you and Charlotte Hamilton. About Daisy. About how you and Alison started your affair five years ago when we were here on the Cape trying to rekindle our marriage. How the two of you plotted out Elizabeth Temple's arrest. Bryant would turn the madam in and you'd cut a deal for her. Then your girl-friend would take up where Temple left off. Only you were the one who's really been running the show. Prostitution, drugs, blackmail. And now murder. Multiple murders."

"It couldn't be helped, Fran. The murders, I mean. Char spilled the beans about the kid to Jessie. It was spite. Because she heard through the grapevine that Jessie and I were getting it on. Ali took it in stride, but Char. She was one fucked-up lady." He shrugged. "I had to get rid of Char because who knew who the fuck else she'd tell. Not just about the kid—bad enough word got out the DA fathered a druggie/prostitute's kid. Char also knew why I'd cut a deal with Ali. She knew I was behind the whole operation. I couldn't take any chances. And then Jessie started getting on my case. She wanted a kid, too." He laughed harshly. "Yeah, that's all I needed. But I strung her along. Problem was, lovely Genevieve had a big mouth, too. She told her brother-in-law she was gonna be tying the knot soon even though I told the dumb bitch it was supposed to stay our little secret for a while."

He rubbed his jaw. "It all just mushroomed." Joe Keenan sounded tired but unfettered by even a modicum of guilt or regret. "I should have taken care of Ali first. That was my big mistake. But I really thought I had her in line."

"And you were counting on her to cinch the case against Car-lyle," Nat said.

Keenan's features registered pure hatred. "I busted my balls getting the scum of the earth locked up—"

"Making a big name for yourself in the process," Robie cut in dryly.

But Keenan wasn't listening. "And that fucker went and let 'em out like they were Boy Scouts or something." He sneered at Nat. "Bet you think Carlyle's a Boy Scout himself. Well, guess again, sweetheart. He's got his price just like the rest of us."

Jack groaned in pain. His eyelids fluttered open. "Hold on, baby. We're going to get you to a hospital," Nat said softly, her eyes riveted on Keenan. "I need help to get him into my car."

"Wilson," Fran called out.

The disheveled middle-aged detective stepped into view at the open doorway. He, too, had his weapon in hand. Behind him were two more armed cops.

"Drop the gun, Joe. It's over." Robie ordered.

"Help Nat, Wilson," she snapped. "Take him in the cruiser. Radio ahead to Cape Cod Hospital that you're coming in with a gunshot-wound victim."

Wilson hesitated. Joe Keenan lowered the gun.

"Do what she says," Nat snapped. Jack's eyes were closed again. His breathing was shallow, coming in fits and starts. His blood was seeping through her sweater into her skin. It felt like it was seeping into her very core. She was losing him.

By the time Wilson got to them, Nat had already started lifting Jack on her own.

As she and the detective carried Jack across the room to the open front door. Nat's eyes met Fran Robie's. The police captain smiled, but Nat had never seen a smile etched with so much pain and sorrow. "Like minds do think alike, Nat."

The second pop came just as she and Wilson stepped onto the porch with Jack in their arms. Nat looked back into the room.

Joe Keenan was lying on the floor, blood pouring out of the self-inflicted wound in the precise center of his forehead. Francine Robie had not moved from her spot. She still had her weapon trained on her ex-husband, her finger still poised—or was it frozen?—on the trigger. Even though she must have known, as Nat did, that she was aiming at a dead man.

. . .

At first Nat thought it was Jack's blood, but after he was whipped off down the hospital corridor on a gurney she realized it was her own. It was running down her legs. Spreading like a puddle on the floor. And the pain—the physical pain—was just catching up with her. She started to sway. Wilson caught hold of her.

"Steady on."

Nat started to cry.

"Hang in there, Ms. Price," the detective said. "He's gonna pull through. You'll see."

But it was Wilson who didn't see.

Nat clutched his sleeve. The room was spinning. "Get Leo," she gasped before she passed out.

She was trapped in a burning apartment. A recurrent nightmare. The remnants of a traumatic real event, playing like a film she'd seen so often she knew it by heart. Every frame.

Only this time it veered midway through. The flames became blood. So much blood. And commotion. People everywhere. Poking, prodding, pulling on her. She couldn't breathe. They were suffocating her. Torturing her.

Don't hurt me. Don't hurt my baby.

"Shhh. You're fine, Natalie. You're fine now."

Leo's voice. So soft. So reassuring. She didn't want this to be part of her nightmare. In her nightmare everyone was leaving her. Everyone was dying. Nat didn't want to lose him, too.

His hand, cool and strong, on her forehead. How could he bear the heat of her skin?

Nat could open her eyes now. She knew she was truly awake. But she was afraid. Afraid that one look at Leo and she'd have the answers to the questions she could not bring herself to ask.

. . .

Leo smiled tentatively as he entered her hospital room the next day. He was carrying a delicate orchid plant in one hand, gripping a huge sheet of white posterboard in the other. He turned the poster around to face her.

In the upper right-hand corner there was a big yellow sun with thick yellow lines radiating all around it. A smiley face was painted on the sun. Birds fluttered in the puffy white sky. And beneath the sky, a little boy with arms outstretched and X's all around him.

And printed in big letters in a child's hand across the bottom, Natalie, Here's My Big Get Well Hug with Lots of Kisses. I Love You. Your Boy, Jakey.

The tears came. Nat didn't try to stop them. She had plenty of reasons to cry.

Leo sat on her bed and held her in his arms, kissing her hair, her eyes, her neck. Hugs and kisses from her other boy.

It was just the three of them in the hospital chapel. They all shed tears. They each said their silent prayers. Their silent good-byes.

Nat made the decision not to find out about paternity. She figured both of them—Leo and Jack—had fathered the baby girl she'd lost. Leo had accepted her decision immediately. Perhaps he knew there was nothing he could say that would change her mind. Perhaps it was his way to show his love, damaged as it had become. Jack, on the other hand, was Jack. He argued it was a cop-out; he thought he had a right to know—that they all had that right. But, in the end, he relented. No. In the end, he gave her his support. *Whatever you want, I'll live with it, Nat.* Trying to give her what she needed.

Only she was so far from knowing what she needed anymore. . . .

"Ready?" Leo asked softly.

"Yes."

He helped her up from the pew. Her body still had that empty feeling inside. Each day, she told herself that she was slowly healing. But it was a lie. She doubted that she would ever heal. Doubted whether any of them would.

She put her hands on the rubber grips of her deputy's wheelchair. "Are you ready too, Jack?"

"Ready as I'll ever be."

epilogue

AGAINST ALL ODDS, FRAN ROBIE AND Nat became friends. In the weeks
since she'd been home recuperating, physically and emotionally,
Fran dropped by often. During a visit early on, she shared with
Nat that she, too, had suffered a spontaneous abortion several
years back. Like Nat, she was riddled with guilt and self-blame.
Like Nat, her obstetrician had insisted there was nothing she'd
done or hadn't done or could have done to prevent it. And while
Nat thought it striking that their miscarriages had both been
brought on by what their doctors termed chromosomal abnormal-
ities resulting in nonviable fetuses, she'd come to learn it was the
most common cause of first-trimester miscarriages. The good
news was it wasn't a condition that was any more likely to cause a
second miscarriage than if it hadn't happened in the first place.
Good news, but Nat was far from even considering the possibility
of another pregnancy. Truth was, she was having trouble considering whether to even bother getting dressed when she got up each
morning.

Tonight, Fran was bringing over Chinese takeout and a video. Girl's night in. Nat hadn't had any of those since her friend Maggie Austin died. She could smell the wafting aromas of Szechwan pork even before Fran got to the front door. So could Hannah. Her dog was panting at the door by the time Nat got there.

Fran wasn't wearing her dress-for-attention clothes tonight. She had on a pair of jeans and a sweatshirt under a down parka that was flecked with snow. First snow of the season. Her hair, which was brushed back in a girlish ponytail, was flecked, too. She didn't have on a drop of makeup. She looked terrific.

"I saw Steve Carlyle today," she said a while after they'd settled on Nat's sofa, cartons of Chinese open, chopsticks protruding from them.

"How is he doing?"

"Okay, considering," Fran said.

"Considering his wife filed for divorce and his two sons moved out?"

"And considering he handed in his formal resignation to the commissioner yesterday."

Nat gave Fran a surprised look. "He did?"

"He admitted in his resignation letter that he'd received payoffs to influence the Parole Board to approve parole for a handful of inmates over the years."

"One of those inmates being Peter Grayson."

"Getting the Grayson conviction was Joe's first major coup," Fran mused. "We celebrated big-time when that jury came in with the guilty vote. I know he took it as a personal affront that the inmate got paroled first time out."

"Carole Nelson, the head of the Parole Board, not only told me that Stephen Carlyle had been instrumental in persuading the board to grant Grayson's parole, she gave the same information to Joe Keenan. So Joe knew it was Carlyle's doing. Carol said the DA was livid when she told him."

Fran sighed. "Funny the things that come to you in hindsight. Remember some time back when you asked me about that charity ball Joe and I were at last spring?"

"Yes. I certainly do."

"Joe happened to spot Carlyle at another table and he made some remark to me about how he believed the deputy commissioner was on the fix and he was going to nail the bastard."

Nat looked over at Fran. "He almost did."

"He almost nailed you, too, Nat." She must have seen Nat flinch because she gave her shoulder a gentle squeeze.

"I visited Jack today at the rehab hospital," Nat said quietly.

"How's he doing?"

"He's coming along, but it's slow going. And Jack Dwyer is not a patient man. This is tough on him."

"And on you," Fran said softly.

"On a lot of people," Nat said. But she was sure Fran knew she meant Leo. Things were different now between them. In ways Nat could sense more than she could put into words. He came by a lot. He called. His concern and caring were as constant as ever. But Nat knew she'd lost Leo's trust. And she had no idea how to get it back. Sometimes she lied and told herself she wasn't even sure she wanted to.

"Any news about Daisy?" Nat asked.

A shadow of sadness played on Fran's face. Nat was asking about Fran's ex-husband's child. "She's staying with her grandfather full-time. He plans to file for legal custody. I think she's going to be okay." This last comment was filled with more hope than certainty.

"Did you suspect Joe before Alison Bryant blew his cover?" Nat asked her.

She nodded slowly. "When you accused me of lying about Rob Harris's statement . . . I knew then."

"Why didn't you say right away that Joe was the one who supposedly got that statement about Alan Carlyle's SUV from the Harris boy?"

"I was once married to the guy. I thought . . . I hoped . . . there was some explanation. I never even got to call him on it. Alison Bryant settled it all when she came in and made a clean breast of it."

"Will the acting DA cut a deal with her?"

"I doubt it." She picked up a container of fried rice. Nat picked up the Szechwan pork and hit play on her video remote.

"A couple of good things," Fran said as the film started. "That screw, Barker, admitted Joe was the one who paid him to start that fight with Elizabeth Temple."

Nat didn't chastise Fran for calling Barker a screw. "So it wasn't the name Landon I saw scribbled on that pad. It was Keenan."

"But speaking of Councilman Landon, guess what?" Fran said, smiling. "He's decided not to run for a Senate seat after all."

Nat smiled as well. Probably her first real smile in weeks. Maybe she was beginning the healing process after all.

The film title rolled. *Tender Mercies.*

Nat glanced over at Fran. "Good choice," she murmured softly.